THE
HARBOR

THE
HARBOR

Katrine Engberg

Translated by Tara Chace

SCOUT PRESS

New York London Toronto Sydney New Delhi

Scout Press
An Imprint of Simon & Schuster, Inc.
1230 Avenue of the Americas
New York, NY 10020

First Scout Press hardcover edition February 2022

SCOUT PRESS and colophon are registered trademarks of Simon & Schuster, Inc.

For information about special discounts for bulk purchases, please contact Simon & Schuster Special Sales at 1-866-506-1949 or business@simonandschuster.com.

The Simon & Schuster Speakers Bureau can bring authors to your live event. For more information or to book an event, contact the Simon & Schuster Speakers Bureau at 1-866-248-3049 or visit our website at www.simonspeakers.com.

Interior design by Jaime Putorti

Manufactured in the United States of America

10 9 8 7 6 5 4 3 2 1

Library of Congress Cataloging-in-Publication Data

Names: Engberg, Katrine, 1975– author. | Chace, Tara, translator.
Title: The harbor / Katrine Engberg ; translated by Tara Chace.
Other titles: Vådeskud. English
Description: First Scout Press hardcover edition. | New York : Scout Press, 2022.
Identifiers: LCCN 2021005009 (print) | LCCN 2021005010 (ebook) | ISBN 9781982127633 (hardcover) | ISBN 9781982127640 (trade paperback) | ISBN 9781982127657 (ebook)
Subjects: GSAFD: Mystery fiction.
Classification: LCC PT8177.15.N44 V3313 2022 (print) | LCC PT8177.15.N44 (ebook) | DDC 839.813/8—dc23
LC record available at https://lccn.loc.gov/2021005009
LC ebook record available at https://lccn.loc.gov/2021005010

ISBN 978-1-9821-2763-3
ISBN 978-1-9821-2765-7 (ebook)

To Cassius.
My anchor, my hourglass,
my little sun that shines.

MONDAY,
APRIL 15

PROLOGUE

After spending his weekend in bed, Michael woke up Monday morning with a throat full of glass shards. He had just pulled the comforter up around his fever-laden head and decided to call in sick, when his wife came in to stand at the foot of the bed, crossing her arms and giving him *that* look. Michael got up. After all, she was right. His job as crane operator at the incineration plant was still new, and he couldn't risk making a bad first impression.

Pumped up on a mixture of Tylenol and black coffee, he drove out to Copenhagen's industrial island, Refshaleøen, the car radio alternating between soft hits and crisp commercials, and gradually he started to feel better. He parked the car, nodded to the guards in the lobby, and rode the elevator up to the staff room to change his clothes. Strictly speaking that wasn't necessary, because the negative pressure in the sealed waste silo left the surrounding facility nearly odor-free, but Michael always changed into his boiler suit anyway. He laced up his protective work boots, put on his helmet, and walked through the plant with knees aching from the flu.

The walkways around the silo made up their own world of steel and valves, control panels, boilers, and signs. There were no windows, the incineration plant comprising a closed system that lacked weather or any circadian rhythm. Michael casually ducked under the hot-water pipes, said hello to a couple of coworkers by the steam turbines, and let himself into the crane operator's room. He stuck his lunch in the refrigerator and made a pot of coffee before sinking into his work chair with a heartfelt sigh. A ferocious scene came into view in front of him, one that he still had not fully gotten used to.

A window—the only one in the entire waste silo—offered a view into the heart of the incineration plant: the underbelly of Western civilization, a massive aggregated heap of filthy futility. Michael hadn't worked with garbage before, and on his first few shifts he had felt sick to his stomach, as if he were witnessing the apocalypse and ought to be doing something instead of just watching it. It had gotten better over time. He had even started eating the cookies his coworkers left behind while moving the claw.

The claw! At eight meters across from leg to leg it resembled something from a dystopian world where giant spiders ruled a dead planet. Michael had brought many pictures of the claw home to his six-year-old son, who firmly believed his dad had the coolest job in the world.

In reality, his dad's job was a little boring. The system that controlled the claw—moving it from the chutes where the waste carts were emptied and over to the ovens—was automated. Michael was only there to observe the transfer of the waste from left to right ad infinitum and make sure that nothing went wrong.

"Good morning," said Kasper Skytte as he walked in and sat in the chair next to Michael.

Occasionally the process engineers came to check if there was trouble in the control system. Michael hadn't noticed anything.

"Any problems so far?"

"Nope."

Luckily the engineers rarely spoke to the crane operators or any-one, really, who didn't understand their technobabble. So Michael knew he would be able to work in peace, which was just as well. He felt feverish and hot and perhaps should have defied his wife and stayed in bed after all.

"Coffee?" Kasper asked.

"Thanks, I'm good."

The engineer got up and clanked around with cups and spoons behind him, then yawned loudly and sank back into the chair beside Michael so they were once more seated side by side, watching the silo. Michael pulled his bag closer and dug around in it for some-thing to relieve his sore throat, hoping he still had a couple of loz-enges left. He found a pack of Ricola drops and gratefully popped one into his mouth.

The claw approached the window with a full load. It was always an impressive sight when it swung by really close. Trash dangled from its enormous grabbing arms, like tentacles on a jellyfish: a rope, a dirty tarp, a sneaker.

Michael leaned closer to the glass, squinting. That shoe was attached to something. Just as the load passed right in front of the window, an arm emerged, flopping out of the trash and dangling limply from the claw. Next to him Kasper spat his coffee at the win-dow.

Then Michael slammed the dead-man button.

SATURDAY, APRIL 13

TWO DAYS EARLIER

CHAPTER 1

The ocean closed over his head, and he sank to the bottom, away from the light at the surface. A kelp plant caressed his arms, inviting him deeper. He was tempted to just let go, exhale one last time, and fall, let his body dissolve into motes dancing in the sea's vertical rays of sunlight and surrender to the mermaids of the bottomless blue.

But the gray waters of Snekkersten Marina were far from the bottomless blue. Jeppe Kørner pushed off from the bottom and stretched his arms up toward the light. Seconds later, he broke the surface and inhaled.

"I was starting to think you would never come back up."

Jeppe shook the water out of his ears and squinted up at the figure on the dock. Above the surface the world was warm and bright. He swam to the ladder and searched with his feet for the slippery bottom rung, then he looked down one last time. The cool depths of the sea always stirred a longing in him, some kind of death wish perhaps.

"I don't understand how you can stay in so long. Ten seconds and I'm freezing." Johannes Ledmark shivered in his bathrobe and held a towel out to Jeppe. "Let's hit the sauna and warm up before the senior crowd arrives. I can't stand the sight of all those varicose veins."

He winked as if to take the sting out of his harsh remark and headed for the sauna. Jeppe dried himself and stuck his feet into the slightly too small sandals Johannes had found for him to use.

Johannes, renowned actor and one of Jeppe's oldest friends, was renting the ground floor of an old brick house by the harbor in Snekkersten for the summer while he looked for a new place to live. His repeated attempts to save the marriage with his husband of twelve years had failed, and the inner-city condo they owned together was now for sale. Meanwhile Johannes was licking his wounds far from the prying eyes of the public in the old fishing village of Snekkersten, north of Copenhagen. The run-down house was leaky and the yard overgrown, but Johannes seemed to thrive in the makeshift chaos overlooking the waters of the Øresund. He had even begun attacking the yard with a hedge trimmer and loppers, stubbornly insisting that mowing the lawn and weeding the patio felt meditative.

"Ha, I think we lucked out. The sauna's empty."

Johannes held the door of the little black-painted building on the breakwater open for Jeppe. They made themselves comfortable on the sauna's wooden benches and let the oven's dry heat rise up through the wood and bring the life back into their cold bodies. The early spring weather had been unusually sunny and warm for Denmark, but there was still a bite to the air, and the water temperature hadn't crept up above the midforties.

"Would you look at us, all grown up, winter bathers in the sauna," Johannes said with a chuckle. "We're just a pastrami sandwich and a senior pass to the Louisiana Museum away from turning into our parents."

"What's wrong with pastrami?" Jeppe asked, squeezing the salt water out of his short hair with his hands to stop the chilly trickle down his back. "I'm afraid we turned into our parents a long time ago. You just haven't noticed yet, because the guys you pick up are half your age."

"Oh, would you stop?" Johannes snapped a rolled-up towel at Jeppe's arm, and Jeppe responded by punching him on the shoulder. They rubbed their bruises, laughing.

"Besides, my young boyfriends keep me fit. Look, I've never been hotter than now!" Johannes smiled enigmatically. "Youthful, and only ever lonely on Sundays. How about you? You practically have a wife and kids now. How's that going?"

Jeppe looked down at his feet, which pearled with beads of sea-water and sweat. Indeed, he had got in Sara what he might call a package deal, one that he had never pictured himself signing up for, and he often found himself walking the very fine line between love and irritation.

"We haven't moved in together yet," Jeppe said. "It's not so easy when there are kids involved."

"On the other hand, it's a way to have kids." Johannes tipped his head to the side and dried his ears on the towel. "That is something you've always wanted, after all."

Jeppe shrugged. He had lived through three failed rounds of fertility treatments with his ex-wife before they decided to split and she had a baby with someone else. Since then he had pretty much given up on the idea of becoming a parent.

"When you don't have kids yourself, the whole thing can be a little overwhelming," Jeppe admitted.

"Honestly," Johannes said, eyeing him skeptically. "Can you ever really learn to love someone else's children?"

Jeppe pictured eleven-year-old Amina, who had awakened the household that morning—along with most of the neighbors—by playing K-pop at concert volume and throwing a temper tantrum when Sara turned the music down.

"They're both great girls."

"I'll take that as a no." Johannes laughed. "I figured as much, but I get it. Most kids are just as unbearable as their parents."

"Wait," Jeppe protested. "That's not what I mean. I'm very fond of Sara's kids, we just need to get used to one another. They need ample time to adjust to Mom having a boyfriend, who is not their father . . ." He felt a wave of heat rise up his spine and hit his cheeks, turning them a glossy red. "Say, shouldn't we be talking about your divorce instead? How's it going with divvying up the assets? Are your lawyers on speaking terms?"

"Okay, okay, you win." Johannes raised his hands in the air, like a white flag of surrender. "Let's go have some breakfast. I got croissants from the good bakery."

"First we need to go back into the water." Jeppe stood up, a drip of sweat falling from his chin to the floor. "Just a quick dip."

"No way! I'll die if I have to go into that freezing ocean again."

"A little dying won't kill you. Come on, old friend!" Jeppe pulled Johannes out of the sauna and pushed him down the breakwater toward the swimming dock. He was already longing for the cold darkness below the surface. Jeppe hung the bathrobe over the railing and was on his way to the swim ladder when he heard his phone ringing. He walked back and plucked it from the pocket of his robe to see who was calling. The wind raised goose bumps on the bare skin of his arms. It was the police commissioner.

HER SHOES SANK into the soft sand, immortalizing each point of contact between her rubber soles and Greve Beach in a trail of footprints. Anette Werner let the dogs run on ahead and enjoyed the feel of her body working, lungs pumping oxygen in and out. The ocean lay like a bluish-gray belt, sending in whiffs of seaweed-scented air with the surf and mixing it with the sharp smell of beach gorse. The morning sun already stood well above the horizon. Anette breathed hard and pondered how the things that make us feel happy and alive generally also involve pain. Like becoming a parent, for example. Having little Gudrun a year and nine months ago was hands down the hardest—sometimes even the most boring—thing she had ever attempted. Even so, she loved her daughter so much that she began missing her the very second she waved goodbye every morning at the day care.

The dogs started barking up ahead. She could see them by the water's edge and sprinted the hundred or so yards to her three eager border collies, running so fast she could taste blood in her mouth by the time she reached them. The dogs were growling and jostling one another, alternately jumping up or lying down flat in the sand. Anette separated them and crouched down to see what they had found.

A dead bird lay in the coarse sand. She recognized the sharp black-and-white markings, the green on its neck, and the delicate orange on its breast, a male common eider. It was lying on its back with the head turned to one side, like an infant. Its plumage was pretty much intact, it almost looked like it was sleeping. But between its yellow legs, where the abdomen should have been, there was just a bloody hole. The bird was dead. Maybe it had been migrating from Saltholm, headed north for the summer and left behind by the flock.

The sun glistened on its glossy feathers, and Anette resisted an impulse to run her finger over the beautiful animal. It was just a dead bird after all, not so different from the chicken Svend had made for dinner the night before.

She called on her dogs, and they followed her obediently back to the car, antsy at having to leave the bird behind but too well trained to defy her. In the parking lot she cleaned off their paws and they gracefully leaped into the back of the car, already seeming to have forgotten their find. But as soon as Anette turned on the engine, they started whining and whimpering and kept it up all the way home, as if they had left a part of themselves behind on the beach.

At Holmeås 14, Svend stood in the front yard, greeting her with Gudrun in his arms. Even from a distance, Anette could see her daughter struggling to get down and go explore the world, ever impatient, only at rest when she was asleep. *Just like her mother*, Anette thought with pride. As she turned off the engine, Svend set their little girl down and let her toddle off into the bushes without looking back, her diapered butt swaying and those short arms sticking out, like a tightrope walker's balance pole.

Anette let the dogs out of the car and went to kiss her husband. She put her hand up to the back of his head, prolonging the kiss.

"You're all sweaty." He gently pulled away from her embrace, caressed her cheek, and herded the dogs toward the front door. "But sexy!"

And as she peeled off her running clothes in front of the mirror, for the first time in their twenty-five-year-long relationship, she agreed with him. She had always had what her mother consistently called strong bones, maybe to protect Anette from the uncomfortable fact that she was fat. She had been the biggest girl in her class, the tallest with the broadest shoulders and the beefiest thighs. The one who won all the athletic disciplines and got picked first whenever they chose teams. Anette had never considered her size a problem, and Svend had never given her reason to think that he saw her as anything other than perfect, no matter how chubby she had been at times.

But now, looking in the mirror, she saw a new body. The nursing and many months of maternity leave had sucked off the excess pounds, with the result that at the age of forty-six she was in better shape than ever before. Still with meat on her bones, but firmer and stronger. And prettier. It surprised her how good it felt. In the shower, she allowed her hands to pay attention to the body they were lathering up for once, and felt a strong sense of well-being touching the firm skin over her abdomen. She dried off in front of the full-length mirror and dressed with her back half turned so she could appraise her butt. Having considered her body a tool for most of her life, rather than something decorative, there was something heady about feeling attractive.

"Your phone's ringing!" Svend called from the kitchen, and Anette hurriedly pulled up her pants and ran to answer it.

Gudrun sat at the little dining table, now strapped into her high chair, throwing fruit yogurt at her father, who received the bombardment with a smile. He had always had a calm temperament, but since becoming a father, his patience had extended as a wad of chewing gum in the sun. Anette shuffled across the room, buttoning her pants, and grabbed the phone, which lay buzzing on the kitchen table next to Svend's freshly baked sourdough rolls.

"Werner here!" She realized that she had managed to step in a glob of yogurt and cursed under her breath.

"Sorry to have to disturb your weekend, but we have a situation. Well, a possible situation anyway. I've just spoken with Kørner." It was PC's voice. Anette's Saturday mood began to tank, plummeting down toward her mixed-berry-covered toes. The commissioner—who never went by anything other than "PC," even though her name was Irene Dam—was deeply professional and would never have called on a Saturday if the "possible situation" wasn't very likely real. Anette saw their planned family outing fade into uncertainty.

"What happened?"

"We have a missing young man, or to be more precise, a fifteen-year-old boy, Oscar Dreyer-Hoff. Last seen when he got out of school yesterday afternoon at a quarter to three. His parents thought he spent the night at a classmate's house, but that turns out not to have been the case. They didn't realize it until he didn't come home this morning as agreed."

"Why are *we* getting involved?" Anette asked, looking around for something to wipe her foot. "It's pretty common for a fifteen-year-

old to be missing for a day or two if he wants to go to a party his
parents won't let him attend or whatever. If we're getting involved,
there must be an indication of something fishy?"

"The family received a letter."

Anette made eye contact with Svend. They had been through this
so many times before that he knew instantly what the look meant.
The family picnic was going to happen without her. He shrugged
and gave her a smile of encouragement, before he hid behind his
newspaper again and then suddenly popped his head out, causing
Gudrun to burst out laughing.

"Was he kidnapped?" Anette asked.

"We don't know for sure," PC sighed. "But the family is . . . shall
way say, *prominent*? They own that auction house, Nordhjem. And
they have received threats before. We've had them on our radar for
several years."

Anette heard her daughter's laughter fill the kitchen.

"I'm on my way."

CHAPTER 2

Behind Langelinie Pier's steady stream of cruise ships and the world-famous Little Mermaid sculpture, a small pleasure-boat marina, Søndre Frihavn, was tucked between warehouses and the sort of modern apartment buildings where the stainless steel–clad refrigerators are always empty because their owners are in Hong Kong.

Jeppe Kørner scowled at the pier, past the restaurant with the outdoor seating underneath dark green sun umbrellas, toward the red and gray concrete buildings, where the Oslo ferry docked at the end. This area might be considered desirable, fashionable even, but Lord knows it certainly wasn't pretty.

Dampfærgevej, PC had said. The Dreyer-Hoff family lived at number 24B. Anette Werner would meet him on the street out front at eleven.

He walked along the water, glancing at the small gathering of Folkboats, yawls, and yachts made of fiberglass and wood that were moored in the little marina. Their rocking and sloshing in the breeze brought an echo of life to the desolate area.

A hundred yards farther down the pier he spotted Anette in front of a modern brick building. She was standing near the breakwater, inspecting an older wooden boat that was wrapped up in tarps and looked like it was being overhauled. Jeppe contemplated her with a smile. He never thought he would be saying this about his partner, but she looked good. Still as big as a shed, and yet even so, she seemed longer now and with a slenderness around the hips, which made her broad shoulders look sporty. But it wasn't just that she had lost weight. Anette had a new twinkle in her eye lately, a depth that changed her rather ordinary facial features and made her—well, beautiful. Maybe it had something to do with her becoming a mother, or maybe she was just one of those women who got prettier with age. Jeppe was fairly confident that she would punch him if he remarked on the change.

"What, are you checking out my ass while you've got the chance?" Anette asked him, her back still to him.

"Would be foolish not to."

"I agree." She turned around and winked at him.

Jeppe returned her offered fist bump with one of his own—a compromise greeting, somewhere safely between a hug and a handshake, which suited them both nicely. "What did you have to cancel today?"

"A family picnic. It's fine. How about you?"

"I was out at Johannes's place in Snekkersten."

"Aha, so he's still in hiding from the mean, nasty tabloids?" She pointed to an entrance around the side of the building and started walking. "The front door is around that way."

Jeppe let his partner's sarcasm slide. Besides, there was a grain of truth to it. Ever since Johannes had returned from Chile with a divorce in his suitcase, he had stalled out. Jeppe was starting to worry if he would ever return to the stage.

The intercom button for number 24B revealed that the Dreyer-Hoff family owned the whole top floor of the building. A spotless stainless steel elevator, which made Jeppe think of the Department of Forensic Medicine, brought them straight to the family's condo. On the way up, Jeppe texted Sara to warn her that he might be late tonight. There was no telling what the day would bring.

The elevator doors opened to an impressive room, where wide-plank flooring disappeared under Persian carpets and continued out to floor-to-ceiling windows overlooking the marina. Clean, modern lines were punctuated by colorful works of art and antique, worm-eaten wooden furnishings that looked to have been shipped home from Italian monasteries wrapped in tissue paper. Not a humble home, and the woman who received them also looked anything but humble. Malin Dreyer-Hoff was voluptuous like a Botticelli angel, with big eyes, pink lips, and a green floral dress that sat tight across her chest. When she saw them she called out in a strained voice.

"Henrik, they're here!" She clasped her hands together in front of her, twisting them nervously. Her fingers were stained with some type of blue paint.

"Hello." Jeppe hesitantly held out his hand. "Jeppe Kørner from the Copenhagen Police's Investigations Unit. This is my colleague, Anette Werner."

"I'm sorry. I'm just . . . Thank you for coming so quickly." She responded to his handshake with limp fingers and averted eyes.

"Is there somewhere we can sit down?" Jeppe gazed around the large room with an open kitchen to the left and glass walls all around. It looked like a modern version of the loft apartment he had dreamed of owning ever since he had seen *Flashdance* as a child. It looked like money.

"We'll go join my husband in the living room."

Malin led them to a long hallway with a view of the water on the one side and doors to various rooms on the other. Jeppe peeked in an open doorway and saw more paintings and two sleek computer screens. The Dreyer-Hoff family had built their fortune running an online auction house for art and antiquities. It showed in their home.

The hallway ended in a light-filled living room, nearly as big as the kitchen space. A pink five-seat sofa sat beneath a Kasper Eistrup painting, which suited the space so perfectly that it must be a commissioned piece. By the window stood an easel with a half-finished blue painting, and next to it a tall gray-haired man waited for them with his back to the ocean and his hands in his trouser pockets. He had a vertical crease between his eyebrows but looked put together in a freshly ironed white shirt and beige canvas slacks that closed over a budding paunch. His shoulders drooped in the fashion of someone who spent most of his day at a desk.

He walked over to greet them, holding out his hand.

"Henrik. Hi. Thanks for coming."

Jeppe was puzzled by his choice of words, which would have been better suited for a social call. But worry makes people say the strangest things.

"Have a seat."

Jeppe and Anette sat down on two matching armchairs facing the pink sofa, where the couple then settled. Henrik Dreyer-Hoff put his arm around his wife protectively.

"You still haven't heard from your son?" Jeppe scrolled to a blank page in his notebook.

They both shook their heads.

"When did you discover that he was missing?"

"This morning." Malin took a deep breath. "On Saturdays we usually eat breakfast together, all of us. It's a family tradition. Henrik cooks brunch. . . ."

She looked at her husband, who nodded.

"I love to cook, but I rarely have time on weekdays. So on the weekend . . . Oscar always requests pancakes. The American buttermilk ones with syrup." Henrik stopped.

Malin gave her husband a look, as if he had said something wrong, and turned back to Jeppe.

"I got up early and painted," she said, "while I was waiting for everyone else to get up and for Oscar to come home. But he never came. At eight thirty I called him and texted."

Jeppe noted the time and saw as he did so that Henrik's hand was squeezing his wife's shoulder in a tight grip. As if he were holding her up. Or back.

"Where was he last night?" Jeppe asked. "Or where was he supposed to be?"

"At his friend Iben's, to study for a written Danish exam. They're freshmen. But she says he never showed up. I got ahold of her just before ten. That's when we knew something was wrong." Malin nervously twisted a ring around her finger.

"And Iben doesn't know where he is?"

"She says she just thought he had changed his mind. I think that sounds weird. And her father, who could have done the responsible thing and contacted us, didn't even know about their plans. Or so he says."

"We're going to need Oscar's phone number, and Iben's and her parents'." Jeppe passed his notebook over the table to Malin. She stared at it for a second, perplexed, then slowly began writing, her trembling hands showing her fear of the worst imaginable.

"I think he's been kidnapped." Her voice shook. "Just the thought that he—"

"Where does Iben live?"

"On Fredericiagade," Henrik replied, and looked at his wife. "Number sixty-four, isn't it? With her dad. It takes about ten minutes to walk from here if you cut across the Citadel. Oscar usually does."

Jeppe nodded to Anette, who got the notebook back from Malin, stood up, and walked over to the window to call the friend.

"What about the rest of the family? Were you home last night?"

"Yes," Malin replied after a brief pause. "Well, Victor, our eldest, was out with some classmates, but Henrik and I were home with our daughter, Essie."

"They left this for us." Henrik carefully picked up a sheet of paper from the coffee table. Five typed lines glowing black on a white backdrop. "We didn't see it until today. Then we knew something was seriously wrong, and we called the police right away."

Jeppe pulled his sleeve down over his fingertips, took the piece of paper, and read it.

> *He looked around and saw the knife that had stabbed Basil Hall-ward. He had cleaned it many times, till there was no stain left upon it. It was bright and glistened. As it had killed the painter, so it would kill the painter's work, and all that that meant. It would kill the past, and when that was dead, he would be free.*

THE KEEL SLICED lithely through the water, dividing the waves into an endless V behind the boat. Seagull cries accompanied the motor noise, and the sun played off the tops of the waves, turning the helmsman's pupils into two little black dots. CopenHill, the combined incineration plant and recreational facility, sparkled in the morning light so that one would think there was actually snow on its manmade ski slope. There wasn't, of course. It was spring, and the incineration plant's recreational vision was far from ready, so the city's downhill skiers still had to travel to real, snow-covered mountains for the time being.

Copenhagen's port was quiet. Only harbor buses and garbage boats were out this early. In a few hours the water would be filled with Saturday canal tours, rental boats, and yachtsmen on their way out to fish, swim, and camp on the little islands in the Øresund strait, as well as yawls with beer-guzzling captains and sea kayaks paddled by clear-eyed rowers in windbreakers. By that time he would be gone.

He was steering without any plan or time pressure, the way he preferred it, just leaning into the boat's movements and letting the wind squeeze morning tears from his eyes. Trekroner Sea Fortress came into view ahead of him, the small island smiling red and green and invitingly in the sunlight. Mads Teigen steered the fort's tug familiarly into the little harbor. One lone wooden yawl was moored by the dock, otherwise the harbor was empty. He tied the boat securely, turned off the motor, and jumped ashore. The steep embankments were covered with spring grasses that looked like soft wings of wild-growing green and yellow protecting the old fort.

Trekroner was originally built in 1713 as part of Copenhagen's fortifications, a system of defense structures that included several other forts and which played a key role in legendary attacks like the 1801 Battle of Copenhagen and the 1807 British bombardment of Copenhagen, when the city lost its fleet. The original fort of Tre-kroner was established with three old ships that were sunk and filled with rocks. One of them was named the *Tre Kronor*, and she gave her name to the fort even though most people think it originates from the time, over 250 years later, when the island was sold to the government for three Danish kroner.

Mads picked up a stray plastic bag and scanned the horseshoe-shaped promenade for signs of life but didn't see any. As always his eye lingered on the white lighthouse, which towered over the main entrance to the fort itself. From there the structure extended down two stories belowground. The casemates had served as a base for 750 soldiers during the First World War, and the Germans later used them during the occupation. When standing within those peeling walls in the corridors below sea level, you could still sense the smell of gunpowder and anxious sweat in the air. Panic and boredom had seeped into the masonry and now whispered the tales of hundreds of dead men.

Nowadays the fort was home to only birds, mink, and one solitary fortress caretaker living in the red-painted old commandant's quarters. A hermit on his island—that had become his fate.

Mads walked across the platform, where he was amassing wood for the midsummer bonfire, and up over the ridge to the outside of the embankment. He wanted to check on the pair of swans that was nesting down by the breakwater. From the top of the embankment the view of Copenhagen's towers and spires on the one side and Malmö's Turning Torso on the other was unimpeded. Standing there, he might as well be on his own planet, it was that deserted. An enclave of wilderness in the middle of the capital, separated from the hectic city life by only a narrow band of water.

The pair of swans was brooding; the female sitting heavily on the nest of seagrass, the male circulating warily around her. In a good month's time, the fort would have a new clutch of fuzzy little fledglings that would stick close to their mother to survive the first critical weeks.

Mads smiled at the thought.

He continued along the embankment, past one of the old white-and-red-striped navigation markers, towering on poles atop the ridge. The first bachelor party of the season was taking place around noon today. Mads had already prepared the stations of their treasure hunt in the underground corridors, but an impulse made him walk the route again.

The air between the casemate's thick concrete walls felt cool, as he descended the winding stairs to the low-slung ceiling of the cellar level. His footsteps echoed, as if somebody was walking behind him in the shadows. When he passed the old cell door with a red cross on it, the sound distortion felt so real that he had to turn around and look back. But of course no one was there, only the ghosts in his own head.

Mads checked all twelve of the stations and made sure that the ropes were lashed and the flashlights charged, before he walked back out into the light. He could just fit in a couple of hours in the workshop before the guests arrived. On his way back to the commandant's building, he passed the solitary wooden yawl, which was still moored to the dock. It didn't worry him. Still, he locked the main door behind him. No need to risk being disturbed.

To be on the safe side he also locked the door to the workshop. He hung his windbreaker on the doorknob, leaving his phone in a pocket of it, and switched the sound system on so Tchaikovsky's Sixth Symphony filled the room.

The prospect of an hour of absolute peace and quiet for his next project made Mads breathe a sigh of relief. He took a plastic-wrapped package out of the refrigerator and set it on the workbench. Carefully he unwrapped it, filled a bowl with water, and got the scalpel ready.

CHAPTER 3

Anette watched the parents sitting on the pink sofa and reluctantly remembered the British couple who had lost their little girl while vacationing in Portugal. Despite years of searching, she had never been found. Eventually some people had begun speculating whether the parents themselves had been behind her disappearance.

"The letter was left on the kitchen table," Henrik explained, pulling his wife closer, as if he could physically protect her from the words coming out of his mouth. "We didn't notice it until we realized that Oscar was missing, just thought it was a homework assignment or something like that."

"And it isn't?"

They both shook their heads.

"It was folded in the middle and it had *To M and H* written on the outside. Plus it is typed. See!"

Jeppe turned the paper over and showed it to Anette. She pulled down her sleeve to cover her fingers, just as he had done, took it, and carefully examined the words.

"Could it be"—Malin took a shallow breath—"a ransom demand? It's about killing."

"It seems to be some kind of a quote." Anette looked at Jeppe and knew he was thinking the same thing. Most kidnappers' messages were concrete, not descriptive and lyrical. "Who's Basil Hallward?"

"No idea," Malin replied quickly. "We've never heard the name before."

Anette detected a dismissive note to her voice, as if she thought the police were asking the wrong questions.

"We've received threats before, maybe two years ago? We notified the police. You must have a record of it."

Anette nodded.

"Did those letters resemble this one?"

Malin hesitated and then said, "As far as I remember they were all different, some of them written by hand, others on a computer. But all brief."

"Do you still have them?"

"No." Henrik interrupted before his wife had a chance to answer. "The point is that someone has it out for our family. And now they've taken Oscar!"

On the last sentence his voice wavered. He lowered his head, and his shoulders began to tremble. Malin put a hand on his leg and patted him impatiently. To Anette the gesture didn't seem very affectionate.

"Did the police find out who sent the letters back then?" Jeppe asked.

"No."

"Okay, we'll find the report and take a look at it. Our forensics experts will investigate this letter for potential clues, and then we'll compare it to the earlier ones if we have copies of them on file."

While Jeppe explained, Anette took pictures of the letter with her cell phone, then got up to find her bag and pulled out a brown envelope, slid in the letter, and sealed it. She noticed that Henrik had lifted his head and put his arm around his wife again.

"Were there any signs of forced entry?" she asked.

"We have an alarm, but it wasn't triggered," Henrik answered, shaking his head. "But that's not so surprising, is it? They probably rang the bell, and Oscar let the kidnappers in."

"When was the last time he was seen and by whom?" Jeppe turned a page in his notebook.

"When he finished school at two forty-five yesterday afternoon," Malin responded. "He goes to Zahles School, a private high school near Nørreport subway station. Iben told us that they waved good-bye to each other in front of the school and that Oscar then walked home."

"When did the rest of you get home?"

"Fridays Essie—Esmeralda, our youngest—has dance class. I picked her up and we got home a little after five, maybe five thirty." Malin touched Henrik's hand on her shoulder, as if she wanted him to remove it. He didn't.

"Have you checked with your immediate family to see if they've heard from him?"

"We called my parents and my sister, but none of them know anything. That's all our immediate family. Henrik's parents are dead. But Oscar would never just stay away without letting us know."

Anette sat back down next to Jeppe.

"Can you tell if he came home after school yesterday? Is his backpack here, for example? His computer?"

Malin shook her head.

"Neither is his cell phone."

"What about his passport?" Anette continued. "Is that in its usual place?"

"I checked. All our passports are where they go in the drawer." She pointed to a red lacquered secretary. "What are you planning to do to find him?"

"We'll start searching for him immediately," Jeppe assured her. "If he has his cell phone on him, we'll find him right away. What you can do in the meantime is call everyone who has contact with Oscar on a regular basis and ask about him."

Henrik's eyes grew moist.

"Do you have a good recent photo of your son?" Jeppe asked.

"I'll get one." Malin freed herself from her husband's grasp, got to her feet, and supported herself for a moment on the backrest, as if she were dizzy. Then she left the room.

"Would you mind if we took a peek at his bedroom?" Anette asked.

The father didn't respond. Anette looked at Jeppe, who shrugged in a gesture she chose to interpret as approval, got up, and walked back down the long hallway, opening doors as she went. The first room looked like an office, furnished with heavy wooden furniture. In the next room sat a teenager wearing headphones. He had dark hair and long limbs: a handsome young man.

"Hi, I'm Anette from the police. You must be Victor."

He pulled off his headphones and let them hang around his neck like a backward necklace. A heavy beat filled the room. Anette saw that his eyes were red from crying.

"I'm looking for your little brother's room," she explained over the noise of the drums.

"Just call me Vic, everyone else does." The boy took out his phone from his pants pocket and pressed on the screen. The music stopped. "This is actually his room. I was just sitting here and . . ."

"I'm assuming you don't know where your brother is?"

"If I did, I don't really think you'd be here right now, do you?" Victor smiled apologetically and wiped a tear off his cheek. "Sorry,

I'm not trying to act smart or anything. This whole thing is just . . . weird."

Anette looked around at the room's spartan decor: a desk with a worn wooden chair, bookcases brimming with books, a full clothes rack, and a dresser. That was it. The room was as clean and tidy as the rest of the condo, but nowhere near as cozy.

Prefab frames hung close together over the desk, displaying black-and-white images, charcoal drawings of human forms, naked bodies, faces with downcast eyes, and limbs that faded into black.

"Did Oscar draw these?"

"Yeah, he drew all of them. He's damn good. When we were younger, he always used to try to teach me. You know, he would put a vase of flowers in front of me and demonstrate how to draw in perspective and do shading, the little stinker. I could never do it, and he would get all grumpy and say that I was messing it up on purpose, to tease him."

Anette smiled.

"When did you last see him?"

"At breakfast yesterday," Victor answered hesitantly, his voice sounding brittle, on the verge of breaking the whole time. "We ate in the kitchen like we usually do—with my little sister—and then we went to school together. Oscar and I go to the same high school. He's a freshman, and I'm a senior."

Victor fiddled with his headphones.

"Mom says someone took him. Do you think that's right?"

"It's too soon to say."

Something snapped off the headphones, and the boy looked at the little piece of plastic in his hand, puzzled.

"We had agreed we would walk home together, but I . . . I had to talk to someone at school. Maybe if I had stuck to our plan . . ."

He eyed her pleadingly. Anette wished she could reassure him, but she didn't know any more than he did. And maybe he was right.

He took off the headphones and tossed them on the floor.

"One of my friends says that he saw my little brother talking to someone in a black car outside the Botanical Garden after school."

Anette held her breath.

"What's the name of your friend?" she asked.

"Jokke. Well, Joakim. He's in the same grade as me." Victor held up his phone and showed it to Anette. "I wrote to everyone I know on Messenger a little while ago. He just wrote me back."

She handed him her own phone.

"Could you please type in, uh, Jokke's phone number for me?"

He complied.

"Do you think Oscar could be mixed up in something he shouldn't be? Maybe with a friend your parents don't want him to see?" She smiled amenably to signal that he wouldn't get in trouble.

"No! My little brother is a good kid."

Anette looked around the room again, at the pictures, the desk, the dresser, and the room's only chair, in which Victor was sitting.

"Uh, where does he sleep?" Anette asked.

"In the family bed."

She looked at him blankly.

"Our parents believe that the pack should sleep together, so when I was little, they built a huge bed for all of us, fifteen feet wide. I have my own now, but Oscar still sleeps there."

Anette felt a cold breath of air on the back of her neck.

A family bed?

BOWLS OF CHIA seed porridge sat congealing on the kitchen table—breakfast prepared by a father with no appetite, for a family that wasn't home. Iben ought to be here, sitting with her elbows on the table and her mouth full, laughing at his bumbling attempts to prepare the vegan fare that she herself had introduced to the household. But in spite of her best friend being missing, she had gone to a morning rally at the Danish Youth Council. Iben was active in their environmental organization. His daughter, idealistic and stubborn as hell.

Kasper Skytte tilted his head back and downed what was left of the Fernet-Branca. The burning sensation in his esophagus felt good, as did the subsequent wave of nausea. He wasn't particularly fond of Fernet-Branca, especially not in the morning, but today of all days he needed liquor and the blissful indifference it spread through his body. Kasper didn't have a drinking problem—his addiction wore a different face—but he knew that he sometimes drank too much. That his already ample wine consumption had escalated to something decidedly unhealthy in the seven years since his relatively amicable divorce. That he only coped with being a single parent by having a drink and a couple of hours alone in front of the computer screen to look forward to at the end of the workday.

When his ex-wife moved to San Sebastián with her new boyfriend six years ago, she had agreed to let Iben remain in Denmark. Kasper had gotten the condo, their daughter, and—much against his will—the dog, a Coton de Tulear named Cookie that he had begrudgingly walked twice a day until it finally kicked the bucket last year. In other words, he had gotten everything and she had walked away with nothing but her freedom.

And yet she seemed to have taken some part of their daughter with her, for with every passing year the emptiness in Iben's eyes grew. At least when she was looking at her father.

The gate banged shut in the front yard, and he looked out the window to see if it was her. It was the upstairs neighbor. Iben had promised to come straight home after her meeting, and now she wasn't even answering the phone when he called. He started throwing away the remaining porridge but gave up on doing the dishes. They would just have to wait for later.

Oscar was missing, and the police were coming to question his daughter. That was reality; he couldn't run away from it. Kasper prayed she would be home in time for him not to have to face them alone.

He went into the cramped living room and turned on the architect lamp over the small desk that he had squeezed in despite Iben's protests. True, there wasn't a lot of space, but where else was he going to put it? If he were to be home to greet her from school, to prepare their meals, and be a parent, he had to be able to work when she went to sleep. Hanging on the wall over the desk was a drawing of Copenhagen's new incineration plant, the ambitious CopenHill, or more formally, the Amager Resource Center, a.k.a. ARC. His workplace for the past year and what occupied most of his waking hours, besides Iben.

He spread out four sheets of paper on the desk and leaned down over the rows of numbers. They specified the preceding week's emissions from the plant's six internal pipes, called the scrubbers. These pipes cleansed and led the smoke from the ovens to the 123-meter-tall chimney, so it could puff out clean, white steam over the city. Kasper was employed as a process engineer to design data pathways and keep an eye on harmful emissions of toxic substances from burning the trash, but also to optimize the use of the energy the incinerator produced. He oversaw all stages of the incineration process, from garbage pickup around the city to the computer-controlled claw in the waste silo itself.

ARC was unique in a lot of ways. Under the motto "We take and we give back," this incineration plant had been considered much more than a garbage dump from the beginning. Designed by world-renowned architecture group BIG, the plant had a roof that was built as an eighty-five-meter-high ski slope, complete with lifts, a café, and a unique Italian plastic underlay that made it possible to whiz down the slope without a single snowflake. Copen-

Hill was the city's new recreational gathering place and landmark. The roof project alone was rumored to have cost three hundred million Danish kroner.

But the slope's opening had been delayed several times already, and the press seemed to magnify every single little misstep, as if they had no appreciation for the size and significance of the project. One of the cleanest incinerators in the world, and it was working impeccably. Even so, the plant kept running into headwinds. A favorite story was how they had to import trash from England to be able to deliver enough district heating to the city. The plant was oversize from the beginning, and Copenhagen's waste volumes were decreasing. The journalists were all over that, of course. But upscaling the plant had been a political decision to avoid ending up with a plant that would be too small in ten years.

Kasper held a magnifying glass to the paper and read the NO_x catalyzer's latest emissions numbers. Nitrogen oxides are significant environmental health hazards, so they are strictly regulated around the world in order to minimize smog and acid rain. He and his colleagues were some of the leading engineers globally in smoke purification plant construction, and they had already been contacted by incineration plants in Canada, India, and France regarding potential consulting gigs. The goal before long was to be able to capture all the CO_2 from the plant's smoke so that it could be deposited into an underground geological formation. The technology already existed. It was only a question of time.

He looked at his watch and called Iben again. Still no answer. Kasper tossed his phone down, and when it bounced off the desk onto the floor, he was forced to shamefacedly pick it up and check for cracks in the screen. The police would be here soon, so she had to come home.

He leaned over the desk again and started drawing lines with numbers next to them. Pathways and values, illustrated with cramped little symbols. But his fingers kept writing the wrong things, and he swore to himself, leaned back in his chair, and looked up at the ceiling, listening for the key in the door.

He shouldn't. He had promised himself he would lay off. But the idea of turning the computer on grew in his head, until he could hardly read the numbers on the paper in front of him. If he logged in, it would be easier afterward, then he could stay off it for a while. Kasper felt a burning sensation in his body like an inflammation that spread from his stomach through his bloodstream out into his skin, making it tremble. He fetched his laptop, breathlessly logged in, and felt the world falling back in place.

BY ØSTERPORT STATION, where the train tracks run underground alongside the park Østre Anlæg, the trees shone white with flowers against a carpet of green and small dots of yellow. Branches of half-open flower buds pointed eagerly up at the sky, defying gravity, and their scent filled the whole area. The white ones must be mirabelle plum trees because it was too early for bird cherry or hawthorn, and the yellow, forsythia. Early spring blossoms were covering the city. It was more than life-affirming, it was pure-happiness heroin.

Esther de Laurenti breathed in the scent. She had turned seventy, and with every passing year, as she moved closer to the end of life, the arrival of spring felt like winning the lottery. She pulled on the single dog leash with only one pug at the end and felt a little stab of pain. Twelve-year-old Epistéme had caught a cold over the winter, and the cold had turned into encephalitis, which the pug hadn't been able to shake. Now only Dóxa was left. She had whimpered at the loss of her partner for a few weeks, then it had subsided. Now she trotted down the path in fine form, without any visible signs of grief. Strange how death could come so close without leaving any serious harm behind.

Esther bent down to scratch the dog behind the ears and continued her walk past the National Gallery, along the Botanical Garden, and to the Lakes. The sun was reflected brightly on the water, forcing her to squint her eyes to narrow slits. She smiled at a group of young people sitting on a bench, holding beer cans, their eyes luminous. *Copenhagen is at its best right when it wakes from its winter hibernation,* she thought, *unlike us humans, who have to go through countless morning rituals before we're good for anything at all.*

Gregers, her eighty-five-year-old housemate and friend, was a prime example of a slow starter. Sometimes he would sit in the kitchen of their place on Peblinge Dossering, grumpy till almost noon. And it was only getting worse with age. As time passed he moved less and complained more. He still walked to the bakery on Blågårdsgade every day for exercise, but even so he was losing weight, the flesh melting away from his once strong bones, and his mood rarely made it above freezing point.

Esther pulled Dóxa gently away from the bench and let her thoughts wander back to what she spent most of her time thinking about these days: her writing. She had only an incipient idea for a book, but still it was so exciting that she couldn't shake it. The idea had come to her at Christmas when she was placing a bouquet on her deceased friend Kristoffer's grave. It had snowed that day, and the plot was covered with ice flowers. She stood for a long time in the cold trying to establish a connection with her friend, feeling stuck and dejected.

Why do we deal with death so poorly when it's the one inescapable condition we all have to face? Where do you put your grief once all the rituals associated with death are over and everyone is busy moving on?

These thoughts buzzed around in the back of her mind like a stubborn wasp that would neither sting nor go away.

Esther had begun reading about death rituals in other cultures, about grieving and funerals. One morning in March she had woken up and gone straight to her computer to write—just disconnected thoughts about death to begin with, but now a text was starting to take shape. Her stomach tingled at the thought of her budding tale.

She leaned her head back and looked up at the new chestnut leaves, dangling limply from the branches like puppy ears. It was impossible to picture how they would soon lift themselves up to form resilient, bright green parachutes.

Death rituals and budding springtime greenery. Esther couldn't remember when she'd ever felt better.

CHAPTER 4

The grayish-blue ocean waves crashed on the rocks along Langelinie, splashing salty sea spray on Jeppe's and Anette's cheeks. On the horizon they could see Trekroner Sea Fortress and the industrial buildings on Refshaleøen, and to the right, farther into the harbor, the old navy barracks on Holmen and the controversial opera house. Jeppe stopped by the Little Mermaid statue, where flocks of tourists were trying to take a decent picture in front of the disappointingly small statue, and threw away the rest of the hot dog that had made up today's lunch. He tasted the oniony breath it had left behind and began fishing around in his pockets for cigarettes.

"Are you going to smoke *now*?" Anette asked him disapprovingly. "The Skytte family is waiting for us."

Jeppe held the pack of cigarettes out to her with a smile. No one is more fun to tease than a former smoker. She shook her head and stuck her hands in her pockets while he lit one up and inhaled deeply.

First wave of the search operation was up and running. A team of officers was looking through digital channels, doing door-to-door searches in the neighborhood, and calling Oscar's relatives and class-mates. The second wave would take an hour or so to activate. Canine patrols, helicopters, and media assistance all took longer to set in motion. They had decided to sit on the letter and their suspicions regarding kidnapping, at least initially. Until one knows the kidnap-pers' demands, it can do serious harm to involve the rest of the world in the situation.

Their hope was that Oscar would turn up unharmed before it became necessary.

"What are your initial thoughts?" Jeppe asked.

Anette pursed her lips.

"That it didn't look like a classic ransom note."

"But given the previous threat pattern, it's likely what we're deal-ing with," Jeppe said, squinting out at the water.

"Well, maybe," Anette began, kicking a pebble so it skittered across the asphalt. "Is it just me or did you get a weird vibe between the parents?"

"Isn't that to be expected?"

She shrugged.

"What do you think about the concept of a *family bed*?"

He exhaled a delicate column of smoke toward the horizon.

"Well, I guess it's not exactly normal to sleep in the same bed as your teenage son. But every family is different. I presume they're doing what they think is best for their children."

"I think it's creepy," Anette said, shuddering demonstratively. "And who says that Malin Dreyer-Hoff is in tune with her kids? She doesn't seem like the empathetic type."

Jeppe raised an eyebrow, impressed.

"Knock it off, Jepsen! You don't hold a patent on decoding people just because you read a book once."

Jeppe smiled wryly at his partner and put the cigarette out on his heel.

"Come on, let's go," he said.

The neighborhood around Amalienborg Palace reeked of old money. They passed white plaster facades, cobblestone streets, and thick brass nameplates before they turned onto Fredericiagade. The fashionable atmosphere slowly faded the farther they got from the water and the castle, where the budget for maintaining the old buildings was obviously lower. At number 64, a relatively humble entrance around the corner from Borgergade, Jeppe found the name *Skytte* on the intercom and pressed the button. The door opened into a little courtyard between tall apartment buildings. A blond man of medium height, and with a full beard, was waiting in the doorway of what turned out to be a ground-floor apartment with direct access from the courtyard. Jeppe wiped his feet on a floral doormat and offered him his hand. Chewing gum didn't quite mask a trace of alcohol on the man's breath.

The apartment itself had a low ceiling and felt dark but was pleasantly furnished with pine furniture, rag rugs, and faded children's drawings on the walls. The decor was functional and unpretentious—there couldn't have been more of a contrast from the Dreyer-Hoff family's meticulously designed luxury penthouse.

"Let's sit in the kitchen. Iben just got home." Kasper Skytte pushed open a wooden door with the knob missing and led the way in.

In the kitchen, a young girl with dark blond, shoulder-length hair and a childish face sat leaning over a cup of tea. Anette remained standing by the kitchen table shooting a sidelong glance at the dirty dishes in the sink, Kasper found a chair next to his daughter, and Jeppe sat down across from him. The father turned to the girl, and a fist-size birthmark came into view on his left temple, extending from the edge of his beard up to his hair.

"Iben, sit up straight," Kasper instructed. "The police are here."

Jeppe held his hand out to the daughter. She took it slowly, as if the gesture was unaccustomedly grown-up for her.

"Hi, Iben. I'm Detective Jeppe Kørner with the Copenhagen Police. As you know, your friend Oscar is missing. He told his parents that he was going to spend the night at your place . . ."

Iben looked down into her cup.

"But he didn't. Do you know where he is?" Jeppe continued gently.

The girl rotated her teacup without looking up, and Kasper put his arm around her shoulder comfortingly.

Jeppe noted that she withdrew from his touch.

"If you know anything, now's the time to tell us," Jeppe said. "This is a very serious situation. Oscar could be in danger."

"I don't know where he is."

"That's okay, Iben." Jeppe smiled reassuringly. "When did you last see him?"

"In front of the school, right after the last class yesterday. A few of us hung out for a few minutes and talked about what we were doing over the weekend. There were some people from our class, as well as a few seniors. Oscar was waiting for his older brother, but he never showed. After about ten minutes we started walking home. I crossed over Nørreport Station, and he went off toward the Botanical Garden."

"Weren't you going to hang out?"

"Yeah, but he wanted to go home first and drop off his backpack and then come over to my place later. For dinner, you know, just normal stuff." She answered quickly and smoothly.

"Why didn't he just walk home with you?"

"Like I said, he wanted to get a change of clothes, okay?"

Iben scrunched up her nose, and Jeppe sensed that there was a temper behind her innocent exterior.

"But he never showed up," Jeppe said. "Did you try calling him?"

She lifted her chin disapprovingly, as if the question was stupid.

"Of course I did! But he didn't pick up, so I figured he'd probably started gaming or drawing instead, or that he had fallen asleep, or whatever. We see each other all the time, it wasn't like a plan that was written in stone—"

Anette interrupted the girl.

"One of the seniors, Joakim, says that he saw Oscar talking to the driver of a black car. Did you see that, too?"

Iben shook her head.

"And you never wondered why he didn't cancel?" Jeppe insisted.

"No." She looked at him with a teenager's disdain for the conformity of adult life. "I just figured he would call me when he woke up this morning"

Kasper eyed her seriously.

"Have you been lying about sleeping over at each other's places?" he asked.

A pulse began beating in the middle of the birthmark on the father's temple, and it occurred to Jeppe that the man was exerting himself. As if he had to rein in the strength that ran through those muscular arms so that it fit in the small apartment without breaking anything.

Jeppe turned back to Iben and asked, "You have no idea where he might have gone?"

"No." Her eyes were back on the teacup.

Jeppe was overcome by a desire to yell at the indolent teenager, to make her grasp the seriousness of the situation. *He's been kidnapped. Help us!* But of course he didn't. Witnesses must be treated with care, otherwise they clam up.

"You have no idea where he slept last night?" Jeppe said calmly.

Iben sat still for a second and then shook her head.

The kitchen faucet dripped monotonously onto the dirty dishes in the sink, and Jeppe counted the drips in his head. One heartbeat. Two heartbeats. Three heartbeats.

His next question broke the rhythm. "Oscar's parents found a note with a quote on it, printed out on a piece of paper. Does that ring a bell?"

"I don't know anything." Her voice thinned and faded into a whisper.

Kasper put his arm around her again, and this time her reaction to the physical contact was impossible to miss. She hit his arm away like a small child who doesn't yet have the words to express boundaries.

Anette took out a card.

"If you happen to think of anything you want to tell us, call this number right away. The sooner we find him, the better."

It was Kasper who took the card. He looked at them nervously.

"Do you think he could be in danger?" he asked.

Jeppe waited just a bit before responding.

"In the vast majority of cases like this, people turn up again unharmed."

That wasn't a lie, he thought, while saying goodbye to the father and daughter. Most missing people turn up unharmed within the first twenty-four hours. After twenty-four hours, the odds drop significantly.

In other words, they had two and a half hours to go.

"INTO MY ARMS, *O Lord. Into my arms . . .*"

Nick Cave's husky vocals filled the little atelier. Jenny Kaliban turned up the music and closed her eyes, smoked, and sang along, letting the music alleviate the restlessness in her body the way only music can. Under her rib cage the fear gnawed like a parasite, threatening to devour her. Her worries were starting to show in the fine wrinkles around her eyes and mouth, in her graying hair and her worn knees. Today she had woken up with a knot of regret in her chest and was having a hard time shaking off the sorrow. As a mantra, she tried to tell herself that she didn't have much to lose, but of course that was a lie. Everyone has something to lose.

She opened her eyes, switched off the music by pressing a button on the old-fashioned boom box, and tossed her cigarette into the sink. Today was a rare full day in the atelier, and she shouldn't waste it on self-pity and negative thoughts. Finances were tight, if not to say disastrous. She had to start teaching evening classes again, take more shifts at Thorvaldsens Museum, find new sources of income. The job as a custodian suited her well enough, but it didn't pay much. Her landlord's notice to vacate lay on the filing cabinet, smoldering like a stubborn fire that threatened to burn her life to the ground.

Jenny pulled a smock off the hook by the door and looked around at the little workroom. It was situated on the first floor of a dilapidated town house that had been left standing in the Østerbro neighborhood, when all the other ones had been torn down in the sacred name of modernization. One entered from the courtyard at the back of the building. The dusty windows didn't let in much light, and over the years she had filled up the room with pictures, sculptures, and drawing materials. The art filing cabinet with its deep drawers took up a lot of room, and so did the little kiln she used to fire ceramics. She had put shelves in front of the windows for etching needles, pastels, and charcoal sticks, each in their own jar. The darkness and denseness suited her fine. The light she needed came from the paper and the music—from inside—not from the sun in the sky.

The front of the building was a clothing shop, the back below the atelier was the shop's storeroom. They had just closed for the day; she would have peace and quiet to work for the rest of the afternoon and evening. In here no one commented on the mess, the music, or the turpentine smell. The atelier was her biggest luxury and her only necessary expense. Jenny would rather give up her tiny apartment near Nørrebro Circle than do without this place.

She pulled a sheet of thick watercolor paper off her Canson pad, secured it with clips to a plywood board, and set it on the easel. Placed charcoal sticks and powdered charcoal ready on the floor, got out rags and the spray fixative to set the work once the drawing was finished. She hummed to herself. The preparations that preceded the actual artmaking were so ingrained in her fingers that she became one with them. Once everything was ready she chose a charcoal stick from the jar and brought it to the blank paper without hesitation.

Her students often asked about inspiration, where it came from and how it got converted into art. Jenny never knew what to answer. For her, drawing and painting were as intuitive and natural as breathing. She just did it, let her fingers be the link between soul and paper. The picture took shape on the canvas without her conscious awareness. She was often surprised at the scenes that materialized before her, even though they had been created by her own hands.

She listened to the scratch of the charcoal stick against the paper. When she stood like this in front of the easel, time literally disappeared. Morning turned into evening and night became noon without her registering it.

Jenny took a step back from the easel, forcing herself to snap out of her trance and look at the nascent picture. She saw a familiar form, a body with its face turned away and pale, naked limbs. She recalled the countless exhibits of Rodin's drawings, Duchamp's elementary parallelism, and Picasso's portraits that her gallery-owning parents had dragged her and her sister to throughout their childhood. Those images had forever become embedded in her flesh. They lived in her and comforted her when she felt lost.

*   *   *

JEPPE'S OLD OMEGA Seamaster showed three o'clock when he and Anette let themselves into their office on Teglholmen. The streamlined corridors of the Violent Crimes Department were deserted, and not just because it was Saturday afternoon. Last year all investigative units had been moved from the historic police head-quarters downtown to this new so-called super police HQ on the newly built Teglholmen, south of the city. But the move hadn't been so straightforward to implement. The new facilities were inadequate from the start, and despite their modern appearance investigators were finding that conditions at the new location weren't really con-ducive to either getting their work done or thriving while doing so. Plus, it had no soul. Even though the old headquarters had been run down after more than a hundred years of use, a spirit inhabited the old walls and the vaulted ceilings that no new construction could replace.

Jeppe's office chair hissed efficiently beneath him as he sat down at the desk and turned on his new computer with a nostalgic sigh. Twelve years he had worked within the dark wooden paneling of the old headquarters. Teglholmen's bland glass and brick was going to take some getting used to.

He placed the picture of Oscar Dreyer-Hoff that Malin had found for him on his desk. A skinny boy with dark hair, brown eyes, and skin that looked like he didn't get enough fresh air. A face that was still caught in the teenage span between baby fat and finished features. He had intelligent eyes, if deducing that kind of thing from a photo made any sense. It had been taken in the sunlight, possibly out on the water, and the reflections made the boy squint. He looked skeptical.

Jeppe opened POLSAS and made a report with the day's notes about the missing boy. Anette, who sat across from him, had started calling neighbors and classmates one by one, drawing a line through their names on a list as she went. They had already gotten hold of most of them, but no one knew where Oscar was. Victor's class-mate Joakim, who thought he had seen Oscar talking to the driver of a black car by the Botanical Gardens, hadn't noticed the make or license plate of the car, and after some consideration he wasn't sure whether it had happened on Friday or maybe Thursday.

Jeppe sent a brief email to Detective Thomas Larsen and asked him to run a background check on the Dreyer-Hoff family, focusing on the threatening letters they had reported and the family's business affairs and finances. If someone had taken Oscar, the reason was likely to be related to either the family's money or its history.

Jeppe went out to the coffee machine in the hallway, made himself a double espresso, and poured a splash of milk in it. Who knew what the rest of the day would bring? The thought of a possible autopsy on a dead teenage boy turned his stomach. Children should outlive their parents, period.

Back at his desk, he printed out the picture Anette had taken of the mysterious letter. The original was on its way to the forensic scientists to be examined for prints and other evidence that might tell them something about its origin. This printout, though, looked quite inconspicuous. Ordinary machine-written letters on ordinary white paper, it could have been typed on any computer and printed on any printer.

Jeppe skimmed through the words one more time.

As it had killed the painter, so it would kill the painter's work, and all that that meant. It would kill the past, and when that was dead, he would be free.

They reminded him of something, maybe something he had read. He typed the lines into the search field on his browser and received a whole page of links about the author Oscar Wilde. Oscar? Was the shared name a coincidence or a hidden message?

Jeppe seemed to remember that Esther de Laurenti had mentioned and quoted Wilde more than once; maybe he should check with her. Normally he was reluctant to ask her things that had to do with his policework. Their friendship had been founded in the course of a murder case three years ago, and back then her assistance had almost cost her her life. Esther had helped him since, but he was always vigilant about not exposing her to potential danger.

He called her.

"Yes, hello?"

He heard music in the background, opera.

"It's Jeppe. I hope I'm not calling at a bad time." He took a tentative sip of his coffee and made a face.

"Jeppe, how nice to hear from you." This was followed by a brief pause, as if Esther moved away from the phone. When she spoke again, she sounded more distant. "Let me just turn this down." The music was silenced. "There, that's better. What can I do for you?"

"As a matter of fact I'm calling to ask if you're familiar with an Oscar Wilde quote that I came across. I could ask Sara to look it up online, but I need to know the context and to understand what it might mean. Can I try reading it to you?"

"Of course!" She responded with an academic's excitement at being challenged on her home turf.

"'He looked around and saw the knife that had stabbed Basil Hallward. He cleaned it many times . . .'"

Jeppe didn't get any further than that.

"*Do I know it?* I wrote my master's thesis on Oscar Wilde. The quote's from *The Picture of Dorian Gray*, Wilde's tribute to youth, his satirical skewering of the vanity of his era."

A crash sounded in the background, as if a dish had fallen and broken.

"Gregers, what was that?" Esther exclaimed. "Oh dear, we had a little accident here. Gregers dropped a glass and now there are shards and milk all over. Dóxa, no! Jeppe, can we talk later? Or do you have time to meet?"

"Thank you, Esther. Tomorrow afternoon? Maybe around five?"

"Yes, just come on over!"

By the time Jeppe hung up, his coffee was cold. He threw away the cup and looked over the table at Anette, who was also wrapping up a phone call. She waved at him impatiently.

"Sure, Søndre Frihavn, got it! We'll be right there." Anette removed the phone from her ear. "That was Dispatch. Oscar's backpack has been found on a boat dock a few hundred meters from the family's apartment."

"How do we know it's his?"

"His name is in it," Anette said. "The forensic specialists are on their way. Let's go!" She clapped her hands as if hurrying a child along.

Jeppe got up and grabbed his jacket with a rush of the energy that his coffee had not yielded. A clue!

CHAPTER 5

Anette leaned forward in the driver's seat and looked past the parking lot's modern yellow-brick buildings toward the water. A group of rumbling motorcycles sped around a corner nearby, probably on their way back to the city from the traditional biker ice cream place at the end of Langelinie Pier. The air was buzzing with weekend vibes and people doing pleasantly purposeless things.

She and Jeppe got out of the car and walked toward Søndre Frihavn's little marina. Anette hung back slightly, feeling a pang of guilt at the sight of families having fun. But Svend, Gudrun, and the family weekend would have to wait. That was part and parcel of policework: she didn't get to enjoy time off with her own kid when someone else's kid had been abducted.

A narrow ramp led them from the quay down to the dock. They walked past sailboats, houseboats, and yachts with inflatable swim toys secured to the deck.

"Hey, ladies, how's it hanging?" Anette waved to the forensics crew.

Clausen, the crime scene technician, a wrinkled, balding fifty-nine-year-old man, looked about as far away from being a lady as one could get. But he shared her old-school sense of humor.

"Ah, if it isn't Kørner and Werner, our favorite wonder twins. Good to see you both!" He held up a black nylon backpack in his latex-clad hands. "This is it. No visible signs of violence, no tears, no blood. We're taking it to the lab to have a closer look at it. You'll get it back afterward, of course."

"And his name is in it?" Anette asked.

Clausen opened the backpack and pointed to a label on the inside with Oscar's name and phone number written in black marker.

"His name is in the textbooks, too, and this must be his laptop. I assume that should go to Saidani?" Clausen waited for a nod and then continued. "We'll check it for prints right away, so you can take it. Beyond that, there's just a pencil case and an empty water bottle."

He automatically shook open a plastic bag with one hand and put the backpack into it with the other.

"Wait!" Jeppe beckoned to him. "Let me look at the books."

"Sure." Clausen reopened the backpack and carefully took out a book with his gloved fingers. "Why do you want to see them?"

"He's out of comic books and doesn't have anything to read on the john," Anette joked. "Where was the backpack found?"

Clausen nodded toward the shore.

"It was tucked under the ramp," he said. "Between some brooms and buckets that the boating association stores there, not particularly well hidden."

"Who found it?"

"A caretaker guy from out at the fort. I asked him to wait for you. He's over there." Clausen nodded in the opposite direction, back out toward the water.

It took Anette a second before she spotted him in the stark after-noon sunlight, standing in a boat, leaning against the railing. She left Jeppe to look at the books and walked toward him, squinting her eyes, but could make out only the outline of a tall man, backlit, wearing coveralls, as far as she could tell. She shaded her eyes from the sun with one hand. The boat was compact, black and yellow, and looked mostly like a little tugboat. STÆRKODDER was painted in all caps on the side.

"Were you the one who found the backpack?"

"Who's asking?" the man retorted, his face still obscured by the sunlight behind him.

"The police."

He moved along the railing and hopped onto the dock.

"It was under the ramp. I found it when I went to grab a broom. Recognized the name from the coast guard's search alert and called you guys. I have no idea how it got there."

The man had thinning hair and broad shoulders with muscular tattooed arms, a slightly tousled look, and friendly, if sad-looking eyes. He held out his hand; it was strong and warm.

"Mads Teigen. I'm the caretaker at Trekroner Sea Fortress."

"Anette Werner, investigator with the Copenhagen Police."

He looked her right in the eye without blinking, his gaze the color of the ocean with little flecks of green.

Why am I noticing that? she wondered, and looked away.

"So you actually live at Trekroner Sea Fortress?"

"Yup, alone on a deserted island, the harbor's own Robinson Crusoe, that's me." He smiled shyly, like he had said something pre-sumptuous that he now regretted.

Anette squatted down to touch one of the blue mooring lines lying on the dock next to an empty slip. It was warm and dry in the sun. She peered out over the water.

"If you have a slip here, can you see if any of the regular boats are missing?"

He shook his head apologetically.

"As you can see," he said, "there are a lot of empty slips. Some of them are out sailing, others haven't been put back into the water yet after the winter. It's not the kind of thing you can keep track of."

"Okay." She got back up. "Have you seen anyone sailing around the fortress with a teenage boy? Or anywhere else in the harbor in the last twenty-four hours?"

"I see a lot of young people. It's getting popular, boating in the harbor, drinking and partying. Really dangerous if you ask me, but, no, I haven't seen anything that looked suspicious." He squinted up at the sun. "So you guys have no idea where he could be, the missing boy?"

"Why, do you have any information you'd like to share?"

"No, no. If I did, I would have told you, of course. I was just . . . curious."

Anette got out one of her business cards and handed it to him.

"If you see him or happen to think of anything that might help with the investigation, please let us know."

He took her card and studied it carefully, as if it might tell him something about her that he wanted to know.

Anette studied his broad fingers holding the agency's white card stock and felt an impulse to reach out and touch him, but at the same time an urge to run away.

"As I said, call if you see anything!"

She turned around and walked back to Jeppe, suddenly eager to get home to Svend and Gudrun, home to hugs and pasta and snuggling on the sofa in front of the TV.

"Had he seen anything?" Jeppe asked, starting to walk up the ramp.

"No. He just happened upon the backpack."

"And we're sure he didn't plant it himself?" Jeppe asked, looking back over his shoulder.

"What are you talking about?" Anette frowned. "Why would he plant Oscar's backpack and then call the police? That doesn't make any sense."

"Hmm, maybe."

Anette shook her head behind her partner's back.

"I'll just call PC and brief her on the backpack." Jeppe put the phone to his ear. "We need to start a door-to-door around the dock, ring doorbells and stop passersby. Someone may have seen Oscar and his kidnapper in the harbor."

"Tell her I say hi!"

Anette unlocked the car and opened the driver's-side door. Before she got in, she gazed back down at the dock. Mads Teigen was still standing by the boat holding her business card, looking after her.

THE SCENT OF risotto Milanese spread through the apartment on Peblinge Dossering. Esther de Laurenti had sautéed onions and rice and stirred in white wine and stock, and now the dish was simmering over a low flame while she sat at her computer. In a few minutes she would finish it off with butter and Parmesan, but until then she could fit in a little work.

The idea for her book had finally fallen into place around New Year's, when she read an old article online about funerals and was reminded of the legendary Danish anthropologist Margrethe Dybris. Esther had met her once or twice at the university but had never gotten to know her. Dybris had traveled through Southeast Asia in the 1960s and '70s, researching death rituals, taking pictures of the locals, and exhibiting her photos afterward.

Esther had checked out one of the anthropologist's scientific articles from the main library and was sold. Margrethe Dybris, who unfortunately passed away in 2017, seemed like an exceptional person. She had never married; instead she had traveled alone to some of the most primitive corners of the planet at a time when most women were chained to their stoves and children. She had later adopted two of her own, settled down as a single mother on Bornholm, and continued her research.

Esther ended up borrowing everything she could find about Margrethe's field trips to graveyards, about mummified corpses and death masks. She read the material with a growing admiration and also indignation.

Why hadn't anyone ever written a biography of Margrethe Dybris? Such a remarkable pioneer who had lived and breathed feminism, long before the concept had been divided into waves and watered down.

Esther had done only a few weeks of research before realizing that that was the book she would write. Margrethe's book.

Now she was studying up and gathering information for a biography of the anthropologist and her life's work, confident that the writing would come once she had thoroughly researched the topic and inspiration truly struck. She was in a good phase, leaving pages of notes and ideas all over the apartment.

Esther learned that Margrethe Dybris had lived with the Torajan people in Indonesia on multiple occasions. They mummified their dead and lived with them for years before burying them. She did a search for the tribe and read about their death rituals, kept going, and found an article about relics of the dead exhibited at a museum in Warsaw. She took notes.

It looked as if there might be an exhibit of death masks at Thorvaldsens Museum right here in Copenhagen that she would have to go see. A new link led her to a sales notice for a carved wooden relief of a funeral procession, beautiful but gloomy, with crying children and a skeleton among the mourners. It was for sale at the auction house Nordhjem for an astonishing sum, not exactly in her budget. A new link led her to pictures of reliquaries; she found herself scrolling past crosses and birds and eventually stopped at a picture of a light-skinned doll.

"Did you take the scissors?"

Esther nearly jumped out of her chair. Gregers was standing right behind the desk, looking at her accusingly.

"They're not in the kitchen drawer where they usually go."

"I haven't seen them, Gregers," she said, putting her hand over her racing heart. "I wonder if they aren't in your room?"

"Oh, please! If they were, I'd hardly come in here asking you about them, would I?" He pointed to the stacks of paper on the desk. "I can't believe you put up with this mess."

Esther got up from her computer with an audible sigh. For the most part, living with Gregers was pleasant and unproblematic, but every once in a while his crankiness got on her nerves.

"Come on, let's go look in the kitchen," she suggested. "I need to stir the risotto anyway."

Gregers led the way, and she followed, contemplating his dwindling frame. He had lost weight again. His appetite wasn't what it used to be, and sometimes he forgot to eat altogether, so Esther had started preparing dinner for both of them a few times a week. It was more fun cooking for two anyway, even if Gregers complained about her Mediterranean dishes.

"They're right there!" Esther said, pointing. "In the middle of the table."

"They weren't there before," Gregers said, scowling at the scissors. "You must have moved them!" He snatched the scissors and angrily shuffled away down the hall, toward his own room at the back of the apartment.

"Dinner will be ready in fifteen minutes!" she yelled after him.

Esther poured herself a generous amount of shiraz and got out the butter. Things seemed to be getting worse with Gregers.

She turned on her favorite recording of Verdi's *Rigoletto*—the one with Caruso—and let "Bella figlia dell'amore" accompany the scent of melting Parmesan. She drank an ample mouthful and then topped off her glass, realizing to her dismay that the bottle was already half-empty. She would probably have to lay off drinking wine on weekdays for a little while, however sad that was. It was so tedious to not drink.

The paper lay open on the dining table, several sections spread out side by side. Esther set down her glass and walked over to take a closer look. Square holes gaped like eyes in the pages, clipped at random without consideration to where the articles started or stopped. The cut squares lay in a neat pile. Esther picked up the top square. It was an ad for sunny vacations in Egypt, clipped right through the middle so the pyramid was cut in half and the headline unintelligible.

A little creature slowly unfurled in her gut. Not only had Gregers had the scissors all along, he had also been using them for something incomprehensible.

The word *dementia* hit her at the same time as the smell of risotto burning on the stovetop.

CHAPTER 6

"You want to park, and I'll go order for us?" Jeppe asked.

He got out of the car and left Anette to find a parking space while he headed for Oscar Bar. Yet another Oscar, Jeppe thought as he crossed the cobblestones. The renowned Copenhagen LGBTQ+ bar and café was right next to city hall, a stone's throw from the old police headquarters, and over the years it had become their haunt for after-work drinks. Neither the relocation of their offices nor a missing boy was going to change that.

Jeppe had forgotten that it was Saturday night until he opened the restaurant door to find loud music and dancing patrons wearing bright colors and tight leather. He took a seat at the bar and ordered two bottles of beer while Donna Summer belted out "Hot Stuff" and the bartender sang along.

Oscar had been missing for more than twenty-four hours and they were still without a single relevant witness statement or any contact with the alleged kidnappers. His backpack's location on the boat dock could indicate that he had been taken out to sea. PC had gotten the chief superintendent to grant assistance from the emergency management agency, whose search and rescue units and divers were now heading out on the water. The navy's helicopter could make it about an hour in the air over Copenhagen Harbor before it got dark. The alert had gone out to the various caretakers and attendants of the forts and islands, lighthouse keepers and pilots up the coast on both the Danish and Swedish side of the strait. The Swedish Search and Rescue Services in Malmö had offered their assistance. A search on Danish soil didn't get any bigger than this. However, none of it would help if someone was holding Oscar hostage indoors.

"Oh, man, that Carlsberg looks refreshing! *Skål!*" Anette appeared beside him and took a long drink of her beer. "I just got a call on my way in—the door-to-door didn't turn up a thing. No one has seen Oscar since he left school yesterday." She glanced over her shoulder and raised one eyebrow as a comment on the bar's party mode. "Any clues on the letter?"

"Let me see . . . Yes, Clausen just wrote." Jeppe tapped his phone and opened the crime scene technician's email. "The paper is run-of-the-mill white twenty-pound bond copy paper, and the text has been printed on an ink-jet printer, not a laser printer. The font is Times New Roman. There is a faint roller mark on the top of the page suggesting that it was printed on a large machine, not one for home use. Likely the kind of copy machine or printer you would find in any business office."

"Or at a school," Anette suggested. "Fingerprints?"

"A few. They found both Henrik's and Malin's. But unfortunately the others aren't clear enough to be used. You know how it is with prints on paper." Jeppe put away his phone and smiled at an older couple who had started dancing in front of the bar. There was something liberating about the unrestrained atmosphere around them, so innocent and untroubled by their concerns. "Esther de Laurenti confirmed that the quote is from a book by Oscar Wilde. I'm going to stop by her place tomorrow to hear more."

Anette shook her head and drank again.

"What kidnapper leaves a quote from a book before forcing the victim onto a boat? I don't believe that piece of paper has any connection to Oscar at all."

"Unless he wrote it himself?" Jeppe suggested. "Fifteen-year-olds can be quite . . . cryptic."

She gave him a knowing look and said, "I'm damn sure *you* were when you were fifteen. Cryptic and a pain in the butt."

"Oh yes. A sensitive young man full of words and dreams."

"Good thing I didn't know you back then," Anette said, winking at him. "I mean, it's hard enough to put up with you as a grown-up."

"Seriously, though, his backpack could be an indication that he was abducted against his will. Why else would it be stashed on a dock? He didn't leave it there while going for a swim, did he?"

"I still don't buy it," she said, shaking her head. "Kidnappers are nervous and blunt in their messages. If this was being done for money, we'd have heard from them by now—I mean, in a concrete way."

"So where does that leave us?"

"I say the parents did it." Anette drank and then wiped her mouth with her hand.

"Did what?" Jeppe countered. "You can't just toss out an accusation like that!"

"Well, all you do is come up with half-baked theories." She laughed wryly. "No, in all honesty, there's something off with that family. Time will tell whether it's the father, who swatted him too hard, or the mother, who has Munchausen syndrome by proxy. But I'm afraid that Oscar's lying on the bottom of the ocean with something heavy tied to his legs."

"If there's anyone who has Munchausen, it's you! Those poor people are dying of fear for their missing son. Give them a chance, would you!" Jeppe set some money on the bar. "The threats against the family are real enough, so they're probably related to Oscar's disappearance."

"That's what they want us to think anyway," Anette said.

Jeppe rapped his knuckles on the bar.

"Well, that's it for me. I'm going home to Sara. . . . You know, another possibility is that Oscar has gotten messed up in something online, through a chat or online game."

Anette finished her beer, sighed, and then said, "So, what you're saying is that some internet psychopath on a surfboard left the parents a nice letter, then took the boy out to sea and vanished into thin air?"

"Yes, Werner," Jeppe said, getting up. "That is exactly what I'm saying."

DIRTY SOCKS, SINGLE sneakers, tote bags, hats, schoolbooks, unopened envelopes, and comic books. The apartment looked like a garbage dump. All items lay scattered about in a way that robbed them of their original purpose, as if the things had lost their value by virtue of their location and had turned into garbage on the living room floor.

Sara Saidani surveyed the chaos with growing irritation. She wasn't a super-tidy person and had always lived with piles of this or that, but lately the mess had escalated to a point where even she could no longer stand it. She shared a nine-hundred-square-foot apartment in Copenhagen's Christianshavn neighborhood with her two daughters and, on most days, her boyfriend, too, and keeping it in even moderately decent order was starting to feel like holding a tsunami at bay with nothing but a roll of black trash bags.

She spotted a brown, half-eaten apple in one corner and rolled her eyes in disgust. Oh, what rotten filth wouldn't she find once she got going? With a weary sigh, she started cleaning.

A pair of floral-patterned cotton underwear landed in the hamper along with the yellow hoodie that Amina had whined for weeks to get and which was already stained and had been demoted to loungewear only. And here was one of Jeppe's T-shirts—normally he took his laundry with him when he went. Sara brought the white cotton shirt up to her nose and inhaled the scent of boyfriend but then quickly wadded it up and tossed it in with the rest of the laundry. After all, there were limits to how sappy a woman could act when she was a mother of two. Single parent, police investigator, and in love with her coworker—not an optimal trio.

She carried the hamper to the laundry room, squatted down, and started stuffing a load into the machine. Their cramped living quarters combined with the challenge of integrating Jeppe into the family was beginning to wear on her. For as passionate as he was about her, he seemed equally disengaged when it came to her kids. Sara sometimes felt like she was so busy forcing them all into a family relationship that she no longer knew how she felt about it herself.

Jeppe would be here soon. Sara wasn't on call herself, but after he had texted her this morning, she had turned on her police radio. The boy was fifteen years old, missing since yesterday afternoon. It could be serious but also quite harmless. Hopefully he would turn up again soon and in good shape.

The washing machine rumbled, and she watched it meditatively as it filled with water, while she picked at the Pippi Longstocking Band-Aid that covered a scrape on her knee. Little Meriem had applied it for her, concentrating, her tongue sticking out of the corner of her mouth.

The bathroom door creaked, and Sara could sense Jeppe even before she turned around to face him.

"There you are," she said, getting up. "Have you found him?"

"No. No witnesses, and no one knows where he is."

"Oh, poor parents. How are they taking it?"

"As you might expect."

Jeppe held her face between his hands and kissed her. Sara felt the familiar mix of tingly new-love excitement paired with the exhaustion that hit her every night after the girls had been put to bed. "Love isn't like in the movies," someone had sung and they were right. Only when the children were asleep and the Violent Crimes Department was far away could love be like in the movies, even if just in little glimpses. If only she weren't so tired.

"How was your day?" He tucked one of her curls behind her ear.

"Fine, same old, same old. I took the girls to see a film. Come on, let's go in the living room. I'll get you a beer."

She closed the French doors behind them. "Look, I cleaned the place up."

Jeppe looked around the living room, which seemed to be its usual messy self.

"Okay, okay!" Sara confessed. "So I didn't get very far. It's scary how little I get done even when I'm not working."

He smiled, looking like he was holding back. It wasn't something they said out loud, but they both knew their differing standards for neatness was one of the many stumbling blocks on their road to possibly moving in together.

"I brought Oscar's computer," Jeppe said, flopping onto the sofa. "I know you're actually off tomorrow, but . . ."

Sara considered for a second, mostly for her own consciousness' sake. She already knew that work would win over family time.

"I'll take a look at it. Maybe I can get my mother to watch the girls for a couple of hours." She sat down next to him. "Has it been checked for fingerprints?"

"The crime scene technicians found several sets, not just Oscar's. They're in the process of comparing them to the family's to see if there are any we can't identify." He opened the beer and drank with a sigh of satisfaction. "There was a letter to the parents. No sender, just an Oscar Wilde quote about something about a knife and the past having to die."

"A ransom note?"

"We don't know yet." Jeppe shrugged. "No contact yet, and no demands."

Sara shook her head, then reached over for his beer and took a swig.

"You don't like talking about it?" he asked.

She tilted her head evasively and said, "It's just, you know . . . a child going missing . . . When you have kids, that's the worst thing imaginable."

Jeppe took back his beer, emptied it, and set it down.

"I can't think about it anymore, either. Let's go to bed."

She let him pull her into the bedroom. Protested half-heartedly, but at the same time enjoyed the feel of his hands and eyes on her body. She succumbed.

"Mommy, I had a nightmare."

Meriem was standing in the doorway looking at them, perplexed. Sara wrapped the bedspread around her shoulders and got out of bed, squatting down to hug her daughter. Jeppe disappeared under the covers.

"Aw, sweetie, well, it's over now. Come on, let's put you back to bed. I'll sit with you for a bit."

Sara carried Meriem into the bedroom that the two girls shared and tucked her into the floral bedding in the bottom bunk. She sat on the edge of the bed, holding her daughter's hand, and tried to stifle her irritation that she couldn't just let Meriem sleep in the double bed with her. Would it be different if Jeppe were her father? Or just a little bit more interested?

She stayed, looking at Meriem, feeling the warmth of her small palm. When she finally slept again, Sara snuck back into her own bedroom.

Jeppe had fallen asleep.

Darkness surrounds the boy's body like a heavy quilt, stifling. He closes his eyes and opens them again, but it makes no difference. His heart is racing in his chest. He tries to breathe slowly to calm himself down, but the blindness makes it hard. It is cold around him, and he is shivering in his thin denim jacket. He tries to stop himself from shaking, knowing that it will only make him feel colder.

It is a claustrophobic little room. The ceiling is low, the space cramped. It is hard to get his bearings in the dark. The walls crumble under his fingers, and it is dripping from the ceiling. He can hear the ocean, but he can't see it anymore. He is hungry. And tired.

He sits down on the floor and leans against the wall. He tries not to think too much about the confined space or the darkness; that is no use. There is no way out. He is trapped.

The boy knows he is here to die. He has given up hope and just wishes it will happen quickly now, that his suffering won't drag on.

He knows what awaits.

When his heart stops, the blood in his body will stop circulating and slowly cool down to the temperature of his surroundings. His skin will grow clammy and change color, turning pale and yellowish. His eyes will either be closed or open, the whites reddish and runny. Livor mortis will appear first where his body is in contact with the surface below. If a long time passes before they find him, the pathologists will scoop reddish, yellowish fluid out of his lung cavities with a ladle.

The boy tries to think of the process as natural, like a biology assignment, a condition of getting to be alive at all. But he is still scared. Not so much of what awaits on the other side, but of what he has to go through before then.

SUNDAY,
APRIL 14

CHAPTER 7

"We haven't found him yet. I'm so sorry." Jeppe let the words fade. This morning's status report from the emergency management agency was discouragingly unambiguous.

Malin Dreyer-Hoff responded with more of a sound than an actual word. Then she cleared her throat.

"Okay, thank you," she said. "We haven't heard anything, either."

The echo of a tiff in the kitchen between Sara and Meriem reached the bedroom, where he was sitting. Jeppe hoped that the conflict wouldn't be audible on the other end of his phone call.

Where there is strife, at least there is life, he thought, and closed the door.

"I . . ." Malin sounded as if she, too, were walking away from someone or something. "I have something I'd like to show you. Do you think we could meet?"

"I could come by"—Jeppe looked at his watch—"in about an hour?"

There was silence on the other end. He was about to repeat his offer when she responded.

"Meet me at work, Stockholmsgade forty-one. It's also in Østerbro."

At work, now? he wondered, but didn't ask.

"Okay, I'll be there at nine o'clock."

He hung up and sent a text to Anette and Thomas Larsen, telling them to meet him at the office in Teglholmen at noon. It had been forty hours since Oscar Dreyer-Hoff had last been seen. They were going to have to work parallel to the search and rescue teams, exploring every conceivable option, even on a Sunday. Just as he received their *okay*, he heard the bathroom door open and hurried out there before Amina had a chance to get back in. Sara's older daughter was in the habit of occupying the bathroom for a half hour or more at a time. On top of that she was chronically morning grumpy. He showered quickly amid an array of scented bathing items, got dressed, and sat down at the table next to Meriem.

"Did you sleep well?" He never quite knew how to act with the girls. He wasn't sure if he could stroke Meriem's cheek and felt shy about his lack of knowledge as to how to talk to an eight-year-old.

"Answer, sweetie! Jeppe asked you a question!"

"Fine." Meriem sat reading a comic book and didn't look up. She turned the page and stuck a spoonful of oatmeal into her mouth, dripping some milk on the table.

Jeppe pushed the bowl closer to her. She pushed it away, her eyes on the comic book.

"She's just tired." Sara set a cup of coffee in front of him. "Have they found him?"

"No." He took a sip of coffee and burned his tongue.

"Found who?" Meriem looked at them, suddenly attentive.

"No one, honey. Eat your breakfast!" Sara caressed her daughter's hair and turned back to the toaster where slices of rye bread were starting to smoke. "I have managed to get a couple of hours to work this afternoon. My mom's coming. She might take the kids to the pool."

"Yaaaay, the pool!" Meriem squealed with joy. She jumped up, accidentally knocking over her bowl.

Sara swiftly found a rag and wiped the milk up off the floor.

"Look now! Ugh, as if it wasn't messy enough around here."

Jeppe tried to take the rag from her, but she waved him off. Meriem started crying.

"Okay, enough. No harm done. I'll give you a new one. See?" Sara hurriedly scooped more oatmeal into a bowl and got out the milk.

Amina came in and leaned against the kitchen table with her arms crossed.

"Did I hear you right that Grandma's taking us to the pool? I'm not up for that!"

Jeppe got up and put his cup in the sink. "Well," he said, "I'd better be off. . . ."

Sara shot him a look and turned back to her eldest daughter.

"I hear what you're saying, Amina, but you're still going. I don't want you to forget how to swim."

"As if that has anything to do with it!" Amina scoffed. "You just have to work."

Jeppe stopped in the doorway and said, "Remember, we're having dinner with my mother tonight."

"What?" Amina glared at him with her mouth hanging open.

"I told you about this, young lady." Sara waved to Jeppe over her shoulder.

"You did not! Why doesn't anyone ever ask me what *I* want to do?" Amina snapped.

"Have a good day!" Jeppe found his bag in the hallway and walked down the stairs into Christianshavn's fresh morning air. When he reached the street, he took a deep breath and exhaled.

*   *   *

JENNY KALIBAN BUTTONED her uniform and got ready to open Thorvaldsens Museum to the first of Sunday's museumgoers. The ocher building stood like a temple in the shadow of Christiansborg Palace, its facade frieze depicting Thorvaldsen's return to Copenhagen from Rome reflecting in Frederiksholms Canal. Bertel Thorvaldsen, the world-renowned sculptor, had helped design the building but died before it was finished in 1848. Now he lay buried in the internal courtyard of the museum, making it both an extensive collection of his art and his mausoleum.

Jenny pulled her graying hair into a ponytail and rubbed her face to get some blood into her cheeks. Yesterday had been a frustrating day of work in her atelier, followed by an even more frustrating evening. At three in the morning she had had to smoke two joints to be able to fall asleep. Now she was tired and out of sorts and certainly not ready to lead the guided tour at ten fifteen. She plodded from the staff room and down the vaulted corridors, past statues whose vacant eyes were all turned toward the courtyard. Her heavy footsteps echoed under the star-bedecked sky-blue ceilings, displaying a new zodiac sign in each vault, and she smiled as she passed Scorpio, the sculptor's sign as well as her own.

Art historians generally found Thorvaldsen to be too Scandinavian, chilly and chaste, but Jenny knew better. The museum was full of secret symbols and romance that revealed Thorvaldsen had been anything but frigid and boring. Take the axis that ran from the west-facing door past the Scorpio sign, straight through the ivy-covered burial monument, and out to the Christ figure by the east door. From birth to death and resurrection in one line, illustrated so subtly and smoothly. Not to mention all the erotic details and the humor that lurked everywhere just below the surface. When Jenny gave tours, she consistently described Thorvaldsen as a philosopher of love, emphasizing his freewheeling, erotic life with his many girlfriends and lovers outside the formal bonds of matrimony. Often people couldn't see beyond the dead gazes of the marble statues and found the museum boring. If they only knew! Eroticism has many faces.

Jenny opened the doors and let the spring light stream into the lobby, followed by eager visitors. She welcomed them, pointed them toward the ticket window, and let them know about her upcoming tour in a few minutes. Then she stood ready, legs apart and hands behind her back, below the plaster statue of Pope Pius the Seventh, the marble counterpart of which stood in St. Peter's Church in Rome.

At ten fifteen a group of eight people had assembled—seven of them gray-haired, wearing eyeglasses and practical footwear—and she began her tour. By way of introduction, she told them about Thorvaldsen's humble beginnings in late eighteenth-century Copenhagen, where he'd gained a reputation as a child prodigy and began studying at the Royal Danish Academy of Fine Arts when he was only eleven, winning countless silver and gold medals. Then she moved on to his prominent friends, including the poet Adam Oehlenschläger and author Hans Christian Andersen, his journey south by ship via Malta, and the forty years he spent in Rome. Jenny pointed to paintings and sculptures as she led the group around, and then guided them out into the courtyard. Here she told them about the burial chamber deep underground, allegedly sky blue and decorated with roses and lilies, featuring a cross on the floor and two crossed palm fronds on the cover plate over the coffin itself. That's how it was depicted in the architect's blueprints. Here she paused for dramatic effect before continuing:

"But there's no way to prove it, because the grave has never been opened."

Throwing in a bit of Dan Brown–style symbolism here and there always put the tour groups in a good mood. People loved mysteries.

Jenny led the group onward to the marble statue of Ganymede with Jupiter's eagle, which was tucked away in one of the museum's richly colored little exhibit rooms. She had mixed emotions about the beautiful sculpture of the young man kneeling in front of the eagle, his hands outstretched. His skin was so smooth and flawless, his eyes trusting and unaware that the eagle was actually the god Jupiter, who was about to kidnap him to Mount Olympus, rape him, and make him cupbearer to the gods.

THE DOOR TO Nordhjem's office on Stockholmsgade was painted in a color Jeppe remembered as Copenhagen green, gleaming as if it had been buffed within the last couple of hours. He was buzzed into an elegant hallway lined with high-quality wood paneling and climbed a flight of stairs to the first floor, where Malin Dreyer-Hoff greeted him.

"Thank you for being able to meet me so quickly," she said, even before he had made his way to the top of the stairs. "I had to get out of the house for a bit."

"That's understandable." Jeppe accepted her outstretched hand and stepped onto the herringbone parquet floor. He couldn't help tilting his head back and admiring the artfully painted ceiling with gold detailing and a Venetian glass chandelier. Two pink sofas that matched the one the Dreyer-Hoffs had in their home and big canvases of modern art accentuated the regal style. It didn't look like the kind of office Jeppe was used to.

"Malin, Oscar's backpack has turned up in the harbor just below your apartment."

"His backpack . . . What does that mean?" She stiffened.

"We don't know yet. There weren't any marks on it, everything looked normal. It was stashed underneath a ramp leading down to one of the boat docks."

She opened and then closed her mouth.

"That's where our boat is moored," she said.

"You have a boat?"

"Just a little daysailer. It's Henrik's."

"Does Oscar know how to take it out on his own?"

She hesitated.

"I don't think so," she said. "Maybe."

"Would you ask Henrik to check and see if the boat is in its slip? Right away."

She hesitated for so long that Jeppe was about to repeat his question.

"Of course. I'll call him."

Malin called up her husband and spoke in a quiet, staccato voice, no soft words among all the hard ones. After two minutes, she hung up abruptly.

"He's going to check now."

She walked over to the pink sofas, sat down, and tugged on the hem of her blouse. It was a habit Jeppe associated with women who felt insecure about their weight, but maybe it was something else that made her fidgety. He sat down on the sofa across from her and pulled out his notebook.

"What does it look like?"

"The boat? A twenty-footer, wood, painted white, named Frida, after my mother."

He jotted it down without looking up.

"It's Henrik's pet project," she continued. "I'm not a boating fan. But he loves new toys—cars, racing bikes, and since last year, a boat, too."

Jeppe smiled at the description. Men and their gadgets.

Her phone beeped. She skimmed the message and set her phone down on the table, screen down.

"The boat's gone, and the keys aren't hanging on their hook. Although they could very easily be in a pocket or a bag somewhere. We're not exactly organized at our place. Things do go missing sometimes."

"Please look carefully and let us know if you find them." Jeppe paused and watched her nod slowly. "So you had something you wanted to show me?"

"Yes." She tugged on the hem of her blouse again, leaned down to pick up her purse from the floor, and pulled out a plastic folder. She held it for a moment before passing it over the coffee table. "Henrik doesn't think we should confuse matters, but . . ."

Jeppe took the folder and read through the clear plastic.

A pig like you doesn't deserve to live. A pig like you needs to look over his shoulder. That's not an empty threat. I'm going to shoot you Monday on your way home from work!

"The infamous threatening letters, I presume? So you did have them after all."

Malin ignored that.

"How long does it usually take before a demand for a ransom is made?" she asked.

"I can't really give a specific answer to that. A few days, sometimes longer." He patted the folder. "But maybe we'll find the kidnappers now that we have these letters. Thank you. Oh, and by the way, does the author Oscar Wilde mean anything to you? The quote comes from one of his books."

"No, I've never read anything by him." Her pink-varnished fingertips twisted the many gold rings on her hands anxiously. "The thought of not knowing where my child is. That he's scared, maybe suffering . . ."

Jeppe leaned forward and put his hand on her arm.

"Every resource we have is searching for him, I promise you that."

She put her hand on his and gave it a grateful squeeze, holding the eye contact. He knew there wasn't anything he could offer her that would make her feel better but the safe return of her son.

"We'll investigate the letters and search for the boat. It must be in the harbor somewhere. I assume a small boat like that couldn't go very far?"

"I have no idea."

"That's okay. I'll ask Henrik." He gently pulled back his hand, and they both stood up.

A framed drawing of a face hung over a curved leg console table. The features were young and pretty, the gaze turned away from the observer, as if out of shyness. The drawing had been made with assertive black lines, the paper's planes varying in tones of gray. Jeppe stopped.

"I don't know how obvious it is, but that's a picture of Oscar, actually." Malin stood beside him and admired the drawing of her younger son. "He was so cute when he was little. Do you have kids?"

It was one of those questions that one can only answer with a yes or a no. Jeppe hadn't quite decided yet.

"No."

He smiled at her, and she reached for him. Her eyes reminded Jeppe of the panther at the zoo. Trapped by her own worst fear.

"It'll be all right, Malin."

The kiss was unexpected. Soft and inviting, tasting of coffee and fear. Jeppe pulled away from her and she looked down.

"I'm sorry. I don't know why I did that. I'm just . . . Things are so—"

"That's okay. I understand," Jeppe said, even though it was unclear to him why she had kissed him. A need to feel soothed, perhaps, to think about something other than what was haunting her? But why didn't she seek that comfort from Henrik?

"We'll find him."

Jeppe cast one last look at Malin before he opened the door. They would definitely find Oscar. The question was whether he would be alive when they did.

CHAPTER 8

CopenHill glowed in the bright spring morning light, the shiny metal facade reflecting the sun. Way up above the steeply inclined roofline the chimney top shone red like an evil eye. Copenhagen's new landmark resembled a flashing, living animal, lying in wait among the bushes and trees of Refshaleøen.

Kasper Skytte took a swig out of the bottle in his hand and contemplated his workplace through the windshield of his parked car. Lukewarm Aalborg aquavit—he hadn't been able to find anything else to brace himself with. It burned the whole way down to his stomach. Still, he kept drinking.

Working at the plant this past year had turbocharged his life in every sense. He had never been under more pressure, been more successful, or had more struggles than now. It felt as if existence had sped up, that life was flying by, and all he could do was try to hang on with a pounding heart. Race through the city to make it home and buy the groceries for dinner, wake up every morning to fifty new emails, decipher emissions numbers, develop new software, research, mop the floor, and be a dad without failing too much at any of it.

They say that he who works a lot makes a lot of mistakes. But was that really a comfort? An excuse perhaps, even?

It was too late to change it.

He had stood at a fork in the road and made a choice. That always sounded great in books, as if someone were actually standing on a mountain divide and could choose to go either north or south toward new adventures. In reality here he was, sitting in his worn-down family car with a blood alcohol level as sky-high as the incineration plant's chimney. And he could no longer turn back and confess.

When Iben was little, life had been simple. Her arrival in the world had put everything in perspective and cranked it up, so that black and white were lucidly clear. Back then he had never had any doubts what was right or wrong, what kinds of values he would pass along to his daughter, and what kind of a world he wanted her to inherit. Now he didn't know anything anymore.

Kasper took another swig and swallowed a belch of stomach acid. His cell phone rang. Again. He didn't answer it. As if he needed a reminder of how fucked he was.

He threw the bottle out of the open window. Then he started the car and drove toward the plant's fire.

"HEY, WHAT'S THE deal? Where is everybody?" Thomas Larsen set a bakery box down on the cafeteria table and looked from Jeppe to Anette. "I thought we would have a whole team here. I bought twenty cinnamon rolls so there'd be enough for everyone."

"Well," Jeppe said, screwing a lid onto a freshly brewed carafe of coffee, "that makes plenty for us, then. Look, I'm sorry, Larsen, but we're going to keep the investigation small and efficient for the time being. It's just us three and Saidani, and she's working from home today. The search for Oscar is going full force, but as long as we haven't heard from the kidnappers, there's not a whole lot *we* can do. I only dragged you two in here on a Sunday because Werner has . . . let's call it a hunch."

Larsen sat down at the table without taking off his leather jacket.

"A *hunch?*" he complained. "I just spent four hundred kroner at the bakery."

"Oh, it's worth the money, I promise you." Anette grabbed a chair beside him. "What are we celebrating? Not that I'm complaining, but why did you bring goodies?" She raised the lid of the box and selected a cinnamon roll with a particularly large amount of icing on it and transferred it to her plate.

"Yeah, well, I was going to make an announcement, but I suppose there's no getting out of it now." Larsen sighed, looking like a little boy whose sandcastle had just collapsed. "Mette's pregnant. I'm going to be a father."

Jeppe caught Anette's eyes from across the table and suppressed a laugh. There was something involuntarily comedic about Larsen's self-importance, which tickled them both. A rare combination of good looks, carefully honed ambition, and no sense of humor whatsoever. Jeppe knew that his desire to laugh at Larsen also involved a touch of envy. Now this detective who was ten years younger would be a father before him. He pulled himself together.

"That's wonderful. This really is a cause for celebration."

Anette patted Larsen on the shoulder and said, "Congratulations, old boy!"

"Well, now, it shouldn't all be about me," Larsen said, looking mollified. "Let's hear some more about Werner's *hunch!*" He put air quotes around the word.

"Malin and Henrik Dreyer-Hoff are convinced," Jeppe said, pushing his plate aside, "there's a connection between the threat letters they received two years ago, Oscar's disappearance, and the current quote that was left for them. They believe this is a kidnapping case, but Werner is not convinced."

"I think they're lying," Anette interjected with her mouth full. "If he was abducted for ransom money, we would have heard from the kidnappers by now."

Larsen was about to say something, but Jeppe interrupted him.

"On that we can agree. The family's boat is missing. That could mean either that someone forced Oscar onto it or that he took it out on his own."

"Unless," Anette continued, "the backpack on the dock and the missing boat are red herrings planted by his parents and meant to lead us astray."

"At any rate," Jeppe said, nodding, "we should have a look into the family's—" He was about to say *skeletons in the closet* but stopped himself.

"Into the *family bed*!" Anette exclaimed, rolling her eyes.

Larsen looked back and forth between them and seemed to be considering whether they were somehow pulling his leg.

"So, Larsen, let's hear it!" Jeppe gave him a smile of encouragement. "That's the situation. What have you found out about the threatening letters?"

"Oh, so you *do* want to know?" Larsen opened his logo-adorned bag and pulled out a folder holding about ten sheets of paper that he spread out on the table. "A little under three years ago, a customer went to the police suspecting dirty tricks in Nordhjem's auctions. The media picked up on the story, and a number of other customers came forward with their suspicions. It ended up turning into more than twenty individual cases. Because the story broke in the middle of a long business holiday it was able to simmer along for quite a while. You could definitely call it a shitstorm."

He took a bite of cinnamon roll and wiped his mouth with a neatly folded paper napkin before continuing.

"That can't have been fun for the family—the business is theirs, built from the ground up, not run by some venture capital firm. The couple founded the auction house just six years ago, so they've been quite successful in a short time. She came from the art world as a gallery owner, and he had been the manager of an electric company, and they maintained that division of labor. She's the creative director, and he's the administrative ditto, but they do overlap each other's areas of responsibility. She mostly handles acquisitions, and he's responsible for online sales and marketing and all the finances."

Larsen raised the cinnamon roll to his mouth but changed his mind and set it back down again.

"The crisis hit three years ago. The accusations were about so-called shill bidding, which basically means making fake bids on an auction item to inflate the price. The bids come either from the seller or from an accomplice and are incredibly hard to uncover or prove."

"But was it proven?"

"The state prosecutor for serious economic and international crime, SØIK, investigated the case and confirmed the suspicions that the auctions had involved widespread fraud. At one point the district attorney's office became involved. They obtained a search warrant and raided Nordhjem's offices. My contact says—off the record—that they were sure the family knew about the scam and may even have been involved. They certainly made plenty of money off the artificially inflated prices."

Larsen found a document on letterhead from the Copenhagen district attorney's office. The text had been heavily redacted, with a lot of sections blacked out.

"But they didn't find anything concrete, and the case was closed. My guess is that they simply couldn't prove it and had to give up. The threatening letters came in the period that followed. A total of nine letters over the course of a year; the last one was received two years ago. They were written on different paper, either by hand or on a computer, but they were all about the family—especially Henrik—being terrible people who deserved to die."

"So it's plausible that the scandal triggered the threatening letters. Was the sender ever found?"

"No." Larsen smiled meaningfully. "The family never surrendered the letters and ended up withdrawing the report."

The three detectives looked at one another over the cinnamon rolls. When people withdrew reports, it often suggested that they had something to hide.

"Does the letter the family found yesterday look anything like the threatening letters?" Anette asked.

"Not specifically." Larsen searched for the right words. "In the report the family describes the letters as very direct threats, expressed in blunt language."

"But they're still our best bet of finding a possible kidnapper." Jeppe pointed to Larsen. "Look into the consequences of the auction scandal. Monetary losses, employees who were fired, anything that might have given someone a motive for getting revenge on the family."

"I'll get to it." Larsen put the folder back into his bag with an expression that suggested he might have expected more applause from his audience.

"The parents could easily have taken Oscar somewhere by boat and killed him, maybe by accident." Anette broke a piece of icing off a cinnamon roll. "A fight that ended badly. A person could easily fall down the embankments at Trekroner Sea Fortress. That happened to a young guy a few years ago, and he died. They could have gotten rid of the body and the boat. Mads Teigen says there are a lot of private boats sailing around in the harbor. It would have been easy to hide among them."

"That guy, the one who found the kid's backpack?" Jeppe raised his eyebrows. "Whether we believe the parents' explanation or not, we have to focus on the threat letters. They could even have come from someone close to the family."

Anette reached for the bakery box, and Larsen hurriedly closed the lid.

"It's probably worth questioning the immediate family," he said, eyeing Anette disapprovingly, "friends, and employees of the company. There could be conflicts we're not aware of. Henrik's parents are dead. Malin's parents live north of Copenhagen, and she has a sister as well. Plus there's Oscar's siblings."

"I'm meeting Henrik in a few—" Jeppe was cut short by a ringtone.

Anette pulled out her phone and looked at the caller ID, then shrugged as if she didn't recognize the number.

"Werner," she answered.

Jeppe saw her eyes light up. After a brief exchange, she hung up and got on her feet.

"That was Search and Rescue. Oscar may have been spotted on the island of Hven."

"On Hven?"

The Swedish island, located in the strait between Denmark and Sweden, had already been scoured by the search and rescue crews without any results.

"One of the residents claims to have seen both him and the boat as recently as an hour ago. And he wasn't alone in the boat. I'm going to head out to the island right away." Anette started for the door.

"How? Are you going to swim? Shouldn't I come with you?" Jeppe smiled at his partner, who was bouncing from foot to foot in the doorway, flushed and eager.

"No, that's fine. Let's spread the work. You deal with Henrik, I'll sail to Hven with Search and Rescue, and we'll meet up later." She waved and vanished out the door.

Jeppe yelled after her, "Hey, Werner! Don't you want to bring your jacket?"

CHAPTER 9

A scent of fermenting seaweed hit just as Kyrkbacken's white lighthouse came into view. Nesting swans were tucked in among the concrete and boulders of the little harbor, and behind them towered a one-hundred-foot-tall grass-covered slope with a whitewashed church on top. The dimensions were Danish—small and quaint—but the atmosphere typically Swedish all the same. Maybe it was the string of small black and red wooden buildings with shingle roofs lining the pier, maybe it was the signs in front of the kiosk, advertising hot dogs with crab salad. Anette tasted her childhood memories of blueberry-picking outings on family trips to Sweden and remembered the giddy feeling of running zigzag through the heather so the adders wouldn't bite her.

The keel of the aluminum boat slid through the surprisingly full marina, where sailboats and motorboats were moored close. Standing at the helm, the crewman maneuvered them safely into an available slip at the innermost end of the marina and deftly tied the fore and aft lines with loops of strong rope.

"I'll just go find the witness." Anette hopped onto the wharf and moved through throngs of children eating ice cream, heading toward the harbormaster's office. Inside, a man in a faded blue T-shirt stood behind the counter watching soccer on his phone.

"Copenhagen Police," Anette said, showing him her laminated ID badge. "We got a call from a witness here who—"

"Building next door," the man said, looking up only briefly from his phone screen. "Nicklas, he's out back."

Anette appreciated the Swede's nearly accent-free Danish, sure to make day tourists from Copenhagen feel right at home on the island.

"Ah, thanks."

"No problem."

She walked the few steps to the building next door, which was decorated with a sign that read FISKBODEN, as in the Fish Shack, passed the locked door, and proceeded around to the back of the place. A man in his forties, with a receding hairline and earrings in both ears, stood painting the wooden facade with dollops of paint. As soon as he saw her, he set down his brush, wiped his hand on his pants, and held it out to her.

"Nicklas, hi. Welcome to Hven."

She shook his hand.

"You saw the boy we're looking for?"

"I saw him over there." He nodded toward the far side of the harbor. "In a wooden boat—white, right? It was a little before nine. I was coming in from Norreborg, where I live. They were just tying up."

"Are you sure it was him? Who was he with?"

He looked at Anette as if she must be a couple of condiments short of a sandwich.

"I was about a hundred meters away, so, no, I'm not sure. But it was a young man with dark hair in a white wooden boat and a second person, who had blond hair. So I called my friend Mads and asked if that matched the description of the missing boy, and he relayed it on to the search and rescue folks in Copenhagen." The man picked his paint brush back up and dipped it in the pail of rust-red paint.

"Over there, you said?"

"The boat's still there." He went back to painting with a sideways glance at the tourists in the harbor area, as if to demonstrate that he was too busy getting ready for the upcoming summer season to talk to her anymore.

Anette thanked him and returned to the search and rescue boat, where the crewman and the two volunteers were waiting.

"It's over here. This way!"

They walked by the pleasure boats, past the restaurant, the public bathrooms, and the swimming dock, around to the opposite side of the harbor. Sure enough, hidden behind a pretentious yacht, a white wooden boat was moored to the wharf.

"Don't you usually put the name of the boat on the stern? It's supposed to be called the *Frida*, but as far as I can tell there's nothing there."

The crewman hopped down onto the boat, grabbed the railing, and leaned over to study the side facing away from the breakwater.

"No name back here, either. It's actually required by law, but boat owners still don't always get the name on." He inspected the open boat. "There's nothing here besides some rope. It's empty."

Anette straightened up and looked around at the harbor, along the coastline, up to the church. How far could one get on foot in a couple of hours? Where could one even disappear to on such a small island as this?

"Maybe you ought to walk up to the church and get an overview," a voice suggested from right behind her.

Anette turned around and found herself looking into sea-green eyes. Mads Teigen.

"What are you doing here?" Her surprise made her sound gruff.

"I was the one who called the search and rescue folks. I know Nicklas from the fish place, who saw the boat. I thought you could probably use some assistance."

Anette contemplated the crewman from Search and Rescue Services and the two volunteers. Mads had a point. It was kind of a ragtag bunch.

"Maybe we could." She looked at the white church on the top of the hill, shining like a sign in the sunlight. An arrow pointing up to Our Lord, an outstretched hand to a searching soul, perhaps? "Is the view good from up there?"

"You can see most of the island," he replied.

"Okay." She pointed to the crewman. "You guys search the harbor! Ask everyone you meet if they've seen him! Meanwhile, the fortress caretaker and I will walk up the hill and get an overview."

She nodded to Mads and asked, "Shall we?"

The road curved its way out of town and looped around the hill, turning steeply upward past beautiful houses with neatly tended patios in terraces going up the slope. They fell into stride, and Anette was thankful to be able to keep up with him without getting winded. At the top of the hill, they reached the church and its surrounding cemetery. Mads stopped with one hand on the handle of the wrought iron fence.

"Did you know that *isola* originally stems from the Latin word for 'island'?"

Anette sensed that she was not meant to respond.

"People who go to an island, go specifically to *isolate* themselves and be alone." Mads stayed with his hand on the handle, his broad shoulders forming a wall in front of her.

"Is that why you live on Trekroner . . . ?"

He didn't answer. After a brief moment, he pushed down on the handle and opened the gate into the cemetery at the Church of Saint Ibb.

Anette watched him walk in. Then she followed.

*   *   *

"ANYTHING TO EAT?"

Sara shook her head and ignored the server's pointed look. She had been sitting for half an hour over a single pot of tea and knew that her bill would not help Paludan Books & Café pay their rent. Around her, groups of friends were gossiping over extended Sunday brunches, and she did her best to shut out their conversations and the aroma of their pancakes. Oscar's computer sat on her café table beside the teapot. Her mother had ended up staying home with the girls, because Amina flat out refused to go to the swimming pool, and Sara was forced to leave the house to find somewhere to work.

In front of her an image of two dead birds with black feathers dotted with app icons filled the computer screen. The dock held the expected word-processing programs and apps for music and social media. Oscar played *Fortnite* and *World of Warcraft* regularly—games that Sara was very familiar with and knew could potentially put a child in contact with a whole world of sketchy acquaintances. Pedophiles offered kids skins and other perks in exchange for nude pictures. But there were no immediate indications that Oscar had gotten to know anyone through the games who might have lured him astray, no suspicious chats or invitations that she could see. She went through his emails and calendar, but found only sparse information.

On Oscar's Facebook page he had posted paintings of Francis Bacon, links to art exhibits, punk music videos, and environmental policy updates about the effects of meat production on the ozone layer, endangered rhinos, single-occupancy vehicles, and CO_2 footprints.

There were conversation threads with his classmates in Messenger about parties and homework. One of the threads revolved around a subject-focus day at the high school two weeks earlier, where Oscar had apparently given a presentation on plastic in the world's oceans. Several classmates praised him with flexed biceps and heart emojis, but a few also mentioned a subsequent debate, where things apparently got a little heated. Someone named Karla wrote, *You're the one who's right. They are being totally ridiculous!* and someone named Gabriel added, *Hang in there! If our generation doesn't sound the alarm, the world's going to be screwed in ten years.*

Sara scrolled through to see if Oscar had commented on the subject but didn't find anything.

There was a folder on the computer's desktop that turned out to contain school assignments. Sara browsed through them. One paper in his social studies folder was titled "Brexit, and How It Could Affect Northern Ireland," and another was called "Hurry!" with the subtitle "If We're Going to Save the World." She opened and skimmed the assignments; they were articulate, and showed that he was a good student and engaged in his schoolwork. One title in the Danish folder gave her pause. "In His Image—Oscar Wilde."

Sara opened the document. It was an essay for Danish class. She skimmed the text but didn't find any quotes that sounded like the one Jeppe had mentioned. Still, there had to be some connection. His Danish teacher had written comments and given him an A at the end of the document. The teacher's comment was signed *Malthe Sæther, Zahles School.*

A quick search of the name yielded a phone number and an address. Sara called, but no one answered, nor did the call go to voice mail. It just kept ringing and ringing. Did she have time to pay him a visit? He lived at Vendersgade 19, on the fifth floor.

She looked at the time. It was almost two. She could probably be gone for another half hour without pissing her mother off. Sara sent her a text saying that she was on her way, slid the computer into her bag, and headed for her parked bicycle.

Vendersgade was a only few minutes away, practically on her way home.

Oh, Copenhagen, you wonderful, village-size capital!

She pulled her bike out into traffic and rode down Nørregade toward Nørreport. Six minutes later she stood in front of the teacher's building, breathing hard. The facade had been freshly plastered in a delicate pale yellow shade, which probably wouldn't stay clean for very long in the middle of the Nørreport area's heavy traffic. A sign that read SÆTHER in blue ballpoint pen sat next to the buzzer. She pushed it and waited. No answer. Looking up the front of the building she saw one of the top windows open in what must be his apartment. She pressed the doorbell again and waited.

"Who are you looking for?"

Sara turned around and saw a woman of indeterminate age, sitting with a cigarette on the top step of the cellar boutique next to the door. Her mouse-brown hair was pulled into a messy ponytail, and she was wearing a loose-fitting African-print bodysuit.

"Malthe Sæther, up on the fifth floor."

"He's not home."

"Do you know where he is?"

The woman seemed to size Sara up and apparently concluded that she was harmless, because she said, "Probably at his girlfriend's place. She lives in Odense, two hours away. He spends most of his weekends there."

"Oh." Sara nodded automatically and pulled a folded grocery list out of her pocket. "I just have a note for him that I wanted to poke through his mail slot."

"I can let you in." The woman stood up and pulled out a key. "It'd be silly for you to have to come back."

The woman opened the front door for Sara, who slipped inside with a smile, shaking her head to herself at how gullible people are.

She jogged up the stairs. On the fifth floor she found a white door with a laminated cardboard name sign stuck on it. A child had written *Malthe Sæther* in a wobbly line with alternating capital and lowercase letters and added a rainbow. Sara knocked and waited. Still nothing. She found his phone number, dialed it, and then put her ear to the door. No ringtone from inside the apartment. She squatted down to the mail slot and sniffed. The apartment smelled faintly of soap-treated wood floors, nothing else.

Sara got back up and checked the time. The magical boundary between late and too late was rapidly approaching. With an exasperated sigh, she jogged down the stairs to her bicycle, the traffic, and her daughters waiting at home in Christianshavn.

A STIFFENED WELCOMING committee of tombstones stood just inside the cemetery gate. Anette walked closer. A dark stone named *The Deaf-Mute Bengtsson Sisters*, followed by their first names and birth and death dates.

How little space we take up when we die, she thought. *A stone with a few words and some numbers to cover a whole life story.*

She lifted her gaze and saw Mads Teigen standing on the hill's highest point, in front of the church, looking out over the town below. In the sunlight, his body drew a sturdy silhouette against the sky, like a mythological hero with strong arms. The little hairs on Anette's arms stood up. Here by the church, far from the bustling harbor area, it was deserted and they were all alone. The thought made her feel strange, as if she were seeing herself from the outside, a woman and a man with no onlookers.

"Enough now!" Anette snapped out loud to herself, and kicked at a box hedge. She continued along the path behind the church without waiting for her traveling companion. One of her strengths had always been the ability to see the big picture without emotional quivers, but now it seemed as if her thoughts were all backing up. Maybe some vital part of her brain cells had been lost while breastfeeding or from the lack of sleep.

Behind the church the burial sites extended toward a wilderness of trees and bushes that continued along the ridge of the hill. Footpaths were trampled down in the tall grass, and the air hummed with insects. Anette tromped through the idyll, still flummoxed by her unwelcome reflections, and so preoccupied with her own thoughts that she didn't see him till she practically stepped on his foot.

A young man lay in a clearing between the bushes. He was naked, his skin gleaming an unnatural white in all the yellowy greens around him. Next to him was a backpack and articles of clothing strewn about like wreckage on a stormy sea.

Anette instinctively took a step back and tried to get her shocked breathing under control. She could hear Mads approaching from behind her and held up a warning hand to slow him down in time.

"He's here." She whispered without at all knowing why. Some strange form of respect, maybe.

He caught up, and they both bent down over the body in the grass. Just a big kid, really, with a hint of stubble on his jaw and grass stains on his skinny knees. His hair was dark and his face covered in freckles. A deep snore broke the concentrated silence in the clearing.

"Well, at least he's not dead," Mads commented dryly.

Anette couldn't hold back a relieved smile.

"What are you doing here?" A young girl appeared from the bushes, wearing only her underwear. "Gösta, wake up!"

The boy blinked a few times and stared at them in shock. Anette pulled out her police badge and showed it to the two young people.

"Put on your clothes. We have a couple of questions for you."

"What's the problem?" The girl pulled a dress on over her head.

"Is that your white wooden boat moored at the far end of the harbor?"

The boy responded in the singsong Scanian dialect of Swedish. "My dad's. We sailed it around from Bäckviken this morning."

"Bäckviken?"

"Yeah, on the east side of the island. That's where we live." He glanced shyly at his girlfriend.

Anette hesitated. The boy was Swedish, lived on Hven, and didn't look anything like Oscar Dreyer-Hoff. Even so, she pointed at him.

"And you're sure that that boat didn't come from Copenhagen? From Søndre Frihavn, for example?"

The boy shook his head fearfully.

"My dad built it himself! You can ask him."

Mads thwacked Anette on the arm.

"Okay, then. We're sorry to bother you. You two have a good day!" He started walking back toward the cemetery entrance.

Anette stayed for a moment looking at the teenagers. Then she gave in.

"Yeah, sorry. It was a misunderstanding. Well, goodbye."

Anette and Mads walked back down the hill in silence. Anette was stung by disappointment. Now that she herself was a parent, it felt as if she bore a certain responsibility for all children's safety. But apparently she couldn't help Oscar, couldn't do a darn thing.

At the foot of the hill she pulled out her phone and called Jeppe.

"Kørner here."

"It was a bust. The boy was Swedish and just out for a little jaunt with his girlfriend."

"Damn it!" She could hear him take a drag from his cigarette. "I'm on the dock waiting for Henrik. Are you still on Hven?"

"Heading home now. I just need to find the search and rescue folks . . . no idea where they went. Where do I meet you?"

"Go home, Anette!" Jeppe said after a pause. "It'll be four o'clock by the time you get back to the harbor. Spend some time with your family, and we'll meet tomorrow morning."

"Okay." She hung up and looked around the harbor for the search and rescue people.

Mads cleared his throat.

"I can take you back to Copenhagen, if you like? We can call Search and Rescue from the boat."

"Thank you, that would be great."

He led the way to the fortress's tug and cast off. As they sailed out of the harbor, Anette stayed on deck to let the wind blow her thoughts out of her head. Mads stood at the helm in the wheelhouse, a lit cigarette between his lips.

He exhaled smoke and looked at her.

"You want me to just drop you off by the boat dock in Søndre Frihavn?"

"Yes, please." She leaned against the railing. "What island is that?"

"Off the starboard side? That's Fort Middelgrund, one of Copenhagen Harbor's old sea forts. It was built around the turn of the century—well, the previous century, that is—to protect the city from a maritime attack. It's huge, three or four stories tall. When it was built it was the biggest fort in the world."

She went to join him in the wheelhouse so they didn't have to shout over the wind.

"What's it used for today?" she asked.

"Well, it's been basically abandoned for many years, but a fund bought it recently, and they're going to fix it up and turn it into a place for young people, Youth Island."

"*Youth Island?* What in the world is that?"

"The plan is to use it for scouting events and vacation camps. But renovations have ground to a halt because they've run out of money." He shifted his weight from one foot to the other, causing their shoulders to touch. Anette pulled away discreetly.

"I wonder if the search and rescue teams have searched out there."

"I'm sure they have. Plus there are surveillance cameras in the fort's harbor, just like on Trekroner. If Oscar were there, they'd have found him on the footage. And the boat would be moored in the harbor."

"Oh, right. Of course."

Anette fell quiet. She had so hoped that the boy on Hven would be Oscar. He should have been standing next to her right now with a blanket around his shoulders and a look of relief in his eyes. Ahead of them Copenhagen Harbor opened up and she watched the city's spires and domes with a thorn in her heart. And empty hands.

CHAPTER 10

When Henrik Dreyer-Hoff showed up on the dock at three o'clock sharp, he was noticeably burdened. His posture was slumped, and his firm handshake had been replaced by a vague nod of greeting.

"Malin took Vic and Essie out to her mother's place. We can't have them at home right now with things the way they are. It's better for them that way."

The father looked tormented. But something lay behind his expression that was deeper than shock or worry, Jeppe thought. Guilt has a very particular smell, and it hung heavily around Henrik Dreyer-Hoff.

"Did the keys to the boat turn up?"

"No." Henrik stuck his hands into his jacket pockets and shivered, even though the breeze was positively mild. "I'm pretty sure they were in the bowl in the front hall, but they're gone now. Just like the boat." He nodded over at the empty slip.

And Oscar, Jeppe thought.

"Is that your slip?"

"Yes, number B-thirteen. That's our spot. I used to joke that the thirteen would bring bad luck, that someday we would sink."

"When was the last time you took her out?"

"Thursday afternoon, just a quick little joyride on my own. It was chilly, and none of the others wanted to join me." He raised his hand toward Langelinie Pier. "That's how we go from the dock here, around and under the bridge and out into the harbor proper. Going right you pass the Little Mermaid and on toward Christianshavns Canal. If you turn left you head out toward Trekroner and the open sea. But the boat isn't intended to cross the shipping lane. It only goes up to five knots, so we mostly stay in the harbor."

Jeppe followed his finger as he pointed out their usual routes.

"How often do you take the boat out?"

"During boating season, I try to get out two or three times a week. Even just a quick jaunt in the afternoon energizes me for days. But I can't always get the kids to come along. They have so much other stuff going on."

"And what do you usually do? Are there any outings you take regularly?"

"Well, it depends on the wind, and whether we want to fish or swim. Sometimes we head out to Flakfortet or over to Trekroner. . . ." Henrik lowered his chin and held his breath for a moment before continuing. "Oscar loves going there to explore. He brings his sketch pad and draws. We've gotten to know the fortress caretaker. He often takes the time to show Oscar around."

A note sounded in the back of Jeppe's mind.

"The fortress caretaker? What's his name?"

"You know, I can't remember," Henrik said, his brow wrinkled in concentration. "We've met him only a handful of times. But he's friendly and very knowledgeable about the fort's history. And about birds."

The note grew in intensity and started chiming in Jeppe's ears.

"How do you operate the boat? Is it hard? I mean . . . I'm sorry if I'm asking a stupid question, but I've never tried it myself."

"It's not a sailboat. You just turn on the motor with a key, like in a car, and put the boat in gear," Henrik explained. "You cast off the mooring lines and push away from the dock. The hard part is bringing the boat in again without damaging it. Steering it is easy. You just use the tiller in the back of the boat."

"Do you think Oscar could do it?"

"That . . . I don't actually know. Victor's a good sailor, but Oscar has never been so keen. Why, do you think he sailed off on his own?"

"We're keeping all options open for now." Jeppe resisted an impulse to soothe the father at all costs. There was no point in giving him false hope. "Can you think of anyone in your own circle of acquaintances who would want to harm Oscar? Or you?"

"For money, you mean? A ransom?" Henrik eyed him quizzically.

"Well, yes, money. Or revenge?"

Henrik shook his head.

"The only thing I can think of is envy. Someone who wants something from us."

"There are no old family feuds that we should be aware of? Problems with the auction house?"

A cruise ship blew its horn and pulled away from Langelinie Pier nearby. It looked like an iceberg breaking free from the icecap and gliding away.

Henrik blinked. A burst blood vessel in one of his eyes made the white look pink.

"You've obviously heard about our . . . difficulties at the auction house a few years back," Henrik said. "The accusations came out of nowhere, and the police didn't find any grounds to take it to court, but people believe what they want to believe. Malin and I gave interview after interview to explain ourselves and clear the air, but it didn't do much good. People just bashed our lifestyle instead, our decor, our parenting."

Jeppe nodded. He was already familiar with the anatomy of a public shitstorm, thanks to his friendship with Johannes. But it's a long way from a shitstorm to a kidnapping.

Henrik was talking himself up into a heated state.

"A well-known so-called family counselor even said on prime-time TV that we were unfit to be parents because we co-sleep with our kids."

"Your oldest son did mention that you sleep together in one big bed. A *family bed*, I think he called it . . . ?"

"And?" Henrik said with a shrug. "Why would kids benefit from sleeping by themselves in their own rooms? Can you explain that to me?"

"It's just unusual for older kids—teenagers—to sleep with their parents."

"What are you trying to insinuate?" Henrik eyed him angrily.

What did Jeppe know about raising teenagers anyway, or any kids for that matter? Not a goddamn thing.

ESTHER FOUND THE bottle of port in her glass-front cabinet, poured ground coffee into the French press, and set out some can-tucci biscotti on a Royal Copenhagen blue fluted plate. Jeppe was expected at 5:00 p.m. and even though it felt a bit silly to have coffee and cookies this late before dinner, it had become a bit of a tradition when he visited.

"I'm not feeling so good."

Esther looked up from the steaming kettle in her hand.

"How do you mean, Gregers?" she asked.

"I don't really know." He opened and closed his mouth several times. "It's like everything is flipped the other way, the wrong way. Isn't the kitchen table usually over there, or have you moved it?"

"What do you mean? You can't move the kitchen table. It's attached to the wall. . . ." Esther noticed how rapid and shallow his breathing was, like a baby bird's. "All right, here's what we're going to do. Tomorrow morning, first thing, I'm calling your doctor, and I'll insist that they fit you in right away. We need to get you looked at. Okay?"

"I'm going to go lie down," he said, nodding slowly.

"Okay, just come get me if you need anything."

Gregers shuffled down the hall toward his bedroom and closed the door behind him.

Esther finished brewing the coffee and poured herself a glass of port. She deserved it. She needed it, at any rate.

Just as she brought the glass to her lips, someone buzzed from downstairs. A minute later, Jeppe stood in her front hall, out of breath. He kissed her cheek and walked in an arc around the barking Dóxa into the living room. When Esther brought in the coffee, he was standing at one of the windows facing the lake.

"Not a view you get tired of, is it?" he asked.

"Not in my lifetime anyway. Have a seat. You'll have some coffee, won't you?"

He obediently sat, took a cup from the tray, and held it out to her.

"I'll always say yes to your coffee. Thank you."

She poured them both a cup and sat down in her peach-colored wingback chair. There was an unsettled energy about Jeppe today, but of course, he had a lot on his mind. She took a sip of coffee and cleared her throat.

"So," she began, "what's all this about *Dorian Gray?*"

Jeppe set down his cup with a smile.

"Right to the point, as always. I appreciate that. We're looking for a teenage boy who has been missing since Friday afternoon."

"Oscar Dreyer-Hoff, right?" Esther asked. "I saw it on the news."

"Exactly. His family found this letter." He handed her a piece of paper. "This is a copy, you can touch it."

Esther took the paper and read it carefully. She recognized the words and enjoyed their eloquence, read them again.

"Is this a suicide note?"

"We think he might have been kidnapped and that the abductor left the note."

Esther got up and walked over to her shelves, which covered the whole end wall of the living room and were stacked with books from floor to ceiling. She searched briefly and then pulled out a volume. It had the picture of a young man on the cover.

"Here it is. *The Picture of Dorian Gray*, one of the best books in the history of the world if you ask me. Like I said, I wrote my master's thesis on Wilde back when I was a student eons ago."

She handed Jeppe the book and he dutifully flipped it over and skimmed the back.

"Yes, thank you, Professor. But why do you think the quote could be a suicide note?"

She smiled over the edge of her coffee cup.

"Turn to page two hundred fifty-five!" she said.

Jeppe found the passage and read it aloud.

"'As it had killed the painter, so it would kill the painter's work, and all that that meant. It would kill the past, and when that was dead, he would be free.'"

"The quote comes from the end of the book, just before Dorian Gray takes his own life. Hence it might be a suicide note. There's that curious coincidence of the names, *Oscar* Wilde and *Oscar* Dreyer-Hoff as well."

Jeppe drank some coffee and contemplated the young man on the cover of the book.

"Remind me how the story goes again?" Jeppe asked. "There's something about a painting, right?"

"Exactly! The handsome young man, Dorian Gray, has his portrait painted and is so enamored with his own beauty that he trades places with the picture so that he remains young and the picture ages. All his misdeeds—and age, as it comes creeping up on him—are visible in the painting, but Dorian's own face doesn't change. Finally he can no longer stand to look at the truth of the painting, and he destroys it. But as he thrusts a knife through the canvas, he himself dies. A subtle form of suicide, if you will." She threw up her hands and for a moment felt like an academic again, driving home her point.

"But would a fifteen-year-old think like that?" Jeppe asked with a skeptical wrinkle in his brow.

"What were you like as a teenager?" she asked.

That made him smile again.

"You're one smart cookie, Esther de Laurenti."

"Oh, please." She topped off their cups and realized she was blushing. "But seriously: if I were you, I would investigate whether the missing boy has reason to want to disappear."

"Suicide?" Jeppe asked, his skeptical wrinkle back.

Esther set the French press down carefully on the coffee table.

"Do you have a better explanation?"

CHAPTER 11

At Holmeås 14 the evening meal was being served earlier and earlier with every passing week. Anette sometimes had the feeling that both she and Svend were unconsciously pushing the dinner hour so that they could all go to bed earlier. As a confirmed night owl, she opposed cutting the evening short and giving up that potential adult time, but in all honesty she could use the extra sleep.

Special Forces soldiers, she thought, *who brag about not sleeping for multiple days straight, should try having kids.*

Gudrun had long since cried her way into their double bed and now slept regularly in the sweet spot between her parents. That meant unrestful sleep for all three of them as well as constituting a massive threat to her and Svend's sex life. They often agreed that their daughter had to learn to sleep on her own soon, but she resisted ferociously, and they didn't have the energy to insist. Besides, having her snuggled between them was cozy. So far their discussions about moving her had led to nothing.

Anette watched her husband clear the table while he played peekaboo with Gudrun in her high chair. At least their child was alive and at home.

"Now, honey, maybe we should let Daddy clean the kitchen while we go take a bath?" Her daughter started wailing in response, her screams ricocheting between the smooth surfaces of the kitchen. Anette picked her up out of the high chair and tried to soothe her protests with calming words.

Svend stopped them.

"Actually I promised that *I* would give her her bath today."

"Da!" Gudrun exclaimed, and lunged for her father, who accepted her with an apologetic smile. Gudrun immediately calmed down and laid her head on her father's shoulder. He gave Anette a pleading look that still managed to be ever so slightly reproachful. As if it was somehow her own fault that their daughter preferred to be bathed by him.

"Shouldn't I . . . ?"

"You bathe her next time. Go take the dogs for a walk instead and get some fresh air!" He looked affectionately at Gudrun. "Kiss Mommy bye-bye, princess, and then let's go find the tub toys."

Anette was allowed to kiss her daughter on the hair before they disappeared off to the bathroom. Disappointment chafed at her, but she refused to let it take over, even though fatigue left her feeling raw. It was normal that her daughter currently preferred the parent who spent the most time at home. As long as Gudrun was safe and happy it didn't mean anything. She fetched the leashes and called the three border collies. They ran straight to her, no doubt about who *they* preferred.

Out on the street the late-afternoon air was thick with pollen; she could practically smell bark and musk and spring seeds. The sky was high and bright, and spring so palpably around the corner that it was impossible not to feel giddy. The dogs jumped about, tugging impatiently on their leashes. When they reached the marsh, she let them loose so they could sniff around and run off their exuberance, while she relaxed on a bench. She felt a pack of cigarettes in the chest pocket of her fleece from back when she used to smoke and took it out, shook out a cigarette, and set it tentatively between her lips. It was like putting on her very best old jeans, and she felt both disappointed and thankful that she didn't have anything to light it with.

The image of Mads Teigen at the helm, smoking and smiling, appeared out of the blue. Or rather: it had popped into her head quite a few times over the course of the afternoon, but now she permitted herself to dwell on it. There was something unusual about that man, a reticence that she just couldn't decode. He was reserved, no doubt about that, but at the same time a darkness burned in those green eyes; a gloom that seemed strangely alluring to her. Anette had to admit that she found him exciting, and she had no idea what to do with that feeling. Even the fact that he smoked made him interesting in this sanctimonious parent phase of her life. She sighed heavily at her own silliness. It was probably just the spring going to her head. The spring and her fatigue.

Her phone rang. It was Kørner.

"What is it *now*?!" Anette laughed to make it clear that she was kidding. Her partner could be a little dim sometimes. "Anything new?"

"No. But I have a couple of details I'd really like to discuss with you if you have time. You're not in the middle of making dinner, are you?"

Anette heard him light up a cigarette and felt a sharp pang of longing for the way things used to be.

"No," she said, "it's fine. Let's hear it!"

"I was just talking to Esther de Laurenti. She thinks that the letter to Oscar's family might be a suicide note."

"You are saying that he killed himself?"

A group of laughing teenagers walked past Anette's bench. She moved the phone over to her other ear.

"The father can't rule out that Oscar is able to operate the family's boat."

"What the hell, Jepsen? That makes no sense. If he committed suicide, we would have found him and the boat by now. Or at least the wreckage." Anette spoke with more conviction than she felt. None of their theories seemed really plausible.

"There's something else, too. That fortress caretaker guy, the one who found the backpack . . . The guy who was also on Hven—"

"Mads Teigen, what about him?"

"Do you know how long he's been working at Trekroner?"

"No, why?" Anette stiffened.

"There's some indication that he knew Oscar. The Dreyer-Hoff family went to Trekroner often. Henrik mentioned the guy but couldn't remember his name."

"I'll ask him. Anything else?"

"That's it," Jeppe replied. "Say hello to everyone for me!"

Anette hung up and returned her phone to her pocket, tossed the unlit cigarette into a bush, and summoned her dogs.

THE TABLE WAS set with his grandmother's old silver, which Jeppe knew his mother usually kept stored in her safe-deposit box. A candlestick gleamed in the middle of the table. There were single-serving portions of dessert on individual plates, surely store-bought and then arranged at the last minute. His mother had pulled out all the stops. Jeppe just wished that she had put a little more thought into the fact that 50 percent of the guests were children instead of so obviously trying to impress the grown-ups.

She started the evening off by asking Sara enthusiastically about her upbringing in Tunisia, only to hijack the conversation with a monologue about Carthage, the Phoenicians, and the ethnic minority of the Berbers. After that she moved on to her favorite topic, culture, and started fishing to see if Sara was more interested in theater or opera, art or literature. Sara admitted without batting an eye that she didn't really have time for any of it, a confession that Jeppe knew automatically placed her in his mother's blind spot.

"Oh, but you absolutely must read out loud to your daughters! Otherwise they'll end up being cultural illiterates. Choose one of the classics, *Alice's Adventures in Wonderland*, for example, or its sequel, *Through the Looking-Glass*. That's a wonderful choice for that age group. I have a copy you can borrow. I think it might even be Jeppe's from when he was a boy."

Sara smiled and drank a sip of water without making any move to continue the conversation. Jeppe felt a drop of sweat trickle down his spine. There was a crash as Meriem accidentally knocked over a glass with one of her Transformers action figures.

"Maybe we should excuse the girls from the table while the rest of us have dessert," his mother suggested.

"It's just water." Jeppe gave her a warning look.

"We don't like the cake anyway," Amina said, her arms crossed. She looked like she had spent the last hour being subjected to Chinese water torture.

"Okay." Jeppe ignored his mother's raised eyebrow and stood up. "Come on, girls. Let's go in the living room. Meriem, bring your toys along!"

"Can I watch YouTube?" Amina directed the question at her mother.

Sara nodded, and Amina leaped up and retrieved her phone from her jacket out in the hall. She came into the living room with her nose glued to the screen and plopped down onto the sofa, immersed in the K-pop music videos she was into at the moment.

Jeppe helped Meriem set her action figures up on the carpet and then returned to the table, where the conversation had stalled. He felt briefly irritated at the women in his life, who only really tolerated people who were like themselves.

They could at least try! But that's not how we humans are. And the older we get, the more we insist on our right to have our quirks and preferences left in peace.

He contemplated his mother, who had raised him all on her own with lots of discipline and not very much money. She had cared deeply, but after her long workdays at the university there hadn't been much time and energy left for him.

In a way, he felt like he instinctively understood Oscar. Even though he had never met him, Jeppe recognized a sensitivity in the boy. As a fifteen-year-old, Jeppe Kørner had often spent hours or even entire days lying in his bed with a thick book and the curtains drawn. While his friends played soccer and got together to secretly drink beer and talk about girls, Jeppe had withdrawn from socializing and retreated into self-imposed solitude. He remembered his teenage years as the worst of his life, brimming with doubt and self-loathing, his reflection in the mirror one of chronic insecurity and weakness. It was a wonder that he had survived that period.

Jeppe looked at his watch. It was eight o'clock. At dusk the search and rescue crews would suspend the search for the day. Everyone knew that passing the forty-eight-hour mark without any sign of life from Oscar likely meant that he was dead.

Where are you, Oscar? he thought, sticking his fork into his tiramisu. *Where the hell are you?*

Hunger has set in for real now. The boy has never tried going without food before. It frightens him, how the pain in his stomach fills his whole being. More than the cold and his fear of the sounds he hears. Rattling and footsteps around the clock, and yet no one comes. He is alone.

He is lying down now. The strength to sit or stand is no longer there, and he no longer knows if it is night or day. Here it is dark all the time. Not the kind of darkness he knows—the night sky lit with stars and the moon reflecting on the surface of the ocean—but black as if he has lost his sight.

He tries not to think about his family, but it is hard. His thoughts revolve around his siblings; they talk to him in the dark and plead with him to come home. His stomach hurts even more when he hears his little sister's voice, and he clenches his teeth hard to force her away.

Breathe. As long as he focuses on breathing, he doesn't think about anything, not even death. But he knows it is thinking about him.

MONDAY,
APRIL 15

CHAPTER 12

Monday morning Kasper Skytte showed up for work feeling anxious. A guilty conscience battled with fear to overtake control of his body, and he had to muster all his energy to be able to focus on the task at hand. Today was allocated to sitting with the crane operator and supervising the computer-controlled sorting system in the waste silo. They had to nip problems in the bud to keep the whole incineration process from coming to a standstill. Right now that would be catastrophic in more ways than one.

At eight fifteen he walked through the bright, airy lobby and took the elevator up to his office, grabbed his work laptop, and continued on to the silo. His footsteps echoed across the metal bridge and up the stairs until he stood in front of the orange door that led to the crane operating room. He hesitated for a second before he let himself in, greeted Michael the crane operator, and took a seat next to him, with the computer on his lap and an unobstructed view of the trash.

Kasper wasn't a big fan of looking at trash, and every time he was forced to sit here, he mostly thought about when he could leave.

"Any problems so far?" Kasper brought up the morning's statistics on his screen.

"Nope."

Michael wasn't a talkative guy, and today that suited Kasper perfectly. The silence made it easy to look back and forth between the numbers and the claw. The claw moved the trash from the sluices, where the garbage trucks were emptied, over to the ovens, from left to right ad infinitum. Once he had watched it for a while, he started to see things. An umbrella frame became winter branches, a frayed plastic bag became loose hair, and black trash bags turned into severed limbs. He stood up.

"Coffee?" he asked Michael.

"Thanks, I'm good."

Kasper poured himself a cup. He checked his phone and gratefully remembered that there was no service in this part of the plant before turning back to the window. He blew tentatively on the hot brew and took a sip. The claw glided by right in front of them with a full load, monstrous, unpleasant, and fascinating. Strange objects that had once been colorful but were now gray.

That's when he saw it.

Kasper felt the coffee approach his windpipe. He coughed and pointed.

A second later, Michael hit the dead-man button.

"MAKE SURE YOU put on these suits, safety shoes, and a face mask before you enter the silo. The air in there isn't fit to breathe, so keep it short. When you get in, you'll find a plateau with a long gap on either side of it. Those gaps lead to the ovens. They're off right now, but they're still very hot, so keep well clear of those! As soon as you come back out, we'll be ready to disinfect you."

Anette accepted the two white bundles and handed one of them to Jeppe. They normally wore protective suits to avoid contaminating the discovery site, but today it was the other way around, to protect themselves from being contaminated by the discovery site. While she was pulling on the suit she wondered whether she had ever been in such a horrifying place before. A set of massive double doors before them led into the waste silo, to the plateau between the ovens that normally burned at a thousand degrees. Even out here the heat was intolerable. The thought of walking into an even hotter, dark, contaminated room to inspect a dead body was more than unappealing. Good thing she wasn't sensitive.

She pulled her face mask into place and checked to make sure that Jeppe was ready, then opened the door and stepped through the airlock and into the silo. Anette could hear Jeppe gasp as the wave of scorching hot putrefaction hit them, and she had to swallow a few times herself to keep it together. A world of garbage lay far below them, enclosed within the silo's solid metal walls and with the crane operator's window as the only eye. It was astonishingly quiet in here, but quiet in the way of a road paver who pauses to wipe the sweat from his brow before thundering onward.

The claw hovered over the plateau, hugging trash in its enormous embrace and forming its own round planet in a spooky universe. A bright work light was aimed at it, and next to that stood a tall, thin figure, whom Anette recognized as Professor Nyboe, the medical examiner, along with another figure who was taking pictures. They both wore protective gear like hers and were moving quickly and efficiently.

She and Jeppe walked closer to the light. Sweat was already trickling down her spine and forming a little puddle above her butt. She resisted the impulse to yank off her face mask so she could breathe properly and focused on the trash in front of her. Between a wad of cardboard and some cans, a slim, white-skinned human leg stuck out. Portions of the trash had been dug away from around the leg, and a body could vaguely be made out, a neck, and a head.

"Can't we just open the claw?"

Nyboe turned around.

"Ah, there you are! Horrible this place, horrible. The claw contains five and a half tons of trash, so we have to dig the body out very carefully. If we open the claw, it'll simply vanish in the muck."

"Is it a man or a woman?" Jeppe's voice sounded far away, even though he was standing right next to her.

"We don't know anything yet." Nyboe removed a chunk of plastic with a pair of long-handled pliers. "Except that it is a human being."

The corpse's cheek came into view. It was covered with a thick layer of dust and looked like a statue, smooth and unconcerned and very, very dead.

"Do you have any idea about the cause of death yet?"

"I'll give you my opinion when we have gotten the body safely out and I can examine it properly. This place isn't fit for living creatures!" He swore to himself and dug yet another piece of trash out of the claw.

Jeppe poked Anette on the shoulder and pointed toward the door. "Let's get out of here!"

Once through the double doors they pulled off their masks and greedily breathed in the air. Anette felt her eyes stinging and was about to rub them when an employee in a boiler suit stopped her.

"You need to be disinfected. Come with me!"

He led them down a flight of stairs to a staff room where they could remove the protective gear, wash off perfunctorily using a little washbasin, and wipe with disinfectant. Getting out of the foul-smelling clothes helped, but the stench in their noses wasn't as easy to get rid of.

"Unbelievable! How long were we in there? Two minutes, five? How the heck can we stink like this already?" Anette spat into the sink and promised herself she would spend a full hour in the shower if she made it home tonight. "Could you tell if it was Oscar?"

Jeppe sat down on a bench and spread hand sanitizer over his hands for the third time in a row. Her partner, the hopeless germophobe!

"I had really hoped that it wouldn't end this way, that we would find him alive." He responded without looking up, sounding deflated.

"Ditto." Anette sighed and rubbed her eyes. "*If* it is him. . . ."

"I know what you're going to say," Jeppe said, standing up. "*If* it is Oscar, how did he end up in a garbage dump on Refshaleøen?"

"Exactly." She spat once more and felt like she might never be really clean again. "And where the hell is the boat?"

A SMALL GROUP of burly men in rugged overalls sat clustered around Michael, the crane operator, as Jeppe and Anette entered the tech crew's employee lounge. There was coffee on the table and a clear liquid in paper cups that Jeppe guessed to be some sort of alcohol that they probably weren't allowed to drink at the plant. The crane operator spoke quietly to his colleagues, his face an agitated flush of red, before downing the last of whatever was in his paper cup. He took out a tissue and blew his nose noisily.

Jeppe, who had been about to offer him his hand, patted him on the shoulder instead.

"Jeppe Kørner. How are you doing?"

"Well, I guess I'm okay. But I have to admit that I've had better Monday mornings than this."

His coworkers murmured their consent around the table.

"But I think Kasper took it even harder," he continued. "He had to go lie down on one of the couches in the cafeteria."

"Kasper was with you in the crane operator's room?"

Michael nodded.

"We'll give him a chance to recover, then. Are you up for giving my colleague and me a tour? Show us the plant while we ask you some questions?"

"What do you want to see?" Michael asked, getting up willingly. He looked almost a little relieved to have something to do.

"We don't really know, actually," Jeppe said hesitantly. "But what we need to understand is how the body could end up in your claw, where it could have come from."

"Then let's start on the tipping floor. Follow me!"

He led them over to a stainless steel elevator, and after that down corridors and stairs, through the interior of the incineration plant. Jeppe and Anette followed, ducking quickly under pipes and wires to keep up. The body would be removed from the claw soon and transported to the Pathology Department. Because of the correlation between the body and the disappearance of Oscar, the autopsy would be performed right away instead of the following day, as was customary.

Michael walked out onto a platform that offered a view over the large, well-lit tipping floor. One entire wall of the space was open to the outside, and Jeppe could see the ramp that led the garbage trucks up from Kraftværksvej. A man dressed in a fluorescent yellow vest stood arguing with a group of drivers, whose trucks were parked around the tipping floor.

"I bet they're grumpy because they can't dump their trash and move on." Michael pointed down along one wall of the vast room. "See the trench that runs along the wall? That's where the trucks normally unload the trash. The silo is on the other side of that wall. You've seen that from the inside."

"How does it work?" Jeppe asked, pulling out his notebook.

"The floor supervisor directs the truck to a bay, and then the driver backs into it until the load is over the trench. There's a button in the driver's cab that opens the rear and pushes the trash out so it falls down into the trench."

Anette leaned over the railing and pointed to a garbage truck in the bay below them.

"Does that mean the garbageman doesn't look at the trash at all?" she asked.

"We call them sanitation workers now, not garbagemen," Michael responded, clearing his throat self-consciously. "But yeah, at this end of the process, he doesn't see what he's unloading. It just lands in the trench and ends up in the silo on the other side of the wall."

"At this end of the process? What do you mean?"

"Right. Well, as he follows his route to pick up the trash, he opens the lid of each trash can to see if it needs to be emptied. If there was a body in one of them, well, first of all, it must have been a pretty good-size container, maybe a six-hundred-liter or even a commercial dumpster, otherwise there wouldn't be room. Second, the body must have been wrapped or covered somehow. The driver might have been surprised at how heavy the container was, but the cart lifter on the truck would have done the actual lifting, so it probably wasn't something he gave too much thought to. Right, then the compactor crushes the trash and it gets driven out here to the incineration plant."

Jeppe hurriedly jotted down the key words in sloppy all caps only he would be able to decipher later on.

"Is it possible to trace where in the city the body was thrown into the garbage? How big is a six-hundred-liter container? Are they common or only found in certain locations?"

Michael smiled wryly.

"They're used all over the city for regular old municipal waste. I couldn't really say how many there are, but if I had to take a guess, I'd wager we're talking thousands."

"Okay. So the trash that was emptied at the plant this morning, what part of the city did it come from?"

Michael shrugged his shoulders.

"You'd have to ask the different waste management companies to find out exactly, but Monday morning is a big trash day. Municipal waste comes in from all over downtown and the suburbs."

"So you're saying that it'll be hard to track where the body came from?" Jeppe asked, looking up from his notepad.

"No, I'm saying it will be *impossible* to trace a specific item back to a specific trash can. The claw grabs from the top layer of trash, and since the body was picked up on a Monday morning, it's pretty likely that it was dumped in the silo today. But you can't even know that for sure." Michael nodded down toward the trench. "If you want to get rid of something, this is the right place. Everything disappears."

In the cafeteria, Michael pointed to a shape lying on a sofa, his face to the wall. Two employees, a man and a woman, were standing over him looking concerned.

"That's Kasper," Michael whispered to them. "It doesn't seem like he's feeling better."

The female employee looked at them and sighed.

"He's out cold," she said. "I think we might have to take him to the hospital."

Jeppe walked over. The man had a big birthmark on his temple, and it took him but a minute to remember where he'd seen him before. He and Anette exchanged looks.

"Kasper, this is the Copenhagen Police talking. We'd like to ask you a few questions."

The man moved slightly, opened his eyes, then quickly closed them again.

"I'll . . . Just give me a second." With his coworkers' help, Kasper began to slowly sit up.

Jeppe and Anette stepped a few paces away from the sofa.

"What the fuck?!" she hissed under her breath.

"Keep your voice down!"

"Iben's father works *here*, where Oscar's body was dumped? Can we just agree that that's—"

"Kasper, are you okay?" Jeppe turned back to the sofa and squatted down in front of it.

Kasper Skytte eyed him waveringly. His face was the same color as beaten egg whites.

"It's just the shock," he mumbled.

"Do you think you can handle a few questions?"

Kasper nodded and swallowed hard.

"We're a little surprised to see you here. How long have you been working at the plant?"

Kasper closed his eyes.

"He started last summer." One of the coworkers answered for him. "So, a little under a year."

"Kasper, take a deep breath," the coworker said. She sat down next to the engineer and put an arm around him.

Kasper opened his eyes and looked at Jeppe, groggy as a boxer in round ten.

"Is it Oscar?"

"We don't know yet," Jeppe said after a moment's hesitation.

Kasper's head fell. His coworker worriedly pulled a trash can in front of him.

Jeppe's phone rang, and he got up and walked away from the sofa to answer it.

"Kørner speaking."

"Nyboe here. We're back at the department and have just started washing the dust off our dead friend here so we can see what we're doing. I haven't begun my exam yet, but I thought I should let you know my first impression right away. . . ."

Nyboe paused for dramatic effect, long enough for Jeppe's stomach to have time to turn.

"I think we have what you would probably call a bingo. The body from the claw is male. Light skin, dark hair, and very young."

CHAPTER 13

One, two, three slow steps and then a small pause, masked as a glance toward the horizon and some fumbling around in his jacket pocket for a lozenge. Esther was shocked at how impaired Gregers's walking was. He usually took several walks a day. How could he be this out of shape? Or was the snail's pace rather a sign of reluctance to face the upcoming appointment?

"Are you nervous about seeing her?"

She gazed up at the nondescript medical building on Øster-brogade while she waited for him to put a tissue pack back in his trouser pocket. On the third floor his doctor's office waited for them. Esther had had to be very persuasive to get an appointment right away, and now they were running late for it.

"Maybe it's just the flu." His voice sounded almost hopeful. "As a matter of fact I do feel a little hot."

"Let's hope so, my friend." Esther tucked her arm around his elbow and gave it a squeeze. "Come on. It's this way."

They entered the building and found the elevator. The closer they got to their goal, the longer Gregers's pauses lasted.

Esther noticed that he had put on the blue plaid shirt that he usually only wore for festive occasions and that he had combed his thinning gray hair.

The waiting room had fewer chairs than people and seemed to buzz with a restless energy. Esther let the receptionist know they had arrived and towed Gregers into a corner where they would be as out of the way as possible.

"Why did we have to hurry so much if they're just going to make us wait?"

Esther noted that he seemed less confused and more like his old, crotchety self. A chair became available, and she was just about to nab it for him when the doctor's door opened.

"Gregers Hermansen?"

The doctor was wearing casual jeans and a knit top. Even so, she managed to look more efficient than everyone else in the place combined. Her healthy mien identified her better than any lab coat could have.

Esther nudged her roommate into the doctor's office, trying to avoid taxing the doctor's patience. The doctor offered her hand and then showed them a seat in the sunshine-yellow-painted office, where cobalt-blue art posters adorned the walls.

"Well, Gregers, it's been a long time, hasn't it?" she began. "How are you doing?"

"I'm doing great." He sat up very straight.

"That's wonderful to hear. So how can I help you today?" The doctor rolled her office chair closer to him, ready to get to work.

"That's a good question!"

"You've had trouble breathing," Esther said, patting him on the arm. "Don't you remember?"

"I'm doing great." He smiled derisively.

"Well, since you're here, how about I give you a listen anyway?" the doctor said, getting her stethoscope ready.

"By all means."

Gregers scooted forward in his chair so the doctor could access his chest. She got to work with the stethoscope and instructed him on his breathing.

"Well, Gregers, I'd like to run a couple of blood tests. I'm picking up a little bit of noise in your lungs, and we need to find out what's causing it. Do you smoke?"

"No, never have."

Esther knew that was a lie.

"Gregers, you used to smoke when you moved into my old place on Klosterstræde, a pack a day. We argued about it because the smoke wafted up into my apartment."

"I've never smoked," Gregers insisted, shaking his head.

Esther made eye contact with the doctor, who raised her eyebrows, and got up to fetch vials and sterile needles.

"Roll up your sleeve, Gregers, and I'll draw a blood sample."

The doctor cleaned his skin and found a vein, inserted the needle, and started filling the labeled vials with dark red blood. Gregers waited, his eyes averted.

"Have you been feeling confused at all lately? Had trouble remembering things? Strange dreams at night, perhaps?"

"Maybe a little," he said with a shrug.

The doctor finished her blood draw and put a Band-Aid on his arm.

"Call me after noon tomorrow for the results. I can see from your file that you're taking a blood thinner. It would probably be a good idea if you had some help remembering to take your medicine for the next few days." She looked at Esther. "Is that doable?"

Esther nodded. She knew it would be a struggle to help him with his pills, but she was ready to insist.

"Thanks for coming in today."

Gregers stood up and shook the doctor's hand before shuffling over to the door, followed by Esther.

"Stupid cow!" he whispered on the way out.

"Gregers!" Esther protested.

"What the hell kind of a waste of time was that?" he fumed, glaring at her. "What was the point? What am I doing here?"

ALL THE COWORKERS shook Thomas Larsen's hand and expressed their subdued congratulations on his pending fatherhood in the small Violent Crimes break room. Despite the seriousness of the situation, congratulations were in order. PC had asked Jeppe to lead an investigative team consisting of Anette, Sara, and Thomas, as well as eight other officers, who for a start would assist with taking witness statements and gathering material. Until they knew the victim's identity, they had to treat the case as a new, unrelated murder investigation running parallel to the search for Oscar.

Jeppe poured himself a cup of coffee and scooted around chairs to the table, where his laptop, phone, and notebook were already laid out. He drank from the bitter machine espresso as he watched his coworkers getting settled, and made eye contact with PC's dark gaze at the opposite end of the room. Then he knocked the table lightly.

"As you know, two ARC employees found a body in the waste silo of the incineration plant at eight forty-five this morning. The victim has not yet been identified, nor do we know the cause of death. But it is the body of a young man. Nyboe is preparing the deceased for autopsy as we speak, so hopefully we'll know more soon."

He nodded at Anette, who stood leaning against the wall. She took over.

"Unfortunately, it's hard to say how the deceased ended up in the silo. The body was wrapped in plastic and could have been brought in by any of the first hundred garbage trucks that dumped their loads this morning prior to seven a.m. If it wasn't there all weekend, that is. We'll have to see what Nyboe has to say."

"Are there other ways the deceased could have ended up in the silo?" Larsen asked. "Can't pretty much anyone just drive in and dump trash at the plant?"

"No, there's no unauthorized access to the area," Jeppe responded. "We have someone going through the surveillance footage from the tipping floor where the trucks dump their loads. So far they confirm that only authorized garbage trucks have been at the plant since Friday afternoon. If the body was planted in the silo in some other way, it must have been done from inside the facility. At any rate, the discovery site indicates that we're dealing with a homicide. I have a hard time seeing how anyone could end up in that claw by accident."

He pointed to the eight officers.

"We need to locate and talk to any potential witnesses—starting with the staff at the plant. It's a big place with a lot of employees who move back and forth between offices, machine rooms, and the roof area. We'll divvy up the group, so four of you will go to the plant and start at one end. The rest of you, get in touch with the waste and resource workers' industry association, DAKOFA, and figure out the best way of locating potential witnesses among the sanitation workers. There are multiple private operators involved in garbage collection in Copenhagen. Find them, and ask about their routes and pickup times. We are specifically looking at this morning, but anything unusual would be of interest. One of their men very likely transported the body from a large trash can or dumpster in Copenhagen and even though he may not have been aware of it, it's still possible that he might remember something suspicious if asked."

The officers nodded, jotted down notes, and started divvying up the tasks among themselves.

"Werner and I will attend the last part of the autopsy after lunch. Everybody, be ready to look into the rest—family, residence, coworkers—as soon as we have a definite ID on the victim."

"You haven't heard the best part yet!" Anette interrupted. "Guess who discovered the body, along with the crane operator? Kasper Skytte, the father of Oscar's best friend since childhood! Turns out he works as an engineer at the plant."

"You're kidding, right?" Larsen exclaimed, sounding impressed.

"Nope, not kidding."

"Could he have dumped the body in the silo?" Larsen asked, brushing the hair out of his eyes. "From somewhere inside the plant?"

"Well, it is certainly a bit of a coincidence that he works at the place where we may have found Oscar's body." Anette pointed to Larsen for emphasis.

Jeppe quieted the agitation that was spreading through the room.

"I know what we're all thinking," he said, "but you also know that we need to do this in the right order. No leaks to the media, is that understood? We can't risk the family finding out too soon." He stood up. "All right, let's get to it!"

The crew started getting up to exchange relevant names and other information. The phone on the table in front of Jeppe rang. He looked at the number on the screen. Pathology.

"Kørner speaking."

"Nyboe here." This introduction was followed by a sigh and, for Nyboe, an extremely uncharacteristic pause. "I have bad news. Or good. It depends on how you look at it."

"Let's hear it." The conversation around Jeppe faded away as if Nyboe's serious tone on the other end of the line could be felt in the room.

"We've had a look at him. Look, Kørner, you've got the body of a dyscrinic man on the table, i.e., small in stature . . . you know, a young man who isn't producing a lot of sex hormones. In the old days people would incorrectly use the derogatory term *hermaphrodite* . . ."

"Nyboe, what are you trying to tell me?" Jeppe felt his colleagues' eyes on him.

"What I'm trying to tell you is that the deceased is *not* Oscar Dreyer-Hoff."

"What?!"

"It's not a boy at all, but a grown man in his twenties, slight of build and underdeveloped in terms of his—"

"But," Jeppe heard his own voice, like an echo, "if it's not Oscar, then who is it?"

The team fidgeted uneasily. Jeppe turned his back to them.

"My forensic chemist found his fingerprint in the system." Nyboe rustled some paper. "He filled out one of those background forms that people who work with kids have to sign. You know, to make sure they're not pedophiles. The deceased was a schoolteacher, a guy named Malthe Sæther."

CHAPTER 14

He really did look very young, the man on the stainless steel table. Skinny, smooth cheeks, and thick, dark hair. His head lay at an odd angle, and his legs were bent in a fetal position. There was a dirty sneaker on one foot, otherwise he was naked. Scratches and bruises competed with purple livor mortis on the body, and his skin had a faint greenish tint.

"How old did you say he was?" Anette asked, leaning in over the inert form of Oscar Dreyer-Hoff's Danish teacher.

"Twenty-seven. But his physique is almost like a teenager's. See the narrow chin and the underdeveloped Adam's apple? Clear signs of a low testosterone level." Professor Nyboe sounded defensive. Anette knew he didn't like to be wrong.

"Don't touch him. The skin might come off!" Nyboe warned.

Anette pulled back. She thought she detected a taunting twinkle in Nyboe's eyes, but it was gone again before she could be sure.

"It was falling off him when we were cutting off the remains of the plastic," he explained. "When the immune system stops working, bacteria spreads from the stomach and intestines throughout the entire body and starts to consume it. Certainly aided in this case by all the bacteria in the surrounding trash. Can you see those fluid-filled pustules beneath the epidermis here and here?" He pointed a gloved finger at the body. "That's where the cells have started to leak."

"What does that tell you about the time of death?" Jeppe came and stood next to Anette by the table, tapping a ballpoint pen against his notebook.

She could smell the cigarette he had smoked right before they walked into the Teilum Building to attend Malthe Sæther's autopsy. Even now, in these surroundings, bending over the body of a dead young man, the smell of smoke triggered her urge to light one up, too.

Nyboe checked to make sure the Dictaphone in his hand was turned off. He was addressing them, not filling in his report.

"It's hard to say precisely. There are a lot of factors to consider. The abdomen and face are still only mildly swollen with methane gasses, rigor mortis is subsiding, and the decay process is slowly beginning. That means death took place more than twenty-four and less than thirty-six hours ago. However, the body was wrapped in plastic, and—am I correct in understanding this?—might have been lying in a trash can or a dumpster before it was found in the silo?"

"There is some evidence to suggest that," Anette confirmed.

"It's still cold out at night, all the way down to around freezing. If he was in a trash container outside, wrapped in plastic, that may have delayed decomposition. Do we know when he was last seen alive?"

"I contacted his girlfriend, Josephine, to notify her," Anette said with a nod. "Their registered address is here in Copenhagen, but she lives in Odense part-time. She says she talked to him on the phone Friday at around five p.m. After their phone call, we don't have any confirmed signs of life from him. Not yet, anyway."

Nyboe pointed to the bent neck and tucked-up legs.

"If you look at the body's position, there are signs that rigor mortis occurred while he was lying in the trash container. But again, it's a little hard to determine after all the bruising from the claw."

"If he was transported out to the incineration plant by a garbage truck—and that's the most likely scenario, because it's hard to gain access to the waste silo other than via the trash chutes—then the body would also have been squeezed by the compactor in the garbage truck," Jeppe added.

"Yes, he's quite battered." Nyboe paused, resting the Dictaphone against his chin as he thought. "My provisional statement is that he died Friday evening or sometime overnight, but I won't be able to pin it down until we've opened him up and had a look at his stomach contents and so on."

Anette caught Jeppe's eye. Friday night. The same day Oscar disappeared without a trace.

"I would wager that he was wrapped in plastic and placed outside, presumably in a garbage container, sometime Friday night or early Saturday morning. He lay there until the garbage was picked up this morning. If he had been in the silo all weekend, I would expect the decay process to be even more advanced."

"So a dead body has been lying in a trash can in the middle of Copenhagen all weekend?" Anette's face contorted in a spasm of disgust. "Without anyone noticing it?"

"Why not? A big plastic bag at the bottom of the container isn't anything unusual, and the stench is there already." Nyboe turned his Dictaphone back on. "Fortunately the manner of death looks easier to determine. Presumed cause of death: asphyxia. Traumatic, it should be noted. Pronounced stasis phenomena and lividity marks on the neck. In the internal examinations, we'll look for acute emphysema and any breaks in the hyoid bone, fractures of the thyroid horns or injuries to the cricoid cartilage."

He let go of the Record button and nodded to the forensic technician, who was preparing stainless steel bowls for the body's organs.

"Could we just get a close-up shot of the neck?" Nyboe instructed. "Both sides, if you can access them."

The forensic technician got out the camera and took pictures while Nyboe explained.

"Manual strangulation. It's very likely that he was strangled, from the front, with both hands." He demonstrated as he spoke. "One of the most common homicide methods, typical for crimes of passion and other impulsive killings. Plus he was naked inside the plastic—well, apart from the sneaker. No immediate signs of sexual activity or assault prior to or subsequent to the moment of death."

Anette tried to picture skinny little Oscar strangling his teacher with his bare hands. It didn't seem like the most obvious scenerio. And yet at the same time, it was just that. She leaned over to Jeppe and spoke softly.

"Don't you think it would be a good idea to inform Oscar's family of Malthe's death? See how they react . . . ?"

"Good thinking, Werner." He nodded. "I'll send Larsen and Saidani up to the grandparents in Charlottenlund right away—that's where Oscar's siblings are. And then you and I will inform the parents ourselves when we're done here."

"Check."

The forensic technician set aside the camera and returned to the stainless steel bowls by the wall. Nyboe stepped back to the table and leaned down close to the deceased's face.

"Oh, there's something else . . . a bit odd."

The tone of his voice made Anette prick up her ears.

"Maybe I'm just being old-fashioned, but I definitely don't see this very often here in the department." He pointed to the deceased. "His face is covered with a type of light face powder. He's wearing makeup."

*   *   *

THE FARTHER NORTH of Copenhagen one goes, the taller the
trees. Around Hellerup the crowns of beeches and oaks begin to seriously dominate the skyline. Even in people's yards, the tree trunks
stand like Grecian columns casting shadows as well as glamour over
the neighborhood. A sign of prosperity, Sara thought, looking out
the passenger's-side window at the lucid green colors flickering by.
Just like obesity used to be, until the Industrial Revolution changed
the ideal body. In the subsidized housing in Helsingør where she had
lived with Mido and the girls until their divorce, the trees had come
up to only about fence height. Big enough to climb, but too small
to block out the light. Here in the affluence belt, the trees obviously
couldn't get tall enough.

"I'll have a place out here in the next three years, either in Hellerup or Charlottenlund, possibly Ordrup in a pinch," Thomas
Larsen said, naming some of the suburbs close to where they were
driving, along the eastern coast north of Copenhagen. "A big, fat box
of a house with a patio, a carport, and a trampoline in the yard."

Larsen slowed down and rolled north on Bernstorffsvej, his nose
pressed to the windshield, as if he were actually house hunting for his
new place right now. Clad in a plaid blazer and a tasteful white shirt,
he almost looked like a caricature of the kind of person who would
live in these parts.

"I thought you liked living in posh old Frederiksberg," Sara said,
glancing at his cuff links.

"Well, now that we're going to be parents . . . children need a
yard to play in, a safe environment."

"And you can't get that in the city? Like, say, in Christianshavn?"

"We all have our own way of doing things," he said, smiling pla-
catingly. "Why don't we just leave it at that?"

"Only your way is better than mine?"

"Let it go, Saidani! It's your own choice to interpret my attitude as looking down on your way of life. I just want to give my family a green, quiet home."

Sara rolled down her window and let the drizzle soothe the tension around her eyes. Not a week went by when she didn't ask herself how safe it really was to live in the middle of the city, a stone's throw from Christiania—Copenhagen's anarchist, hippie commune—with two daughters who were growing bigger every time she blinked. Amina already acted like a teenager, more interested in her friends and K-pop than she was in spending time at home. Would she be safer out here under these tall trees? Not that it was a financial option, but *if* it were?

"It was Johannevej, right?"

Larsen slowed down and turned left, rolled slowly ahead, and parked in front of number 10. A modern yellow-brick house stared blankly at them with curtainless windows on either side of the front door's mouth. Two short trees flanked the entrance symmetrically but unostentatiously. This house could have been placed anywhere in the Greater Copenhagen area. It was far from the prospective buyer's fantasy that Larsen had just shared a couple of minutes ago—just a completely normal middle-class house with a fancy-pants zip code.

The woman who opened the door, on the other hand, looked expensive. She was discreetly dressed with her mouth set in a firm line; short, clean fingernails; and an elegant gray haircut. The skin around her eyes looked transparent, as it does when one has been crying but is trying to hide it. *Dignified* was the word that came to Sara's mind as she held out her hand and introduced herself and Larsen. The woman looked dignified.

"Sara Saidani and Thomas Larsen with the Copenhagen Police. Thank you for agreeing to see us on such short notice."

"I'm Frida Dreyer. Oh, but then you know that. Come in. My husband is in Sweden today, but my grandchildren are in the conservatory."

She led them through the modern house and its eclectic interior style of rustic peasant furniture and chic, clean-line design. Sara ducked under a copper chandelier in the entryway, which would have hung beautifully in a front hall with a high ceiling but seemed unwieldy and out of place here. Victor and Esmeralda Dreyer-Hoff sat in a glassed-in sunroom on either end of a floral-upholstered sofa, each with a blanket over their legs. A stack of magazines lay between them, and on the bamboo coffee table an empty pizza box had leaked oil at the corners.

"My angels, the police are here."

"Have they found him?" Victor asked, his voice sounding hopeful.

"Unfortunately not."

Victor blinked. His hair was disheveled and black, his eyes dark with long eyelashes, and his lips full. He was an uncommonly handsome boy, Sara thought, and pointed to a bamboo chair.

"May we have a seat?"

"Oh, I'm sorry," Frida said, throwing her hands up in the air, flustered. "Of course. Please, sit. Put the comic book away, Essie. The police want to talk to us."

Her granddaughter put the comic book in her lap and stared at Sara. She tried to smile reassuringly to the girl, but it didn't seem to have any effect. Frida walked over to Essie and sat down on the arm of the sofa so she could hold her granddaughter's hand. Her other hand fumbled nervously with the slipcover Essie was leaning on.

Sara and Larsen sat down. The bamboo chairs creaked, the sound massive in the tense silence of the conservatory.

Larsen began. "Early this morning the body of Malthe Sæther was found at Amager Resource Center."

"Who's that?" Frida looked confused.

"Malthe is a teacher at Zahles School," Larsen continued. "He teaches Oscar Danish. Victor's class has also had him as a teacher."

"Do you know him, Vic?" Frida asked, looking even more confused.

Victor looked as if he had been turned to stone, hardly breathing. Then in a sudden gesture he flung the blanket aside, put his feet on the floor, and sat up straight, as if the topic were too serious for such a relaxed posture.

"Fuck!"

"Are you okay, honey?"

"Yes, yes, Grandma," he said, shaking his head. "It's just . . . What the hell is going on? Do you know who killed him?"

"Is this related to Oscar in some way?" Frida asked, eyeing Sara with suspicion.

"We don't know yet," Sara replied. "We'd really like to ask you a few questions. You've probably already answered some of them over the phone. Will that be all right?"

They nodded, one by one.

Sara opened the Notes app on her phone.

"First of all," Sara said, "we'd like to know where you all were Friday night."

"My husband and I were home," Frida hurriedly replied. "We watched a movie, I think, or maybe that was Saturday night. But we were home all weekend. What about you, sweetie? You were probably home with your mom and dad, right?" She stopped toying with the pillow to run her hand over Essie's hair.

Essie nodded.

"Were all four of you home?" Sara asked. "The whole night?"

"Mom and I were," the girl said, looking uncertainly at her brother. "Dad was at work."

"He always is," Victor explained.

Sara jotted that down. "And what about you? Where were you Friday night?"

"Out, of course." Victor blinked a few times. "Friday night we played air hockey at the Electric Corner. It's a bar."

"Who were you with?"

"Friends from school. Kids from my grade, the usual gang. We stayed until closing." He stuck his hands in his pockets. "We probably finished playing a little before four."

Larsen smiled knowingly, as if he were still young enough to hang out in town until the wee hours of the morning.

"Do you know if Oscar has been in contact with Malthe outside of school?" Larsen asked.

"Can you tell me what this is about?" Frida asked, looking alarmed.

"I need some air." Victor stood up, knocking the pizza box off the table. "You can come out in the yard with me if . . ."

"I don't know if that's a good idea." Frida turned to Sara. "He's only seventeen."

"It's fine, Grandma." Victor opened the glass door to the backyard.

Sara nodded to her reassuringly, and she and Larsen followed Victor outside. Maybe there were things Grandma didn't need to know.

They walked across the wet lawn to a little gazebo, where Victor slumped down on a built-in bench. He pulled out a pack of cigarettes and lit one before putting the pack back in the pocket of his gray sweatpants.

Sara sat down beside him, leaving Larsen to stand in the doorway. Victor smoked intently, until the ash hung from the end of the cigarette in a gravity-defying balancing act.

"If he did anything to my brother . . ."

Sara looked at the teenage boy's profile, at his long eyelashes and the sculptured jaw, which clenched every time he inhaled.

"What do you mean, Victor?"

He took another drag, and this time the ash floated down onto the tiled floor of the gazebo.

"A couple of weeks ago I was looking for my little brother at school. I had forgotten my lunch money. They were in the library."

"Who? Oscar and Mr. Sæther?"

"Yes." Victor's dark gaze met hers. "They were standing with their arms around each other."

CHAPTER 15

The red bricks of the Geological Museum flew past the car window. Anette took a right turn in third gear, and Jeppe had to hold on to the door handle to keep from tipping over into her.

"Malthe's girlfriend, Josephine, is on her way to Copenhagen," she said while Jeppe struggled back into his seat. "We can meet with her in an hour."

"Has the rest of his family been informed?"

"His parents live way up north in Hjørring. They're divorced, but they live two streets apart in the same neighborhood. Larsen talked to the mother. Nice lady, he said, completely devastated, understandably. The murder is a shock. Malthe was a happy, healthy young man, athletic and idealistic. There have never been any problems with drugs or crime."

"Are they coming over?"

"That depends on when the body can be released to them. The local police there are taking care of them and will let us know if they learn anything relevant to the case."

Anette was speeding as usual, pushing the car to the limit and beyond. To Anette a yellow light was merely an invitation. Over time Jeppe had grown used to it.

"Does Kasper Skytte know we're coming?"

"He didn't answer when I called." Jeppe threw his hand up to the dashboard to avoid being flung through the windshield. "But the emergency room said he went home."

"Well, then we'll just have to surprise him," Anette stated, and leaned on the gas pedal.

"Whoa." Jeppe made a show of grabbing the driver's seat. "Larsen and Saidani are contacting Sæther's colleagues at Zahles School. Since we haven't found his phone, we need to start there and then get the names of his friends from his girlfriend."

"According to the school, he's been employed for two years. He moved to Copenhagen when he got the teaching job at Zahles." Anette reached over to rummage around in the glove compartment without slowing down whatsoever.

"What do you need?"

"I don't know," she snapped, slamming it closed again. "Gum, licorice, cocaine. Anything that will take away this damned urge to smoke."

Jeppe shook his head at her and exhaled audibly.

"Why do you think he was wearing makeup?"

"Maybe the guy just liked to wear makeup," Anette suggested, and turned left on yellow, ignoring the resulting concert of honks.

"Would a young teacher really wear makeup? Not many men do. What would his students say?"

"Maybe he only wore it when he wasn't working. Who knows? We'll have to find out."

A pedestrian appeared on the crosswalk in front of the car, and Anette slammed on the brakes and honked aggressively.

"She had the right of way," Jeppe pointed out.

"Yeah, but she still should have looked!"

They waited in silence for the light to change. The traffic signal clicked like a metronome, a countdown. Jeppe realized that he was drumming along on the dashboard.

"What do you think happened, Werner? If you had to guess, just between us, without needing to back it up in any way. It stays with me."

"I'm not a big fan of guesswork, Jepsen. You know that. If your gut is telling you something, it's usually just that you're hungry."

Jeppe couldn't help but laugh.

"But if you insist," she continued, while starting to drive again, "I think Oscar killed his teacher and then took off. I don't know why he did it, but it seems like the most obvious explanation to me. His parents know, and they're protecting him. That's why they're behaving the way they are. There you go . . . logic. In other words, no emotional claptrap from me."

"A talented fifteen-year-old from a wealthy family kills his teacher, writes a mysterious goodbye letter, and sails away? That's what you call logic?"

Anette slammed on the brakes yet again, flinging Jeppe into his seat belt.

"You are assuming that he's happy and talented, because they have money and because that's what they're telling you? What happened to your critical eye, Jepsen?" she asked.

"Aren't you the one sensing things now?"

"I'm just connecting the dots where the distance is the shortest."

"Logical and straightforward," Jeppe said, smiling at his partner. "But that's not how life is. Everything organic sends up shoots and branches, and twists in unexpected directions, crimes included. There could even be a totally different perpetrator who killed Malthe and maybe Oscar too. Although now that you mention it, you're right about one thing. Life in the Dreyer-Hoff family might not be as harmonious as they want it to appear."

"The *family bed*." Anette sneered and stopped the car across from Fredericiagade 64. "It's just freaking weird."

Jeppe unbuckled his seat belt and said, "What I find seriously weird is Kasper Skytte. Can it really be a coincidence that he was the one who found the body of Oscar's teacher?"

"Let's go in and ask him."

They got out of the car, crossed the street, and buzzed him on the intercom by the building's front door. No answer. Anette leaned heavily on the doorbell. Still no response. They waited two minutes in case he had been asleep and needed time to get up. Then Anette buzzed his apartment again. Jeppe looked at his watch. It was two o'clock.

"Not at work, not at the hospital, and not at home. Where the hell did he go?"

THORVALDSENS MUSEUM WAS deserted. The afternoon sunbeams fell on the statues, making the white marble shine like newly fallen snow. Esther strolled through the exhibit spaces. The vaulted ceilings swallowed up the noise of her careful footsteps as soon as she trod them. She walked through the red, green, and yellow rooms and stopped in front of a statue of a boy with an eagle.

"You have the place to yourself today."

Esther turned toward the voice and discovered an attendant right behind her. She was wearing a dark blue uniform and stood with her hands crossed behind her back.

"We're usually closed on Mondays," the woman explained, coming over to stand next to Esther. "Today is a new pilot program, so most people don't know we're open." She nodded at the statue. "Do you like it?"

Esther looked at the marble eagle again.

"Uh, I haven't really had a chance to think about it. Actually I'm here to see the museum's collection of death masks, but I can't seem to find them. . . ."

"Why do you want to see those?"

Esther hesitated.

"I have a professional interest in them . . . for a book I'm writing," she said.

The attendant nodded slowly, as if in approval.

"The museum doesn't consider them art. Who's to say? I work with images myself, and I have no damn idea what's art and what's not."

The attendant had a ravaged face, wrinkled and swollen, but it was evident that she had once been very beautiful. Before life's concerns and the passing years had taken their toll.

"The death masks aren't on display. We store them up in the attic. They're not available to the public." She started walking out of the room.

Esther followed. "Isn't there some way to apply for permission? I just want to look at them. It doesn't have to be for very long."

The attendant kept walking, unmoved.

Esther tried again. "I would be happy to pay . . . if it required extra staffing costs?"

The attendant stopped and turned around. She regarded Esther, biting her lower lip.

"How much?"

"I'm sorry?"

"How much would you pay?"

The question struck Esther as both rather crass and inappropriate. At a street market in Bangkok maybe, but here?

"For five hundred kroner, you can have a private viewing right now. We're not exactly crowded today, so they can do without me on the floor for a bit."

Afterward Esther had trouble recalling why she had said yes. A combination of surprise and embarrassment, she supposed.

"Okay. I'll just run to the ATM when we're done."

The attendant nodded contentedly and held out her hand as if to seal the deal.

"Jenny Kaliban," she said. "Nice to meet you."

"Esther de Laurenti."

"We're going upstairs." Jenny turned and started walking rapidly, emphasizing the sense that they were up to something shady.

Esther looked over her shoulder before following.

On the second floor, Jenny opened a panel that was hidden in the doorframe and typed in a code. A red metal hatch in the middle of the ocher-colored wall opened with a little click, and an automated ladder slowly unfolded.

"After you, ma'am!"

Esther forced herself to smile and climbed up the precarious-seeming ladder. After ten rungs, it led to a brick staircase that extended up beneath the roof of Thorvaldsens Museum.

"Watch your head!" Jenny warned. "We're going to that bookcase over there. Can you see it?"

Esther saw rubble, crates of paintings, and exposed Rockwool in all directions. She ducked under a rafter with painted helmets sitting on it.

"From the war," Jenny explained from behind her, "the resistance movement. The masks are over there, to the right."

On the shelves of an old bookcase stood boxes made of wood and cardboard with either numbers or ornately handwritten cards on the front. There were about forty boxes in all, as far as Esther could tell. One right in front of her was very clearly labeled *27*, and above the red number a name was carefully penciled in. She read *A. GOETHE* and then continued to another box. *KARL XII.*

"Is that . . . are these masks really of the people whose names are on the boxes?"

"Yes, crazy, isn't it?" Excitement crept into Jenny's voice. "Look at that one!"

Esther followed Jenny's index finger and read *NAPOLEON BONAPARTE*.

"*Napoleon's* death mask is here?!"

"It is. It's only what they call an 'original copy,' and Thorvaldsen wasn't the one who made it. But, indeed, it's here, hidden away in a box in the attic."

"That's kind of a shame."

"I agree! From my perspective, art isn't just about aesthetics. It's a form of cognition that tells you something fundamental about being human. But who bothers listening to me?" Jenny put on a pair of cotton gloves and carefully took one of the wooden boxes from the shelf. "I'll show you one of the best ones. Georg Zoëga, Thorvaldsen's mentor. It's from 1809."

Jenny removed the lid from the box and scooped out the protective foam pellets handful by handful, until she was able to lift up an object wrapped in tissue. Carefully she removed sheets of wrapping paper from around the mask and presented it to Esther, as if it were a newly hatched chick.

The mask was gray and cracked in places, but otherwise well preserved, looking like a hollow-cheeked male face with closed eyes and a hooked nose, its mouth slightly open. He could have been sleeping, and yet without even knowing why, Esther had no doubt that he was dead.

"And they were made shortly after the moment of death?"

"With plaster of paris on the face of the dead, yes. Then used as a cast. In the 1800s many artists made casts of prominent dead people so that they could later carve a statue with a good likeness. A death mask." Jenny carefully turned the mask over to show the handle on the back. "In the old days, people hung them on the wall for decoration, but we're too prudish to do that kind of thing now. We're so terrified of death that we would rather ignore it."

Esther leaned closer till the mask was only a handsbreadth from her eyes.

"Do you think some essence of the deceased remains in the mask? That it can sort of build a bridge between the world of the dead and the living?" Esther asked.

Jenny looked at her as if she were crazy.

"I have to get back down to the floor again before my boss notices I'm gone." She set the mask back in its box, carefully returned the foam pellets, closed the lid, and put it back on the shelf.

"Right, of course." Esther stood up straight.

"So then we just need to deal with the payment."

"I'll go find an ATM and be back in a second."

Esther followed Jenny back under the rafters, along the raw masonry to the stairs and back down to the museum lobby. She hurried out the main entrance and headed for Højbro Square. There had to be a cash machine. As she hurried along, she thought about what she had just experienced in the museum attic. Not just the death masks but the woman who had shown them to her. Jenny Kaliban. What a strange character.

A POLAR BEAR wearing a tuxedo, bow tie, and white gloves stood in front of a golden wall of human faces in textural relief. The polar bear held its paw to its forehead, as if surprised or possibly outraged by the golden faces behind it. Jeppe turned his back to the bear and looked at Anette. She seemed to be having fun. Malthe Sæther's girlfriend, Josephine, had suggested they meet here at the artsy café Bankeråt, because it was right around the corner from Malthe's place. She was going to pick up her things from the apartment, but as long as it was full of forensic investigators gathering clues, they couldn't question her there. Thus Jeppe and Anette were now sitting at a marble-topped table between the café's taxidermied animals and doll-head light fixtures, waiting for her. Jeppe was opposed to questioning a witness at a café and particularly at having to sit here with Anette, looking ridiculously square in this cool rock and roll scene.

"Are you with the police?"

A young woman stood beside the table, looking at them earnestly. She was skinny and not particularly tall, with jet-black hair, rings through her eyebrows, and heavy eye makeup. She had a deep, hoarse voice that seemed ill matched with her slight stature.

"I'm Josephine," she said with a nod.

"Hi, Josephine. Thank you for meeting us so quickly. Should I order you something?"

She shook her head and sat down in the chair next to Anette. Despite her heavy makeup, the skin around her eyes and nose looked red.

"I have to warn you that I'm feeling rotten. I've just said goodbye to the dead body that was supposedly my Malthe." She closed her eyes. "Actually I don't know how I can even keep it together."

"We'll make this quick. Do you have someone you can be with after this? So that you don't have to be alone?"

She nodded.

"You said that you last spoke to Malthe on the phone at five o'clock on Friday." Jeppe opened his notebook to a blank page. "What did you talk about?"

She took a deep breath and began hesitantly.

"He called to postpone our date. Malthe and I usually take turns visiting each other on the weekends. As long as I'm living in Odense—I'm an intern there at a bookstore on the pedestrian shopping street—we have to do it that way. He was going to come to Odense Friday night, but he canceled."

"Did he say why?"

"He had to stay in Copenhagen because one of his students was in trouble and needed help."

Oscar, Jeppe thought, but didn't say aloud.

"Malthe didn't say who it was or what it was about, but I could hear in his voice that it was serious. Otherwise he wouldn't have spent his time off doing it. He was very dedicated, but . . ." Josephine blinked and looked down.

"Was he with someone when you talked to him?"

She shook her head.

"Who did he socialize with here in Copenhagen?" Anette asked. "Friends, colleagues?"

"Malthe doesn't have a big social network in Copenhagen yet. We spend our weekends traveling back and forth. When you're apart all week, you become a little stingy with the time you have together." Josephine dabbed at her eyes with a crumpled tissue from her pocket. "But he spoke highly of one colleague named Lis. I don't actually know her last name. And he drank coffee with several of the people from his building. He sang with a chorus once a week. A men's chorus that practices in a church in Vesterbro. He really enjoyed that."

Jeppe made notes.

"Do you know the name of the chorus?" Jeppe asked.

"Allegro, maybe? Or Axis? Something like that. I never got to hear them sing."

"What else did he do in his free time?"

"Hung out with me, like I told you," she said, one corner of her mouth rising ever so slightly. "On the weekends anyway. Malthe hasn't worked as a teacher for that long and still spends most of his weekday nights preparing for work. Apart from chorus on Tuesday night and long bike rides. He's always biked a lot, but here in the city he hardly has time to keep it up. He's always prepping for class and grading essays."

"Do you know of any conflicts he may have had? Did he have any enemies?"

"No." Josephine laughed nervously.

Jeppe waited, but she didn't elaborate.

"There wasn't anyone he didn't get along with?"

She shook her head.

"Did he ever socialize with any of his students outside of school?"

"Of course not!" She sounded indignant.

Jeppe and Anette exchanged a glance over the little café table, then he asked, "Has Malthe ever mentioned a student to you by the name of Oscar?"

Josephine thought about it and then shook her head.

"He never mentioned an Oscar Dreyer-Hoff?"

Her face lit up.

"Dreyer-Hoff?" she said. "If you mean Victor, then yes."

"Are you sure it was Victor Dreyer-Hoff Malthe talked about?" Jeppe looked at her, confused. "Not Oscar, his little brother?"

She nodded so that her eyebrow rings tinkled.

Jeppe leaned back in his uncomfortable café chair and asked, "So what did he tell you about Victor?"

"Well, Victor was a freshman at Zahles when Malthe started teaching there. The boys in his class all looked up to him, cliques formed, there was bullying, and the weaker students didn't fare so well." She showed with her fingers that *weaker* was up to interpretation. "Malthe was determined to do something about the problem. He talked to the students and tried to persuade them to be more accepting."

"Did it help?"

"Just the opposite. The headmaster reprimanded Malthe and told him to stick to teaching. It was so unfair! Who knows, maybe Victor's parents are best friends with the board of trustees or something. Malthe ended up being reassigned to a different class." Her cheeks looked a little flushed under the pale makeup. "He talked to Lis about it a lot. I know that. But apart from her, his colleagues weren't much help. That was the most disappointing part, he said. When you're in a new place, you hope that the teachers will stick together. But he doesn't think too much about it anymore. He loves the school"—she corrected herself—"loved."

Jeppe jotted down notes. The young woman cleared her throat, then continued.

"After the headmaster reprimanded him, Malthe found a dead bird in his bag in the teachers' lounge!"

"A dead bird?"

"A dove. Isn't that gross?! He was sure Victor's clique was behind it, but of course he couldn't prove it." Josephine tugged on the collar of her plaid shirt, then let go of it.

Jeppe wrote VICTOR DEAD BIRD? in his notebook.

"And you are sure Malthe didn't have any enemies?" Anette insisted.

"Positive!"

"No one held a grudge against him? Debts? Some old score to settle?"

"No! Just no. Malthe is the nicest, kindest person I know." Josephine looked down at her lap and exhaled heavily. Her skinny shoulders made her look like a baby bird.

"Maybe you should go get some rest," Jeppe said gently. "Did you need to pick up something from the apartment?"

She nodded without looking up.

"We'll walk you there."

"Okay. I just have to stop in the bathroom first."

She got up, grabbed her canvas tote bag, and steered toward the bathroom. Anette watched her walk away.

"What's with the war paint?"

Jeppe smiled and found his phone to check for new emails.

"Nyboe writes that Malthe Sæther died Friday night around midnight, give or take two hours either way, so between ten p.m. Friday and two a.m. Saturday."

"That's five to nine hours after the last confirmed sign of life. So now we need to find out what he did after his phone call with Josephine." Anette looked at her watch. "Do you mind if I don't walk to the apartment with you? I think I'd like to pop over and see Mads Teigen at Trekroner. I want to find out how well he actually knows Oscar."

"Now? By yourself?"

"Don't worry, Jepsen. I can tackle him with one arm behind my back if it comes down to that."

"You want me to break the news of Malthe's death to the Dreyer-Hoffs alone?" Jeppe asked with a sigh.

"I'll try to be back in time, but if not, I'm sure you can handle it without me." She got up.

"Don't do anything stupid, Werner."

"Never!" Anette winked at him and headed for the door. Jeppe saw her lift her face to smile up at the afternoon sun, and then she disappeared around the corner.

When he turned his head, Josephine was once again standing at the table, her canvas bag over her shoulder. She had touched up her eye makeup and applied fresh powder to her nose.

"Unfortunately my partner can't join us," he said, standing up. "Are you ready?"

He escorted her out of the café and onto the sidewalk. For such a small person, she walked extremely fast. He had to pick up his pace to keep up with her. In front of Malthe's building, Jeppe stopped by the bike racks.

"Can you see his bike?" he asked her.

Josephine scanned the rows of bikes and shook her head.

"It's a mint-green road bike, but it's not here."

"Okay, thanks."

Jeppe greeted the officer at the front door, and they climbed the stairs to the fifth floor. In the doorway of the apartment they were met by a smiling Clausen, the crime scene technician, who handed them both a pair of latex gloves and blue plastic shoe covers to pull on over their shoes. Josephine clutched the doorframe and looked like she might not be able to let go again. Clausen gently loosened her hand and walked the young woman into the apartment. A few minutes later they came out.

"I can't do it, I have to get my family to come pack up my things. I never want to come back here!"

In her hand Josephine held a photograph of herself and Malthe. She looked like someone who just wanted to pinch herself and wake up from the horror she was experiencing.

"Does anything in the apartment look strange? Anything out of place?" Jeppe asked.

"It looks the same as always." Her eyes teared up. "Can I go now? My mother lives in Rødovre. I want to go see her now."

"Of course. I'll have an officer drive you. Just make sure we have a way to reach you."

She removed her shoe covers and handed them to him.

"One last question," he said. "If that's okay?"

She nodded.

"Did Malthe ever wear makeup?"

"*Makeup?*" She looked at him in surprise. "You mean like me? Goth?"

Jeppe shrugged.

"*Makeup?*" She shook her head. "He would just never do that. Please, he's a country boy from Hjørring."

"POOR GIRL!" CLAUSEN approached Jeppe as he stood in the doorway, peeling off his latex gloves.

"Yes, I feel sorry for her."

"We're just about done, Kørner, so you can have the place to yourself in a moment. We haven't found anything unusual—there are no traces of violence, nothing broken, no mess or blood anywhere. The place is clean and tidy, the plants have all been watered recently, and there's food in the fridge. We've collected fingerprints from glasses and the remote control and packed up his hairbrush and toothbrush for DNA profiling. We'll take his computer as well and look it over. I assume Saidani wants it when we're done, right?"

"Right, Clausen. Have you found his cell phone?"

"Nope, no phone. But his wallet is here with his driver's license and ATM card in it, so wherever he went, he wasn't planning on driving a car or needing money. Unless he had cash on him."

"Any smut?" Jeppe was referring to the usual sorts of pornography and sex toys that the police found in nine out of ten residences— usually hidden in an underwear drawer or a shoebox in the closet.

"No smut."

"Okay, thanks."

Jeppe walked past Clausen into the apartment. Two other technicians dressed in white were on their way out, their hands full of brown paper bags, headed back to the labs with their forensic specimens. He closed the door after them.

The apartment was furnished just the way he would expect for a young couple who had moved in relatively recently. White walls and furniture of the temporary, financially conscious kind. There were IKEA folding chairs stacked behind the kitchen door and a row of sneakers on the floor in the front hall. A framed poster hung on the wall with a retro drawing of a bike rider dressed in yellow. White melamine shelves contained books on pedagogy, etymological dictionaries, and a nice collection of Danish and European literature from this and the last century, all in alphabetical order.

On the wall over the kitchen table was a collage of travel photos, Malthe and Josephine in front of temples, rock formations, and sunsets.

Jeppe walked over. They were an unusual couple. Malthe looked sunburned and red-cheeked in most of the pictures, Josephine pale and heavily made-up. He looked like a skinny but healthy young man from North Jutland, she an autonomist antifa from Copenhagen's Nordvest neighborhood. But they looked happy together.

Josephine had mentioned a chorus. People were always full of unpredictable interests. Apparently this young bicycling enthusiast from North Jutland liked to sing. Allegra, or something, maybe Jeppe could find a pamphlet somewhere. He flipped through a binder of bills and correspondence from Malthe's workplace and his union, looked through his nightstand drawer and in a stack of magazines by the TV. Nothing.

He lucked out in the kitchen. In between some local newspapers was a green handbill, about five by eight inches, advertising the chorus group's retreat at the end of May. Jeppe read on the back of the brochure that the chorus was called *A-choir* and that it was for men only. All ages were welcome, but applicants had to submit an audition recording to join plus be able to spend every Tuesday night rehearsing at Absalon's Church.

Jeppe set the pamphlet in a folder and put it in his bag. Just as he was leaving the kitchen he noticed a drawing hanging with magnets on the fridge. It depicted two men in some kind of wrestling match, drawn with charcoal and pencil on white paper. Both men were naked. He recognized the lines right away.

The drawing looked like the ones in Oscar Dreyer-Hoff's room.

CHAPTER 16

"What a pleasant surprise. And so late in the day, too. It's almost seven, don't you ever knock off work?" Mads Teigen held out his hand to help Anette ashore from the boat. She pretended not to notice and hopped off on her own.

"During an investigation like this, there's no such thing as knocking off work."

"Of course." He found a soft pack of cigarettes and lit one.

The short boat ride had passed in silence. Anette had to work up her courage to ask the question she had come for, and it annoyed her.

"So what can I do for you?"

That intense look again, that sea-green gaze, that electric charge. Anette averted her eyes.

"How long have you worked here at the fort?"

"Almost a year."

"Do you know Oscar, the boy who's missing?" The words stuck in her throat.

"What do you mean?" He froze, the cigarette in the corner of his mouth.

"Henrik Dreyer-Hoff said that you have shown them around the fort several times, that you have spoken with Oscar and told him about the birds."

Mads looked at her. It was impossible to tell what was going through his head. Those dark brows moved together over his nose.

"I'd remember it if I'd met him multiple times. It's possible they've been here and I haven't noticed them, but I don't *know* them." He inhaled and smiled at her. "It must have been the previous fort caretaker."

His smile was disarming, his explanation so straightforward that Anette felt a sense of relief spread through her body. Mads hadn't even worked here a year, and the family probably hadn't taken this boat out all winter. It was more than likely that Henrik Dreyer-Hoff was talking about Mads's predecessor.

"When were the search and rescue crews out here looking for Oscar?"

"Saturday and Sunday. And I do rounds morning and night, every single day. He's not here."

Anette regarded the empty harbor, the grassy embankments, and the fort itself, its contours already obscured by the twilight.

"But maybe he *has* been here and left behind some trace that you haven't discovered. How do you usually check the place?"

"I just start at one end with a flashlight. It can take anywhere from twenty minutes if I'm tired to an hour and a half if I really do a thorough job. It's called an inspection round."

"Let's do one together. We'll look in all the nooks and crannies, even the places you don't normally check. We know from his father that Oscar loved to explore the casements." Anette reached into her pocket and pressed a piece of nicotine gum out of the blister pack, a recent purchase that embarrassed her. She stuffed it into her mouth and chewed it tentatively. Substitutes like this weren't normally her thing.

"Sure you wouldn't rather have one of these?" Mads asked, showing her his lit cigarette.

"Hey, don't tempt me. I'm trying to stay the course." She laughed, then clapped her hands together. "Where do we start?"

"First we need flashlights. Come on!" He walked up the dock, heading for one of the red buildings, the commander's residence. Anette swallowed the unpleasant taste of nicotine and peppermint and followed him.

Inside, the residence had high ceilings and old-fashioned decor, with solid wood furniture and sea chests. In the gathering twilight, the rooms seemed strangely abandoned, as if time had come to a halt and no one really lived here. Mads disappeared into a storage room, and Anette waited in the entry hall.

"Let me just find a couple that work. It'll take me only a sec."

"Fine, fine."

Anette eyed a collection of yellowed black-and-white photos stuck on the wall over a chest of drawers and walked over for a closer look. Soldiers at dining tables and in smiling groups, all of them long since dead and buried. Next to the chest of drawers there was an open door into a room that looked like a kind of workshop with a workbench and shelves along the walls. She poked her nose in.

On the shelves taxidermied birds stood close, many of them with their wings spread as if in flight. Seagulls, swans, eiders, and crows with glossy feathers and dead eyes.

"Are you ready?" Mads reached in behind her and closed the door to the workshop so that she had to take a step back. They were standing so close she could feel his breath. He handed her a heavy flashlight, smiled shyly, and then stepped over to open the front door.

"I could only find one with batteries in it, so we'll have to share. And we'd better get started."

Anette walked out and heard the door slam behind them. The air felt crisp and refreshing.

"Let's start in the rabbit hutch." Mads walked toward a little grassy hill right next to the building and unlocked the hutch door.

Anette shined the light into what clearly served as storage for the island's summer café with chairs, tables, and brooms.

"What we're looking for is food wrappers, a sleeping bag, anything he might have left behind," Anette instructed. "Maybe he wrote something on the wall. You know the place inside and out—keep an eye out for things you haven't seen before."

They proceeded across the island, opened every door and shined the light into every corner, inspected the lighthouse and buoys, but didn't find any sign that Oscar had been there. They moved on into the darkness of the casement building and made their way down to the cellar level. Their footsteps crunched on the porous concrete, the beam from their flashlight lifting dreamlike images out from the shadows. Mads ducked under an arched doorway.

"Maybe we should throw in the towel, huh?" he suggested. "Like I already said, I've been over the island thoroughly several times, both with and without the search and rescue crew. If there had been traces left behind, I would have found them."

Anette's light hit some colorful drawings on the curved walls. Elements of blue and red formed a bird snatching a pancake in the air, a fat cat by a pile of fish bones, and a sign that showed the way to the Cell of Death.

"What *is* this?"

He grinned in the darkness.

"In the 1930s, the island was temporarily turned into an amusement park for Copenhageners. The wall paintings are from that era. Here, pass me the flashlight! Over here one could throw balls through the old ventilation duct. Three balls for twenty-five øre."

He shined the light over the near-hundred-year-old remnants of carefree fun, and Anette felt a pang of that same hopelessness she sometimes felt when holding her sleeping daughter in her arms. What good is it all for when we're going to die anyway?

"Isn't there somewhere we haven't checked? I mean, there must be a trillion corridors and secret rooms—have you really been over the whole thing?"

"Yes. And I still haven't found anything." Mads opened a door and shined the light on the floor, showing the way out and up a flight of stairs into a bigger corridor with higher ceilings.

Anette stepped over a pile of delicate bones, presumably from a dead bird. A boat sailed by outside. Its lights shone through the mullion windows, drawing black lines on the ceiling.

Mads turned off the flashlight. "Pretty, isn't it? Sometimes I come over at night just to see that."

They watched in silence as the patches of light slid over the vaulted ceiling. Once the boat passed, it went completely dark again.

"Is it true that you guys found a body out at the incineration plant?" he asked. "Or is that just a rumor?"

"I'm not at liberty to discuss current investigations. Unless you know something you want to share?"

He didn't respond.

Anette suddenly felt tired of it all. "All right, man, turn on the light!"

"Should we call it quits for today?" Mads said, switching the flashlight back on.

Anette turned to face the now-black window and the sea beyond it. Whatever had happened between Oscar and Malthe Sæther, people always left something behind—trash, wreckage, bodies.

"What about one of the other forts in the harbor? Fort Middelgrund, which is being renovated? You said it's pretty much deserted. . . ."

"But as I said, also under video surveillance, not to mention thoroughly searched by Search and Rescue. He's not there." The flashlight flickered and Mads shook it with a sigh. "I think people need to start preparing for the possibility that he may never be found."

*   *   *

MALIN DREYER-HOFF PULLED Jeppe into a hug and rested her head against his neck. The intimacy was unexpected but so sorrowful that after a brief hesitation Jeppe put his arms around her. He stood awkwardly still with his coat on, sweating, afraid of getting too close but also wary of rejecting her. The apartment was dark and quiet, and slowly her breathing calmed down.

He patted her on the back and pulled away gently to check her face. Her pupils were small, like a hunted fox's.

"Isn't Henrik home?"

"He had an errand. As usual . . ."

Jeppe nodded. Maybe the couple just couldn't stand being together right now.

"Could we sit down somewhere?" he asked. "As I said, we still don't have any concrete news about Oscar, but something has happened that we need to discuss."

She dried her eyes with the backs of her hands, not wearing any makeup and clearly long past any kind of vanity.

"I tried to paint a little," she said, "just to think about something else. But I can't focus. I think we have a nice bottle of rum in the kitchen. Will you join me?"

Jeppe hadn't had dinner yet, and his stomach rumbled aggrievedly at the thought of pouring alcohol into it.

"Thanks, why not?"

Malin found a bottle in one of the kitchen cupboards and turned on the lights over the table with a surprised expression, as if she had only just realized that it was getting dark outside. Jeppe sat down at the kitchen table and accepted a beveled glass with a generous helping of rum in it.

"I'm here because a body was found early this morning. Malthe Sæther, a teacher at Zahles School, is dead."

She drank a sip of her drink and closed her eyes but made no move to say anything.

"That doesn't surprise you?"

"Nothing surprises me anymore," she said with a weak smile. "My son is missing. As far as I'm concerned, you could tell me the sun won't be rising tomorrow." She shook her head. "I'm sorry, I don't know what I'm saying. That's terrible, of course. How did it happen?"

Jeppe looked at her. Did she understand the implication of the coincidence of the timing between Malthe's death and Oscar's disappearance?

"He was strangled and thrown in a garbage can."

"No?!" Malin stopped, the glass midair. "Really? That's horrible."

"Do you know him—Malthe?" Jeppe took a sip of his rum, ignoring the protests from his stomach.

"I met him once at a parent-teacher conference, but nothing beyond that. He was friendly, young, from somewhere in Jutland." She shrugged her shoulders to indicate that that was all she knew.

"What did Oscar think of him?"

"I haven't heard him complain about his teacher, but then Danish is one of his favorite subjects." She inhaled and held the breath, then shook her head sadly. "Oh dear! What is happening to the world?"

"You didn't get the impression that they might be friends beyond the usual teacher-student relationship?"

She gave him a strange look.

"Oscar's never mentioned Malthe to me."

Jeppe pulled a folder out of his bag and set the drawing from the teacher's fridge on the table between them.

"Do you recognize this?"

She looked down without leaning forward, as if she wasn't willing to commit fully.

"No, not at first glance. It looks like one of Oscar's drawings."

"I found it on Malthe Sæther's fridge."

She drank again but didn't say anything.

"Do you have any idea how it could have gotten there?"

"Oscar often gives away his drawings. He's so talented."

"Yes, it's very good," Jeppe said with a brief smile. "But isn't it an unusual drawing for a high school student to give his teacher? Considering the subject."

"Isn't it just having an imagination?" Her blue eyes took on a hostile gleam. "He also likes drawing dragons and monsters."

"And Oscar didn't socialize with his teacher outside of school?"

"No!"

There was no mistaking the hostility now.

Jeppe put the drawing back in his bag and let her recover for a second before he flipped backward through his notebook to the interview with Malthe's girlfriend, Josephine.

"Have you heard about the conflicts in Victor's class when Malthe Sæther was his teacher?"

She hesitated and then said, "*Conflict* is really too strong a word to use. There were a few students who weren't happy. Malthe tried to turn that into an issue for the whole class."

Jeppe watched her closely, trying to assess whether she was deliberately playing it down or rather refusing to acknowledge her children's problems.

"There was something about a dead dove in Malthe's bag?"

"Victor didn't have anything to do with that." Malin shook her head exasperatedly. "Wasn't it someone from another class? At any rate, the whole thing got blown way out of proportion."

"Are you saying the teacher overreacted?"

"Let's just say that Malthe was young and eager. . . ." She shrugged and emptied her glass.

"Okay. Remind me again: You and Henrik were both home the whole night Friday, weren't you?" Jeppe's esophagus was starting to burn from the rum.

"We talked about that already!" Malin set down her glass with a little clink. "I told you, we watched TV and then went to bed early. Why?"

"Henrik didn't go out anywhere?"

"No."

"Thank you for the drink," Jeppe said, getting up. "I'll call you as soon as there's any news."

She looked at him nonplussed, as if she had been expecting him to stay, then hesitantly got to her feet. A slight stagger made it clear that the rum was beginning to challenge her balance. Either that or her emotions were knocking her off course.

"You're just leaving?"

"I think that's probably best."

Jeppe pressed the elevator button and hoped it got to him before she did. The ding sounded right away, and he stepped in with a relieved *goodbye* to Malin's silhouette in the kitchen. His job was to find her son, not be her comforter.

The elevator lighting transformed his reflection in the shiny metal walls into a yellowish ghost. Narrow face, short dark hair— he could easily have played the grown-up Oscar Dreyer-Hoff in a movie.

If there was ever going to *be* a grown-up Oscar Dreyer-Hoff.

CHAPTER 17

Hair strands fell in the sink, slowly covering the white porcelain in a woolly layer. In the bathroom mirror Kasper Skytte's jawline was hummed into view under the beard trimmer. He puffed out one cheek and ran the trimmer over it—up, down, and diagonally, until his beard was only an eighth of an inch long. Though it was a struggle, he forced himself to meet his own eyes. Grooming helped his self-esteem a little, even if the extra padding around his gut and the bags under his eyes were starting to pull his appearance in the wrong direction. He wasn't an ugly man. Even the birthmark, which he had hated so intensely when he was younger, had turned out to score him points in the eyes of the opposite sex.

"Dad! Are you almost done? I have to pee." Iben knocked on the door, hard.

"Yes, sweetie. Just give me a minute!"

He *knew* she knew something. Obviously Oscar had blabbed. The question was how much she knew and where her loyalties lay when it came down to it.

His phone had been ringing all day, and in the end he had turned it off. They had even come by and rung the doorbell. The police, presumably. He was under pressure from all sides. Kasper took a swig from the small bottle next to the sink. Aquavit again today, brought home from a hotel minibar. It was lukewarm and already tasted of tomorrow's regret, like so much did these days. He had been drinking since he came home from the ER, and knew he would have to stop soon if he was going to preserve some modicum of functionality for tonight.

Kasper cleaned the hair out of the sink, turned on the water, and rinsed the last remaining clippings down the drain, then wrapped the empty aquavit bottle in toilet paper and put it in the bottom of the trash can. He should have been relieved, but he felt anything but. If only he could say that his guilty conscience was eating him up from inside, but that would be yet another lie. Though he was certainly struggling with feelings of guilt, mostly he was just afraid of being caught.

The police. He would have to talk to them sooner or later, even if the thought was inconceivable. Maybe he could call them tomorrow morning and explain that he had been so shocked by the corpse in the claw that he had taken a sleeping pill and gone straight to bed. What could they say to that?

"It's all yours, honey!" he called.

Iben came out of her room and headed straight for the bathroom without looking at him. He reached for her, but she dodged around him and slammed the bathroom door behind her. He heard her lock it and stood for a moment watching the closed door; he considered knocking and trying to get his daughter to talk, but dropped it. It would just make her hate him even more.

When had she started treating him like a leper? Was it when his addiction had escalated, or simply when she had become a teenager? It felt like only a moment ago that she would sit on his lap while he read her a bedtime story. She used to kiss him ten times on the lips before he was allowed to turn off the light.

Kasper pulled a clean T-shirt over his head and went to his desk in the living room. On the way he bumped into the blue floor lamp, knocking it to the floor, and the bulb broke. He had better drink some water.

As he leaned down to the tap over the kitchen sink, he realized how seriously drunk he was. The corners of the room were blurry and swimming—if it weren't for the nausea rising up his throat, it would have been hilarious. He returned to the desk and the computer and congratulated himself on his fortitude, as he did every time he managed to abstain. Instead, he checked the account as he had done daily since the bank transfer two weeks ago and smiled at the number that appeared on his screen.

He *was* relieved—he just had to get through the discomfort of this first phase, then surely it would all work out.

A *ding* announced an incoming email. He opened his in-box and carefully skimmed it. It was a press release from the office, and he could already tell from the header that it was one of the news items for which he himself had provided the information.

ARC saves the environment from the equivalent of fifty thousand cars' worth of NO_X emissions. The catalytic converter turns toxic NO_X into standard nitrogen, which means we are now emitting only a tenth of the NO_X released by the old incinerator. It is a sensational achievement.

Kasper skimmed the text, his pulse speeding up. Everything was great. He should be proud and happy, inviting his coworkers to dinner and toasting them all with champagne while discussing future projects and trips. And yet here he was alone, drunk as a skunk and scared stiff. He knew that communicating in writing was danger-

ous, but given that it was his ass on the line, he refused to bear sole
responsibility if it was discovered. He opened Messenger and wrote:

What do I do if they find something?

Then he hit Send.

JEPPE RAN UP the stairs to the fifth floor. There was no elevator in
this old apartment building on the shadow side of Nyhavn. The door
flew open and hit a moving box of vinyl records and paperbacks that
needed to go up to the attic. That box had been sitting in the entryway for six months now. Maybe he should just throw it out.

He entered his apartment and breathed in the stagnant air that
is found in homes where no one lives. He didn't bother turning on
the light—after all, he was only here to pack up some clothes for the
next few days. His apartment was on the very top floor, right under
the roof, with a view of the Charlottenborg museum. It had been his
for almost a year and a half now, but he had never really moved in.
In the beginning, he and Sara had tried to alternate back and forth
at each other's places, but it had been too complicated with the kids.

Now he commuted between work and Sara's apartment in
Christianshavn and lived out of his sports bag. He stopped by his
own place once or twice a week to do a load of laundry and pick up
his mail, but he only stocked the fridge at Sara's, never here. Jeppe
pulled jeans and T-shirts off the drying rack and folded them, then
put away half and packed the other half into his sports bag. A life as
free as a backpacker's, but perhaps a little measly, too.

Jeppe noticed that the sofa had been made up as a bed, which
must mean that Johannes had been by recently. He had given him
a key so his friend had a place to spend the night when he was in
town and didn't feel like making the trip all the way up the coast to

Snekkersten. Sara was right that it was silly not to use this apartment properly. It was big and expensive. Maybe they should just take the plunge and find a place together. How difficult could it be, after all, to be a stepfather to her two daughters? Besides, he was getting a little sick of living out of his sports bag.

He slung the bag over his shoulder, locked up, and jogged back down the stairs. The evening was clear and mild, and he decided to walk over the bike bridge to Christianshavn. That walk along the water always did him good, even now, when he couldn't help searching the harbor for a white boat.

In the middle of the bridge he set down his bag and gazed out past the Opera House and Langelinie Pier, toward Trekroner Sea Fortress and the open ocean. He tried to follow Anette's theory through to the end. Oscar in some kind of jam with Malthe Sæther, maybe an unhealthy relationship? They had seen each other Friday night, argued, and then Oscar had strangled his teacher, thrown him in a trash can, and taken the boat out on the sea to disappear.

Or had someone murdered both him and Malthe? Maybe Oscar's body was lying in the trash silo, rotting under those heaps of garbage. If so, they would probably never find him.

Jeppe picked up his bag and set off again. On the other side of the water he turned right and walked along the canal toward Overgaden Oven Vandet. He loved this section of cobblestone-lined pier with its houseboats and wooden dinghies under the old linden trees. In the mild evening air, the street glowed like some tale from the gilded days of Copenhagen's past, before it had turned the cloudy gray it was now. When he reached Bodenhoffs Square he turned onto it and headed toward Burmeistersgade and Christiania. In just a few yards the feel of the neighborhood transformed from bourgeois idyll to scruffy chic, including big muscle dogs and the smell of pot.

He could hear laughter from the newsstand at the corner and muted music from someone's phone.

Jeppe smiled as he walked through a crowd of teenagers. *Nothing says spring like idle young people on the streets.*

He stopped. In the group, amid all the hoodies and beer cans, sat Amina, ducking down. It was nine thirty at night. She should be in bed.

"What are you doing here?" Jeppe tried to keep the shock out of his voice but failed.

A girl in a cap who looked like she must be fifteen, sixteen, maybe even seventeen, eyed him with suspicion.

"Who's he?" she asked.

"My mom's boyfriend," Amina mumbled at the ground, refusing to look him in the eye.

"Chill, man!" The girl in the cap laughed. "She's spending the night with my little sister tonight, and they're both here with me. We're on our way home." She stood up and got Amina and another girl Amina's age onto their feet. "Come on, girls. Let's go."

Jeppe stopped them.

"Does your mother know you're all down here?" he asked.

"Everything's fine. We live right over there. We're going now." The girl in the cap waved for her little sister and Amina to follow and started crossing the street.

"I'll walk you home."

Jeppe followed the three girls and ignored the titters from the group of teenagers behind him. He felt at a loss. Should he take Amina home no matter what the consequences for her might be?

Fifty yards down the street the girl in the cap unlocked the front door of an apartment building. Jeppe put his foot in the doorway.

"I'll come upstairs with you and say hi to your mother."

She shrugged indifferently, but he could tell she didn't like it. On the second floor a smiling woman with bleached-blond hair came out to meet them with a cat in her arms. She spoke only to the girls.

"Ah, there you are. Good, it's bedtime."

"I understand that Amina is spending the night?" Jeppe said, looking at her with concern.

She confirmed this with a nod.

"I'm a friend of her mother's. I don't know what rules your kids have, but Amina isn't allowed out on the street late at night, certainly not with a bunch of teenagers drinking beer."

"I hadn't noticed how late it had gotten." The woman nervously scratched the cat between its ears. "But they're home now, right?"

She backed into the apartment and closed the door with a faint smile at Jeppe, who stood indecisively in the stairwell until he finally walked back down the stairs and out onto the street.

His springtime buzz had evaporated.

The boy lies on the concrete floor in the narrow passage between two walls. It is no more than a crack, just wide enough for a person to be able to stand in. Or lie down.

The daylight never makes it in, no plants grow here, and no one comes by. And yet. A scratching sound grows out of the darkness, blending with the sounds of the surf and the wind. A crow has found its way down into the depths. It hops cautiously closer and examines its prey.

The crow is an intelligent bird, one of the only birds able to use tools— digging food out with a stick, for example. Normally it lives primarily off grain and eggs from other birds' nests, but that doesn't mean it turns up its beak at some carrion. You could almost call it opportunistic. It cleans up nicely after the rest of us, making sure there aren't any corpses lying around. Nature's little garbagemen.

The crow hops warily closer, waiting. It's used to being cautious, but the boy isn't moving anymore. The bird approaches his face and looks at him, contemplating where it should slash its beak into the flesh and take a chunk.

TUESDAY,
APRIL 16

CHAPTER 18

The Tuesday morning mood at Burmeistersgade was positively cheerful. There was no line for the bathroom, and Meriem chatted happily at breakfast. Jeppe tried not to ponder too much on whether the household peace was due to the fact that Amina wasn't home. Sara smiled at him as she poured their coffee, and he felt a sense of peace spread from the pit of his stomach all the way to his earlobes.

"Did you sleep well?"

"Like a log!" Sara's expression lit up the room. "How about you?"

"Okay. I'm a little stiff. That mattress is still too soft for me, but there is nothing wrong with my mood." He got the milk out of the fridge and gave her a quick kiss, which she leaned in to.

"Would you be able to look at Malthe Sæther's computer today? Clausen's sending it over this morning."

Her smile stiffened. As a rule they didn't talk about work in front of the kids.

"I will."

"Thank you." Jeppe tried to get her to smile again, but she wasn't going for it. He sat down, drank his coffee, and tried to focus on the tasks ahead instead of the subtle shifts in his relationship.

To find a perpetrator, first he had to get to know the victim. The key to Malthe's death was in all likelihood hiding somewhere in his life—at school, in the chorus, with a friend—they just had to find it. The first item on Jeppe's agenda for today was to question Lis Christensen, Malthe's fellow teacher from Zahles, then later the choral director, and hopefully Kasper Skytte. But first, he had a personal matter to attend to.

At ten minutes to eight, he stood waiting by the fence in front of Christianshavn School. Boys and girls on scooters and in hoodies with low-hanging backpacks passed him in a steady stream without looking up from their shoes and their phones. Parents in tight black jeans dropped off their progeny from cargo bikes with kisses and eager waves, before hurrying off to work.

Amina came walking along behind her friend, as if she were hiding, which she probably was. Jeppe edged his way through the crowd and pulled her aside before she was able to enter the school grounds.

"Good morning, Amina," Jeppe said. "Could we have a quick chat for, like, two minutes?"

She avoided making eye contact.

"I just want to hear what you were doing out on the street so late last night."

"Did you blab to my mom?"

"No."

The decision to keep Amina's secret at the expense of Sara's trust had been instinctive. He already regretted it.

"Amina, I'm just worried about you. You were hanging out on a street corner at nine thirty at night with teenagers who were drinking beer. You know you're not allowed to do that."

"I didn't drink anything."

"Oh, believe me! If you'd have been drinking, I would have dragged you home." Jeppe put his hand to his head. "You're eleven years old! *Eleven!* You were playing circus with your little sister, like, five minutes ago."

She raised her face and looked at him, eyes narrow, and the corners of her mouth curled downward.

"Who do you think you are? You come slinking in every night after we're tucked in to screw our mom. You think that gives you the right to tell us what to do? To play house?"

"Amina, you don't mean that!"

"Forget it! Just fucking forget it!"

She pulled away from him and headed for the school.

Jeppe watched her go, then turned around and started walking. Where there had been a knot of worry in his chest before, it now just felt hollow.

At Christianshavns Torv he went down to the subway. For once, people's morning grumpy pushing and shoving suited his mood just fine. On the train the burden of his inadequacy felt heavier, station by station. Of all the ungrateful little brats in the world, why did Sara have to have a daughter who just refused to give him a chance?

He got off at Nørreport Station and tried to stomp his frustration out on the stairs as he made his way up to street level.

On Nørre Voldgade, elegant gold letters on a tasteful facade revealed the location of Zahles School, one of Copenhagen's finest old high schools. Malthe's coworker Lis Christensen had promised to meet Jeppe at the front door at quarter past eight, and just as he arrived, an older woman walked out the glass doors and approached him. She had a neat dark brown haircut and a pained look in her eyes.

"Is it you?"

That one existential question you basically always have to answer in the affirmative. Jeppe smiled and held out his hand.

"Jeppe Kørner from the Copenhagen Police's Investigations Unit."

"Yes, I'm Lis. Would you mind if we stayed out here in the fresh air? There are benches in the park." She pointed toward the entrance of Ørstedsparken and began walking slowly and with difficulty, clearly suffering from arthritis or an injured hip.

The sky over the city had become overcast and looked as if it might rain any minute. In the absence of the sun, temperatures had dropped sharply and people were back to wearing wool coats and scarves again. Jeppe assumed that Lis wanted to have their conversation on a bench more out of discretion than a desire for fresh air. She walked slowly along the gravel path, huddled over in the morning cold, and Jeppe matched her pace until they reached a bench with a view of the pond and a lacy canopy of light green branches.

They sat down. Lis lifted her head and squinted. Even on cloudy days, the light over Copenhagen is always sharp and bright.

"Is it true that Malthe was murdered?" The question tumbled out of her, as if she had been thinking of nothing else since the news of the teacher's death had hit the previous day.

"Yes, I'm afraid it is."

She nodded briefly, almost politely, a controlled reaction—obviously the way to safeguard her against this horrible news.

"I'm sorry. How well did you know him?" Jeppe asked.

"We weren't friends, but I spoke with Malthe often in a professional context, right from when he was first hired two years ago. He was a sweet young man."

Lis didn't seem bothered by the low temperatures, even though her breath showed in the chilly air when she spoke.

"He didn't have an easy start at the school, although I did my best to help him. Malthe and I had many conversations about teaching and how to tackle problems in the classroom."

"What kinds of problems?"

She looked at him skeptically, as if the question were somehow inappropriate, and it took a little while before Jeppe realized that that was just her neutral expression. A long life of teaching naughty kids had left its mark.

"Malthe was idealistic. People often are when they arrive fresh out of the university. Full of ambition and ideas. That's great of course, but the reality of a classroom is . . . something else." She sighed and smoothed the fabric of her pants with her hands. "Young people don't sit on the edges of their seats, eager to learn. School bores them. And unlike when I was young, they're not exactly receptive to discipline. Well, sorry."

"No need to apologize!" Jeppe said with conviction. "Was Malthe well-liked among the faculty?"

"Yes, definitely. He was easy to get along with and had great ideas for subject-focus days and ways to vary the teaching. Some coworkers may have found him to be a bit of a handful with all his energy, but there wasn't anyone who *didn't* like him."

She turned and looked out at the pond. A gray heron flew in low over the water's surface and landed on the bank.

"Can what I tell you remain between us?"

"Not if it contributes to our investigation," Jeppe replied. "But I'll do my best to make sure your name isn't mentioned."

She contemplated him skeptically but collected herself. It was clear that she had decided to share her thoughts, even before they met.

"We had an episode at the school about six months ago that Malthe was involved in, an episode with a student . . ."

"Victor Dreyer-Hoff?" Jeppe guessed.

She nodded.

"Malthe very nearly got fired over it." She took a breath as if to continue, then looked away and sighed, clearly affected by what she was telling him.

"What kind of episode?"

"There were rumors that at the fall dance last year, Victor, who's a senior, molested one of the freshman girls. I wasn't at the dance myself, and neither was Malthe, but the story made its way through the hallways all the way up to the teachers' lounge and the headmaster's office. The girl never reported it. She refused to name him or even make a statement, and none of the other students had seen anything, so it never got any further."

"Molested?"

Her hands flew up from her lap to her face, where she held them protectively over blushing cheeks.

"Yes, you know, sexually. I don't know if there was anything to it, but Malthe insisted on getting to the bottom of it. He talked to both Victor and the girl to get to the truth."

She paused.

Jeppe gave her space and waited until she seemed ready to continue.

"What did the school do about it?" he asked.

"That's the point!" she said with a scornful laugh. "Not a darned thing. Oh, I mean they lifted a finger, and there was a little window dressing, but there was no will from the headmaster to look into the case, quite the contrary. Malthe received a direct order to stay out of it and leave the students alone. Victor is popular, student body president and active on the basketball team and the prom committee, from a prominent family. And of course these kinds of incidents are bad publicity."

Jeppe leaned back on the bench and tried to get the information to add up. Rumors of an assault, Oscar's disappearance, Malthe's death.

"Did you ever talk to Malthe about Oscar, Victor's little brother?"

"Malthe liked him a lot," she said with a sad nod. "It really tells you something about how Malthe operated, that he never let his conflict with Victor spill over onto Victor's little brother. Oscar is a good boy, but even so, Malthe could easily have chosen to keep him at arm's length. Especially when you think of Iben."

"Iben?"

"Iben Skytte." Her eyes wandered. "She and Oscar are best friends, so it was a bit of a wasp's nest to stick his hand into. But Malthe wasn't scared."

"I'm not following." Jeppe shook his head, confused. "How is Iben related to all of this?"

"Well . . ." She hesitated. "She was the one, at the fall dance. The girl Victor allegedly molested was Iben Skytte."

THE OLD ADAGE aptly says that we don't know what we've got till it's gone. Anette was so used to waking up to the scent of coffee and freshly baked bread that Tuesday morning's lack of aromas seemed as wrong as tartar sauce on liverwurst. The bedroom was empty. Svend must have gotten up with Gudrun, but clearly he hadn't started making breakfast. Disoriented, she got up and opened the bedroom door. Not a sound. Wherever Svend had gone, he had taken the baby and the dogs with him.

She staggered into the shower and turned the temperature way down in an attempt to wake up. The night had been one long series of dreams about naked skin and water, and she had woken up several times with a body quivering with sexual shivers. Had she had an actual orgasm in her dream? She forced her head under the water. The road back to reality was foggy and difficult, but the cold on her scalp helped a little. She gasped, turned off the shower, and rubbed herself with the towel until she was warm and clean, free of dirty dreams and foggy fantasies. She got dressed and listened for voices, halfway hoping that she would be able to leave for work before her family came home.

As she stood at the kitchen table pouring cereal into a bowl, the front door opened and the dogs raced in with wet paws and hungry devotion. She petted them, got out kitchen towels to wipe their muzzles and their paws, poured food into their bowls, and gave them fresh water. Just as she was pouring milk into her cereal, Svend appeared in the doorway.

"We got caught in a downpour. Could you just take her?"

Anette took her daughter and put a big kiss on her rain-soaked cheek before carrying her into the bathroom to dry her off, tickle her, and dress her in dry clothes.

When they were done she found Svend in the kitchen with a cup of instant coffee and the newspaper open in front of him. She put Gudrun in her high chair and buttered some crispbread for her, sliced an apple into wedges, and poured her some milk.

"Good morning by the way. Where were you guys?"

"Went for a walk," Svend answered with his head buried in the newspaper. "To get the paper. She's exhausted, so I'm keeping her home from day care today."

Anette turned on the electric kettle and spooned ground coffee into the French press.

"You didn't bake this morning?"

He didn't respond, just shrugged, as if it was trivial. Which it would have been for anyone else, but not for Svend. He hadn't even kissed her good morning!

Anette sat down with her bowl.

"Is something wrong?"

He looked slowly up from the paper, his eyes glazed and distant.

"I'm just a little tired. Gudrun was up at five a.m. again."

Svend kept reading, and Anette ate a spoonful of cereal. It expanded in her mouth into a pasty mass that was hard to swallow. Maybe he *was* just tired. She really couldn't blame him. Tomorrow morning it would have to be her turn to get up with Gudrun.

"We should take that weekend in Paris, shouldn't we? We've been talking about it for ages. Once I'm done with this case? Just you and me and a bottle of red wine in the hotel bed? Your parents would be happy to watch Gudrun."

Svend made a smiling, humming sort of sound but didn't look up.

Anette set down her spoon and watched her reading husband with a growing sense of worry.

"He still hasn't been found, the missing boy."

That made him lower his newspaper. "That's terrible! Those poor parents. How long has he been missing now?"

"Since Friday afternoon, so three full days and a night. I was out looking for him myself yesterday. At Trekroner Sea Fortress. With the fort caretaker out there." Anette bit her tongue. What kind of sick need made her tell Svend about the man who was haunting her nighttime fantasies?

"Trekroner Sea Fortress? That would be a stupid place to hide. Way too many people go there. If you really wanted to hide in Copenhagen Harbor you'd choose someplace else like Fort Middelgrund or Prøvestenen." Svend buried his nose in the paper again.

"Prøvestenen? What's that?"

"Oh, it's another one of the old sea fortresses, just not so well known. It's on Petroleum Island, surrounded by heavy industry. You know, back behind the ARC incineration plant. Unless you work there the only way to get to it is by boat."

He yawned and went back to his reading.

Anette gave up on her cereal, cleaned up after both herself and Gudrun, and got out the DUPLO blocks for her daughter.

"I have to run to work now. Will you be a good girl for Daddy?" She kissed her toddler's peach-fuzz cheek and turned to Svend to say goodbye. He still sat, engrossed in his article, and let her hug him without much response.

"I'm slipping off to work, honey. Gudrun is in the living room, I'll keep the door open so you can keep an eye on her. I'm meeting Kørner at Vesterbro in half an hour. I'll text you if I can't make it home for dinner. Have a good day, you two!"

The kiss Anette blew from the doorway still hung in the air as she got into the car. Svend was tired. That was probably all that it was. Her guilty conscience over the unwanted thoughts was probably playing tricks on her.

When was the last time they had sex? It had been quite a while. She would have to get serious about that getaway to Paris so they could have a little time together again as a couple.

She started the car and checked the time on the dashboard. They were questioning Malthe's choral director at ten. Maybe she could convince Mads Teigen to meet her after and take her out to Prøvestenen. Her midriff buzzed at the thought, and she hit the dashboard to rein herself in. What the hell was this fascination with a random man with sad eyes and strong hands all about? She wasn't a freaking teenager anymore! Pushing the thoughts forcefully away, she wrote a quick, cool message to Mads to see if he was free to help her search at noon.

Svend, she thought, *my good, loving husband, who is reliable, who makes me laugh, who never has bad breath. I do love him!*

But the thought had been planted in her like a malicious virus: Was their love waning?

CHAPTER 19

The distinctive hum of *Ark Futura* often woke Mads Teigen in the early-morning hours. The massive freighter's propeller had its completely own sound, deeper than those of the other freighters that passed through the harbor. Usually he went back to sleep again, but today his sleep was poor and plagued by nightmares, and he ended up tossing and turning until well into the morning. The sounds of Trekroner had long since become familiar to him: the hoarse cries of the gulls, the seaplanes, and the horn of the Oslo ferry. Lying in bed he registered it all without really hearing it anymore. It had become the backdrop of his life.

A life without any prospects of change. Not that he wanted change. Mads had stopped expecting more from his existence. The grass on the embankments needed to be mowed, the mink population controlled, the fort maintained. Routine, no variation.

And yet.

Yesterday had been a variation. For a second he had opened the door to his heart chamber and let the light shine on the swamp that it was. That had been a mistake. It wouldn't happen again. He had been punished for it all night, and now there was only one thing to do. The same thing he always did: shut down and move on.

He got out of bed, ran through his mental checklist under the shower, and got dressed. Today was Tuesday, and there wouldn't be many visitors on the island. Apart from the regular rowing clubs, he would probably be left to work in peace today. The coffee trickled through the filter. He poured himself a cup, took it out into the morning light, and drank it under the tall beech tree in the yard, his eyes on the horizon.

Today was day 266 on his calendar.

Mads did the morning rounds. He started at the cannon emplacement, where a goose was nesting on top of the old ammunition depot. He knew the eggs would hatch soon. The geese always incubated for twenty-five days. If one of the eggs was late, it risked being left behind for the crows' hungry beaks. Only yesterday he had tried to save a gosling from another nest; it had been lying on its back, unable to roll over. But the attempt hadn't been successful. So now it was lying in his fridge instead, waiting to be preserved.

On the other side of the island, he checked the sunken barge off the shore, where a little colony of seals had been living these past weeks. Yesterday they were suddenly gone, probably because they had eaten all the fish in the water and had moved on. He missed their big-eyed doggy heads on the surface. Six or seven years ago, he remembered, someone out in a sea kayak had thought he saw a seal on the breakwater by the sunken barge, but when he brought his kayak closer, it had turned out to be a body. A waiter from a restaurant on one of the forts who had run afoul of some gang members, Mads recalled.

Seals and dead people, rare birds and paddlers—if he waited long enough, the whole world came by Trekroner.

Mads crossed the fort's upper level, past the lighthouse and back to the southern flank. Here he had found a spot where he could stand against the casemate building in the lee of the wind and the noise from the city and see all the way from Fort Middelgrund on the left, past the offshore wind farm, and over to Refshaleøen and the incineration plant on the right. There was a special energy here that encouraged peace and contemplation. Mads was a carpenter by training and had always considered himself to be a pragmatic northern Jutlander with his hands screwed on right. He liked the outdoors, fishing, and hunting, a practical man without too many frills. Until his life had come crashing down, and—with the help of one of his old hunting buddies—he ended up here.

During this last year, he had developed a sort of sixth sense. He didn't know what else to call it. A connection to the other side, perhaps. When he stood here facing the sea, that connection blared loud as a car alarm and couldn't be ignored. The dead child spoke to him in a clear voice. Without blame, without fear.

He closed his eyes and breathed in the sea air. Kelp, salt, wind, rain. Flying sand grains that prickled against his cheek and lyme grass that whispered about the transitory nature of everything.

It wasn't my fault, he told himself, but deep down inside he knew that was a lie.

A SCHOOL HAD moved its sports class out onto one of the basketball courts on the grassy median strip on Sønder Boulevard. The cheerful shouts of the students merged with the morning rain, as Jeppe and Anette met up in front of Absalon's Church, like a collage of youth and hope.

"Howdy," Anette called out when they were about five yards apart, "is this the place? Was he in a church choir, or something?"

"The church is no longer in use. It's a community center now. They host all sorts of activities—bridge and communal dining and tango lessons. And apparently choral singing."

"How modern." She squinted up at the skies. "Are you going to smoke before we go in?"

"So you can mooch off my smoke?" Jeppe laughed. "Forget it, Werner. It's raining! By the way, have you been in touch with Kasper Skytte?"

"No." Anette frowned. "Is he still not answering his phone?"

"Nope! Come on, it's this way."

They walked up the stone stairs to the church's big wooden door and opened it. Inside, the high-ceilinged former church greeted them warmly, its walls painted salmon pink and blue and green. Long tables filled the floor space, where church pews must have once been.

"The choral director said we could find him in the bar," Jeppe said, making his way between the tables.

"A bar in a church . . . ?" Anette mused, following him. "We certainly don't have that out in suburban Greve Strand."

"Oh, how would you know? When's the last time you went to church?"

"Granted, it's been a while. But now that you mention it, I think we actually did drink a little shot of schnapps at the altar."

Jeppe laughed.

"Are you calling the blood of Christ a shot of schnapps?"

"Tasted awful. I haven't been back since."

In a room to the side of the former altar they found a bar counter with shelves of liquor bottles behind it and a commercial dishwasher. A board listed the day's bar snacks, and the draft beer dispenser could be heard humming under the table—they could have been in any hotel bar or nightclub in the city. A collection of milk crates in the middle of the floor, containing food supplies, indicated that the bar was currently closed.

"What's his name, the choral director?"

Jeppe checked his notes.

"Sigurd Vejlø."

"Sigurd?" Anette giggled at the somewhat unusual name. "Sigurd the choral singer!"

Just then a door behind the bar swung open and a young man walked through carrying an empty milk crate in his arms.

"Ah, there you are. Have you been waiting long?" He set the crate down and wiped his hands off on a dish towel.

"Are you Sigurd?"

"I am indeed."

"Jeppe Kørner and Anette Werner from the Copenhagen Police's Investigations Unit. We spoke on the phone."

Sigurd shook their hands.

"Let's find a seat at one of the tables. There's a Spanish class that starts at eleven, but until then we have the church to ourselves."

He removed his apron and walked toward the chapel, Jeppe and Anette following him. The choral director was tall—maybe six foot six—and very slim, with short platinum-blond hair and gold rings in both earlobes. A multicolor tattoo with angels and demons poked out from under his short-sleeved shirt and extended all the way down to his wrist.

They sat down.

"So you're the choral director, *and* you work in the bar?" Anette asked.

Sigurd smiled at her.

"To start with I was hired as a bartender, but Absalon likes to make use of the full range of their employees' abilities. It truly is the people's house. I also manage a music quiz night once a month."

"All right, A-Choir . . . ," Jeppe said, pulling out his notebook. "How did the choir start, and how many members do you have?"

"I started the choir last spring, and there are twenty-two of us. Men only."

"Tell us a little about it," Jeppe said.

Sigurd hesitated.

"Well, I'll be happy to and all, but do you mind telling me why you're interested in us?"

"Of course. We're here because one of your members has suffered a serious injury—Malthe Sæther. I'm afraid he's dead."

"No!" Sigurd brought his hand to his mouth and sat frozen. His eyes teared up.

"Did you know him well?" Jeppe asked, as gently as he could. This was a much stronger reaction than he had expected.

"No . . . ," Sigurd mumbled. "I'm sorry, I'm just . . . in shock. I really liked him."

Sigurd rubbed his face and took a deep breath. Jeppe and Anette exchanged glances.

"How long had you known each other?"

"Malthe joined the choir just under a year ago, so almost right from the beginning. What happened to him?"

Jeppe sighed. There was no easy way to say it.

"Malthe was murdered. We don't know all the details, but he died late Friday night."

Sigurd looked away, his already pale cheeks losing color.

"When did you see him last?"

"Tuesday night for choir. Oh God, this is terrible!" Sigurd shook his head. "Malthe is just the nicest guy. He sings tenor, beautiful blue eyes. Everyone loves him."

Jeppe offered the choir leader a pack of tissues from his pocket.

"Did you ever see him outside of the choir?" Jeppe asked.

"No." Sigurd pulled out a tissue and wiped his nose. "He often stayed after and had a beer, but nothing more than that. Sometimes we biked home together—he lives on Vendersgade, which is on my way home. I live in Østerbro."

"And where were you Friday night?"

"At home." His answer came without hesitation. "I'm in this phase where I focus on taking good care of myself. I'm eating healthy, staying in, and I go to bed early. That's what I did all week-end."

"Do you live with anyone?"

Jeppe could tell that Sigurd knew why he was asking.

"No, alone. Unfortunately I don't have anyone who can corrobo-rate that I was home."

"It's standard procedure for us to ask."

"I understand." He nodded.

"And you haven't spoken with him since Tuesday night? Any phone calls . . . or text messages?"

Sigurd appeared to think back and then said, "No, there hasn't been anything."

"What about the other chorus members? Do you think any of them might have seen him during the week?"

"I don't think so." He shook his head. "Malthe came to sing and have a good time; that was it. As do most of us. It's not like a dating scene."

Jeppe smiled.

"Did you ever discuss personal stuff?"

"No, not really. Although there was one night when he seemed down, a couple of weeks ago." Sigurd was crumpling up his tissue into a little ball as he spoke. "We talked about the challenges the younger generations face today, and how social media makes new types of bullying possible. The topic really seemed to strike a nerve with Malthe."

"Did he say why?"

Sigurd shook his head.

"He's required to keep certain things confidential. But I got the clear impression that one of his students had experienced it first-hand."

*   *   *

ESTHER COULD NOT find peace. She moved through her morning routines—long shower, oatmeal with raisins, and a walk around
the Lakes with Dóxa—and settled at her desk with every intention
of working on the biography she was writing. But she kept getting
up for more coffee and found herself lost in her own thoughts at the
keyboard. She went to the window to look out at the Lakes, where
rain showers speckled the surface of the water, then sat back down
at her desk again.

The notes she had written yesterday about the death masks at
Thorvaldsens sat on her desk, as a reminder of her encounter with
Jenny Kaliban. Esther tried to identify what it was about the woman
that stirred unease. Her bluntness, of course—she had been almost
rude, but there was something more than that. Her body language
maybe, her vibe? There was a tense energy to Jenny Kaliban that
Esther interpreted as egocentric.

Esther decided to allow herself five minutes to satisfy her curiosity. Five minutes and then she would get to work! She typed Jenny's
name into the search field on her browser and received a string of
links to galleries, museums, night-school classes, and a Wikipedia
article that she opened and read. The article was brief and relatively
light on content.

Jenny Kaliban née Dreyer was born in Frederiksværk, about an
hour north of Copenhagen, on November 6, 1968. Her parents were
both gallery owners and art teachers. Jenny was named after the
Swedish opera singer Jenny Lind. From an early age she was active
in the local art society, which met in a gallery owned by the Dreyer
family.

In 1990, she and her sister founded the artists' commune Kaliban
and organized exhibits and events in the local area. A link to the
local paper in Halsnæs led Esther to the revelation of a joint work in
the library. The photo showed Jenny at an easel in front of a white-
painted brick wall. She looked young, in her twenties, and was strik-

ingly pretty in a white suit with her eyes focused confidently on the camera. A smiling young woman stood on the other side of the easel: her sister, in a floral summer dress.

Esther zoomed in on the caption, yanking her chair a bit closer and disturbing Dóxa, who was napping at her feet.

The sister's name was Malin Dreyer. Wasn't she the mother of the missing Oscar Dreyer-Hoff?

Esther closed the article and read on about Jenny in random posts. Accepted in 1995 to the Royal Danish Academy of Fine Arts in Copenhagen. Group exhibition at Den Frie in 1999. Interview in the international arts magazine *Apollo*. Invited to participate in the Venice Biennale in 2005. Cofounder of the Art as Protest movement, which put on an event in front of Christiansborg Palace in 2008. Commissioned to do a piece for the town square in Frederiks-værk in 2009. After that the references thinned out a bit.

Esther found a link at the bottom of the page that led to an article from *Weekendavisen* from not quite three years ago. The title read, "Museum Cancels in the Eleventh Hour," and the article was about the Arken Museum of Modern Art, which chose to cancel Jenny Kaliban's solo exhibit with only a couple months' notice. The museum director refused to comment on the specific case, and Jenny Kaliban was also silent, but the journalist speculated that it might have had something to do with the scandal at the Nordhjem auction house, which was owned by Kaliban's sister.

So she *was* Oscar Dreyer-Hoff's aunt!

Esther continued to browse but didn't find more of interest about Jenny Kaliban. What she'd discovered, though, suggested an artistic career that had foundered before it ever really took off.

Just like my own, Esther thought, closing the browser with a guilty sigh.

*   *   *

"DO YOU MIND if I just drop you off?" Anette pulled over to the curb in front of the super police HQ and put the car in neutral.

Jeppe looked at his partner in the driver's seat.

"Where are you going?" he asked, surprised.

"I'm meeting Mads Teigen, the fort caretaker from Trekroner."

"Again?!"

Anette blinked, for a second looking uncharacteristically hesitant. One would almost think she was insecure.

"He promised to help me look for Oscar at that fort called Prøvestenen. And before you say anything—I *know* it's a shot in the dark, but I think the Search and Rescue crews might have overlooked it. I saw them in action on Hven and, honestly, I wasn't impressed. Only three men turned up, and two of them were volunteers."

Jeppe rolled his eyes at her.

"Can we agree that you have a control issue? Say, do you check whether Svend folds his undies the right way, too?"

She didn't laugh.

"I just have a . . . hunch. You of all people know what that's like."

Jeppe got out of the car, bracing himself against the rain.

"Just be careful, Anette!" he urged. "Remember to wear a life jacket."

She winked at him, waited for him to close his door, and then raced away. Jeppe saw her speed around the corner, then turned to face his workplace.

The sight of the modern office building in the rain automatically muted his serotonin level and made him wish that he could travel to some warm country and stay there. Walking to the front door he glanced up at the facade and felt the weight of the soaked bricks deep in his soul. This was his new reality. He had no choice if he wanted to keep his job, and he loved his job. In other words, he had to find a way to—if not love—then at least accept the new police building in Sydhavn.

In the shelter of his office he hung his jacket over the back of his chair to dry and tried to look at the bright side of things. At least he and Anette shared their own office and didn't have to sit in an open-office layout like many of their coworkers. He went to fetch a cup of coffee from the machine and found Thomas Larsen and Sara Saidani in their cubicles down the hall.

"Larsen, Saidani, everything all right?"

"Yeah, thanks. I brought Malthe's computer in," Sara replied, and smiled at him in a way that was not strictly professional. Her look warmed his heart. "It came back from the crime scene technicians at NKC this morning. No prints other than his own. And so far there's nothing to be found, everything seems normal."

Jeppe drank his coffee. It tasted very faintly of dishwashing soap.

"I met with one of Malthe's colleagues this morning, a Lis Christensen. She claims that there have been problems between him and some of the students, including Victor Dreyer-Hoff."

"Whereas Victor insists that he saw Malthe and Oscar hugging in the school library two weeks ago," Sara replied with a frown.

"Could Victor be making that up because he has a bone to pick with the teacher?" Jeppe set his coffee cup down on Sara's desk. "Lis also told me that there were rumors of an episode at the fall dance last year. Victor allegedly sexually molested Iben Skytte. Lis didn't know if it's true, for now it's just a rumor. But we need to ask Iben if there's anything to it."

"I'll handle her," Sara said with a nod.

"Before you get going," Larsen interjected, "I checked Victor's alibi, and it seems to hold water. His friends confirm that they were together all of Friday night until the early-morning hours on Saturday. Does this Lis seem like a reliable witness?"

"She does, but who knows?" Jeppe perched on one of the vacant desks nearby and put a hand on his sore neck, rubbing it cautiously. "According to Malthe's choral director, he was preoccupied with a problem among his students, something to do maybe with bullying or sexual harassment. That's consistent with what Lis told me."

"So what are you saying, Kørner? That Malthe tried to resolve a heated situation with the students and somehow came between the two brothers and was murdered?" Larsen sounded skeptical. "If so, Oscar did it and not Victor, because Victor was out playing air hockey at the Electric Corner all Friday night."

"And then Oscar took the family boat and sailed away," Sara added.

"That could be the case," Jeppe admitted. He knew that was the most plausible theory they had. Even so, he nursed an instinctive antipathy toward it. Maybe he just didn't want the sensitive young boy, who reminded him of himself, to be guilty of murder.

"Have any of you been in touch with Kasper Skytte? He's gone underground since Werner and I saw him at the plant yesterday. Our agreement was that he was going to call ASAP."

Sara and Thomas Larsen shook their heads.

Jeppe walked back to his office and dialed Kasper's number yet again. This time the phone was answered.

"Hello?" The voice sounded distant and sleepy.

"Hi, Kasper. It's Jeppe Kørner from the police. We've been trying to reach you since yesterday."

"I'm sorry about that." He cleared his throat. "I felt so terrible when I came home from the ER that I took a sleeping pill. I slept straight through till now. It must be the shock."

"Aha." Jeppe paused. He could hear Kasper Skytte swallow. "We need to question you about the discovery of the body as soon as possible. Can we stop by?"

It was Kasper's turn to be quiet now. Then he mumbled, "Of course. Do you mind if I shower first?"

Jeppe looked at his watch. It was a little past one. But he felt obliged to give the man a chance to wake up properly.

"I'll be there at three. See you then." He hung up.

Jeppe had left his coffee behind on Sara's desk but couldn't be bothered to go get another cup. He contemplated buying a sandwich until he remembered that there was nowhere in the neighborhood to get food besides a horrible fast-food joint around the corner.

He walked over to the window and watched the smoke billowing up from a factory smokestack on the horizon, letting his thoughts drift with the smoke, until the ringtone from his cell phone reverberated through the office.

"Kørner."

"Hi, Jeppe. It's Esther. I hope I'm not disturbing you."

"It's fine." He dumped himself into his office chair, and it sank slightly under him with a hydraulic hiss.

"I'm calling to ask if you've talked to Oscar Dreyer-Hoff's aunt, Jenny Kaliban?"

Jeppe sighed. What was Esther up to now?

"Not yet. Why?"

"Well, you see, I happened to meet her at Thorvaldsens Museum yesterday, and she left me with a strange impression, so I read up on her a little. Are you familiar with the Nordhjem auction scandal?"

"Yes, Esther, I am." A little irritation crept into Jeppe's voice, and he took a deep breath before continuing. "We're investigating all aspects of the missing boy's life." And his dead teacher's, he thought, but chose not to say that part out loud.

"It's just, because . . . well, the aunt had a large exhibit canceled following all the bad press in the media and the legal charges against the auction house, and I think it is conceivable that that caused a dispute in the family. In the sense that one sister's business ruined the other sister's career."

"Hmm," Jeppe replied noncommittally.

"She has an atelier in Østerbro . . ." Esther hesitated, and he knew that she was debating how hard to push him.

He looked at his watch again. Strictly speaking they should talk to the aunt to find out if she knew anything about Malthe Sæther. He could probably just squeeze her in before questioning Kasper Skytte.

"Do you have her address?"

She supplied it to him in an apologetic voice.

"She doesn't have a cell phone as far as I can tell. I'm really not trying to get mixed up in your work, you know. I'm just curious."

"I have to talk to her anyway," Jeppe said, smiling against his will. "By the way, Esther, since I have you, I want to ask you about something . . . personal."

The words tumbled out of him before he really had a chance to reflect. Why would he be asking advice specifically from her? Even though they were friends, they rarely discussed their personal lives this way.

"Um, well . . . If a person discovered something about a child— an eleven-year-old girl—which her mother would be furious to learn about, and would seriously chew the child out if she knew, should this person tell the mother or not?"

Esther was silent. He was just about to backpedal when she cleared her throat and said, "Is it important to you that the child trusts you?"

Jeppe thought about that. He was surprised to realize how unequivocal he felt.

"Yes, it's very important to me that she trusts me."

"Then the answer is obvious. Unless—"

"Unless what?"

"Unless the secret puts her in danger."

CHAPTER 20

The clouds hung low over the water, ominous and dark, as Mads Teigen moored *Stærkodder* in front of Prøvestenen sea fortress. Anette knew better than to try to help him with the routine tasks and hopped onto the concrete dock. The harbor was completely empty apart from the two of them, not a single boat or person in sight. In front of them the fortress loomed low, with the smoke-stacks and silos of Petroleum Island rising up behind it, gray and forlorn. Crumbling rock, an antenna, a tipped-over trash can. It looked like some sort of cross between a North Atlantic island and a sci-fi movie.

A good place to go missing, she thought, and realized that Mads was standing right beside her.

"Are you okay?" He put his broad hand on her shoulder and let it stay there. His touch sent an electric jolt through Anette, and she didn't dare respond, for fear that doing so would divulge the effect he had on her. She pulled away and looked out at the horizon.

"A-okay, just a little tired. How about you?"

"I'm doing well." He smiled. "Better than in a long time, actually."

Anette returned his broad smile and regretted it right away. Why couldn't she just relax?

"Do you want to have a quick cup of coffee before we get going?" He pointed with his thumb to a thermos that sat on the deck. "Have you had lunch? I brought a little along in case you're hungry."

"That was nice of you, but I'm not hungry. Let's just get started, if that's all right with you."

He nodded in the direction of the fort in a sort of *ladies first* gesture. Anette felt his eyes on her back, and her heart started pounding in her chest. The fort's facade was worn and weather-beaten. She touched a crumbling window frame and watched her finger go right through it. The place seemed totally abandoned.

"It's probably easier to get in from the back."

Mads pointed to the end of the fort, and they walked around it to a big, open area, which was covered with sand. A small excavator was left in the sand, and behind it a gigantic white silo leaned against the masonry like some invasive species that had grown bigger than its host.

"Wow, it looks like we landed on the moon!"

Mads frowned and said, "I don't think we can get into the fort. All the doors are barricaded."

"Wait, maybe it's easier from up there."

Anette walked back to the end of the building where a staircase led up to the roof of the fort. She took it two steps at a time, up to a poured-concrete plateau with shielding concrete bunkers and soft cushions of grass. Mads followed her.

"You brought the flashlights, right? I think we can get in over here."

She pointed to an open metal door with a staircase peeking out from inside it, the steps of which must lead down into the fort. Mads passed Anette a flashlight and turned on his own.

"Ready?"

He nodded.

"Let's get going."

Anette peered in the doorway. The top of the staircase was lit by the daylight from outside, but by the third or fourth step, the contours blurred into a black hole. Her heart skipped a beat, and she groaned, exasperated by her own timidity. What was there to be scared of?

She looked up at the gray sky one last time, turned on her flashlight, and proceeded into the darkness, with Mads right on her heels.

SMOKE FROM THE joint hung thick under the low ceiling of the atelier, obscuring stacked canvases and jars of paintbrushes. Jenny Kaliban breathed easily and leaned back, until the back of her head touched the wall. The noise from the restaurant next door slowly faded. She closed her eyes and enjoyed the remote sounds of life that didn't have anything to do with her. She was an observer, a role she was comfortable with.

A knock on the door disturbed the calm. Jenny put out the joint and struggled to her feet. Her legs felt stiff and heavy. She must have been sitting there for longer than she realized.

A man she hadn't seen before stood in the doorway. He was tall and skinny with dark hair and the kind of eyes that told tales of sorrow. He held a laminated ID card out to her.

"Hello! I'm not sure if I'm in the right place. I'm looking for Jenny Kaliban." He gave her a questioning look, and she nodded, poised. "Jeppe Kørner, pleased to meet you. I'm from the Investigations Unit with the Copenhagen Police. Do you have a minute?"

Jenny hesitated. She could see the weed smoke billowing out into the stairwell. The last thing she wanted was to invite a policeman into her inner sanctum. Apparently she hesitated for too long, because he began to explain.

"It's about Oscar Dreyer-Hoff, your nephew. As you probably know, he has been missing since Friday."

"Have you found him?" Her voice sounded shrill even to her, but she couldn't control it.

"Unfortunately not. There's no news."

Jenny steeled herself, took a step back, and opened the door. "Come in!"

The policeman entered the atelier, stopped a few feet inside the door, and looked around. Jenny saw the mess and dust through his eyes; the blacked-out windows, and the generally shabby condition of the place.

"Let me just air the place out a little." She scooted around him and opened the window to the courtyard, letting the light stream in and the smoke out. She smiled apologetically. "It's good for the creativity."

He nodded politely and refrained from commenting, then pointed to her old armchair.

"Do you mind if I sit down?"

"Oh, please do. Can I offer you something? Instant coffee?"

"No, thank you."

He took a notebook out of his pocket. Casually brought his ankle up to rest on his other knee, and used his calf as a table of sorts as he thumbed through the pages. It made him look elegant, almost like a French intellectual, and quite handsome in a way. It was something to do with his sensitive eyes and the way he turned the pages. Maybe she was just a little stoned.

"I understand from your sister, Malin, that you don't know where Oscar is, either. I presume that hasn't changed?"

"The whole family is falling apart," Jenny said, shaking her head. "It's so awful."

"Of course. We're still searching high and low for him." He clicked his ballpoint pen ready. "The reason I've come is that Oscar's teacher, Malthe Sæther, was found dead yesterday morning."

"Dead?" She felt the floor disappear underneath her.

"Murdered, I'm afraid. Did you know him?"

She released the breath she had been holding for the last many seconds.

"No, I don't know any of Oscar's teachers."

"Has Oscar told you anything about his Danish teacher? He and Mr. Sæther seemed to be close."

"I can't remember having ever heard that name." Jenny looked down at her hands.

The policeman turned the page even though he hadn't written anything yet.

"Are you close in your family?"

She tried to focus on the question, but her mouth was so dry it was hard to speak.

"Well, *close* can mean so many different things. We might not be in and out of each other's houses every five minutes, but we're a family. My sister and her husband are busy, you know, so often a little time goes by between visits. But I've always loved the kids. Oscar's interested in drawing, actually. Vic doesn't have any artistic ability, but both Essie and Oscar have potential, and they're eager to learn."

"Your sister's company ran into some adversity a couple of years ago. . . ."

Jenny waited. Where was he going with this?

"I'm thinking about the accusations of shill bidding and the subsequent press coverage. Has that had an effect on the family?"

"Of course. It was like being hit by a bus. My sister and brother-in-law are still struggling with the fallout from that case."

He glanced at the easel and the sketch she was working on.

"Has it affected you as well?"

Jenny felt the blood drain from her head, flowing toward some unknown point in her body. She remembered how she had screamed at her sister, pummeled her brother-in-law in the chest with her fists, and pleaded with them to do something. Hold the Arken Museum accountable, threaten the journalists into silence, whatever it took to curb the forces that were choking off her career.

"No, it hasn't." She looked him in the eye.

He eyed her inquisitively, then turned another empty page in his notebook.

"When did you last see your nephew?"

Jenny thought it over.

"It's been a while. He's gotten so big and takes interest in other things. It was probably a few months ago, maybe six months. I can't remember for sure."

"Where did you meet?"

"Uh, probably here. Oscar used to come by and draw sometimes. Mostly when he was little. Sometimes he would spend the night."

"Here?" The policeman pointed around with his ballpoint pen, looking like someone who would rather die than let his child sleep in a place like this.

"What's wrong with my atelier? Don't you find it acceptable, or what?"

He raised both eyebrows in surprise.

Jenny took a deep breath and tried to smile. She needed to get better control of herself!

"It's a little messy at the moment. I usually tidy up if I'm expecting visitors. But a certain amount of creative chaos fosters inspiration."

The policeman noted something down. Jenny tried to swallow.

"Like I said, it's been several months since I saw my nephew, but I didn't think he seemed all that happy when I last saw him."

He looked up from the notebook.

"But I don't know for sure. A teenage boy doesn't discuss his emotions with his old aunt."

"He didn't tell you about having problems at school?"

"No."

"Even so, you could tell that something was wrong," the policeman continued. "Did you suspect anything specific?"

Jenny turned her back to him and walked over to the sink, slowly poured herself a glass of water, and drank. What would happen if she told him about Henrik?

She turned back around.

"No. I didn't suspect anything specific. If I had, obviously I would have told my sister."

CHAPTER 21

At quarter to three, when the freshmen at Zahles School got up from their chairs and started scrambling out, Sara Saidani stood at the ready in front of Thomas P. Hejle youth center five hundred yards away. Grimy yellow buses rumbled past every minute, jogging the guilty conscience Larsen had managed to plant in her after all. Of course it was better for children to grow up somewhere green and peaceful, with vegetable gardens and neighbors who said hello. Her decision to move from Helsingør to Copenhagen had been about her career. She hadn't taken the girls' happiness into consideration, not really. Amina had been particularly upset about the upheaval, which had happened shortly after Mido moved back to Tunisia. Without a father, living in completely new surroundings—it hadn't been easy for her.

Sara brushed the thoughts aside. Being a single mother meant living with the sword of doubt planted solidly in her heart. If she got stuck thinking about all the things she wasn't doing well enough, she would never get anything done at all.

"Are you Sara?"

Sara turned around and saw a young face with no makeup, gray eyes, and a small button nose that she recognized from Iben Skytte's Facebook page. The girl in front of her looked like the teenager she was: a searching young woman with eco-friendly labels on her clothes. And acne.

"Hi, Iben. Thank you for coming. How are you doing?"

Iben rolled her eyes sarcastically as if this were too serious a time to be asking something so shallow and light.

"Everything's going to hell. How about you?"

There was an anger in her voice, controlled but clear. Sara read aggression in every cell of the fifteen-year-old girl's body.

"I'm asking because I genuinely want to know, Iben. And I have plenty of time to listen to your answer."

Sara could see from the girl's response that she had said the wrong thing or maybe used the wrong tone of voice, spoken down to her without meaning to.

"If you really want to know, I'm going to hell, too. My older daughter pretty much won't talk to me anymore. She and my boyfriend can't stand each other."

Iben smiled wryly, as if she appreciated Sara making an effort, even though she saw the underlying agenda. Sara had to be on her toes with this girl. She was sharp.

"Do you play table tennis?" Iben asked.

The unexpected question made Sara laugh.

"Uh, sort of?" Sara replied.

"Okay, then, come on!"

Iben led Sara under the main door's pink neon sign, down hallways and stairs, until they stood in a rec room with a nonslip floor and four Ping-Pong tables.

"This is the table tennis room. I play several times a week." Iben took a paddle from a shelf and handed it to Sara. "Take off your jacket and let's play a set! Your serve."

Sara was reminded of how she felt when arguing with Amina: it was no longer her who was calling the shots. This teenage girl, who was already bouncing a table tennis ball into the air, was manipulating the interaction and making her feel insecure in a way no broad-shouldered man could do. Sara set her jacket on a chair and walked over to the table, wondering if this was what happened to kids who grew up with a single parent.

"As long as we talk while we play, okay. I'm here to ask you about something important."

Iben tossed a ball over the net.

"As long as we play, we talk." She encouraged Sara to serve with a nod.

Sara felt her palms grow clammy with sweat and gritted her teeth. She raised her paddle and hit the ball at the table so hard that it bounced through the room into a corner.

Iben immediately tossed her another ball, and this time Sara succeeded in keeping it in play.

"They say table tennis is the only ball sport that activates both hemispheres of the brain. It exercises strategic thinking, fine motor skills, and long-term memory all at the same time." The young woman smashed the ball so it bounced off the very edge of the corner next to Sara. "And you never know until the last second where your opponent will send the ball."

Iben laughed gloatingly. Sara retrieved the ball from the floor and set it on the table, then eyed Iben seriously.

"There's a rumor going around your school that something happened at a party last fall. With Oscar's older brother. Is that true?"

Iben's facial expression didn't change.

"Serve the ball!" she instructed, and raised her paddle, eyes locked on her opponent.

Sara bit her lip to stop herself from swearing and served the ball. They volleyed back and forth in silence, then Iben grabbed the ball.

"You're not so bad, actually," she said. "You should practice more, though."

"Iben, is there any truth to the rumors?"

The girl inspected her paddle, looking dissatisfied, then set it down with a little sigh.

"I don't want to talk about it. What happened at that party stays between Vic and me. It's nobody else's business."

"I wish you were right. But Malthe Sæther has been murdered, and Oscar still hasn't been found." Sara looked the teen in the eye. "What happened between you two?"

"It has nothing to do with this," Iben said, her gaze flickering.

"Did Oscar see you and Victor together at the party? Was he a little in love with you?"

"Oscar and I are just friends. Anyway, it has nothing to do with Malthe's death."

Sara sensed that the blank look on Iben's face was there to hide something.

"Oscar gave a presentation on plastic in the oceans at a subject-focus day at school two weeks ago. Do you remember it?"

"Of course." Iben blinked. "He spoke at the opening. I painted one of the posters. Oscar's really shy, so it was a huge struggle for him to speak in front of everyone. The parents were there, too."

"Is it true that there was a debate after his presentation? Did someone criticize him?"

"Maybe." Iben picked at her paddle.

"Can you remember who it was? Or what it was about?"

Iben shook her head. Sara resisted an impulse to shake the girl.

"Does Oscar attend meetings of the environmental group that you belong to?"

"He might have gone along once." The girl blinked. A wariness lurked in the corner of her eyes.

"What about you?" Sara tried smiling. "How did you get interested in the climate crisis?"

Iben shrugged and tossed her paddle onto the table, yet again taking refuge behind an armor of unapproachability.

"I don't feel like playing anymore. Can you find your own way out?"

"WHAT DO THE police think happened to Oscar?"

Kasper Skytte sounded as if he were trying to make the question seem casual. He was standing at the counter, pouring tea into two mugs. One of them was perilously close to the edge, but he obviously hadn't noticed. The steam rose up around him and softened the smell of alcohol with notes of jasmine and chamomile.

Jeppe looked at his watch. It was a little past three in the afternoon, ostensibly only two hours since he had woken Kasper up, and yet the man was slurring his speech. He must have been drinking heavily to get this drunk so quickly.

They were standing in the Skytte family's small kitchen, where the daylight never properly penetrated. The lights were on, but still the room was as gloomy as a winter night.

"I mean, do you think that he murdered his teacher?" Kasper put the mugs of tea on the little dining table and sat down.

"We're still considering all possibilities." Jeppe pulled his mug closer and turned it halfway around, so the chips on the lip were on the far side. There was old residue around the edge from something that looked like tannins, and he had to overcome his discomfort to be able to drink out of the mug. Being sensitive isn't always convenient.

He flipped through to a blank page in his notebook and clicked his ballpoint pen.

"Yesterday morning at eight forty-five, Michael activated the dead-man button in the trash silo at ARC. Tell me what happened before that."

"*Man in silo*, that's what we call it. We've never pressed it before, not even in training." Kasper drank his tea with an apologetic smile. "I got to work around eight a.m., changed my clothes, and went into the crane control room. I had some error codes in the sorting program that I needed to check out. But I hadn't been there for very long before I saw"—he gulped and then cleared his throat—"before I saw the leg in the claw . . . and well, then Michael hit the switch."

"Were you surprised?"

Kasper stared at him incredulously.

"What the hell do you mean by that? Did I expect to find human remains at work, or what? Yes, absolutely, I was surprised. Shocked!"

Jeppe nodded as he made notes.

"That's right. You did have to go to the hospital."

"Why do you make it sound like there's something wrong with me? I was in shock! I came home, took a sleeping pill, and slept for twenty-four hours. That's how upset I was." Kasper got up, fetched a container from the kitchen table, and stirred two spoonfuls of sugar into his tea.

"At that time, did you know whose body it was?"

"No."

Jeppe turned the page. The paper rustled momentarily in the silence between them.

"But as we later discovered, the body belonged to Malthe Sæther, your daughter's Danish teacher. How well did you know him?"

"Not at all, I would say. Perhaps I've exchanged a total of three sentences with him over all of last year at some parent-teacher meeting. Iben is a big kid, I don't get too involved in her schooling."

Jeppe jotted that down. He could sense Kasper trying to read what he wrote as if it made him feel insecure.

"Hey, I get how it looks: my daughter's teacher turns up dead in the silo . . ."

"*You* found him," Jeppe clarified.

"But it was a coincidence! Everything that gets thrown in the trash anywhere in Copenhagen comes to the incinerator. It doesn't have anything to do with me."

"What does your job actually involve, specifically?"

Kasper raised his eyebrows in surprise. "I'm a process engineer. We're a team of three engineers working together on research tasks. I didn't know the police took interest in that kind of thing."

Jeppe smiled.

"Do you normally sit with the crane operator?"

"Only if there's something wrong with the claw's control system. Normally I sit with my coworkers in an office on the sixth floor."

"And do what? Just generally speaking."

"Well, we work to reduce the plant's flue gas emissions, specifically CO_2 and NO_X. ARC has a threshold limit value of fifty percent compared to all the other refuse incineration plants in the country, and we emit only fifteen percent of the permissible amount. That's a savings equivalent to having fifty thousand fewer cars out driving around on the roads. These flue gases are known to cause cancer and acid rain." He nodded proudly. "We're one of the cleanest waste incinerators in the world."

"Impressive."

"Thank you."

Jeppe watched him calmly. His red cheeks, the spit accumulating at the corners of his mouth, and the smell of booze. He looked like a man under pressure.

"Did Iben ever talk to Malthe Sæther?"

The sudden change of topic clearly confused him. He wiped his forehead on his sleeve.

"You mean privately? Not that I know of. But Iben doesn't tell me that much anymore. You have to drag everything out of her. Teenagers, you know."

"Do you know what happened between her and Victor Dreyer-Hoff at the fall dance?"

"You lost me there." Kasper got up, supporting himself heavily on the table. His eyes swam, and the sweat was beading up on his forehead.

"Everything okay?" Jeppe reached an arm out to assist him. But before he got that far, Kasper stormed out of the room. A door slammed shut, followed by a distinctive sound. Kasper Skytte was throwing up.

THE STAIRCASE ENDED in a long, narrow hallway. Anette's flashlight revealed gray walls and an arched ceiling, and a little way ahead the hallway split in two. Anette took the one on the right and proceeded through the echoing concrete until she came to another junction. She turned around. It was dark behind her. Where had Mads gone?

Annoyed, she retraced her steps, went back to the first split, and chose the hallway on the left. After twenty quick steps, a glimpse of light revealed that he was in a room on the right side of the hallway. Anette saw him shining his light on the wall. He looked absorbed, the shine from the flashlight reflecting back on his face and forming deep shadows under his eyes.

She got control of her breathing and went in. The room was elliptical in shape, like a submarine, and its plaster walls were peeling off in flakes onto hundreds of plastic chairs lined up in neat rows.

"What is this? It looks like drawings of buildings, plans for something or other. . . ." Anette shined her light on a series of posters hanging on the wall. She moved closer, feeling the heat from his body.

"Who knows." He turned to her. Half his face was lit, the other half in darkness. "Have you had enough?"

Anette checked her phone and saw that there was no signal. She straightened her back.

"No, let's keep looking."

They continued in the low-ceilinged hallway and down several steps, deeper into the fort's labyrinthine universe. On a lower level the curved walls were chalk white, and lit chandeliers with electric bulbs hung from the ceiling.

"How can the lights be on?" Anette pointed to the ceiling, confused.

"There must be a generator somewhere running."

"But . . . chandeliers? In a fort?" The feeling of having crossed a threshold between reality and dreams grew stronger and stronger. This place gave her the creeps.

On one wall hung a row of sinks, enough for the members of a whole Boy Scout troop to brush their teeth at the same time. Anette turned one of the faucet handles, and a thin stream of water came out and darkened the gray basin.

"There's running water."

"We've been all over now." A crackling sound, and a glow in the dark told Anette that Mads Teigen had lit a cigarette.

"Wait, there must be pressure relief passageways here like at Fort Middelgrund. My husband says they built passageways to prevent the forts from collapsing if they were attacked by antiaircraft guns."

"He's not here, Anette, and I can't stand anymore. Come on, we're taking the boat back." Mads turned and walked off without waiting for her.

Anette stood there for a second. Damn it if she had come this far, just to give up at the last minute!

She went on through the darkness, along the damp walls deeper into the fort. The air grew colder and damper, rougher and dustier with every step she took. On the bottom level she discovered an opening in the wall she had walked by before. This time she stopped and shined the flashlight in. The opening was almost tall enough for a person and protected by a metal grille door. The light from her flashlight didn't reach the end, just vanished into a bottomless blackness.

She opened the grille door, ducked, and walked in. The space was so narrow that her shoulders touched on both sides. With every step into the passage, it seemed to close in behind her, triggering her claustrophobia. She counted her steps, and when she reached twenty-five, she hit the end wall. The passageway was empty. She turned around carefully so as not to hit her head, and found her way back to the main hallway. When she finally reached it, she breathed in deep like a free diver who's broken the surface.

After a second she continued down the main hallway, until yet another side passage appeared ten yards farther along. The grille door was open.

Her footsteps made a crunchy sound, and she resisted the urge to shine her light down to see what she was walking on. If it was something revolting, she might not be able to keep going by herself, and oh, hell no, there was no way she was going to admit to Mads that she was feeling jittery.

Come on, Anette. You can do it!

She took another deep breath as the light from her flashlight slid over the flaking plaster on all sides, and the walls seemed to narrow in more and more around her. She noted her symptoms of panic and struggled to gain control.

You don't die from sweaty palms and a little shortness of breath.

Maybe that inner monologue was the reason why she didn't see him until he was right in front of her. The shock hit like a gut punch, and she had to bend over and hold on to the wall to keep from collapsing. She was gasping for air.

On the cold concrete floor in a narrow passageway deep within Fort Prøvestenen lay Oscar Dreyer-Hoff, staring blindly at the ceiling.

CHAPTER 22

The military EH101 Merlin helicopter flew in low over Copenhagen and landed on the roof of National Hospital. Clouds still covered the city in a thick layer, and rain was falling heavily in an early storm-induced darkness. The rescue helicopter was a flying emergency room with two nurses and a doctor on board, who tried to revive the patient all the way from Fort Prøvestenen. Detective Anette Werner sat beside them with a blanket around her shoulders, watching.

It took less than five minutes from the landing on the roof until Oscar Dreyer-Hoff's gurney was rolled into the hospital's trauma center. Here a team of sixteen doctors, surgeons, and trauma nurses stood waiting to continue the resuscitation attempt. The cardiologist determined that the patient was more dead than alive. His body temperature was 76.5°F, which meant that he was suffering from third-degree hypothermia. There were scant respiratory motions, and his pupils were not reactive.

The trauma team began CPR immediately, as they slowly warmed Oscar's chilled body and administered IV fluids. With severe hypothermia, it's no good warming patients up too quickly from the outside because then the cold blood flows to the heart and stops it. Instead, the perfusionist hooked Oscar up to a heart-lung machine that took over his circulation, allowing his blood to slowly regain the proper temperature.

A medical secretary walked Anette down the hallway to the family members' waiting room and gave her a cup of hot cocoa. That's where Jeppe found her when he came running through the trauma center's red doors eight minutes later. She looked so very fragile that he walked straight over and threw his arms around her. For the first time in their ten-year partnership Anette put her forehead against his shoulder and allowed him to comfort her. After several minutes she pulled away and dried her cheeks.

"Typical of you to take advantage of a situation like this to feel me up!" she joked.

Jeppe laughed and took a seat on the wool sofa next to her.

"Are you okay?" he asked.

"Yeah, yeah. I don't know what the hell's wrong with me. It was just a real shock, to see him lying there all of a sudden. Life is not all beer and Skittles."

"Drink your hot chocolate. It'll help."

She drank obediently.

"He's alive, but only just barely. The doctors can't say very much yet." Anette shook her head. "I wonder what he was doing out there. I really hope he makes it."

"Have they found the boat?"

"Five minutes ago. At the bottom of the harbor by Petroleum Island. With a hole in the hull, presumably made with a sledgehammer that was found in the wreckage." Anette smiled but still looked enormously sad.

Jeppe gave her a gentle elbow in the side.

"Hey," he said. "Chin up! You did what the search and rescue crews couldn't. You found him! Still alive, no less. Pat yourself on the back."

The door opened, and Henrik and Malin Dreyer-Hoff were shown in by the medical secretary. Malin avoided making eye contact with Jeppe, but considering the mood at their last encounter, maybe that wasn't surprising.

Henrik walked straight to Anette's chair and stopped in front of her. His broad, suit-covered shoulders filled the visitors' room like a pillar of masculine energy.

"Were you the one who found him?" he asked emotionally.

"Yes."

He leaned over the chair and lifted Anette up in a hug. The tips of her toes only barely touched the floor. She protested meekly, resisting this unexpected closeness with Oscar's father.

"Thank you."

"Just part of the job." Anette patted his arm awkwardly from the trapped position within his embrace, looking like someone who had had enough hugging for one day.

Jeppe looked down to hide an involuntary smile. Whether it was from finding Oscar, or his coworker's unusual display of sensitivity, he didn't know, but there in the hospital he experienced an irrational rush of joy. The boy was hovering between life and death and Anette between the floor and ceiling. There was hope.

WHEN THE FRONT door of Fredericiagade 64 finally creaked open, Kasper Skytte was sitting in the dark in the living room, waiting. The armchair's leather had been warmed by his body and the whiskey bottle by the temperature in the room. In the kitchen the vegetarian hash he had made for dinner sat untouched on the table. He could hear Iben rummaging around with her shoes and coat. Then she came in and eyed him warily.

"Why are you sitting in the dark?"

"It wasn't dark when I sat down. Why are you so late?" His mouth was dry, and he had to lick his lips before he continued. "Since when have we become the kind of family that doesn't eat or talk together?"

"I'm going to my room. I have to study," Iben said, looking down.

"YOU'RE NOT GOING ANYWHERE!"

Kasper heard her gasp and regained his composure.

"Please come in and sit down. We need to talk."

A second later the light was switched on. Iben sat down on the sofa, as far away from him as possible.

"You're drunk!" She was pale, and her eyes appeared sunken in her young face.

"And so what if I am?"

"You're fucking pathetic. I'm ashamed of you." Her voice was calm and neutral. The contempt lay in her choice of words.

In the hour he had been waiting for her, he had formulated his questions over and over again, but now that she sat in front of him with her downturned mouth and her smooth forehead, the sentences swam away from him and turned into fog.

"What happened between you and Oscar's older brother?"

"Why do you ask?"

"Why do I ask?! Answer me, damn it . . . Just answer!"

Iben pushed back her hair with both hands and tucked it behind her ears. It was a habit she had had since she was little, and the sight of it hit Kasper like a punch to the kidney.

"I don't understand why I need to face the third degree just because you've suddenly decided to take an interest in my life."

"What do you mean *suddenly*? Since when have I not been interested in you?"

Her eyes narrowed. "Every fucking night when you sit in front of your computer and *work*. Don't think I don't know what you're doing."

"What are you talking about?!" Kasper could hear the panic in his own voice and forced himself to sound calm. "Iben, tell me. What happened with Vic?! I can help you."

The look in her eyes literally took his breath away. Kasper refilled his glass, his hands shaking.

"Yes, Dad, drink some more. That will make everything okay again." She got up.

"Sit down, honey. Let's talk about it. You're everything to me." With the last sentence, Kasper couldn't hold his tears back any longer. He knew how ridiculous he must seem, but there was no helping it.

"That's easy to say, isn't it? *You're everything to me.*" Suddenly she looked like the little girl she no longer was. "But it's a lie, Dad. You don't give a damn who I am or how I'm doing as long as I don't get in the way of your fucking career and pretend like our family is perfect and I have no idea what you're spending all our money on."

"That's not true!" He rubbed his face hard with both hands and cleared his throat. "Have a seat now, honey. It's not too late."

"It *is* too late. I'm fifteen years old. There's nothing left to talk about. What do you want me to say?" Her voice was glass shards and sharp knives. "That it's your fault I don't have a mother?"

"It was a joint decision, that you would stay—"

"*Joint?!*" She was yelling now. "No one asked me what I wanted. Do you think I want to live with—"

She stopped and looked at him, her lower lip trembling with rage. Kasper felt a pang of fear.

"Don't you think I know what you did?"

The pang became an all-encompassing wave of dread that washed through him.

"I did it for your sake. For us!"

Iben's face distorted in a grimace of crying, every bit as fierce as it was unexpected. She shook her head, the tears pouring out of her.

"How could you do it, Dad? Don't you get it? You've ruined everything!"

CHAPTER 23

"So lock all the gates and bolt the chamber door, because nobody leaves or enters anymore . . ."

Esther turned down Al Jarreau's more than forty-year-old hymn, which she always played when she was missing her father, and perked up her ears. She got up and opened the door to the hall. Gregers was standing on the other side with a box in his hand and a sheepish look on his face.

"Yes, um," Gregers began, "I'm sorry to knock so late, but I could hear that you weren't asleep yet."

"It's not that late. Was my music too loud?"

He gestured grumpily with his hands and said, "I just wanted to . . . thank you for your help at the doctor's." Gregers held the cardboard box out to her. "It's chocolate. Although you'd think it was gold at the prices they charge for it."

Esther opened the door all the way and took the box.

"Thank you. You didn't have to do that, Gregers. Should we try some right away?"

"Well, we wouldn't want them to get stale."

"Shall we go sit in the kitchen?" she asked with a smile.

"Well, this room is pleasant too . . ."

"Come in. I have a bottle of red wine open. Would you like a glass?"

Gregers grunted his approval, walked over to the wingback chair, and sat down with a contented sigh. Esther brought the chocolates out into the kitchen, turned on the light, and got out another wineglass. Sure, her roommate could be testy sometimes, but she appreciated his gesture. The clock on the oven revealed that it was a little before nine. Gregers didn't usually visit with her this late in the evening; surely there must be something on his mind.

She brought back a tray with the wineglass and chocolates on it and saw that he had gotten up and was standing by the window, peering out into the darkness.

"We'll sit here on the sofa, right?" Esther set the tray on the coffee table and walked over to stand beside him. "Is everything all right, Gregers?"

He smiled in surprise, as if he had only just noticed she was there.

"Ah, there you are. I was just thinking about life. And death."

"As we all do from time to time." These days Esther's own thoughts circled constantly around death and its rituals, but it wasn't a topic she usually discussed with him. "Do you mean something specific?"

"I think I'm on my way."

At first she didn't understand what he meant, but the look in his eyes caused the penny to drop.

"Gregers, knock it off! You're not dying."

"Oh, little Esther, I'm eighty-five years old. No matter how you reckon it, it can't be that far off. But it's about more than my age. I can sort of *feel* it coming."

Esther sat down and poured them both some wine. His words scared her. Death was only fascinating when it struck far away, not when it came inside one's own front door. But if he felt the need to talk about it, she wouldn't let him down.

"Come, have a seat, my friend. Tell me what you've been thinking."

He sat down and accepted the glass she offered, then gazed at it, as if he didn't quite understand what it was, and set it down on the coffee table.

"I'm no longer sure where the boundary is between my thoughts and reality. I have some dreams that feel so real that they frighten me. For example, we're sitting here in your living room. That's real, isn't it?"

She nodded.

"Is anyone else here besides us?"

"No, Gregers."

"Inger isn't here?"

Esther had to think carefully before she remembered that Inger was Gregers's ex-wife, with whom he had had zero contact in more than twenty years.

"No, Inger isn't here."

"She said it was going to be afternoon at the summer house. We had this lovely little summer house up near Nykøbing Sjælland, when the kids were small. Nothing fancy, but we loved it there. One of the worst parts about getting divorced was that we had to sell that place. Well, anyway Inger said it is afternoon and the sun is shining. We have had beer and schnapps for lunch and I'm lying in the hammock."

Esther interrupted gently, "Is this something that *did* happen, or what?"

He waved her question away, annoyed.

"This is how it's *going* to happen. Anyway, so there I am, lying in the hammock with a bit of a buzz. The kids are playing in the yard, and the dog is alive again and has dragged a bunch of sand into the house. The sun hits my face, someone laughs somewhere, maybe it's me."

He paused and reached for his wine. His voice sounded choked up.

"She comes over to the hammock and takes my hand and kisses me. I close my eyes."

Gregers drank and closed his eyes.

"Then I let go."

JEPPE STROLLED FROM National Hospital by the Lakes to Nør-report Station.

April evenings are cool and clear blue, he thought, shuddering audibly so that a pair of ducks lying on the bank jumped hurriedly in the water. In a month there would be ducklings in the lake and candles on the chestnut trees.

Oscar had been found, and spring was coming.

The train station was closed because someone had been hit by one of the trains on the westbound S-train tracks, and the subway was running only intermittently, so Jeppe ended up walking all the way to Christianshavn. When he reached Burmeistersgade, he was chilled to the bone.

The way Sara opened the door told Jeppe that he was out in the cold in more ways than one. Maybe he had known all day.

"Amina came home today smelling of beer," she announced.

She stood in the doorway looking at him. Jeppe set his bag down on the floor.

"Is she okay?"

"She's sleeping now. But when I wanted to know who gave her the alcohol, she asked me if you had spilled the beans."

Jeppe was about to explain but didn't make it before Sara continued.

"Is it true that you found her out on the street late last night?"

Jeppe nodded.

"But you didn't bring her home or tell me about it? My eleven-year-old daughter was sitting out on the street drinking, and you didn't think that was worth mentioning to me?"

"She hadn't had anything to drink yesterday—"

"She was sitting out on the street at nine thirty at night, and you didn't bring her home?! What were you thinking?"

Sara's expression was more than angry, it showed she was beyond reconciliation. Jeppe looked down. He knew instinctively that it wouldn't do any good trying to explain his attempt to bridge the divide between himself and Amina right now.

She closed the door. Jeppe picked his bag up off the floor, turned around, and left. Every relationship comes to an end. Sometimes its time runs out before the love does. That's when it really hurts.

WEDNESDAY, APRIL 17

If you lie on your arm for too long, it falls asleep. Sensation returns only slowly and painfully, it tingles and prickles as the blood palpably battles the numbness for control. Life hurts when it starts rolling again.

The boy lay for a long time listening to his own breathing. What is a breath? A wheeze, a sign of life. He felt fabric between his fingers. Fabric. He must be lying in a bed. Or a coffin.

He opened his eyes and closed them again, caught a glimpse of a clear plastic tube going into his left arm. Breathing, fabric, tube . . . he had to be in the hospital. That meant he was alive. He felt both disappointment and relief, though he didn't understand how that could be. He tried to move but couldn't. His body was humming. Maybe his bones and muscles had dissolved into a warm liquid that would pour out if someone poked a hole in him.

The light was overwhelming. He had adjusted to the darkness in the fort so much that he had forgotten how demanding light could feel. Vibrant colors stood out against metal and plastic outlines. Clean and frightening.

There was something in his nose bothering him. He tried to lift his hand up to get rid of it but was stopped.

"He's awake!"

The yell pierced his eardrums. Couldn't he just die in peace?

CHAPTER 24

On Wednesday morning Jeppe sat down at his office desk with a sense of moving through water. Slow and heavy. He ran a hand over the laminate surface and inspected it. Not a mote of dust. In a strangely backward way it made him miss the old police headquarters even more. Or to be more precise: he didn't so much wish himself back in his old workspace as he wanted to flee this generic office building in Sydhavn. He had spent the night in his own apartment in Nyhavn for the first time in months, but he hadn't gotten much sleep. As he drank his vending machine coffee with gravel in his eyes, he thought: *They call it a broken heart, but it feels more like having no heart at all. Empty.*

On the far side of their double desk, Anette sat looking expectantly at him, and at the door, Thomas Larsen was leaning against the frame, his arms folded over his chest. Today he had jazzed up an expensive-looking chocolate-colored blazer with a handkerchief poking out of the chest pocket. Its green curlicues somehow contributed to Jeppe's displeasure.

"All right. The last known contact with Malthe Sæther is still the phone call with his girlfriend, Josephine, at five p.m. on Friday,"

Jeppe began with an inward sigh. "As far as we know, he was at home at that time, and he told her that one of his students was having trouble and needed his help. It could be the same student the choral director mentioned, the one who was involved in online bullying. And let me add that the same choral director doesn't have any alibi for the time when the killing occurred."

"But hardly even a shadow of a motive, either," Anette interjected. "So where did Malthe go after the phone call with his girlfriend? We know he was killed sometime during a four-hour window starting at ten p.m. Friday and that he then probably lay in a trash can until he turned up in the silo on Monday morning. His phone is gone, but the information we received from the phone company shows no calls or text messages after the call with his girlfriend. The last registered contact with his cell phone took place at 7:08 p.m. and was picked up by an LTE mast on Bartholinsgade. That may indicate that he was heading northeast. So we just need to locate all the students he had who live northeast of his apartment on Vendersgade."

"We know that he was going to meet someone *connected* to one of his students," Jeppe said. "That doesn't necessarily mean he was meeting the student. It could have been a family member."

Larsen raised his index finger, unintentionally making himself look like a Baptist minister.

"Isn't it still most likely that Malthe Sæther met with Oscar, who for some reason strangled his teacher, threw him in the trash, and then ran off to Fort Prøvestenen? The murder coinciding with Oscar's disappearance can't just be random, can it?"

"Amen!" Anette said.

"But why?" Jeppe argued. "And spare me the usual 'he's crazy' logic. We all know it takes a motive to murder someone."

Anette waved her hand dismissively.

"They could have been lovers or had some other kind of relationship that couldn't stand the light of day. There are a lot of possibilities. We just have to be patient and ask Oscar when he's healthy enough to be questioned."

Patient? Jeppe didn't have any patience left. Not for comatose suspects, teachers wearing makeup, or withdrawn teenage girls.

He got up and went over to the window to cool off. It didn't work.

"Damn it, surely one of you must have something we can use!"

"I'm sorry, what was that?" Anette asked, her chair creaking. "Can we agree that I just singlehandedly found our main suspect in a fucking sea fortress?! What have *you* achieved in the last day or so?"

"This isn't a pissing contest, Werner. Relax!"

"You relax!"

Larsen cleared his throat.

"I actually did find something that strikes me as a little odd. I don't know if it's related to Malthe's death, but there's a funny coincidence between the discovery site and Henrik Dreyer-Hoff."

"Well, let's hear it, then!"

Larsen raised his eyebrows to signal his feelings about Jeppe's tone of voice.

"Yes, okay then, as you know I'm looking into the Dreyer-Hoff family's auction house and its fraud scandal. Henrik is an entrepreneur. He sits on corporate boards, does lobbying work, and that sort of thing. But do you remember me saying that he came from a completely different sector when he and Malin decided to open the auction house around six years ago?" Larsen paused for dramatic effect.

Jeppe sighed and asked exasperatedly, "And . . . ? What, do you want us to guess?"

"I guess not. At first I thought it was an electric company, but as it turns out Henrik was sales manager for the German company Mirnhof and Schalcke. It's a global supplier of industrial process technology–measuring instruments. Its clients include power generating facilities. In that capacity he acted both as part of a collaborative forum and as a personal adviser to the chairwoman of the Danish Waste Association, a political interest association. Her name is Margit Smith."

Jeppe went back to his desk and sat down, rubbed his chin, and was reminded that his shaving gear was at Sara's place.

"Get to the point, Larsen," Jeppe said. "What are we supposed to do with this information?"

"Margit Smith isn't the chairwoman of the interest association anymore. Six months ago she was named CEO of the Amager incineration plant, better known as ARC."

"What does that mean?" Jeppe sat up straight.

"That means that Henrik is close to, possibly even friends with, the CEO of the incineration plant where Malthe Sæther's body was found."

"According to Malin," Jeppe said, glancing down at his dust-free desk, "she and Henrik were home with their daughter the whole night on Friday. He has an alibi for the time of the crime."

"When Saidani and I visited the grandmother, Essie said that her dad was at work Friday night," Larsen protested.

"She did?" Jeppe asked. "Werner, you want to go for a ride? We need to ask Henrik where he really was Friday night."

There was a brief knock on the door, and PC stuck her head in with a polite wave to apologize for the interruption. She craned her neck in a way that made Jeppe think of a cartoon turkey.

"Saidani says hi. She won't be in today, sick kid, but she promises to submit anything she finds on Malthe Sæther's computer in an online report later today."

"Thanks, PC." Jeppe felt the mention of Sara tug at the scar tissue in his heart. "Can we ask Mosbæk to be on standby to go to the hospital with us when Oscar Dreyer-Hoff wakes up? We're probably talking about a kidnapping or a suicide attempt, so we should have psychological assistance ready to go."

"I'll arrange for that."

"Thanks, PC."

Jeppe waited for PC to leave, but she stayed.

"Kørner, a person was hit at Nørreport Station yesterday afternoon at four thirty . . ."

"Yeah, I know. The station was still closed at nine when I was trying to get home. But what does that have to do with us?"

"It appears that you have spoken with the victim. Yesterday morning. An older woman who taught at Zahles School. Her name is Lis Christensen."

OF ALL PLACES in the world, Mads Teigen preferred to be in his workshop. Once again he had woken up early, but this time he had gotten out of bed and gone straight to his workbench, surrounded by the birds. A seagull with its wings spread; a pair of eiders, beaks facing each other; and a rare barn owl with watchful eyes in its white face. They were so beautiful; it consoled his heart.

Taxidermy, unlike mummification, has a built-in aesthetic component: the challenge to create the most lifelike reproduction of the dead. A unique combination of art and science. Celebrities like Carl Akeley added glamour to taxidermy, with his herd of African elephants, which was exhibited at the Museum of Natural History in New York City. The animals' beauty can be enjoyed up close, and if viewers allow themselves to linger in the exhibit they can almost hear the elephants' footsteps and see their ears flapping flies away.

Unfortunately the art form's unavoidable involvement of blood and guts scares most people away. Mads had given up talking about his passion long ago. He didn't have the strength to go through the obligatory stages of polite disgust, stupid questions, and distancing. If he could, he would have explained to people that the birds were what kept him alive. He would have made them understand how his ability to give them new life was what made death bearable.

Now he rolled up his sleeves. They had found the boy more dead than alive, and it was unclear whether he would make it. How long was resurrection possible? Definitely not, he reminded himself, long after a dead body has rotted and turned to dirt.

Mads let his thoughts wander to the policewoman Anette. A warmth spread from his midriff out to the rest of his body, and he felt a tingle in his lap and lightness in his head. He hadn't had thoughts like this in a long time, hadn't permitted himself to think with his body during this self-imposed celibacy. That was a part of his punishment. But now he let the desire flow through him while he worked.

A pretty hooded crow lay on the workbench, ready for resurrection. Not for stuffing. Mads hated that term, stuffing. On the contrary, his goal was to create the illusion of life, a flying bird.

He turned the crow over onto its back and made an incision up the center of its abdomen with the scalpel. He loosened the skin with the plumage attached until it was secured to the body only at the beak and then turned it inside out. Eyeing it affectionately he started scraping the flesh off the bones. After he had washed and dried it, the skin lay sleek and ready between his hands. He took out an appropriate-size foam dummy that he thought would work for the crow's body, and stroked the creature's glossy feathers.

Anette. He could almost feel her skin under his fingers as he turned the bird over and cut a piece of thin steel wire. The thought of her skin made him dizzy. He wanted to hold down her arms and kiss her neck, stomach, breasts, until she yielded to him. Hold her neck as he penetrated her, and look into her eyes as they neared their climax.

Mads pushed the thin wire in, through the bones of the first wing, and then the second. He wrapped cotton wool around a new piece of wire until he achieved the volume of a bird's neck. With his ice pick, he cut a hole in the foam filler for the head, secured it to the neck, and moved it into place inside the coat of feathers, so that it filled out and became a body again. At this point he had to let go of the bird and touch himself. Anette gasped for air beneath him, beaded in sweat and beautiful, and he soon followed, ejaculating and collapsing breathlessly over her. His thoughts swam while the secretions dried into a shameful muck on his fingers.

He lifted himself up from the workbench, removed a stray feather from his cheek, and walked over to the sink to turn on the water. His body was pleasantly drained, but his head teemed with self-recrimination. He had lost all desire to work on the bird.

ANETTE PUSHED THE top button in the elevator and glanced at her partner. He looked worn out, but maybe that was just the fluorescent lighting. Ye gods, he could be annoying sometimes. Although, to be fair, some of her annoyance was probably due to the fluctuations in her own life these last several days.

"Why would Malthe Sæther's coworker kill herself?" Jeppe even sounded strained. "Can you explain that to me? A friendly older woman gets off work, walks down to the subway station, and jumps out in front of a train without warning? I talked to her yesterday morning, and, Lord knows, she didn't seem suicidal. You tell me, how does that make sense?"

"It must have been an accident," Anette said, shaking her head.

"She had trouble walking. Maybe she tripped? Eight hours after I talked to her about Malthe, she dies. Yet another damned coincidence, more unfortunate circumstances."

The elevator doors opened, and light from the Dreyer-Hoff family's apartment poured into it. Henrik was waiting for them with his arms outstretched. Anette tried to reach for his hand, but found herself yet again enduring a hug from the grateful father. He rested his chin on her shoulder and closed his eyes, much too close and too intimate. After a few seconds he gave her a manly pat on the back, released his grasp, and held her at arm's length, his hands on her shoulders.

"I hope your employer appreciates you. In my eyes you deserve a distinguished service medal."

"Thank you." Anette nodded awkwardly. "We're all happy that Oscar is safe."

He held on to her for another agonizing moment, then let her go.

"Can I offer you a cup of coffee? We brought the kids home and are letting them enjoy one last day off from school. They're just having breakfast."

Victor and Essie were sitting at the kitchen counter, each with a plate of scrambled eggs and toast. The sun had come out and was shining on the water down below, letting dappled light dance across the walls of the apartment and onto their faces.

Anette smiled at them.

"Hi, guys. Does it feel good to be back home?" she asked.

"It's okay." Victor shrugged, and Essie nodded shyly.

Henrik affectionately took hold of the back of his son's neck and said, "Vic, why don't you guys take your food into the living room and put on a movie? And I'll talk to the police in the meantime."

"Okay, Dad."

The kids got up and carried their plates in the direction of the pink sofa at the other end of the apartment. Henrik leaned against the kitchen counter.

"Tell me, is Oscar considered a suspect in his teacher's murder?" he asked casually, as if the topic were quite harmless. He appeared to have forgotten about the coffee.

Jeppe sat down on a barstool and laid his hands on the counter in front of him, opening them like a poker player with nothing to hide.

"What makes you ask?" Jeppe said.

"Well, you yourselves were the ones who just found him half-dead of hunger and thirst on a deserted island. Oscar's the victim here, not the culprit."

"What do you mean?"

"You know what I mean." Henrik crossed his arms in front of his chest. "The fact that someone killed that poor teacher doesn't have anything to do with my son."

A tense note had crept into his voice. Anette could see that he was working hard not to get riled up.

"Oscar is a shy fifteen-year-old boy who thinks everything is a little difficult—school, growing up, the world in general. He took the boat out into the harbor to get away from it all. It was stupid and dramatic, and if it weren't for your partner here, the consequences would have been fatal." Henrik nodded appreciatively to Anette.

"Has Oscar told you that that's what happened? Is he conscious?"

"He just woke up, and my wife says he's doing fairly well. But he hasn't yet told us what happened; we worked that out on our own."

"So you don't know for a fact that he wasn't kidnapped?" Jeppe asked, giving Henrik a questioning look.

"No."

"Well, it'll be exciting to hear Oscar's take on things. We'll be heading over to the hospital soon to talk to him."

Jeppe leaned forward on his elbows. Anette knew his body language well enough to see that he was shifting gears.

"Where were you Friday night?" he asked.

"Home," Henrik replied. "Didn't we already discuss that?"

"You didn't just pop into work at some point?" Jeppe asked.

"No."

His answer was prompt, but Anette noticed his gaze flicker.

"All right." Jeppe sat up straight again. "I understand you were employed in a different line of work before you founded Nordhjem, working for a company that supplied industrial equipment. Is that right?"

"That was a long time ago," Henrik said, looking genuinely surprised. "Must be, what, six years ago now, but that's right."

"What was your job title?"

"I was sales manager."

Jeppe nodded the way he did when he was moving in sideways on his victim: his head slightly cocked, his eyes directed toward some point on the floor.

"Is it correct," he continued, "that during that same period you were also personal adviser to Margit Smith . . . who became CEO of ARC six months ago?"

Henrik nodded distrustfully.

"I have great connections . . . in the business community, among politicians, and yes, I also know Margit. . . . I'm sorry, I don't mean to make things difficult, but I really don't understand where this is going."

Jeppe's shoulders came up slightly, and Anette knew that meant he was searching for a crack in the veneer. She thought this would be a good time to step away.

"I'm sorry, I'm just going to borrow your restroom . . ."

She walked down the long hallway, careful to keep her footsteps soft. Essie was sitting on the sofa alone with her plate on her lap, eyes glued to the flat-screen.

Anette cleared her throat.

The frail girl practically jumped in shock and put both hands on her chest.

"I'm sorry if I frightened you. I was just looking for the restroom. Where's Victor?"

The girl looked down at a drop of butter that had spilled on the sofa's pink silk.

"In his room. He didn't want to watch TV."

"Don't worry, it'll come off with water. Look!" Anette dipped her finger into a glass of water on the coffee table and rubbed on the stain, while she prayed she wasn't ruining a hundred-thousand-kroner sofa.

"What are you watching?"

"*Riverdale,*" she mumbled. Everything about the girl radiated discomfort at being around a strange grown-up.

Anette hesitated. The police aren't allowed to interrogate a ten-year-old on her own, but a single question couldn't hurt.

"Essie, you told my coworkers that your dad might have gone to work last Friday. Do you remember that?"

"Dad was home."

"It's just that you told our coworkers that he was at work . . ."

"I remembered wrong." She looked down at her plate.

"Okay." Anette smiled.

"What's going on?!"

Essie jumped, and her plate fell on the floor and broke. Henrik hurried past Anette groaning irritably and started scooping scrambled egg off the floor.

"I was just looking for the restroom."

Henrik stood up with broken shards in his hands and burning eyes.

"I think that's enough questioning for today."

CHAPTER 25

"Here you go, Jenny. I hope you don't take sugar, because we're out. I don't understand where it all goes."

Jenny Kaliban looked from the caseworker, who was taking a seat on the other side of the desk, to the plastic cup of machine coffee she had just put in front of her. A packet of powdered creamer and a plastic spoon sat next to the cup. The woman behind the desk was her age, and had limp curls framing her tired face. Only her fingernails gleamed red and freshly polished, like solitary islands of hope in a dying ocean. You would almost think she had been born to work in the unemployment benefits office, Jenny thought unkindly. Unless it was the grim, sad surroundings that over the years had shaped her in their likeness.

What am I doing here? Jenny asked herself. How had she, who lived and breathed for aesthetics, ended up being forced to turn to these insipid, soul-sucking places year after year with her hat in her hand and a humble look on her face?

She seethed with anger but knew her fury was for herself. She was to blame. Without meaning to, she had fallen out with her family. Now she wasn't even welcome at her nephew's sickbed. But she wasn't the only one to blame—they had failed her first. And society! Artists had always depended on donations from patrons, the nobility, and the upper class, but her generation of artists had been downright degraded. Forced to pander to get by and to endure society's poorly hidden disrespect.

"You still have shifts at the museum, I see. But that doesn't add up to very much." The caseworker typed something on her municipal computer and peered at Jenny over her plastic eyeglasses.

"No," Jenny said. "I can no more live off that than off the supplementary unemployment benefits you give me."

"Well, I'm not the one who determines or pays your benefits." The woman typed on.

"You are the one, though, who evaluates whether I am still allowed to receive a subsidy to support my lifestyle. Isn't that why you have me come to these meetings? To inspect my shabby clothes and hollow cheeks?"

The caseworker typed some more, her lips pursed sternly. Jenny knew she could never make the woman understand, but she couldn't just sit by, couldn't allow the woman's ignorance to persist without commenting.

"The twenty-first century heralds the death of aesthetics. Fuck religion, science, and spirituality! But the human spirit has always dwelled in beauty. Art, words, music. When we lose that, we lose our very purpose for living. We are drowning in discount clothes and plastic boobs. People prefer watching talent shows on TV than listening to Prokofiev's string quartets. *La beauté sauvera le monde!* If only."

"From what I can see, Jenny, you have used up all the supplementary benefits you're entitled to. You can only receive those for thirty out of every one hundred and four weeks; after that they're discontinued."

"What are you saying? I can't get any money?"

The caseworker tilted her head back and squinted through greasy lenses.

"You can requalify for supplementary benefits by working no fewer than a hundred and forty-six hours every month for the next six months' filings."

"But what am I going to live off of?" A pulse started throbbing in Jenny's throat.

"Your job."

"I can't live off the chump change Thorvaldsens pays me. I can't even pay my rent and buy food with that!"

The caseworker propped her elbows on her desk, as if she were about to share a secret.

"Well, then you either have to work a little more or cut back on your expenses. It's not the government's fault if you can't live within your means."

Jenny looked down at her own rough hands. Her nails were short and dirty from the daily toils with canvasses and paints.

"Can't I get cash assistance?"

"Not as long as you're able to work." The woman took off her glasses. "Maybe it's about time you got a real job, Jenny!"

Jenny felt the doors slamming closed all around her. Felt the steadily growing chronic panic, clutching hold of her stomach and squeezing until she could taste the bile in the back of her mouth.

"You're enjoying this, aren't you? Forcing a lazy artist to take a job as a cleaning lady. But you're forgetting one thing: What does art do for society? What kind of a place will the world be without the likes of me?"

"Thank you for coming in today!" The caseworker turned back to her screen and went back to typing.

Jenny stood up, tipping the chair over behind her. She held her head up high and spoke with as much dignity as she could muster.

"You! You have blood on your hands!"

* * *

AT THE ENTRANCE to National Hospital's intensive care unit, Jeppe and Anette were met by a nurse, who led them to the office occupied by Oscar's attending physician at an efficient pace. The doctor was bent over a triangular sandwich, and had her eyes glued to her computer.

Jeppe hesitated in the doorway. "Excuse us for interrupting your lunch. We're from the Copenhagen Police's Investigations Unit. Would it be all right if we asked you a few quick questions?"

"One second. I'll be right with you." The doctor took another bite, then tossed the rest of her food in the trash can, and waved them in as she finished chewing.

"When was Oscar transferred here from the trauma center?"

"An hour ago," she said after checking on her screen. "He has been stable all night and is breathing on his own, so now we're taking over. We are fully staffed around the clock, he's in good hands."

"Is he conscious?"

"He is slipping in and out of sleep right now, but it's normal given the pain relief he's getting."

"But he's going to make it?" Anette asked.

The doctor wiggled her head back and forth noncommittally.

"His age and physical condition make his odds of survival quite strong, but when a person gets so cold and dehydrated, there is a risk of multiorgan failure for several days to come. His liver also appears to have suffered some damage."

Jeppe nodded and said, "I'm assuming that Forensics has been in touch with you about examining the patient. . . ."

"They're coming by later today."

"Excellent. Have you noticed any signs of his having been subjected to violence or force? Marks on his skin, broken bones, anything suspicious?"

"No. Some minor scratches on his arms, bruising, but nothing you wouldn't expect after four days on a deserted island. But . . ."

"Yes?"

"We pumped his stomach. We suspect a possible acetaminophen overdose, but it takes a little while to determine after so many days. The lab needs to analyze his stomach contents before we can be sure, but that's what it looks like."

"Too much Tylenol?" Jeppe asked, his brow furrowed.

"It could be an indication of a suicide attempt." The doctor shrugged slightly. "But pills can also be administered by force. Oscar himself will have to fill us in on that."

"Can we see him? One of our police psychologists is coming to assist us with the conversation."

"He's still very weak, but let's go down to check on him. Then we'll take it from there. His mother is with him."

She showed them to a room at the end of the hall, knocked gently on the door, and went in. They gave her a second to prepare Malin for the visit before following her.

A skinny boy with an IV drip in his arm lay in the hospital bed, his head turned to the wall. Oscar's mother sat in a chair below an out-of-place poster of a walrus, with her eyes focused on her son.

"Don't overdo it!" the doctor urged in the doorway, before letting herself out.

"Hi, Malin," Jeppe said. "Is he asleep?"

Malin shook her head ever so slightly.

"How about you? Did you sleep here at the hospital?"

"On a sofa in the ward's visitors' room."

Trust is an odd element, one of the hardest building blocks of human relationships to fully understand. It demands honesty, reliability, and openness—that much we know. But fundamentally it's either there or it's not. Malin Dreyer-Hoff's trust in Jeppe was gone. Somewhere, somehow in their interactions he had made a misstep, and she had withdrawn. Her wary eyes reminded him how fragile and precarious relationships between people are. Even the walrus over her shoulder scowled at him.

There was a rustle from the door and Mosbæk appeared by the bed. As always, the police psychologist was carrying an overfilled leather bag whose diagonal strap cut across his belly into the plaid fabric of his shirt. His full reddish beard smoldered under the bright hospital lights and he brought with him the scents of autumn woods and vegetable garden.

"Hi, Mosbæk," Jeppe said. "Nice to see you. This is Oscar and his mother, Malin."

"Hello." Mosbæk pulled off his bag and greeted Malin warmly before he pulled a chair over to the bed, elbowing Jeppe and Anette politely but firmly aside.

"Now, if you two go stand in the corner over there, then Oscar and I can have a little peace and quiet."

Jeppe nodded to his partner, and they withdrew to the far wall, leaving the psychologist alone by the bed.

"That's better. Who can think or talk with such a crowd around?" He focused on the boy. "I'm Mosbæk, psychologist with the police department. I used to have a first name, but even my wife quit using it, so you can call me Mosbæk too."

Oscar didn't respond, just lay still facing the wall.

"The reason I'm here," Mosbæk continued, "is to make sure that you make a full recovery. The hospital takes care of your body but people are more than flesh and bones, right? I am here to listen to your thoughts. Do you feel like sharing them with me? You don't have to, it is your choice."

The boy cautiously turned his head.

"What do you want my thoughts for?"

"Well, Oscar, I don't want them as such. But sometimes our thoughts can become our worst enemy, if we don't share them."

Jeppe smiled at Anette. One of the qualities that made Mosbæk so useful was his ability to build trust quickly and get people to let down their guards.

"Do you feel well enough to talk to me?"

"I can't remember very much of the last few days," Oscar said, his eyes wandering. "It's like my brain stopped working right."

Mosbæk found a little notepad in his leather bag and smiled apologetically. "This is just for my own notes. My memory's not so good, either. Let's start with what you *can* remember."

The boy pushed himself uncertainly up onto his elbows and reached for the cup on his nightstand. Mosbæk helped him.

"Well, I remember my family, and where we live, and school, and all that kind of thing. It's not like everything's gone. I'm just having a hard time remembering the most recent part. The days sort of . . . blend. I remember taking the boat out to the fort."

"Did you do that alone?" Anette cut in.

"I think so."

"What were you doing right before you took the boat out?" Anette continued. "Were you with anyone?"

"That's good, Oscar. We'll take it nice and slow." Mosbæk shot Anette a warning glance. "Tell me, how are you feeling?"

Malin sat on the edge of her chair, watching her son, her eyes wide. Maybe she hadn't asked him that simple question yet. Probably no one had.

"I don't know." Oscar swallowed as if to hold something back.

Jeppe could hear Mosbæk exhale through his nose and knew that the psychologist was smiling at the boy.

"That's totally fine. The doctors found some Tylenol remnants in your stomach—can you remember if you took any pills yourself?"

"No," Oscar whispered.

"Why did you take the boat out?"

"Maybe I was feeling down . . ."

"Did you have an argument with someone? Maybe with Malthe Sæther?" Mosbæk asked in a cheerful voice.

"Malthe, my teacher . . . ?" Oscar ran a finger under his nose, looking confused.

Mosbæk turned around to Jeppe and Anette with a questioning look. Was Oscar ready to hear what had happened?

Malin made the decision for them.

"Honey," she said. "Mr. Sæther was found dead, murdered. That's why the police are asking so many questions." She spoke from where she sat, not making any move to get up.

Oscar gasped for breath.

"It's a lot to take in," Mosbæk said, taking the boy's hand. "I get it. Are you okay?"

Oscar looked anything but okay. He looked like a deer, one second before it hits the front bumper.

"Let's take a break." Mosbæk patted his hand.

"What about the note? Did you write it? As a suicide note?" Jeppe received a warning glance from Mosbæk but pressed on anyway. "Malthe Sæther was going to help one of his students on Friday night. Was it you? Or Iben?"

"Is Iben okay?" Oscar began crying. "Can I see her?"

"Not until you're stable and healthy again, sweetie," Malin said, finally getting up.

He put his hands over his face.

"I'll see you guys out," Malin ordered.

Jeppe stopped in the doorway and turned around.

"I talked to your sister, Jenny, yesterday. She confided that Oscar has been having problems for some time . . ."

"How would she know? She never sees him," Malin said, her expression hardening.

"Why not?"

She stood still, her hand on the handle, ready to close the door between them.

"My sister is . . . intense. Jenny tends to create drama around herself and then push the blame off onto other people. She borrows money she doesn't pay back, and I'm afraid she and Henrik don't see eye to eye. I love my sister, but . . . we're very different."

"My impression from her is that she is very close to you. And to the kids."

"Maybe." Malin looked back over her shoulder at her son.

"Malin, what happened in Oscar's life that could have caused him to run off in a boat and attempt suicide?"

"You think I'm a bad mother, don't you?" Her face turned red with anger.

The question was so unexpected that Jeppe couldn't come up with a response.

"You come here with your principles and theories and look down on my family. Disapprove of the way we parent, isn't that so?"

He held up his hands to stop her, but she would not be stopped.

"You think you know exactly how to handle a boy like Oscar and what he really needs." She began closing the door, forcing Jeppe to take a step backward. "But you're wrong. You don't know shit about having kids."

CHAPTER 26

The screensaver came on without warning, and Esther de Laurenti had to click the mouse yet again on the green form to fill in her account information. Sitting here in Copenhagen's main library on Krystalgade fumbling around on a public computer was not her favorite pastime, but since Margrethe Dybris's scientific articles were stored in the library's database and not available online, she had to come in person to print them out.

The library's common area was as noisy as a train station. Even in the middle of the day it was teeming with students and retirees moving in and out of the revolving doors and up and down the escalators of the bright, high-ceilinged hall that was the heart of the library.

Irritably, Esther shook the semi-unresponsive mouse, which only managed to move the cursor about half the time. Part of her was relieved to be out of the house and away from Gregers. He was tough to be around these days, partly because he was uncharacteristically clingy, but also, she had to admit to herself, because his fear of death was unpleasant to be around. She was ashamed to feel that way and even more ashamed about her own growing fear: Who would take care of Gregers if he were to become incapacitated?

She opened and closed tabs and found the three articles Margrethe had written about the Torajan people's funerals and traditions with regard to death and bereavement. Esther skimmed them quickly and sent them to the printer. Seventy-two pages total. That was going to cost her, but she had to have them.

While waiting for the printer, she typed *funeral rituals* into the browser's search field and clicked on *images*. She might as well start thinking about the book cover—the easy part of writing a book.

Esther scrolled through photos of funeral processions and burials, all of them too dull and vague for a cover image. She typed *funerary artifacts* instead. That was better! She scrolled past photos of Egyptian sarcophagi and sculptures to Roman death masks, which citizens would wear during funeral processions to honor their ancestors. One image of a chalk-gray mask made her pause—it looked just like the one Jenny had shown her at the museum—and she clicked on the link below it. That took her to another home page with photos of reliquaries. One picture depicted a pale, light-skinned doll with closed eyes. The picture was very small, so it was hard to see it clearly, but the face of the doll was feminine, its expression dreamlike, and it was lying on dark red velour, which created depth and contrast. That might be something!

She tried to enlarge the photo, but was promptly instructed to log in. The home page was called ninthcircle.com. Maybe she could buy the rights to use the image if she could find a way to ask them. The only question was, how did one do that? No matter what Esther clicked on, she received the same message to log in.

The computer made a sound to let her know her print job was finished. She turned off the monitor, packed up her things, and headed to the printer room.

Ninth Circle. Who could help her get in touch with them?

*   *   *

"HOW ADDLED IS he? Can we count on him telling the truth when he claims that he doesn't remember anything?"

Jeppe kicked at a clod of dirt on the uneven lawn of National Hospital's inner courtyard. The winter had been hard on the grass, or maybe it was the steady stream of kids running back and forth to the castle-shaped play structure, which prevented the young grass from growing. He watched Mosbæk and Anette, who were busy scanning the courtyard's few benches looking for available places to sit, and wondered if it would be wrong to light a cigarette.

"Addled—did you really call him that?" Mosbæk stuck his hands in his pockets and appeared to give up on the benches. "I don't think I've heard that term since 1955."

"What the heck do you call a boy who sails off onto the ocean to die? *Stressed?*"

Mosbæk tutted with a little smile. He was used to being ribbed by his police coworkers, but actually a profound respect prevailed between the detectives and the psychologists they worked with, any mutual distrust from the past having long ago been resolved.

"He may well be experiencing some type of anterograde amnesia delayed reaction."

"Come again?" Anette made a show of putting one hand behind her ear. "Am I supposed to know what that means?"

Mosbæk laughed and shook his head.

"PTSD, a delayed shock reaction to a traumatic experience with subsequent memory loss. Unless of course he's pretending that he can't remember because he has something to hide. I need to spend more time with him to be sure."

A little boy with blond curls, a bandage on his forehead, and a diapered butt toddled between them and looked up their unfamiliar grown-up legs in confusion. Once he had determined that none of them was his mother, he toddled on toward the play structure. Jeppe watched the child head for a woman, his arms raised in the air, clearly expecting to be picked up into the safety of a hug. Ah, how we're born to trust our parents.

"Was Malthe's death the traumatic experience?" Jeppe asked, turning back to the other two.

"The boy could easily be in shock over his teacher's death, possibly even over his own involvement in the death." Mosbæk stroked his full beard, shaping it into a point. "But it's hard to know as long as he doesn't tell us more. Do you know if they were more than just teacher and student to each other?"

"They appear to have been confidants, but we don't know to what extent," Jeppe said with a shrug.

"It's awfully convenient for him to not be able to remember anything," Anette interjected. "But you can't convince me that a boy who sails a boat out to a fort, sinks his boat, and ODs on Tylenol is up to anything other than suicide."

"Unless there was someone along who forced him to take the pills." Mosbæk raised an index finger and then asked, "Is your theory that he killed his teacher and ran off?"

"Yes," Anette replied while Jeppe shook his head.

Mosbæk looked back and forth between the two of them.

"Well, I see that everything is as usual. Don't forget Occam's razor, my friends."

"Is that my cue to ask what it means, so that you can dazzle us with your knowledge?" Anette asked with a sigh.

"Exactly." Mosbæk smiled. "Occam's razor is an epistemological justification, which can basically be paraphrased as "the theory based on the fewest possible hypotheses is the best. You should slice right to the bone and find the simplest theory."

Jeppe looked up at a little swath of sky over their heads, outlined by the gray concrete of the hospital on all sides. The white clouds froze in a snapshot, while happy squeals from children flew through the air like the calls of seagulls.

Like the squeal of train tracks.

"I'm sorry, Mosbæk, but the razor hits a knot." Jeppe looked at Anette. "A knot by the name of Lis Christensen."

"Seriously?" She rolled her eyes.

"We have to at least look into it."

"Uh, is anyone going to tell me who this Lis is?" Mosbæk said, flinging his hands up in the air.

Jeppe got out his cigarettes.

"Lis was hit by a train at four thirty p.m. yesterday while Oscar was lying in Fort Prøvestenen. If she was pushed, there's no way Oscar could have done it."

"Am I supposed to understand any of that?" Mosbæk folded his arms over his chest. "And if you light one of those I will personally headbutt you."

"Sorry, Mosbæk. It's too complicated to explain properly." Jeppe put the pack of cigarettes back in his pocket. "You want to give it one more go with Oscar?"

The psychologist sighed, but then nodded.

"I doubt if he'll remember any more today, though. He's weak, and his mother doesn't seem like she's the best support for him, even if she's trying."

"You're a good guy, Mosbæk!" Anette patted him on the back.

"So are you." He smiled reluctantly. "Just because I want to coax some information out of him, doesn't mean I don't care about his well-being."

"Great," Jeppe said. "I'll call the desk and find out who's on the train case. Maybe Lis Christensen has some next of kin who will talk to us."

While Jeppe dialed, he looked at his partner. Somehow she had grown even slimmer in the last few days and her cheekbones had suddenly appeared like unexpected guests on her face. They made her look worn and raw in an almost romantic way, which was completely unlike Anette Werner.

If I didn't know better, he thought, *I would think she was in love.*

"THE LATEST NUMBERS *reveal an increase in* CO_2 *emissions this year. Despite the Paris Agreement, which was intended to ensure a reduction or at least a stabilization of the emissions figures, there are many signs that global* CO_2 *emissions are on track to set a new record this year. If we do not significantly reduce greenhouse gas pollution in the immediate—*"

Kasper Skytte switched off the radio news broadcast and turned his attention back to the open suitcase on his bed. A pair of shoes, extra pants, T-shirts, and clean underwear for five days, his computer, the most important family photos, the ATM card for the Swiss bank account.

What do you take with you when you don't know if you'll ever come home again? When everything needs to fit in your carry-ons so you don't have to wait in baggage claim and can make a run for it at any given time?

Not very much was the answer; far less than you would want.

He emptied his glass of port and refilled it. A gift from a coworker, probably. He hadn't given in to his craving to log on for the last four days, but then he had been drinking more than ever. The question was if the one addiction was simply replacing the other, but he would have to deal with that once they had reached safety.

Kasper ran through his mental checklist with his eyes on the open suitcase. Now that running was a reality, he felt strangely serene. It seemed safer to be on the run than to stay back and wait to be exposed.

His only problem was Iben.

Running without her wasn't an option. She was only fifteen and not ready to live on her own. Plus he loved her. But how was he going to persuade her to go with him?

He closed the suitcase and checked to make sure it wasn't too full to zip shut. As he set it on the floor he heard the key in the door. It was only two o'clock in the afternoon. She must be ditching her last class. Footsteps followed by a distant rustle told him that Iben had gone straight to her room. It probably didn't occur to her that he might be home since he normally wouldn't be at this hour. Kasper waited, heard her opening drawers and moving things around. She was muttering to herself the way one does when one's upset.

Quietly he sat down on the bed and listened to the sounds his daughter was making. Like he had sat so many times when she was small, listening to her playing. He had tried so hard to make it work as a single father, to be everything she needed. And for a while he had succeeded. Her devotion had been complete, her love boundless, and completely without digs. Now there was nothing but.

He heard her cursing under her breath. People should record their children's voices, he thought. The memories dwell so much more in sounds than images. Carefully he stood up and tiptoed to her room, watching her from the doorway. No longer his little, chubby-cheeked angel, but a lanky, angular teenager with a defiance in her that he couldn't understand. Maybe even with a boyfriend?

Iben didn't see him. She was busy throwing clothes into her big sports bag, pulled stacks of T-shirts and jeans randomly out of her dresser and tossed them willy-nilly into the bag. Kasper couldn't help but smile at the irony of the situation. He had just been going to make her pack her essentials when she got home from school. But he suspected she was packing for something other than their mutual escape.

"Where are you going?"

She jumped at the sound of his voice.

"Dad?! What the hell, you scared me! I didn't know you were home."

"You're packing. Where are you going?" Kasper asked with a smile.

She looked down at her stockinged feet, squirming under his attention.

"Let me guess: some school outing I haven't heard about?" He knew it was stupid to be snarky with her, but he couldn't help himself. "A field trip with Greenpeace that you forgot to tell me about?"

"Dad, stop it!"

"Or maybe you're heading somewhere with your boyfriend? I understand that you're getting into that kind of thing . . ."

She marched over and grabbed the door to close it in his face, but he didn't budge. He held it open with his hand.

"Why do you suddenly care where I'm going? You never do." Iben crossed her arms in front of her chest.

He almost laughed at how desperate the situation was. Bizarre how the most serious moments in life somehow activate our laughter center.

Kasper took a deep breath, put his hands on his daughter's cheeks, and spoke seriously.

"Sweetie. Listen to what I'm saying for once: In less than an hour we leave for Zürich, where I have important business tomorrow. From there we fly to Johannesburg. Pack plenty of clothes and bring your schoolbooks, because it'll be a while before we come back. You can't tell anyone where we're going, not a soul! I'll explain everything later."

"What the hell are you talking about?" she exclaimed, pulling free. "You seriously think I would fly to South Africa with *you*? Forget it!" She turned her back to him and went back to throwing clothes into her bag.

Two steps and he had hold of her. Her skinny shoulders flinched in surprise.

"Ow! Come on, let go of me. That hurts!"

He shook her. In all those years of nighttime crying and tantrums he had never, not even once, laid a hand on his daughter. Now his fingers dug into her flesh as he shook her back and forth.

There was no other way. She had to do what he said. Whatever the cost.

CHAPTER 27

Deceased math teacher at Zahles School Lis Christensen turned out to have been married going on thirty-eight years to retired sign maker Robert Christensen and living in a row house in Albertslund, a planned community just west of Copenhagen. The duty officer was able to report that Lis's death was still being treated as an accident following the autopsy, and to pass on the contact information of her next of kin. Robert was surrounded by his children and grandchildren when Jeppe called, but he was willing to let the police stop by.

Jeppe and Anette knocked on his blue front door amid a rain of children's happy shouts from the little paths between the row houses.

Suburban nuclear family idyll, Jeppe thought, reflecting fleetingly on the life he himself might have had.

There were no children's sounds from inside the row house when Robert opened the door. He was a tall man, balding with wire-rimmed glasses and enormous hands. His blue flannel shirt was creased as if he had been lying down in it.

"I sent the kids home. They have to start making dinner soon anyway." He pointed to the nearby playground. "Both our kids and their families live in this neighborhood. Five grandchildren total. It's wonderful to live so close to each other. Especially . . ." He came to a halt, cleared his throat, and then gestured them in with a wave of his hand.

The row house was a square and functional two-story concrete structure from the eighties. Its modern bones were softened by old-fashioned wooden furniture, full bookshelves, and family pictures on the wall. Jeppe glanced at the shelves and recognized the colorful spines of many crime fiction books, well loved and frequently reread, or so it would appear.

"Have a seat."

Robert sat on a brown sofa and gestured that they could choose between the beech bentwood recliner and a matching brown armchair facing the sofa.

"Thank you for being willing to see us on such short notice. We're so sorry about your wife." Jeppe sat down.

"Thank you." Robert nodded with dignity. "This is a difficult time."

"Obviously. It's good to hear that you have family close by."

He nodded again.

"We're here in connection with the murder investigation for Lis's coworker Malthe. I just questioned your wife yesterday morning."

"Yes, she told me she was meeting you, but she never made it home to tell me about it." Robert cleared his throat once more. "She was planning to retire this summer. We were looking forward to it so much, more time to travel and see friends, spend time with the grandkids."

"It must be rough."

"It's a shock. We're all in shock at her not being here anymore." His voice quavered on those last words.

Jeppe gave him a moment to recover.

"We know that you've already spoken with our colleagues. They informed us that Lis's death is being treated as an accident."

Robert sighed.

"Lis hasn't been able to walk well since her hip replacement. It left one of her legs longer than the other, and she developed back problems before they figured out what was wrong. She refused to use her cane, even though I kept telling her that it was dumb to take chances. That she risked falling and breaking her legs."

Anette discreetly stuffed a piece of gum into her mouth and started chewing. The sound immediately sparked Jeppe's irritation.

He shot her a look, which she ignored, then turned back to Robert and asked:

"I understood from your wife that she and Malthe Sæther had a good professional relationship."

"Yes, they did. It's terrible what happened to Malthe, totally inconceivable. She was devastated to hear about it." Robert smiled sadly. "Lis is an unbelievably caring person, not just to her family, but to her students and coworkers as well."

"But they didn't socialize outside of work, did they?"

"No, Lis steered clear of that kind of thing. When we were younger, we hung out some with the other teachers after work, but we gave it up many years ago. Too much bickering and bantering, you know."

Anette's insistent chewing worked its way into Jeppe's ear canals like a drill, and he struggled to stop himself from asking her to spit out the gum. Some people are annoying because of their deliberate actions, others have no idea how infuriating they can be. The latter group others just have to learn to live with.

"Lis told me that Malthe consulted her when he had problems at work . . . ," Jeppe said.

"Several of the young teachers did. Lis has been a staff representative for most of her professional life; people trusted her." Robert looked proud. "Some of her peers, coworkers who were the same age as her, frowned on it. I assume because they were jealous."

"What sorts of problems did Malthe need help with?"

Robert hesitated.

"I realize that these were confidential conversations," Jeppe continued. "But Malthe has been murdered. It could be important."

"It feels almost disloyal to talk about." He took off his glasses, set them carefully in his lap, and rubbed his face. For a moment he sat, lost in his own thoughts, then he put the glasses back on. "Malthe had challenges with admin because he took the students' interpersonal relationship issues too seriously. Teenagers can be really emotional, and they should be permitted to express that, but adults don't need to keep tabs on all their moods. Lis was trying to teach Malthe that. You need to support them but also know when to act and when not to. Sometimes you just need to let them figure things out on their own."

"Do you mean the trouble with Victor Dreyer-Hoff?"

"Well . . ." Robert turned his palms upward in a dismissive gesture. "Of course that played a part in their conversations, but lately there was something else bothering Malthe, something even more serious. He and Lis talked after school as recently as Thursday, because Malthe suspected that a student had been sexually abused by a family member. He wasn't sure how to handle the situation."

Jeppe's stomach did a somersault.

"Did Lis say which student was being abused?"

"No, Lis is very discreet. I don't know what she advised Malthe to do, either, but I'm sure she urged him to be level-headed. You need to be careful in cases like that. The story really got to her, though. I could tell that."

And now she was dead. Malthe had asked Lis for advice on Thursday. He was murdered on Friday, and she fell in front of a train at Nørreport Station the following Tuesday.

"Well, we don't want to take up any more of your time." Jeppe got to his feet. "Thank you so much for talking to us. We're really very sorry about your wife."

"We had plans to visit Malta this summer, to see Valletta and the Order of St. John's palaces," Robert said, raising his chin bravely. "But now that's off, of course."

He walked them to the blue door and shook their hands before closing it softly behind them.

Jeppe and Anette walked to their car in silence.

Not until they hit the highway back to Copenhagen did Anette speak.

"Whoa, he was so sad," she blurted out. "That poor guy! It really got to me, seeing him like that. . . . Anyway, where should I drop you off?"

"At headquarters. Larsen asked me to come in. Are you coming with me or going home?"

Anette sped up, overtaking a Volvo on the inner roadway.

"Home, if that's okay with you. Maybe I'll just swing by Malthe Sæther's apartment first. I want to see it for myself."

"You just refuse to trust that the rest of us are doing our jobs right?" Jeppe laughed. "And, hey, aren't you done with that gum yet?"

"No and no! You choose which answer goes with which question all on your own."

Jeppe turned and looked out the car window at the cars they were passing. Glimpses of black, white, metal, and glass. A student, sexual abuse, Malthe and Lis discussing the best way to proceed.

"Do you really think Lis's death was an accident, a freak accident that happens to have coincided with Malthe's murder?"

Anette swerved around a truck without using her turn signal, causing a minibus behind her to honk aggressively.

"You know how much I hate guesswork, Kørner. But, no, I don't think her death was an accident. I think she was murdered."

THE AFTERNOON WALK around the lake ended as a mere hundred yards back and forth along the bank. Dóxa was tired and sluggish, and Esther saw no reason to force her. She tried pulling the pug up the stairs, but quickly surrendered and carried her in her arms instead. Those little doggy legs waggled apathetically in her embrace as she climbed the flights back up to her apartment on the fourth floor. Her own knees ached, too, and only her pride prevented her from resting on one of the benches on the landings on the way. The dog whimpered, and Esther shushed her. One old lady carrying another old lady.

Although these days she felt anything but old. The book on Margrethe Dybris was taking shape in her head—a chapter on her early life in Copenhagen; then her travels to Ghana, Haiti, and Indonesia; the men in her life and her decision not to get married in favor of her research career. Her ideas were buzzing eagerly like mosquitoes in a nudist colony.

Back in the apartment, Dóxa trotted into the kitchen to her food bowl, and Esther spoke soothingly to her as she hung up her jacket and removed her shoes in the front hall.

"I'll be right there, sweetie. I just have to make a quick phone call."

Sara Saidani answered right away.

"Yes, hello, Sara. This is Esther de Laurenti. We met each other through—"

"Jeppe," Sara interjected. "Hi, Esther. What a surprise."

She sounded cautious, but not unfriendly.

"Look, I'll keep this short. I'm writing a biography of a Danish anthropologist, and I need a cover image for my book. I mean, sure, it's still in the draft stages, but it's helpful to the writing process to have the format squared away from the beginning. It also makes it easier to present the book to potential publishers. . . ."

Based on the silence on the other end of the line, Esther realized that she was rambling. She tried to focus.

"Anyway, I found a picture on the internet that I'd like to buy the rights to, but I don't know how to go about that. And Jeppe always says you're so good at all that online stuff. . . ."

Suddenly Esther realized that it might be inappropriate of her to call Jeppe's girlfriend and ask for a favor. She was about to backpedal when Sara replied.

"I'd love to help, but I don't think I can do it over the phone. I'm not in the office today. My eldest daughter is home sick, but could you maybe stop by tonight after dinner? Nine o'clock? Then we can look at it together."

Esther, who didn't normally go out at night, accepted gratefully and hung up. The thought of soon being able to submit a pitch to publishers with both cover image and title made her feel positively giddy.

Dóxa whined, and Esther went into the kitchen to feed her. The room was semidark, and it wasn't until she stood in front of the refrigerator that she noticed the figure at the table.

Her heart leaped into her throat. She lunged for the switch and turned on the light.

Gregers was sitting at the table squinting at her in fear.

"What the hell? You scared me!" Esther scolded him, adrenaline making her grumpy. "What are you doing, just sitting there?"

"Well, pardon me for living. I was just composing myself and then you come barging in and start yelling." He pursed his lips prudishly, offended.

Esther took out the kibble and dished up one serving for Dóxa, mixed a spoonful of liverwurst into it, and set the dish on the floor. By the time the dog was happily munching away, she had calmed down. She looked at her roommate and realized that he was wearing his zipped-up jacket and his old driving cap.

"Did you go out?" she asked him. "Is something wrong?"

He looked at her in surprise and then down at himself. Apparently he had forgotten that he was still in his outerwear. There was a piece of paper in front of him.

"What's that?"

"I just wrote down what the doctor said." Gregers looked at the piece of paper, seeming lost.

"Can I see?"

Esther skimmed the notes from his conversation with the doctor. The results from his blood tests. Written in Gregers's unsteady cursive. The words loomed large on the paper.

Further testing
Increased risk
Heightened suspicion
Contrast dye

"Well, that just means they want to do some more testing on you to make sure there's nothing seriously wrong."

The kitchen fell quiet. Gregers took off his cap and set it on the table in front of him, like a busker expecting coins.

"I'm"—his voice trembled—"so afraid of dying."

Faced with Gregers's fear of death, Esther felt acutely awkward. Here she was traipsing around, toying with death as a curiosity, a source of excitement and interest.

She squeezed his hand.

"We all are. But no one is saying you're any closer to death now than you were a month ago. Or than I am, for that matter." She spoke with a conviction she didn't actually feel, and even to herself it sounded hollow.

Gregers looked down at the empty hat sitting in front of him.

"The thing about dying . . . I always thought I would be healthy and happy and then—boom—someone would pull the plug. But now I'm not so sure anymore. It's looking more like one long, grim slide"—Gregers closed his eyes—"into the dark."

*   *   *

THE EVENING RUSH hour traffic was thinning out when Anette pulled up in front of Vendersgade 19, parking the car illegally next to a full bicycle rack. She had texted Svend to ask if she should bring dinner home, but he hadn't replied. Could he read her unfaithful thoughts? When you've been with someone as long as they had, you could sense things like that, could simply smell it. They knew each other so well. Even so, Anette had the strange sense that they were beginning to know each other less well. Everyday life was creating ripples of distance around them and pushing them out into deeper waters. They'd been together for twenty-five years, since they were in school—were they still swimming in the same direction?

She slammed the car door shut and walked to the front door of Malthe Sæther's building, inserted the key with the crime scene technicians' cardboard tag into the lock and jogged up the stairs to the fifth floor, where she unlocked the door and ducked under the crime scene tape. The techs had long since removed all technology, taken fingerprints, and gathered hair and toothbrushes. Jeppe had gone over the place himself with a fine-tooth comb. There was no reason to believe Anette would be able to find anything new, but if she were the type to let reservations like that hold her back, she would never have found Oscar.

Saidani had finished going through Malthe's emails, calendar, and search history, and had noted in POLSAS that she had found nothing unusual. But everyone has secrets, Anette thought. Something had pulled this young teacher out of his harmonious every-day life to end up naked and suffocated in that giant claw at the incineration plant. And the answer *could* be here in the apartment somewhere.

The place already seemed uninhabited, the silence between the walls almost palpable, as if it were here to stay. Anette realized that she was humming to herself to fill up the empty space as she moved from room to room. There really was nothing conspicuous. Exasperated, she opened drawers and rummaged around looking for anomalies. There *had* to be some objectionable letters, secret pictures, a butt plug, for Pete's sake! She browsed through the books on his bookshelf, opened the drawers under the bed, and looked through the bathroom cabinet. Nothing. Even his kitchen rubber bands were neatly bundled together.

Malthe Sæther had canceled his weekend date with Josephine to help a student—that much they knew. He had talked to his girlfriend on the phone, let himself out of his apartment, gone down the stairs, and then what?

Anette closed the apartment door behind her and walked down the stairs, trying to retrace his footsteps: Where had he gone? Had he had an appointment to meet someone, or did he surprise them? Very few people like to be surprised.

On the sidewalk outside the front door Anette stopped and looked at the bike rack next to where she had parked her car. Malthe had loved bicycling. No matter where he had gone Friday night, surely he didn't walk. She knew he didn't own a car, so one would assume he either rode his bike or took public transit.

"Did you come from Malthe's place?"

Anette turned toward the voice and saw a woman in a knit poncho sitting on the steps of a little cellar shop, smoking. The poncho's garish Rasta colors made her Scandinavian post-winter skin look like wet cardboard.

"Do you know him?" Anette asked.

"Yup. I don't live here myself, but I run the shop down here, so I saw him pretty often. Terrible story, can you imagine?" The woman spoke with her cigarette dangling from the corner of her mouth. "Are you with the police, too? There's been a steady stream the whole day."

"I'm a detective with the Investigations Unit," Anette said with a nod.

"Really? I didn't know they let women do that!" The Rasta woman winked to emphasize that she was kidding.

"You haven't seen Malthe's bike, have you? It's an expensive one, a light green road bike."

"Hmm, I'm sure he kept that in the bike room, not on the street." She put her cigarette out and dropped the butt into a jam jar on the step beside her. "But he rode off on it the last time I saw him. It was on Friday night."

"Friday night? You mean this last Friday?" Anette came a step closer. "What time was it, exactly?"

"I was closing up the shop." She pointed down at the glass storefront of her cellar shop, which displayed an overwhelming hodgepodge of African arts and crafts. "It was a little before seven. I was bringing in the pots, when he came down and got his bike."

"Would you mind showing me the bike room, so we can see if it's there now?"

The woman shrugged and pulled out a bunch of keys. She opened a door next to her shop and led Anette first down a hallway to the backyard and then into a low-ceilinged basement room full of bicycles. She looked around.

"It's not here."

"Okay, thank you. Did you talk to him when you saw him last Friday?"

"We chatted a bit, not that much. He wasn't as talkative as he usually is." She reached for something inside her poncho and pulled out a battered pack of cigarettes. Strangely enough, this time the sight didn't elicit any craving in Anette.

"I remember asking him if he shouldn't be wearing a proper jacket. He was dressed in one of those hoodies, and I was already covered in goose bumps myself. But he didn't think it was necessary. He was only going to Østerbro."

The skin on Anette's neck crawled up toward her ears.

CHAPTER 28

The spring light faded over Sydhavn, to be replaced by fluorescent tube lights on the ceilings of those few offices that still held workers. Jeppe regarded the transformation and slid his hand along the window frame. Who ever invented windows that don't open? In trains and buses and office buildings like this one. Sealed rooms with a view of a world that can't be reached and air that can't be breathed. Behind him Thomas Larsen was hacking away on his computer keyboard, the clicking sounds only adding to Jeppe's discomfort. An artificial breeze from the air-circulation system blew gently on the back of his head and he felt a spasm of claustrophobia followed by a vehement aversion to his new workspace.

His cell phone rang, and he answered the call without taking his eyes off the power plant at the end of the street.

"Hi, Kørner," Anette yelled. She was always a loud talker, but even more so when she was excited about something. "I just left Malthe Sæther's apartment. He rode his bike to Østerbro Friday night at about seven p.m. The woman who runs the shop next door chatted with him on the street as he was leaving."

"Well, that fits with the information from the cell signal. Did you find anything else in the apartment? A bloody chain saw the rest of us overlooked?"

Anette sighed. "Go fuck yourself. Oh, and have a good evening!"

"You too, Werner. Say hi to everyone at home!"

Jeppe turned to Thomas Larsen, who was hunched over his laptop.

"A witness says Malthe Sæther rode his bicycle to Østerbro Friday night. The Dreyer-Hoff family lives in Østerbro. Does that mean he was going to meet Oscar?"

"Or maybe some other member of the family," Larsen suggested without looking up from his screen.

"Who do you mean?"

"One sec. I just need to finish buying this." Larsen got out a credit card and typed in his number. "I promised Mette I would buy a baby carrier from this organic baby store. It's twenty-five percent off today."

Jeppe sat down across from Larsen, wove his fingers together on the desk in front of him, and waited until he finally put his wallet away. An organic baby carrier?! Yet another of his colleagues about to be swallowed up into the self-important humdrum of baby life.

"It would explain a few things, wouldn't it? If the father was involved in Malthe Sæther's death." Larsen flicked his hair out of his eyes. "His alibi is as waterproof as a sieve. It could easily be him."

"But why?" Jeppe massaged the worry line between his eyebrows with his thumb. A shrill beep sounded in his right ear. "Let's assume you're right. Henrik tells his wife that he has something to take care of at work, but actually he drives somewhere and meets Malthe Sæther."

"Maybe they actually meet at his office?!" Larsen interjected. "That's in Østerbro, too."

"Great, let's say that. Henrik strangles him and throws him in the trash. What's his motive?"

Larsen looked like a child who had just broken open a piñata.

"I think he killed him because of fraud!"

"Fraud?" Jeppe looked at him blankly.

"Yeah." Larsen nodded. "I have a theory, or at least a hypothesis. It may seem a little complicated up front but give it a second. It's really very simple. Are you ready?"

Jeppe nodded.

"I've been reviewing Nordhjem's accounts from the last three years," Larsen began. "To put it simply, the Dreyer-Hoff family is screwed. Since the scandal, the auction house has been veering toward bankruptcy. Henrik is raising money in all sorts of ways and dumping it into that sinking ship. Here's an example."

Larsen pulled a piece of paper from his monogrammed bag and placed it in front of Jeppe. It looked like an order form with three lines of technical-sounding equipment and a total price in the right-hand column that was in the seven digits.

"More baby gear?" Jeppe joked. "A bit on the pricey side, I'd say."

Larsen ignored the teasing.

"I stumbled across a large payment to one of Nordhjem's subsidiaries that I couldn't explain, so I started digging. What you're looking at there is the purchase of electrostatic precipitators for particle separation, ordered by ARC from the German vendor Mirnhof and Schalcke."

"Where have I heard that name before?"

"That's Henrik's former employer. He acts as the agent between the vendor and the power plant and earns a commission on the sale. There's nothing really underhanded about it. The problem is that the sale doesn't appear to have taken place."

"How do you know that?" Jeppe asked.

"Well, it did require some legwork and a few calls to their accounting department. In German, no less! Mirnhof and Schalcke don't know anything about that order. It doesn't exist in their system. But Henrik was still paid the commission."

Larsen's phone blinked. He quickly typed something and put it away again.

"Sorry," he said. "Mette just wants to know if I remembered the baby carrier. What do you think?"

"About the baby carrier?"

"Come on, Kørner!"

Jeppe put his hands to his head and said, "What in the hot hollows of hell does this have to do with Malthe Sæther?"

"Possibly blackmail?" Larsen said, pursing his lips. "Malthe discovers Henrik's scam, threatens to expose him if he doesn't pay Malthe off, and Henrik ends up murdering him."

"That's a stretch! Everyone describes Malthe as an idealistic young man." Jeppe got up again and walked back to the window that couldn't be opened and the air that couldn't be breathed.

"We'll never get Henrik to talk to us about this. Who at ARC could have ordered the equipment?"

"The plant is closed for today," Larsen muttered, "so we won't be able to call and ask until tomorrow. But the secretary of the Danish Waste Association has been very helpful, sharing good advice and contacts. I'll just give her a try."

"What, now?" Jeppe looked at his watch. It was almost eight o'clock.

"I have her cell number."

Larsen called and introduced himself using only his first name. Judging from the tone of his voice, Jeppe got a clear sense of why the secretary had given him her private phone number. Larsen could be quite charming when he wanted to. He chatted with her briefly, thanked her, and said a heartfelt goodbye.

"Well, that's interesting. According to her, technical equipment orders for treatment plants typically come directly from the process engineers."

"Kasper Skytte?!" Jeppe turned to look at Larsen.

"Looks like it. Skytte and his team."

They looked at each other.

"Let's visit Skytte at the plant first thing tomorrow morning and ask him if he's familiar with this order. I'll write and let them know we're coming. But for now, let's call it a day and go home." Jeppe grabbed his jacket from the back of his chair. It wasn't until he closed the office door that it hit him that *home* was no longer where it used to be.

ANETTE'S STOMACH LURCHED, sending spasms of nausea through her body. Sure, she had experienced situations in life before that had provoked a fierce case of nerves, but only a few times and always for a plausible reason. The physics final in high school, that time when they were waiting for her father's test results, that first ultrasound scan of the baby. Real challenges. Not like this, sitting in the car, afraid to go into her own home to her husband and child.

Anette rested her head against the steering wheel. She hadn't been unfaithful, she must hold on to that fact. There wasn't actually anything for her to feel guilty about, was there? People went on business trips and slept with random strangers left and right, and here she was, on the verge of throwing up over having innocently fantasized about another man. It was ridiculous!

She got out of the car and found her house key. Maybe she'd feel better if she told Svend about it. They could usually talk about anything, maybe he would understand? It was just plain enthusiasm for another person who happened to be of the opposite sex. She had always been curious and had an appetite for life.

That's one of the things he loves about me, she reminded herself as she opened the front door.

The scent of something baking and roasting wafted out to meet her. Bossa nova was playing on the sound system, and she could hear

Svend singing along in the kitchen. Anette hung her jacket on a hook in the front hall and hesitantly moved through the living room. She had anticipated coming home to a dark house and a husband who had fallen asleep while tucking in Gudrun.

She opened the door to the kitchen and saw Svend standing with his back to her, chopping herbs. Pots and pans with wonderful smells were bubbling away on the stove and a browned roast sat on the table. Her husband had poured wine and was wearing his favorite apron. A pair of exposed butt cheeks revealed that he wasn't wearing anything else.

Anette stood frozen in the doorway. Before they had had a child, they would sometimes buy fresh fish or game—skate wings, quail— and alternate for a whole weekend between cooking and making love. One of many things they didn't do anymore. She studied her husband's bare back with an unfamiliar skepticism. Whereas she had lost weight and gotten into shape since the baby, Svend had only packed on the pounds. The apron tie dug into his back fat, creating an upper and lower bulge.

"Oh, hi, honey, I didn't hear you at all." He set down his knife and wiped his hands off on the apron as he came over. He hugged her for a long time and then took hold of her chin. "Hey, I know I haven't been in the best mood lately. I've just been so tired." He kissed her in between the words. "But I feel like the energy is coming back. The extra daylight helps, I think. And sex!"

Svend pushed himself against her. She smiled and pulled free of his embrace.

"Wow, what a welcome! Let me just grab a glass of wine." Anette walked over to the cupboard and got out a glass. "It smells amazing. What are we having?"

"Sweetbreads and tenderloin. The first of the spring asparagus and one big hunk of naked man." He pulled up his apron and let her see what he had to contribute.

"Ha-ha, you're really in fine form today. Do I have time for a quick shower before we eat?"

"If you hurry!"

Svend turned back around to the stove, and Anette hastened to the bathroom and stripped off her clothes. She turned on the shower and let cool water flow over her. Not cold, just cool enough that it felt like a slap. Finally, Svend was looking at her with love again, finally the desire was back. Why then did she have the feeling that it was too late?

As she stepped out of the shower and started drying herself off, her phone buzzed on the edge of the sink. It was a text message from Mads Teigen.

Thinking of you!

She deleted the message and tossed her phone onto the window-sill, wrapped the towel around herself and checked her reflection while efficiently smothering every single butterfly she felt fluttering in her stomach. Then she hurried back to the kitchen and to Svend, who switched off the stove when he saw her.

Anette received his kisses with her eyes closed and the image of Mads on her retinas.

SARA SAIDANI LIKED Esther de Laurenti. She liked the way she came in and hung up her wool coat, as if she were at home, and the way she hugged Sara warmly and matter-of-factly, even though they had actually met only a couple of times.

"Are the girls asleep? Amina and Meriem, right?"

Sara nodded, genuinely touched that Esther remembered their names. She knew how fond Jeppe was of the elderly woman, and she understood why. Esther was sweet. The thought of Jeppe, however, wasn't, and Sara pushed it out of her mind and showed her guest into the living room.

"Would you like some tea?"

"Thank you, that sounds lovely."

Sara boiled water and put tea bags into cups while Esther got settled in the living room. To be honest, she could have used something stronger than tea with honey today. The day's conversations with a hungover and unhappy Amina had planted in her a disgust for alcohol, but at the same time a longing to lose herself in its fog. Sometimes it still surprised Sara that she was the grown-up, the one who was supposed to think rationally and make sound decisions about changing schools, homework, or grounding. She could barely manage her own life.

Esther had gotten comfortable on the sofa, her feet pulled up under her like a young girl.

"Where's Jeppe tonight?"

"Oh, I forgot the honey, one second." Sara turned around and walked back into the kitchen, opened a cupboard, and brought the honey jar into the living room. The last thing she wanted was talk about her love life with a semi-stranger. Unfortunately Esther didn't seem to pick up on her cues.

"Would you like some?" Sara held out the honey.

"No, thanks." Esther set her tea down on the floor. "It's great to see him so happy."

"Okay," Sara said, sitting down next to her with her computer on her lap. "It was something about a picture, right?"

"Ah, yes. Well, as I said, I'm writing a biography. It's about this amazingly interesting anthropologist who traveled around the world for more than thirty years studying death rituals."

"Exciting," Sara said with more conviction than she felt.

"Yes, right?" Esther was beaming with enthusiasm.

"And you wanted to use a specific picture?" Sara asked. Her alarm was set for six fifteen the next morning; she didn't have all night.

"Exactly! I was hunting around for a suitable image for the cover of the book and I stumbled across this web page. It's a doll." Esther unfolded her legs and put her feet on the floor with a small, strained sound. "Ninthcircle.com, but as I said, you can't access it. You need a password."

"Let's see if I can open it."

She typed the address into the browser's search field.

"Hmm, it's just a regular WordPress page. That's the kind of thing anyone could just make from home."

"Do you think you can log in?"

"Not without being a member, it looks like. There's no contact information. That's strange." Sara enlarged a logo in the corner of the screen. "The page is secured by a service called Bulletproof Security Pro. Unusual to secure a homemade page so professionally."

"Ugh," Esther sighed, disappointed.

"I'm happy to see what I can do, but it's not something I can solve right here and now. What's the image that you want to buy?" Sara ignored the insistent request to enter her access code and clicked on the image gallery. A black-and-white photo of a doll appeared, but the picture was less than half an inch square, and she couldn't expand it. "Is it this one?"

Esther leaned closer.

"I don't think so. Try scrolling through."

Sara advanced to the next picture, and they both leaned in closer to the screen.

"Maybe it's that one?" Esther asked.

"Was it a doll without clothes on?" Sara kept going.

"I don't think they were that small when I looked at them at the library," Esther said, somewhat apologetically.

"I may be able to get through the security and get in touch with the page. It'll just take me some time." Sara advanced to the next picture. "Is that it? No, that's not a doll."

Esther's fine wrinkles contracted, making her cheeks look like dumplings.

"But," she protested, "what *is* that?"

Sara squinted and said, "I think it looks like a stuffed bird."

JEPPE POURED BOILING water into his cup of instant noodles, accompanied by Marilyn Monroe and Jane Russell, who were singing their hymn to the broken heart in his head.

"When love goes wrong, nothing goes right."

Some people have good self-care instincts. They observe regular mealtimes, and make sure they have ironed shirts and clean sheets, whether they're in a relationship or alone, happy or sad. Other people eat instant noodles full of MSG standing at a kitchen counter whose top should have been replaced a year ago while telling themselves that they knew from the start it wouldn't work out. As if there was comfort in having predicted the failure of their love.

Being Sara's boyfriend wasn't easy, and not just because of the kids. She was difficult to connect with and quick to shut him out, critical, perfectionistic, sometimes downright prejudiced. But she was also wild and fun and beautiful and razor-sharp, and who the hell falls in love with *easy*? The people we desire can be difficult and complicated, they just need to be worth the trouble. She was.

Jeppe set aside his noodles and contemplated for the one hundred and seventeenth time today whether there was a way to get through the conflict. One cannot just sail off into the blue and lie down to die every time life bared its teeth. But no matter how he tried to look at the issue, he ended up in the same spot: between a bear cub and its mother.

Was that where Malthe had ended up? In the line of fire between Henrik Dreyer-Hoff and his child? Could Malthe have confronted Oscar's father with something that had made him so angry that Malthe had ended up in the garbage dump, strangled and naked?

Jeppe pulled his laptop out of his bag and opened POLSAS, located the report on Lis Christensen's death, and read it. On Tuesday, April 16, at 4:32 p.m., the Farum train pulled into Nørreport's underground station on schedule. But just before the train reached the platform, a person fell onto the tracks, and the locomotive driver pulled the brake and hit the alarm. He had been trying to stop a cup of coffee from tipping over and therefore hadn't witnessed the actual accident itself, just the figure on its way down in front of the train. He couldn't say whether there had been anyone near the woman before she fell. Several people had been waiting for the train, but they had been standing farther down the platform, most of them with their eyes glued to their phones.

"Oh my God, are you here? I didn't think anyone was at home." Johannes's deep voice broke the silence like a hug, unexpected but comfortable. He tossed his keys onto the counter. "If I'd known you were home, I would have called first. Why aren't you at Sara's?"

Jeppe shrugged.

Johannes seemed to understand. At any rate, he didn't ask further questions.

"I went to the movies and didn't feel like schlepping all the way back to Snekkersten. Can I crash on the sofa, or would you prefer to be alone?"

"No, it's nice that you're here."

"Cool." Johannes took off his jacket and tossed it over the back of the chair. "I was actually headed straight for bed. I have to get up early."

"Why? What are you doing tomorrow?"

"I have a casting call for a movie."

"Good." Jeppe smiled. "I was starting to worry that you had completely stalled out."

"Life goes on. There are limits to how long you can fester over a broken heart. I'll just go brush my teeth."

Had Johannes always had that touch of cynicism in him, or had it developed with age? Jeppe couldn't remember anymore, just like he could no longer remember whether his own heavy heart had ever been light and carefree.

"Johannes," he called. "Do you remember that one theater class we took? We must have been seventeen or eighteen. There was a girl in our class."

"Lisa, you mean? Lisa with the long legs?" Johannes emerged from the bathroom in a T-shirt and underwear.

"Yes, exactly! I was so in love with her."

Johannes spread out the bedding and lay down on the sofa. "Yeah, I know. Everyone knew. Including Lisa." He pulled the comforter up to his chin.

"*What?* I didn't tell a soul, not even you."

"You're like an open book, Jeppe. You always have been. To tell the truth, we laughed a little behind your back. You were so . . . shy. It was cute."

Cute? His heart had been near bursting every day at the sight of this girl he barely dared to even talk to.

"Sometimes I feel like I haven't gotten the least bit wiser since then."

"You haven't, my friend. None of us have." Johannes rolled over onto his side with his back to Jeppe. "But at least you have the guts to love. Not everyone does, you know."

"Is that, like, a quality in itself?"

"Yep." Johannes yawned heartily. "Either you can or you can't. You can. It's a gift. Good night."

Jeppe smiled at his friend's back on the sofa. "Sleep well!"

He turned off the light and went into the bathroom to brush his teeth with a stiff, new toothbrush, then made his way through the dark to his bedroom and lay down on a mattress that had not yet shaped itself to his body.

From his bed he could see the city's roofs, like dim shadows against the night sky. He knew that all the thoughts he had ever had would be dancing in a conga line through his head that night. Jeppe closed his eyes to the darkness and tried to find sleep.

So take this down in black and white
When love goes wrong, nothing goes right.

THURSDAY,
APRIL 18

She unlocks her bike and rides along the water. It is early morning, and the air has a bite to it. The girl regrets not dressing warmer. She is wearing her school bag on her back, but she isn't on her way to school. If everything goes well, the others won't even realize that she has played hooky.

Breakfast moves uneasily in her stomach, cornflakes with milk and sugar. When they are home alone, they usually just have something in a bowl with milk on it. Now she wishes she hadn't eaten at all. Later they're all going to the hospital. In our family we stick together, *her father always says,* no matter what.

The wind plays with her hair. She has left her bike helmet at home, and it feels nice to let it blow freely. She is wearing her favorite top and her new sneakers, and she sings while the tires rumble over the cobblestones of the waterfront path and the sun rises over Copenhagen. A song from the radio . . . she doesn't quite remember the lyrics, but that doesn't matter. She sings to calm herself.

At the big intersection she gets off and wheels her bike across the street. Before crossing she looks left and then right and then left again. The cars always drive so fast here, but it is early and traffic isn't that heavy yet. She isn't scared. Well, maybe just a little.

People always think she is the delicate one because she is the youngest. The baby, the girl, the cute one. But they are wrong. She is stronger than they realize. Deep down she knows that she is unbeatable. Brave enough to say things out loud, brave enough to confront a murderer.

CHAPTER 29

The blackbird was singing. When Gudrun woke up, this year's first playful trills were sounding over the roofs of Greve Strand. Anette hurried to her before she woke up Svend, too. She put her in the high chair with a bowl of yogurt and started the coffee maker. There was something particularly lovely about these early mornings alone in the kitchen with Gudrun. She was always so cheerful right when she woke up, and Anette enjoyed turning on the radio to hear her babbling along with the music.

Anette drank two cups of coffee, one right after the other, but couldn't force any breakfast down. She, who always woke up hungry as a bear coming out of hibernation, was gradually losing her good appetite.

Gudrun started whining, and Anette picked her up and got out the stroller. They often took her on a morning walk, so she could rest a little before day care. Anette put on a fleece and decided to leave her phone and its unanswered message behind and just be in the moment with her daughter. But on her way out the door she tucked it into her pocket after all. Wherever her appetite had gone, it had taken her self-discipline with it.

They only made it two hundred yards down the street before Gudrun was sound asleep, but Anette kept pushing the stroller along Greve Strand's network of paths. She needed the fresh air.

Svend had been so sweet yesterday, warm and passionate, lovingly attentive and so fucking grateful that they were finally having sex again that Anette's cheeks burned with shame. If only she could just pull out a big eraser and remove Mads from her consciousness.

Mads.

Anette put the brakes on the stroller and sat down on a park bench. The old pack of cigarettes was still in her chest pocket. She took it out and lit one. The first hits made her light-headed.

He was sensitive and kind, but so was Svend. Strong and masculine, even willful. Was that what she found so exciting? That Mads didn't need anyone, including her? Maybe at the age of forty-six she had finally gotten caught up in that lonesome-cowboy syndrome that many women cultivated, but that she herself had never fallen sway to before. Something about him left her feeling giddy.

She took out her phone, typed a response, and then deleted it for the twenty-fifth time. Felt the anticipation take off and soar inside her until even her toes were trembling. She typed again and sent the message before she could stop herself.

Should we meet up?

Then she put the phone back in her pocket and inhaled to the beat of her pounding heart. She listened for the blackbird, checked on her daughter, who was still asleep, and put out the cigarette before it made her feel sick.

Could it be his artistic side? Was she really that easy, that a man with a workshop and some stuffed birds made such an impression on her?

Because *mysterious*? Because *deep*?

Anette got up, unlocked the brakes, and pushed the stroller down the path. The first joggers of the morning had started zigzagging through the neighborhood dressed in loud colors and breathing heavily. Their focused faces contrasted her own sense of being in the midst of a free fall.

The phone buzzed in her pocket. She stopped, took a deep breath, and got it out.

I'll pick you up at the dock in two hours. Okay?

A single sentence followed by a one-word question. Even so, she felt his desire radiating through the screen like waves from a reactor. With trembling fingers, she wrote Jeppe that she was going to be late.

Anette knew she was heading down a path that led toward the abyss. All the same, she sensed that she would never be truly happy again if she didn't explore this path. That life would feel forever mediocre if she didn't give passion a chance.

Before she had time to change her mind, she responded to Mads: *Okay.*

"ARE WE GOING in *there?*" Thomas Larsen spit contemptuously on the parking lot gravel.

"Don't worry, Larsen, for a waste dump this place is surprisingly presentable." Jeppe looked at ARC's shiny metal facade, where climbing wall grips extended all the way up toward the blue sky above. It still seemed bizarre to him to combine an incineration plant with a recreational facility. "Kasper Skytte still hasn't answered my call, so now we'll just chance it and see if he's here."

They walked toward the entrance and waited for the sliding glass door to open. A burly male receptionist got up as they approached the counter. Jeppe showed him his laminated ID badge.

"We're here to talk to Kasper Skytte. Is he in yet?"

"Let me check." The receptionist looked it up on a screen. "No, it doesn't look like it. Would you like to leave him a message?"

"What about Margit Smith?" Jeppe asked, before he had time to think.

"The CEO?" The receptionist smiled, as if the detectives had just shown up unannounced at a five-star hotel wanting to talk to Madonna. "She's in a course all week." He glanced at the screen again. "Our other two process engineers are here. Maybe one of them could be of assistance?"

"The ones who work with Kasper Skytte?"

"Jim Knudsen and Gitte Mejlhede. They're on the sixth floor. Do you want me to call up and see if they'll have time to see you?"

"Oh, they will!" Jeppe smiled at the receptionist, who picked up his phone and conducted a brief conversation.

"Okay." He slapped two visitors' badges on the counter. "The elevator is over there. Sixth floor."

"Thank you."

On the sixth floor, the open office layout was deserted apart from a group of desks by the window, where two people were waiting for them. A man, who sat looking down at the table, and a woman, who watched them approach with her head held high and her cheeks flushed. She looked like someone who had started her day with either a brisk walk or a quarrel.

"Gitte Mejlhede? I'm Jeppe Kørner from the Copenhagen Police. Thank you for agreeing to talk to us without notice."

She stood up and shook each of their extended hands in turn, her colleague making do with a nod from his seat at the desk.

"Neither of us was at work when the body was found," she explained. "And we've both talked to someone from the police already."

"We would still like to ask you a couple of questions." Jeppe pointed to two empty chairs at the next desk over. "Would it be all right . . . ?"

Gitte apparently couldn't think of any plausible reason to say no, and Jim was of no assistance.

"As a matter of fact we came to talk to Kasper. But he's not in?"
She shook her head.

"Do you know where he is? He's not answering his phone."

The two coworkers exchanged a glance and then mumbled simultaneously, "No."

"Well, maybe you can help us." Jeppe smiled disarmingly. "We'll keep it quick."

Larsen pulled the purchase order out of his bag and set it on the desk.

"Do either of you recognize this order?" Larsen asked.

Gitte picked up the piece of paper and looked at him in bewilderment.

"I'll explain in a minute. Could you just please tell us if you ordered that equipment?"

"But," she said, shaking her head, confused, "we don't even use that kind of ESP here at ARC."

Jim finally lifted his head and stared at his coworker. "We might as well tell them," he said.

Gitte didn't respond.

"If something's wrong, it's going to come out eventually," Jim persisted, leaning awkwardly down over his keyboard.

"Do you really think we need yet another scandal?" Gitte hissed. "Is that it?"

"It's not my fault that the numbers don't match. . . ."

"What's going on?" Jeppe looked from the one engineer to the other.

"After Monday, when the body was found in the silo . . ." Jim began, ignoring his coworker's eye roll. "Kasper has been acting weird. Not just in the way you would expect after something like that, but . . . strange, coming and going as it suited him. He's emptied out his drawers and shredded bunches of papers. He doesn't respond when we speak to him. At first I thought it was just the shock . . ."

Jim shot Jeppe a questioning look, as if to make sure that he really wanted to hear all this.

"You see, measuring CO_2 is a complex process, which is broken up into many different stages, and includes calculating and recording the average readings, which are sent to the plant's database hourly. It would seem unmanageable to all who don't know exactly how to read the numbers. But something's not right. The measurement readings from the monitoring facility are significantly higher than the ones reported to the Danish Energy Authority, and Kasper's the only one who could have altered them."

Gitte looked like she was going to protest, but then seemed to resign herself with a sigh.

"We discovered the discrepancy late yesterday," she said, "and we're not sure what to do about it. Kasper isn't answering his phone, and it seems really drastic to go straight to management."

"What does he gain from reporting wrong numbers?" Jeppe asked, eyeing them skeptically.

The two engineers looked at each other, locked in an unspoken duel over who should respond.

"An embellished CO_2 report saves the plant both money and bad press," Gitte finally replied.

"How does it save the plant money?" Larsen asked.

"When you burn trash, the CO_2 emissions are measured, because they contribute to global warming. With the EU's emissions trading system, CO_2 quotas need to be bought, and they're expensive. Just one year's worth of quotas costs at least twenty million kroner. Are you following me so far?"

"I'm no idiot," Larsen snapped, insulted.

Gitte did not seem convinced.

"The municipality of Copenhagen," she continued, "wants to be CO_2 neutral and demands that we comply with the agreed-upon level of emissions. At the same time, the plant is forced to import waste from the UK to incinerate more and supply more energy, which is how we earn money. So there are conflicting interests. But if you cheat by making the emissions numbers look lower, the plant saves money on CO_2 quotas."

"It can't be that easy to cheat." Jeppe shook his head. "There must be external controls, right?"

"Of course. An outside company collects data and calculates the values at a so-called QAL2-check, which is supposed to detect any major discrepancies. But that kind of check is only done once every three years." Gitte's cheeks had turned red. "The next QAL2 is scheduled for next week, actually. That's why we were looking through the numbers."

Jeppe felt suddenly disgusted by the whole situation. By the fraudulent order and the carbon calculations. By loving a woman who was shutting him out.

"Does Kasper keep a computer here?" he asked. "Can you open it?"

Neither of them answered.

"Let me remind you that we're here in connection with a homicide investigation, and that obstructing or withholding relevant information is a criminal offense." Jeppe looked from the one engineer to the other. "We need to find out what's going on."

Jim got up and walked over to a PC.

"I do have his password," he said. "But under normal circumstances, I would *never* dream of opening up a coworker's computer without their permission."

"You have the police's permission. That should cover it." Jeppe wheeled his chair over next to Jim. "Please open up his email. He may have bought a plane ticket."

Jim found the email program. Jeppe leaned closer to the screen.

"Just go through them slowly," Jeppe instructed. "Thanks."

Jim scrolled through the emails, moving back in time from the present. Meeting notifications and reports slid by their eyes in a soup of inconsequential information.

Gitte cleared her throat.

"Do you think this has something to do with the body in the silo?" she asked uncertainly.

Jeppe didn't respond, his focus entirely on the screen. They had reached Thursday afternoon when a familiar sender's name appeared on the screen.

Henrik Dreyer-Hoff.

"Open that email."

Jim clicked on it nervously. Henrik had sent it on Thursday, April 11, at 4:32 p.m.

He knows about the money and is threatening to blab. I'll take care of it!

That's all it said.

Jeppe pulled out his phone and called Henrik. The call went unanswered. He called Malin instead. She answered with a brusque hello.

"Hi, Malin, it's Jeppe Kørner. I'm actually trying to get ahold of Henrik. Do you know where he is?"

An exasperated sigh.

"I can't reach him, either. He was going to work, but he's not answering his phone. Maybe he's in a meeting."

"Could you ask him to call me right away, when you talk to him?"

"I'm at the hospital, so you'd do better to find him yourself." She hung up.

Jeppe turned around and looked at Larsen.

Kasper Skytte had disappeared, and Henrik Dreyer-Hoff wasn't answering his phone. What the hell was going on?

CHAPTER 30

The tissue paper rustled between Jenny Kaliban's fingers. She wiped her sweaty palms on her pants and continued unpacking. One layer to the side, carefully, then the next. Her fingers were shaking so much that she had to take a break. She lit a cigarette, opened the atelier's window to the backyard, and smoked with the adrenaline throbbing in her throat like an extra heart. It was messed up, doing this on her own. But what the hell was she supposed to do? Until her ship came in, there was no other way to get money.

The smoke burned in her throat and made her eyes water. Jenny let them water. The permanent knot in her stomach was just as much for herself as for Malin. To think that even now, in this situation, they couldn't support each other.

It was Henrik who came between them. The last time she had seen him, two years ago, he had called her a *leech* and said that she wasn't welcome anymore. And Malin hadn't protested. Since then Jenny had seen her sister and the kids only on the sly. She exhaled the smoke. If anybody had backed those two up through thick and thin, it was her. Even when the whole world pointed fingers at their auction con, she had stood by them. And now they had turned on her.

When the going gets tough, you truly discover who your real friends are.

Jenny was still considering whether she should use what she had on Henrik. She had already let him know that his mistakes could benefit her. Not as a threat, just as a warning.

She put out her cigarette and ditched the idea of smoking another. Better to save them for later. There was no one left she could borrow money from. Even with alternative sources of income, she was barely scraping by and would soon be forced to choose whether she could afford to smoke or draw. Unless, that was, her contacts found the right buyers. The material was in her atelier waiting to be sold, and the thought made her chronically short of breath.

But, she reminded herself, *if this works, I can get out of this predicament once and for all.*

The rent for the atelier was expensive, and so were her tools. Every single trip to buy art supplies was a catastrophic hit to her modest budget. When she was around heavy cardstock, markers in little jars, and felt tip pens, she didn't know how to stop. And unlike her artist colleagues, she had always abstained from licking the asses of the board members in the Danish Arts Foundation and had accordingly never even once received any of the grants she routinely applied for every year in January.

Her ambition had never made for a comfortable life. She wasn't interested in predictability and safety.

What is the point of life if not striving to uncover the divine we all carry within? French fries, generic shopping malls, and retirement savings, nothing else.

I'm trying to find God before God finds me.

She smiled at her own profundity and went back to the wooden box. This time she unfolded the tissue paper without hesitating and took out the mask, held it carefully by the wooden pin on the back, and inspected it. She had chosen one of the unknown ones that she knew wouldn't be missed for a while. The face was young and pure, the gender hard to decide; it looked like it belonged to a sleeping teenager. She carefully set the death mask on her workbench and took out her old Olympus. The photo documentation had to be in order, otherwise it wouldn't sell. And then a strong sales blurb, evocative and detailed.

Jenny positioned the mask so that the fine plaster eyelashes could be seen clearly, and started taking pictures.

On November sixth the previous year she had turned fifty, and ever since she had been fighting to keep her faith. Believing that her breakthrough was, if not imminent, then at least still possible was all she had. If she lost that, she might as well lie down and die.

AT TIMES WE lose sight of how those closest to us are doing and only really discover the truth when we observe them in an unfamiliar situation. Across the lunch table at the restaurant in the tower of Christiansborg Palace, amid the massive stone walls and elegant designer furniture, Gregers suddenly looked sick. A used dishcloth among the freshly pressed damask, worn and so incredibly frail.

Esther had invited him out to lunch to cheer him up. It had been intended as a pleasant little outing, but the walk across the cobbled palace courtyard and up the flights of stairs that followed the elevator made it all too clear that he wasn't doing well. He was gasping for breath and complaining of chest and hip pains every ten yards.

Maybe she had been too optimistic. Too excited about her plan to even consider if it was good for Gregers. But now here they were. He had ordered a traditional Danish open-faced sandwich with sliced potatoes and mayo, his beer and aquavit had been poured, and the color was slowly returning to his cheeks. He raised his glass.

"Well, we should have a toast, right?"

Esther clinked her aquavit glass against his and drank.

"Are you feeling better?" she asked.

"What do you mean?" Gregers said. "I'm fine. But I could probably do with a refill on this aquavit once my sandwich comes."

"We'll order another one."

Esther pointed to Thorvaldsen's lion sculptures, which stood
guard over the room.

"Did you know," she asked, "that this used to be a storage room
where the parliament's old statues collected dust? They discovered it
when renovating the roof and decided to make the tower a restaurant. Isn't that lovely? That way everyone can enjoy it."

"Those who can afford it."

Esther sighed. "Have you seen the view?" she asked him. "The
riding grounds, Tivoli, the National Museum . . ."

Gregers glanced at the enormous mullioned window facing the
palace yard but lost interest when the waiter came by and took their
order for more aquavit. Esther made a mental note to make reservations at their local café instead the next time she was taking her
roommate out to eat. She looked back at the lions and remembered
that Thorvaldsens Museum was right next to the palace.

A loud ringtone interrupted her thoughts. She looked around,
but no one responded to the noise.

"Uh, Gregers, is that your phone? You don't usually carry it with
you."

Flustered, he started searching through his pockets. When he
finally sat holding the ringing phone, he had trouble finding the
green button to answer the call.

"Yes? Hello?!" he yelled. "Ah, yes. Hello!"

Gregers listened for a minute, then mumbled a few words and
hung up. He put the phone down and sat with both hands flat on
the table.

"Gregers, is everything all right?"

He looked at her like someone who had just woken up or maybe rather fallen asleep and didn't understand what he was dreaming. The waiter set a fresh glass of aquavit in front of him and he downed it.

"Well, that was that." He set down his glass and blinked, annoyed. "How long does it take to make a sandwich?"

Esther's heart sank.

"Who was that?" she asked.

"That was the doctor. Something called cancer antigens. *CA 72-4*, she said. Mine are so elevated that they want to admit me for some tests right away."

"Right away?" Esther repeated helplessly.

"Yes, well, later this afternoon. I get to pack a bag first."

Esther was about to ask him what it meant but stopped herself. She knew perfectly well what it meant: cancer. In all likelihood the first step on a long journey of suffering and worry. Yet another step along the way toward her own old age and the loneliness that comes when all her loved ones disappear.

She found Gregers's eyes.

Those pale gray eyes told the story of a life lived, of love that had blossomed and faded, friendships, jobs, three children, a divorce. Of little knees with Band-Aids, sack lunches, summer vacations, and late nights out drinking beer after work, of boat trips, failures and misunderstandings, relationship battles, and amputated hearts.

Gregers cleared his throat uncertainly.

"I'm sorry, Esther, but I think I'd like to go home now."

A SEAGULL SOARED past Trekroner's lighthouse and into Copenhagen Harbor like a bright patch of white in the sunshine. Anette tilted her head back and followed its flight.

"That's why I love living out here, the birds, the ocean. Nature becomes a part of you when you're alone with it."

Mads Teigen was standing right behind her, close enough that she could feel the gentle puffs of his breath against the back of her neck. So close that he must be able to see the goose bumps spreading over her arms. Even though she couldn't see him, she could sense his broad frame. Those hands that made her feel so unaccustomedly feminine.

What was she doing here?

Since when did she need to be acknowledged for her appearance? She, who had never given a damn about stereotypical gender roles, and who loved being seen for her courage, toughness, and skill. Was she becoming one of those women who got fake lashes glued on, took selfies at sunset, and cheated on their husbands?

"Come, I want to show you something!"

He took her hand and pulled her toward the red commander's residence. She let him do it. As they walked along the pier, his palm burned against her own. They, too, could be a couple. He caught her eye and smiled. She looked down and tried to regain control of her breathing.

Mads unlocked the building and she automatically wondered why he locked his front door when was he living alone on a deserted island. But then people did come here all the time.

"I don't usually show this to anyone, but I really want *you* to see it. I have the feeling that you'll understand." He exhaled and opened the door to the workshop, stepped aside, and gestured for her to enter.

Anette crossed the threshold into the workshop. It had a workbench in the middle and shelves lining the walls. He followed her in, closed the door, and locked it. Stayed by the door, watching her.

She intuitively sensed that he wanted her to look around, look at the birds. So she stepped over to one of the shelves and inspected the outstretched wings and the swelling feathery splendor of the specimens displayed. She didn't recognize them as anything other than big or small birds, felt unsure of how to react and uncomfortable with their piercing, dead eyes following her around the room.

"Wow! Did you . . . do all of these?"

"Every single one. All of them within the last year."

She nodded appreciatively.

"You've been busy. Is stuffing them difficult?"

Anette could see disappointment in his eyes and realized that she wasn't reacting the way he had hoped. She hesitantly moved closer to a black bird with a white chest and long tail feathers. It had silvery blue contrast feathers on its wings and a little black beak.

"We have these in our yard. Svend always scares them away. . . ."

He looked down at the floor as if she had slapped him and she realized she had probably never mentioned Svend's name to him before. Obviously doing so was a mistake. She reached for the bird and accidentally knocked it off the shelf.

"Oh no, I'm sorry! Nothing happened, I think."

She gathered up the bird and put it back on the shelf. When she turned around, he was standing right behind her.

"Fuck!" She laughed nervously. "Okay, I didn't see you there."

He watched her intently. A deep wrinkle divided his brows, and the look in his eyes was determined. Her mouth went dry. She tried to swallow but couldn't.

Mads grabbed her hand. This time he held it so tightly that there was no doubt of his physical advantage.

CHAPTER 31

Sara Saidani turned the heat down under the pot on the burner and set the egg timer, then put a rye bread out on the kitchen counter and lined up the lunch plates. Jeppe hadn't tried to get in touch with her since Tuesday night, but that was just as well. Her focus needed to be on getting Amina back on her feet and back to school. The episode had rattled her daughter in an unexpected way, unraveling insecurities Amina normally kept hidden. Now that she finally needed her mother again, Sara wanted to be there for her. At all costs.

She went into the living room, opened her computer, and tapped in ninthcircle.com. In all honesty she had neither the time nor the energy for it, but she had promised Esther she would try. The home page with the numerous small pictures came up on her screen, and she leaned in to study them more closely. One looked more like a child, not a doll, a child without clothes on. She browsed on and saw yet another picture of a naked body. This time the little figure was holding a grown-up's hand. You could see a tattooed arm reaching into the picture. Sara's throat tightened. Something was seriously wrong here.

The page didn't offer any contact information if she wasn't logged in. That in itself was unusual if not downright suspicious. Could she hack the log-in? Bulletproof Security plug-ins were notoriously difficult, and it might be a little over the top to do a brute-force attack on the users' encrypted passwords. Maybe she would luck out and find that the server hosting the home page hadn't been updated in a while and therefore would be vulnerable to unauthorized access attempts.

Sara decided to go with a social-engineering attack, and clicked through to the name of the page's host and opened a chat with their customer service, where she pretended to be the page owner. She provided one of her anonymous Gmail accounts and claimed she had been having problems with 500 internal server error messages and the .htaccess file. An automated message informed her that she would receive a response within two minutes.

She leaned back in her uncomfortable dining room chair and looked over at her eldest daughter. Amina was reading the copy of *Through the Looking-Glass* that Jeppe's mother had insisted on loaning them. She was growing up way too fast, and Sara watched her with a double ache in her heart: one for the passage of time, and the other for the oh-so-difficult love.

A chime from her computer drew her attention back to the screen. She read the response from *Bill,* who probably wrote her from a call center somewhere in Pakistan and was likely also someone other than who he pretended to be. Even his first response told her that she knew more than he did. After four messages back and forth she got him to reset the password so she could create a new one.

She was in.

The landing page had a black background and was decorated with a laughing mask that sat propped up against a lit candelabra. Here she found a few concrete facts: The forum had just over ten thousand users who all used pseudonyms like *PiedPiper* and *Jupiterseagle*. The users were active on the page, both posting things and commenting. There was buying and selling, discussions about pictures and specific artifacts like masks and stuffed birds. At first glance it looked like an art forum with a Gothic, almost macabre style.

Now that she was logged in, the images could be enlarged without difficulty. She hesitated for a moment with her finger over the trackpad, then opened one, a white mask. Under the picture it read FOR SALE, followed by a longer text about the item and a link. Harmless enough.

The next picture was anything but harmless. What Esther had thought was a doll turned out to be a child of about seven or eight lying on a red velour carpet. A little girl with her face palely made up and rouge on her cheeks. She was naked. Several images of the same sort followed.

Esther de Laurenti had inadvertently stumbled onto a pedophile ring.

Sara took a deep breath. She had encountered this kind of thing before but had not yet grown immune to the human perversion it represented. And she knew how hard it was to unravel these networks. She had to inform her colleagues in NC3, the National Cyber Crime Centre, immediately.

All of a sudden she wished Amina were far away, safely distanced from the evil the computer was channeling into the living room. Sara clicked through the archive and saw more of the same, artifacts and naked children. One picture made her pause. She zoomed in. Yet another young face, maybe age eight or nine. A layer of white powder accentuated the black hair and resulted in a beautiful Snow White effect.

Sara zoomed in even more and felt a chill run down her spine, an omen of apprehension. The child was several years younger than now, but there was no doubt. She was looking at Oscar Dreyer-Hoff.

*   *   *

AT QUARTER PAST two in the afternoon, a young girl turned up at the police station inside Copenhagen Central Station asking to speak to Sara Saidani from the Violent Crimes Department. When it turned out that Saidani was home with a sick child, she accepted seeing Jeppe Kørner instead, who in turn promised he would be there within the half hour. The girl seemed calm and composed, aside from the detail that she was wearing no shoes. She was shown a soft chair in the waiting room and given a soda, which she let sit, and a sandwich, from which she removed the ham and then ate in small bites.

That's how Jeppe found her when he hurried through the door twenty minutes later.

"Iben?"

She nodded distantly.

"I'm Jeppe Kørner. My partner and I were at you and your dad's place a few days ago, on Saturday."

"I'm not senile," Iben said, setting what was left of the sandwich down on the table. "I remember you. You were looking for Oscar."

He sat down on the only other chair in the waiting room.

"Now we're looking for your dad."

She folded her arms protectively across her chest, but her T-shirt didn't cover the red marks and bruises on her skinny upper arms.

"How can we reach your mother?" Jeppe asked. "I understand she lives in Spain? We want to ask her to come to Denmark, you shouldn't be alone right now."

"Forget about it!" she said, shaking her head. "My mom has a new family. She won't come. I just need a ride and some money for a locksmith, then I can go home."

"I can arrange that, but since you're only fifteen, you can't be home alone. I'll ask one of the officers here at the station to help you when we're done talking. Do you know where your dad is?"

The corners of her mouth curled up into a small, unexpected smile, which was immediately replaced with distress.

"On his way down through Europe with a bottle of booze in the passenger's seat."

"Without you?"

"I didn't want to go." She gathered the crumbs from the sandwich and left them in a little pile. "I ran when we stopped for gas and my dad went inside to use the bathroom, I didn't even have time to put my shoes on. I got a ride, slept in the handicap accessible stall in a café in Vordingborg and then hitchhiked back to Høje-Taastrup and caught the train from there back to Copenhagen."

There was no point in lecturing her about the hazards of hitchhiking alone, even though Jeppe shuddered at the thought.

"Ironic, isn't it? My dad is on his way to Switzerland to withdraw money. My dad, who taught me to turn down the heat and attend climate marches, is on his way to Zürich to empty out his tax-shelter accounts." She shook her head. "*My dad* cheated on the CO_2 numbers!"

Jeppe took out his notebook and wrote Kasper's name on the top of a page.

"Do you know if he did it on his own?"

"Henrik was in on it and probably a few others who want to pollute without paying. The CEO, I think." She flung up her hands. "Oscar was the one who discovered it. He found his dad's notes, figured it out, and called me. They didn't really do very much to try to cover their tracks."

"Did you and Oscar tell your fathers what you had discovered?"

She reached for the soda, then seemed to realize that idealistic teenagers weren't supposed to drink soda, and pulled her hand back again.

"Oscar did. He told his father that we were going to report them to the police if they didn't own up to it."

"Is that why Oscar ran away?"

She looked at him as if the answer was obvious.

"He's afraid of his dad."

Somewhere on the back of Jeppe's head, a blood vessel beat rhythmically, threatening to become a throbbing loop of unwanted background music.

"Iben, was your dad home last Friday night?"

"Yeah, we both were. I couldn't chance it and sneak out since I had promised Oscar we would pretend he was at my place."

"So you covered for him?" Jeppe looked up from his notepad. "Where was he going?"

"He didn't say. It wasn't any of my business, either. Oscar and I have each other's backs, no matter what."

"And you're sure your dad didn't go anywhere that night?"

"Positive! I was in my room, and he was in the living room in front of his computer. He was still up when I went to bed at about one thirty in the morning."

Jeppe drew a line through Kasper's name in his notebook.

"Do you know if Oscar told Malthe Sæther about the scam?"

"Why would he do that?" she asked, looking confused. "We talked about going to the police, but why would we talk to our teacher about it? What would be the point of that?"

Jeppe didn't have an answer. Iben didn't seem like the type who needed a grown-up's help to get things done.

"Is it true," she asked, "that Lis got hit by a train at Nørreport Station? Everyone says she jumped in front of it."

"No one really knows exactly what happened. But, yes, she was hit by a train on Tuesday afternoon."

"Fuck!" Iben put her hands over her face. When she removed them again, her eyes were glossy and red around the edges. "Lis is my favorite teacher. She's tough. A real old-school feminist who has never compromised her ideals. You know, not like all those people who go soft when they get older. Fuck."

"I'm sorry."

"So am I," she said, shaking her head.

Jeppe hesitated.

"Iben, I have to ask you about something else, something . . . unpleasant."

Iben raised her eyebrows.

"An unknown component in an investigation can throw a wrench into our ability to solve the crime. But if it's not relevant to the case, I promise you that what you tell me will stay with me." Jeppe could see that she knew what he was going to ask. "Victor. What happened?"

She blinked uneasily and bit her lip.

"Vic and I were together at the party. In one of the bathroom stalls. One of the other seniors filmed us. He was going to send it to the whole school so everyone could see how good I was at . . ."

Jeppe looked down.

"Victor made him stop before he managed to spread the video too widely." Iben wiped her cheek quickly with her index finger. "That's it. But the video is still out there. It'll be around forever."

Jeppe looked down at the crossed-out name in his notebook and the empty space underneath it. The pulse in his head grew louder; he closed his eyes and tried to think. Iben asked him something, but her voice was drowned out by the pulse and the sound of puzzle pieces that were finally falling into place.

THE RURAL ROAD drifted in and out of focus, its turns coming without warning, unpredictable and unreliable, to put it mildly. Kasper Skytte gripped the steering wheel harder and forced his eyes open.

He had only made it to Hannover the day before, had gotten so tired that he had been forced to scrap his plan to drive through the night and slept at a cheap motel by the highway instead. More than anything it was the emotional strain that drained him—Iben, the fear of being caught, worrying about what Henrik might do. His mind was racing, and that robbed him of the ability to do the most basic things. Even driving a car became an insurmountable challenge.

This morning he had forced himself to lie in the motel bed until nine o'clock, even though he had barely slept a wink. He was dead tired. A shower in the chilly shower stall and a visit to the motel's sad breakfast buffet didn't make it better. The panic returned, threatening to boil over, and keeping it in check took all his energy. His eyes kept slipping shut. He didn't get farther than Heidelberg before going one hundred miles per hour became downright irresponsible, and he had to exit the highway.

At a gas station he bought two chocolate bars and a bottle of Schinkenhäger schnapps in a dusty gift box. That helped a little, especially the schnapps. He got back into the driver's seat and washed bites of chocolate down with big gulps of alcohol that cleared his throat and made his forehead tingle. Cars pulled in and out of the parking spaces around him in a harmonic stream, regular like a unison breath. A breath he was no longer part of. The tears came unexpectedly, a deep spasm from his diaphragm that made his shoulders shake uncontrollably.

Iben had run away. His own daughter was scared to be with him. The thought was unbearable.

Kasper wiped his nose on his sleeve and drank from the bottle. There was nothing to do but take it one hour at a time and balance step-by-step toward his uncertain future. But he'd probably better stick to back roads from now on.

He started the car and continued south, past Bruchsal and Bretten, through Pforzheim and farther south on the winding country roads. Along green fields and drab industrial areas, over rivers and past stucco churches with tall spires and patches of luminous beech

forest. Every five miles he took a swig from the bottle. By the time
he reached the Swiss border, he was totally calm. He turned on his
radio and let generic pop music fill the car.

He would get the money and fly to South Africa as planned,
find a nice hotel in Cape Town, and persuade Iben to come join him.
Once she had calmed down, she would come to her senses. He was
sure of it.

He didn't see the bird until it was too late.

There was a loud bang. The windshield shattered.

Kasper slammed on the brakes and slid across the roadway,
blinded and in shock. He screamed as the car jerked, slamming him
into the steering wheel.

He was breathing hard. There was blood on the shattered windshield, and the radio was still blaring music at him, the noise unbearable. He turned it off, then reached up to touch his face, feeling with
his fingers if it was intact. It left his hands bloody. They were shaking
so hard it took forever to unbuckle his seat belt and get out of the car.

The roadway was deserted. He straightened up, feeling the shock
seep into the ground beneath him until his knees gave way. Skid
marks painted black streaks across the asphalt to the tree that had
ultimately stopped the car. Steam was hissing from the hood, but
apart from that it was quiet among the trees.

The bird lay on the road, looking like a boneless pillow of feathers and guts. Kasper walked over and squatted down. There was a
worm caught in its yellow beak, still writhing and trying to escape.
The bird itself was done trying to escape.

He watched the worm's agony. On the asphalt below his face a
little pool of blood and tears slowly formed.

CHAPTER 32

When Jeppe walked into the Nordhjem auction house a woman wearing an elegant linen suit and chunky glasses looked up from the meeting she was conducting on the pink sofa set.

"I'm sorry, are you hear to pick up the packages? They're waiting down in the courtyard. . . ." She nodded apologetically to the others attending the meeting and got up to speak to him.

Jeppe showed her his laminated ID badge.

"I need to speak with Henrik Dreyer-Hoff."

"Unfortunately he's not in." When Jeppe continued to stand there, she continued. "Do you have an appointment?"

"No."

She was about to protest, but something about the look in his eye seemed to convince her otherwise.

"Wait here!"

She left Jeppe on the herringbone-patterned parquet flooring to simultaneously admire the crystal chandelier and ignore the curious looks from the people on the sofas while she conferred with her boss.

After a long minute she returned and pointed the way to Henrik's office. She didn't look happy.

Neither did Henrik.

When Jeppe walked in, he was closing the door to an adjoining office, looking peevishly at Jeppe as if he was interrupting him in the middle of something important. He locked the door to the other room and took a seat behind a black lacquered desk, his eyes narrow with disapproval.

"Haven't we been through enough? This last week has been hell, our son is still in the hospital. When can we finally have some peace?"

Jeppe pulled out an upholstered velour chair and sat down.

"I'll try to make it snappy."

A cell phone lit up on the lacquered desktop with Malin's name on the screen. Henrik glanced briefly at Jeppe and then answered it.

"Hi, honey . . . No, I haven't heard from her." He spun his chair to face the other direction and lowered his voice. "She probably went for a bike ride after school, you know how she is. Don't assume the worst, honey. The police are here. I have to run." He hung up.

"What's wrong?"

"Essie's late," Henrik said, shaking his head. "My wife must have forgotten a playdate in all the confusion. It's nothing."

"Does Essie have her own cell phone?"

"No, we think she's still too young." Henrik picked up a pen from the desk and jammed it down into the heel of one ankle boot, scratching. "Your question?"

"Where were you on Friday night?"

Henrik groaned.

"I was home with my family, we've told you this a thousand times. I know you're just doing your job and that you're investigating a tragic death, but honestly I have other things to think about right now. And that poor teacher's death doesn't have anything to do with my son or my business."

"You see, that's where we disagree," Jeppe said. "Can I tell you what I think?"

Henrik waved his hand impatiently.

"Kasper Skytte's colleagues are preparing a police report as we speak," Jeppe said, and leaned on the desk, decreasing the distance between them. "It probably won't be long before you hear from the police department."

Henrik met his eyes unflinchingly.

"Late Thursday afternoon you sent Kasper an email saying that someone you referred to as *he* was going to blab. You wrote that you would *take care of it*."

Henrik got up and walked over to a low brass table with a bowl full of fruit on it.

"Apple?" he offered.

Jeppe declined with a shake of his head. Henrik took a red apple and polished it on his sleeve.

"The question is, who was going to blab?"

Henrik took a bite and chewed noisily.

"Was it Malthe Sæther?" Jeppe persisted. "Did you call and arrange to meet him on Friday night?"

The cough was so violent that small pieces of apple flew over the desk. Henrik wiped his mouth, chewed, and coughed again. This time the cough ended in laughter.

"Ah, so that's the theory, is it?! Look, I haven't murdered anyone. And why in the world would a high school teacher care what was going on with my business? That's just ridiculous."

"Maybe he felt the same natural indignation as your children did over your playing fast and loose with the environment. Or maybe he was blackmailing you."

The half-eaten apple glistened in Henrik's hand. He looked at it and then threw it in the trash.

"I'm not even going to comment on that. But since you've been reading my private correspondence, I suppose I'll have to clarify one thing. Even if it disgusts me." He rubbed his temples. "Kasper has always had a bit of a problem. He plays poker online. It has cost him dearly, his marriage among other things. And he has accrued a sizable gambling debt, two hundred and fifty thousand kroner, to be precise. He came to me a while ago to ask for help."

"So what did you do?"

"I loaned him money." Henrik shrugged, as if that were the most natural thing in the world. "But Oscar found out about it and was . . . indignant. He wanted to tell Iben. I promised Kasper I would talk him down. But my son wasn't home Friday night, and then the next day he was missing, and we had other things to think about."

"And Malthe Sæther?" Jeppe asked.

Henrik looked him right in the eye.

"I've never talked to that young man other than at parent-teacher meetings. I didn't have anything against him, and I'm sorry that he's dead. I can assure you that neither I nor my sons were behind his murder."

Jeppe watched the broad-shouldered man, who towered behind his lacquered antique desk, and knew that he wasn't going to get any further without concrete evidence. He couldn't do a darned thing, and he could tell that Henrik knew it, too.

"Does your office have video surveillance?" Jeppe asked, standing up. "If so, we'd like to review the footage from Friday night."

"I'll check with our security service," Henrik said with an exasperated sigh. "Was there anything else?"

Jeppe stood looking at Henrik, at those burly features and dark eyes, regarding him frankly.

"That's all. Thanks."

He left the office and nodded to the woman in the linen suit, who was now standing under the chandelier all by herself. On his way to the door, Jeppe's attention was caught by the drawing over the console table, the portrait of Oscar.

"Ah, an amazing piece of art, isn't it?" the woman said. "You can really feel the love in it."

Jeppe nodded. The averted gaze, the light on the dark surfaces, it really was a beautiful drawing.

"Malin's sister, Jenny, drew it. They're a pair of talented sisters, you've got to admit."

A thought formed in Jeppe's mind, a silent bubble. Without quite understanding why, he got the feeling that he shouldn't be leaving this office.

You can really feel the love.

"THERE'S SOMETHING YOU should know about me."

Mads fumbled and then pulled a picture out of his back pocket with his free hand. The other one was still holding Anette in an iron grip. The picture was of a child, round-cheeked and smiling, with little braids and big eyes.

"This isn't easy for me. I've never talked to anyone about it before . . ."

"Who is she?" Anette let her free hand stretch out to the left, until her fingertips reached a heavy swan display.

"Olga, her name was Olga. She was only four."

She locked her hand around the display. Her left arm wasn't as strong as her right but strong enough.

"She died 268 days ago today. We buried her ashes under an apple tree on my parents' farm." Mads let go of Anette and set down the picture, then covered his eyes with both hands. "My daughter, Olga Marie Teigen. She died almost a year ago. I often wish I had died with her."

"What happened?"

He removed his hand but didn't look at her.

"Melanoma, it happened so fast. Some say we were lucky that way."

Anette let go of the swan display and rubbed her palm against her pants. Her heart was still racing, and she felt dizzy.

"We didn't discover it in time. We thought it was a fungal infection and waited too long to take her to the doctor. . . . By the time Olga was finally admitted to National Hospital, things started moving at the speed of light. She was diagnosed after only a few days of testing and then started getting high-dose chemotherapy right away. But it was too late. Melanoma is rare in children, so we never thought. . . . Maybe if we had caught it earlier, if we had done something right away . . ."

Anette put a hand on his shoulder.

"I'm so sorry for your loss."

What else was there to say? She knew the fear of losing one's child. It dwells in every parent. And Mads was living it.

He lifted his eyes and looked at her.

"I'm telling you, because . . . because I like you, Anette. And I have the sense that you like me, too." He smiled. "But if we're going to be anything to each other, then you need to know about Olga. Even if it's almost impossible for me to talk about her."

Anette beheld the man who this last week had sent her galivanting through the entire spectrum of emotions and made her doubt her marriage. She saw an attractive man, masculine and warm, down-to-earth and sweet. She saw a man in grief.

And there was not even a shadow of attraction left. Whatever had made her fantasize about him in the shower had now been replaced by an overwhelming flood of compassion, nothing else.

"Mads, I wish I could comfort you and ease your pain, but my guess is that no one can. Not yet, anyway."

He nodded, put his hand on hers, and squeezed.

"Let me take you back to the mainland."

"Thank you, you'd better. I have a case to solve."

The girl picks up the little posable wooden mannequin and looks at it, moves its small head around on its axis as she has done so often, then puts it back in its place on the shelf and sits down in the armchair. She's been given a soda, which she drinks in big gulps and gets the hiccups. She hasn't had anything to eat since that morning and is feeling dizzy. The soda doesn't help.

Their talk isn't going as she had hoped.

It begins well, even though she's nervous. She relaxes quickly and says what she knows without being scared. They love each other after all. She has always been told that love is stronger than everything else. Family first. But now the mood seems ruined. She has done something wrong.

The girl feels stupid and has trouble remembering how she had hoped it would go.

She is scared. She wants to get up and run away, but she isn't feeling well. Like that time they took the ferry to Bornholm and it was rocking so bad that everyone got seasick. She has trouble resting her head against the sides of the wingback chair and slides down the seat until she is lying on the floor.

The room is spinning.

A figure comes toward her, its contours blurred by the bright light. She blinks. Then she closes her eyes.

CHAPTER 33

Jeppe was on his way down the stairs from the Nordhjem office when Sara called. The sound of her voice was so familiar that he momentarily forgot their new reality. Her cool tone reminded him that right now they were no more than colleagues.

"I found something, pictures of Oscar on the home page of something that looks like a pedophile ring."

"Pedophilia?" Jeppe stopped with his hand on the door handle.

"I've informed PC and currently I'm trying to figure out who made the page. But as you know, this kind of thing is complex. It never takes long before they start dismantling their sites, so we're working fast. I'll send you screen dumps after I hang up."

Jeppe went out into the street and let the door fall shut behind him. He was at a loss for words. The combination of Sara's frosty tone and the talk of pedophilia zeroed out his vocabulary.

"Okay?"

"Okay."

She inhaled as if she were about to say something but didn't.

"Sara?"

"The pictures are on their way. Talk to you later!"

She hung up. Jeppe stood for a second in the echoes of their conversation. Politely, with no audible undertones, their love had been put on pause.

He crossed the street to Østre Anlæg. Twilight had fallen over the park, and the trees' contours melted together into odd shapes, trolls' arms and bottomless pits. A sweet, melancholy scent of evening blooms hung in the air.

His phone vibrated. Jeppe opened the texts from Sara, ten screenshots in all, with the Ninth Circle logo in the top left corner. The circle for traitors in Dante's hell.

The pictures were hard to look at. Stagings of naked children with powdered white cheeks and red lips left no doubt about their underlying intent. They were explicitly sexual, but at the same time had a clear style, dark, almost Gothic, which made them even more perverse. The pictures of Oscar had been taken in front of a white photo studio background and atop a featureless black carpet. Naked, he'd been photographed sitting, standing, lying down, posing childishly as if someone had instructed him to look extra innocent. The makeup reinforced his childish features. He looked almost like a doll.

Naked photos of Oscar, Malthe murdered, and Henrik deeply involved in fraud. And Essie hadn't come home from school yet.

Jeppe called Malin Dreyer-Hoff, but the phone just kept ringing in his ear. He hung up and immediately made another call. Right now there was only one person in the world he needed.

She picked up right away.

"What the hell, Kørner? Are you still at work? Isn't there some cooking show on TV you need to watch from your couch?"

"Hey, Werner. Where are you?"

At the sound of his tone she grew instantly serious.

"On my way home."

"Can you come meet me in front of the American embassy? I need to discuss something important with you."

She didn't hesitate for a second, didn't even ask any further details.

"I'm close by, I'll be there in ten minutes."

Jeppe took out a cigarette and lit it without taking his eyes off his phone. As the old proverb put it, *you need to have fire in your mouth when you're dealing with the devil.* Or maybe that was just something his father had come up with to justify his daily pack of Lucky Strikes.

He exhaled smoke at the park's blue tree trunks and scrolled through the pictures, until he came to one of Oscar, where he was sitting on a red velour armchair, looking into the camera with an expression that was hard to interpret. Bewilderment? Fear?

Jeppe recognized that chair. He had sat in it himself.

IT WAS ON nights like this that the red wine was imperative. A day full of worry should at least end softly in a warm, slightly time-lapsed buzz. *It's not that I want to drink, but I need to,* Esther sneered at herself and poured yet another glass. Maybe she was just too old to give up her bad habits. Oh, that taste of iron and sharpness in her throat!

If God didn't want people to drink, she should make life a little less difficult, Esther thought, and sat down at her desk. Here in her little cocoon of soft light, Chopin, and tipsiness, she could delude herself for brief moments at a time that the world was friendly and good. Still, she opened her computer with a certain wariness. The screen had a way of reminding her of life's many shadow sides.

The curser blinked blankly on the document that would hopefully someday become a book. Esther's optimism began fading. The road before her suddenly seemed endless, the thought that someone might take an interest in her words, absurd. Her fingers moved blindly over the keys, but found no reason to push down.

Nothing came to mind. An unforeseen fear of the void haunted her from the edges of her consciousness. The fear of having nothing at heart.

Sara Saidani hadn't contacted her, so maybe she hadn't gotten anywhere on securing rights for the picture of the doll. Esther couldn't bring herself to remind her yet. After all, Sara had other things to do besides helping an old woman with author ambitions. She opened the ninthcircle.com home page to look at the picture of the doll again. Maybe it wasn't even suitable as a cover image.

To her surprise the home page opened without asking for a password, and this time the pictures were crystal clear and shown at full size. Someone must have unblocked the site. Maybe Sara had succeeded after all.

A new picture appeared on the screen—apparently some sort of slideshow launched automatically—a white mask that looked like the ones she had seen at Thorvaldsens Museum. The text underneath the picture read FOR SALE. Well, then it certainly couldn't be a museum artifact. She must have been mistaken. The picture faded as the next one appeared. This time it was a carved wooden relief of a funeral procession, also for sale. The mourners included crying children and a skeleton. The next picture was her doll.

Esther let out a scream and stood up. What was this? Had Sara seen these naked children?

She walked over to the window, confused and in shock. A thought appeared in the back of her mind and started floating around just on the perimeter of her consciousness. Down by the lake, in front of her building, streetlights were turning the air blue, ducks quacked, and a laughing couple biked by, holding hands. Nearby, at National Hospital, Gregers lay in bed fasting before tomorrow's contrast exam.

Beauty and pain all in the same frame.

Where had she seen that wooden relief before?

Esther did a breathing exercise half-heartedly and tried to think. Then out of the blue it popped into her head, that sales ad with the picture of the carved funeral procession.

She walked back over to her computer and opened the Nordhjem home page. The auction had ended, but the ad was still there. Identical to the one from ninthcircle.com. The same item was for sale both at a fancy auction house and on a perverted online forum.

Surely the coincidence indicated something important, something wrong. A combination like this of art and perversion always has victims.

She typed two names into the search field. A picture appeared at the top of the page, a photograph from a 1990 exhibit at Galerie Asbæk. Jenny Kaliban, young and beautiful, stood side by side with Henrik, both in relaxed jeans and with big smiles. They weren't touching each other in the picture and yet Esther could see a palpable connection between them. Had Malin Dreyer-Hoff's husband originally been interested in her sister?

Esther's head swam from wine and confusing thoughts. Stolen works of art for sale online with the help of an established auction house? Henrik and Jenny working together to steal and sell stolen property?

The literature professor who had been Esther's mentor had always told her students that art is boundless and must never be hindered by sentimental considerations. We wouldn't have the Sistine Chapel if it weren't for the notoriously evil Medici family. Giza's pyramids would never have been built if it weren't for the suffering of hundreds of thousands of men.

She looked down at her own soft, uncalloused hands. They had never hurt anyone. But then, had they ever created anything lasting?

Esther leaned her head back and emptied her wineglass. Then she opened her email and wrote to Jeppe Kørner.

* * *

ANETTE MET JEPPE on Dag Hammarskjölds Allé in front of the American embassy, winded and out of breath, her hair windblown and disheveled.

"What's up?" she called out to him, causing the guards to turn around and look.

"It's good to see you!" Jeppe held out his phone and showed her the picture of Oscar. "Saidani found pictures of Oscar on a pedophilia site. I know where they were taken."

"Oh, God damn it!" Her face twisted in disgust. "Do you think they have something to do with Malthe's death?"

"They have everything to do with Malthe's death. And with Lis's, by the way."

Anette bent over, bracing herself on her knees while she caught her breath.

"Hey, are you okay?" Jeppe asked.

She stood back up and looked like she was debating how much she wanted to share with him. For a second she looked . . . meek, his hard-boiled partner, sensitive and wide-eyed in the darkness. But just as he thought she was going to fill him in, she clenched her hand into a fist and punched him, hard, on the upper arm.

"All good. Just a little tired. Where are we going?"

"It's just down the road from here."

"You want us to go there now? Unannounced?" she protested.

Jeppe started walking.

"Essie didn't come home from school today. Her parents don't know where she is. I'm concerned."

"Do you have your service weapon with you?" Anette asked, following him.

He pulled his jacket aside and revealed his Heckler & Koch.

"Don't you?" he asked.

She made a noncommittal sound, which Jeppe assumed meant no. He hesitated, then shook his head at her. She still hadn't told him where she'd been all day, but that was going to have to wait.

"It's that way." He pointed.

They walked side by side without speaking through the spring evening. With each step, the tension mounted like a bow being readied to shoot. A bow, that is, that cannot see its target in the dark.

A few minutes later they arrived at their destination.

"We'll ring the bell and ask if we can take a look around," Jeppe said, and pushed the doorbell. No answer. He pounded hard on the door and heard the sound echoing through the stairwell. They waited. Then he took hold of the door handle and shook it. The door yielded slightly but didn't open. He looked at Anette, who nodded faintly. Two steps back and one well-placed kick, and it flew open, revealing a dark stairwell.

They went in and tentatively headed up the stairs, faint music trickling down to greet them. Jeppe pulled his gun out of its holster as he climbed, with Anette right on his heels. On the first-floor landing the door was ajar, revealing bright light and lazy piano notes. Jeppe stayed beside the door and knocked with his arm outstretched.

No reaction.

He knocked again and waited. Finally he pushed the door and watched as it slid open with a prolonged creak, leaned in, and peered over the threshold.

"No one's here," he whispered over his shoulder, raising the gun in front of him. Cautiously he walked in.

The music came from an old tape recorder in one corner. Discordant and dark, it sounded like Tom Waits. A white blanket hung from the top of a shelf, lit so brightly by two floor lamps that it was blinding. There was black Molton fabric on the floor below, bunched up in a heap. The red armchair in which Oscar had been immortalized sat on the other side of the room in front of a camera.

"What's that?" Anette's whisper sounded shrill. She kneeled by the camera. "Shit! Look at this!"

Jeppe kneeled down next to her and saw a spot on the floor. Four inches in diameter, an almost perfect circle of fresh blood. He put his hand to his ear. A familiar ringing sound started drilling into his cerebral cortex.

They were too late.

"Are there other exits beside the one we came in?" Anette grabbed his shoulder.

"I don't know."

They got up and slowly made their way through the room. The blinding lights made it hard for them to get their bearings. Their bodies cast long shadows, and a coat rack in the corner took on a human shape.

"Kørner, look here!"

Anette stood bent over an open drawer. Jeppe came closer and looked over her shoulder. In the drawer a photo printed on letter-size paper was visible.

The picture was of a young man, naked, his head resting at an odd angle against the chair back. His face was pale and his hair slicked back, as if it were wet. He almost looked dead.

Jeppe heard a faint whimper amid the hoarse vocals of the music. He straightened up and looked back.

That's when he saw the feet. They were sticking out of the black fabric on the floor. Sneakers. He grabbed Anette's arm and pointed.

Warily Jeppe pulled the Molton aside. Underneath it Jenny Kaliban lay moaning softly, the left side of her face covered in blood.

CHAPTER 34

Oscar Dreyer-Hoff lay in his hospital bed looking at the ceiling. Over the course of the day there had been a steady stream of family members, doctors, and nurses flowing through his room with blood pressure cuffs and cold fingertips. His body was healing; however, it no longer belonged to him. His thoughts were still his own. But only at night. As long as he was surrounded by people, he had to make sure that he didn't seem too lucid and didn't overspeak. Otherwise they would really start asking questions and demanding answers.

His mother had said good night and gone home a long time ago. He didn't miss her. One didn't have to be particularly perceptive to understand that her cloying attentiveness was an attempt to make up for a guilty conscience. She finally realized that she had failed him. But what was he supposed to do with her shame? He had his hands full dealing with his own.

That shame had become an integral part of him, an independent force circulating like the blood through his veins. He had been on the verge of telling Iben several times, but the thought of how it would forever change her view of him had stopped him every time.

He could no longer recall exactly when and how it had started. He had been lured with extra pocket money and extra attention, that much he remembered, had been told that he was charming and unique. He couldn't have been more than seven or eight years old and full of admiration and respect. Maybe there had even been a little touch of childish infatuation. When they were alone together, there was room for ideas, grown-up music, real conversation, and as many sodas as he could drink. Sometimes he got praise and money, but that wasn't the most important part. The most important part was the way he felt when they were together. The feeling of being talented, of being somebody, of meaning something.

He felt seen.

It wasn't until he got older that it started to feel wrong. Of course, he had always suspected it, but it wasn't until he fell in love with Iben that he understood the pictures were a problem. He had asked to have them deleted, but that had only resulted in threats of having them shown to the school, to the whole world, so everyone could see his double standards. He was told that he would ruin his family if he didn't keep their secret and he knew that was true.

Over time he started hating himself.

Malthe had seen that something was wrong. He was the only adult who he had understood, had looked at Oscar's drawings, and asked how things were going at home. It had come as a shock when Malthe called him into the spare classroom and asked him straight out. Oscar had been paralyzed with fear. But the unaccustomed attention had somehow lanced the boil, and before he had time for second thoughts, Oscar shared his secret.

Malthe was horrified.

I can't pretend I don't know about that kind of atrocity, Oscar. I won't! You're being abused. It must be reported to the police.

At first Oscar had felt relieved. But as the days passed, he regretted his weakness and wished he could take back the confession. It was bad enough that his little sister had once overheard a conversation and guessed what it meant. Her he could control. But not Malthe. And there was a lot to lose. The family would be split in two if his mother found out. His regret turned to despair, but Malthe was adamant.

That was when Oscar reached the end of his rope.

"HER PULSE IS stable, and the wound has stopped bleeding. I think she's okay." Jeppe took his hand off Jenny Kaliban's throat. "Will you call for the ambulance and backup?"

Anette found her phone and walked over to the tape recorder to turn off the music. Jeppe got up and turned around slowly, letting his eyes linger on the canvases and cans of paint, jars of brushes, and stacks of books. Malin Dreyer-Hoff's sister had stuff piled on every horizontal surface in her atelier. He could hear Anette barking commands into her phone and tried to block out her voice.

"Essie," he called out, "we're from the police. I'm Jeppe and that's Anette. Do you remember us? You can come out now. It's safe." He closed his eyes, knew instinctively that Oscar's little sister was here. "You haven't done anything wrong, do you hear me? Nothing is going to happen to you," he tried, and waited.

The whimper was faint, like a newborn kitten's, and it came from the bookshelf behind the white blanket. Jeppe undid the blanket and took it down. Oscar's little sister was hiding on the bottom shelf, her arms wrapped around her knees.

He squatted down and held out his hand. Essie hesitantly took it and let him help her out. She was shaking.

"Werner, bring us a blanket, will you?"

"Help is on the way," Anette said, hurrying over to wrap the black cloth around the girl's shoulders. "We're calling your parents, too."

Jeppe could tell from the tension in her voice that she was as angry as he was.

"Essie, are you okay?" he asked.

"I told my aunt she had to tell the police what she had done, for Oscar's sake. I explained to her that you guys thought *he* had done it, and that he might go to jail." She pulled the blanket around her more tightly. "She agreed and said that she had already been thinking the same thing. We were going to figure it out together. Then she asked me if I wanted a soda."

Essie's eyes looked over at the figure on the floor.

"Then what happened?" Jeppe asked gently.

"I felt so sleepy. When I woke up, Aunt Jenny was standing over me, and she looked weird. I . . . I hit her with the heat lamp. Is she dead?"

"No, she just got a bump." Jeppe smiled reassuringly at her. "Don't worry. Just sit and warm up. Your mom will be here soon."

Essie started sobbing.

"Don't tell her about the pictures. Oscar will be so mad at me!" Her plea was full of childlike desperation.

Jeppe looked over at Jenny Kaliban's outstretched form on the floor. The lowermost circle of hell isn't for traitors, he thought. It's for people who hurt children.

FRIDAY,
APRIL 19

CHAPTER 35

"Thank you for letting me come by. I know it's early." Jeppe stood in the doorway to Sara's apartment, unsure whether he should come in or stay out. "I couldn't sleep."

"Is the little girl okay?"

He nodded.

"She's spending the night at the hospital for tests. She was drugged, but she'll be fine."

"Are *you* okay?"

He thought it over. "No," he said.

"Come in."

He stepped in and closed the front door. Sara didn't make any move to invite him farther into the apartment, so they stayed in the entryway amid jackets and shoes.

"The girls are still asleep."

"I just wanted to see you." Jeppe stuck his hands in his pockets, so they wouldn't reach for her. "The case is solved, the murderer has confessed. Jenny Kaliban will be charged for killing Malthe Sæther after he threatened to go to the police and tell them that she sold naked pictures of her nephew."

"*She* took the pictures of Oscar? His own aunt?!" Sara blinked, looking appalled.

"Yes. Who knows how it came to that."

"Pedophile rings often keep an eye on art pages, anything that has drawings or pictures of children," Sara said, shaking her head. "They start by offering money for innocent pictures of children, then it gradually progresses from there."

"The pedophile ring grooms the artist and the artist grooms the child?"

"A slippery slope. She surely gave Oscar money and praised him for his contributions, so he felt complicit, and then she threatened him when he wanted to stop."

"Who needs enemies when you have family?" Jeppe sighed. "We also found a picture of Malthe Sæther in Jenny's atelier. Naked and made up like the pictures of Oscar and in the same armchair. We think he's dead in the picture."

Sara put her hands over her mouth.

"That kind of thing sells to people who are turned on by necrophilia and snuff. It can potentially be worth quite a lot of money."

"A golden egg for a starving artist."

She nodded grimly.

"The Ninth Circle company has already deleted their home page and every trace of themselves. It won't be easy to find the people behind it—"

"I didn't come here to talk work. Sara, I'm sorry. I made a decision, and it was the wrong one. I'm sorry."

"It's not that, Jeppe. Well, it's not *just* that." She squeezed her eyes shut a little.

He knew that look.

"What are you trying to say?" he asked. "Are we over?"

Her head drooped, but only for a second, then she lifted her chin, determined.

"I can tell that you're trying, but maybe this just isn't what you really want? And it's hard for the girls, too. It's just not working."

The silence resonated in the entryway. Jeppe wished he could reach out and touch her, that she was maybe hoping he would. But he knew that no matter what they both wished, and whether or not she was right, there was no point in discussing it. You never get between a mama bear and her cubs.

"Take care of yourself."

What else was there to say?

Jeppe turned around and opened the door. He walked down the stairs, letting the distance between them grow. Every step he took from now on would lead them farther away from each other, and it was going to hurt, hurt when he thought about her and hurt just as much when he didn't.

He opened the door to Burmeistersgade. Now she was just Saidani to him, a colleague. She wasn't his Sara anymore.

IT WAS THAT kind of spring morning when one felt compelled to take off their jacket and throw it carelessly over one shoulder. Anette slowed down and smiled up at the sun. The air was mild, and the anticipation of summer's arrival seemed even more magical than summer itself.

Gudrun was in a great mood and happily offered a goodbye kiss from the sandbox, so Anette was able to walk away from her daughter's day care without the parental guilt that can ruin the whole day. She strolled home through her residential neighborhood in Greve Strand with a fundamental sense of gratitude. Her suburb wasn't fashionable or chic, but she and Svend owned their own wonderful house here and could create a safe home for their daughter.

The investigation into Malthe Sæther's murder had been wrapped up and the killer taken into custody. She was still in the hospital under observation for a concussion, but as soon as she was healthy enough, she would be charged and face preliminary questioning.

It didn't seem like determining guilt would be a problem. In the hospital late yesterday, Jenny Kaliban had already explained how Malthe had visited her in her atelier Friday night and behaved threateningly. He accused her of having sexually abused Oscar. It ended in a scuffle, and she had to defend herself, but couldn't remember the details of his death and hadn't offered any immediate commentary on what had happened afterward. She had just panicked. It was going to be interesting to hear her try to explain how this panic had led her to apply makeup to the body and photograph it.

Anette crossed the path and turned down toward Holmeås. She stopped by a trash can, found the old pack of cigarettes in her jacket pocket, and threw it away. She wouldn't need it again.

As she walked up the driveway to number 14, she saw Svend in the yard, digging out the old tree stump that they had been talking about removing for ages. His bare arms were glistening with sweat, and he was humming along to a song blasting from the radio on the windowsill. Anette stood watching him until he noticed her. Sure, there were men who were skinnier, more mysterious, and with sorrowful eyes, but Svend was the one she loved.

She walked over and planted a long kiss on his lips.

"I'm really sweaty."

"And I really don't care." She kissed him again, enjoying the taste of salt and the feeling of hope. "Is it heavy?"

Svend laughed.

"Everything is heavy if you choose to look at it that way. So I just don't. You know, like in a cartoon. Gravity doesn't take effect until you look down."

"So the trick is not to look down?"

He leaned on his shovel and looked at her for a long time.

"Well, let's put it this way: At least you get to choose if you want to give in or resist."

Svend knew her inside and out, saw all her foibles, and understood her doubts. And still he loved her without reservation.

He winked at her affectionately and said, "Go grab a shovel and help me dig!"

"SWEETIE, YOU'RE DREAMING again. It's morning." Sara put her arm around her daughter to calm her down. Amina had slept in her double bed for the last three nights.

She, stirred, blinked, and reached for her mother. Sara held her hand and savored having her daughter need her for once.

"Were you having a nightmare, sweetie?"

Her daughter mumbled half-incomprehensibly against Sara's shoulder. "It was like that mirror that you can walk through, only it was different. I was, like, totally old with droopy cheeks."

"What are you talking about, silly? What mirror?" She stroked Amina's arm as she spoke. Her daughter snuggled up to her.

"The one in the book, *Through the Looking-Glass*. Alice goes through the mirror and then everything is reversed and super spooky, and she can't get back to herself. I dreamed that that was me."

Jeppe's book. Sara took it as a painful confirmation that he had a destabilizing effect on their family.

"You watch so many scary things on YouTube, monsters and horror stuff. How can you possibly be afraid of an old book?"

Amina whimpered. She was so skinny and small, still just a child, even though she occasionally tried to act older.

"Good thing it was only a dream!" Sara kissed her daughter on the forehead and got out of bed. "I'll make us breakfast. I'm letting Meriem take the day off too, so we're all going to start our weekend early. But on Monday we're done with all this playing hooky. I need to get back to work."

Sara made her way to the little kitchen, turned on the oven, and opened a pack of the good pita bread from the local produce stand. No oatmeal today. Today breakfast would be shakshuka, poached eggs in a spiced tomato sauce, the traditional dish her own mother had always served whenever something extra comforting was called for.

While the sauce simmered, she opened her computer and wrote to PC that she was taking one last personal day and would be back on Monday. She quickly checked the police report system and read that Kasper Skytte had turned himself in at a police station in Stuttgart and confessed to falsifying documents. His confession would be considered and investigated by the public prosecutor for serious economic crime.

Sara switched off her computer and put the pita bread in the oven to toast. Kasper Skytte would probably take his coconspirators down with him when he fell. His confession would have consequences for others besides himself, particularly his daughter. Poor Iben; she was already at odds with life. Her father being a criminal wasn't exactly going to help her come to terms with her existence.

Sara walked back to her bedroom. In the meantime Meriem had climbed into bed with her older sister and the two girls were lying close together, whispering conspiratorially.

She looked at them and knew that nothing else really mattered.

"Time for breakfast, you two troublemakers!" Sara pulled the covers off them and tickled all the toes she could reach before fetching the food in the kitchen and starting to set the table.

She picked up a book from the floor. *Through the Looking-Glass.* She flipped to the title page and saw how Jeppe had once written his name in childish handwriting. Thoughtfully she slid her finger over the ink as if it could create a connection to him who had once written it, make things right again. But no matter how she tried to make things work, she came up short. She was a package deal, and he didn't seem like someone who wanted a whole package.

Sara clapped the book shut. The blessing and curse of having children was that they always came first. She brought *Through the Looking-Glass* into the kitchen, lifted the lid of the trash can, and threw the book away.

THE SUN PLAYED on the surface of the ocean, sending golden patches of light into the living room of the old house in Snekkersten. Jeppe closed his eyes and let the light play pleasantly over his eyelids. Behind him, Johannes was cleaning out his wardrobe. He could hear him incessantly rattling things and opening and closing drawers.

"Just say if you want me to leave," Jeppe said.

"No, no, it's fine. Aren't you going to work today?"

"Only if it's absolutely necessary," Jeppe said after a moment's thought. "Like, if we need to make another arrest."

"Another?! What's that supposed to mean? I thought the case was closed."

"Not quite." Jeppe opened his eyes and looked out the window toward the sea. "It turns out that Henrik Dreyer-Hoff was helping Jenny Kaliban sell stolen artifacts online."

"You mean to the creepy pedophiles?" Johannes asked, and then slammed a drawer closed behind him.

"Among other people." Jeppe turned around. "It appears that Jenny has been stealing small art objects for years and selling them to collectors with help from her brother-in-law. Via the auction house's own website and through his personal contacts. He even wrote sales texts for her."

"That's like petty fencing. Why would he do that?" Johannes protested. "Pretty risky for a man in his position, no?"

"To help out his sister-in-law, as an alternative to loaning her money. Over time, there has probably been a financial incentive for him, too. Larsen is working to determine the scale of it, and how much he can be held responsible for."

"And in thanks she took nude pictures of his son and sold them behind his back?"

Jeppe breathed deeply and tried to relieve some of the weight in his chest.

"Henrik must have known about that. I just don't see how he could have avoided discovering it. We've found large foreign currency transfers to Jenny's account and a number of simultaneously timed transfers that she's made to Henrik. It looks like they cut off their collaboration two years ago. I'm guessing that he discovered Jenny selling pictures of Oscar and cut her off."

"Without telling anyone?!" Johannes froze, holding a stack of clothes in his arms, his mouth hanging open. "Without reporting her to the police?"

"He couldn't risk Malin finding out. The family couldn't take any more scandals, neither publicly nor among themselves. I guess he wanted to protect both the company and his wife. And since the damage was already done, it was better to just break off contact with her and look ahead. Surely in his own way he was trying to save his family."

"But . . . what about the boy?"

"Oscar tried to kill himself," Jeppe said with a sigh. "He wrote a goodbye note to his parents, but they didn't understand it."

"That's terrible. I don't even know what to say." Johannes dropped his clothes on the floor and sat down on the arm of the sofa.

"Yes, it's depressing what people will do for money." Jeppe looked out the window. He knew that the person who would be hurt the most if the story came out was Oscar. "I've requested a leave of absence."

"You have *what*?" Johannes asked.

"I wrote to PC and asked to take an indefinite leave of absence."

"But why?" Johannes shook his head, confused. "Because of you and Sara?"

"Maybe." Jeppe shrugged. "I just don't see how we could work together right now. But it's also the new headquarters, and . . . I don't know. I just need a break."

"A break?" Johannes stood up. "Okay, I'm sorry, but you caught me off guard with this. What are you going to do?"

"I don't know yet. Travel? I still have some money left from selling the house. Maybe I ought to go see the world, before it's too late."

"Too late in what sense?" Johannes picked up a stack of papers from the coffee table.

"We only get this one paltry life. You've got to squeeze it to the last drop. Isn't that what you're always saying?"

"But what about Sara?" Johannes asked.

Jeppe smiled sadly.

"You can't just give up!"

"Johannes, I can't give her what she needs. There are kids involved. It's not fair to ask her to wait while I try to figure out what I want."

Johannes stared at him blankly, as if he were speaking Korean.

"Now, if you don't object, I'll just jump in the water before I go."

"Suit yourself!" Johannes disappeared into the kitchen.

Jeppe changed into his swim trunks and found a towel and the too small sandals. He walked across the street and out the breakwater to the swimming dock. The little marina was deserted, the masts gleaming silver in the sunlight, making attractive spots for passing gulls to rest. He leaned against the dock's railing and smelled the ocean. The air had a chilly bite to it, but as long as you were in the sun, it was fine.

Had Jenny's hands trembled when she took those pictures? When she strangled Malthe and pushed Lis out in front of the train? Or had she just done what she thought anyone in her situation would do? Forced by circumstance.

His heart sank at the thought of Lis, who had just been helping out a colleague. Malthe must have mentioned Lis to Jenny. In all likelihood, it was Jeppe's own visit to the atelier that had made it clear to Jenny how dangerous it was having Lis around. That it was only a matter of time before Lis realized the significance of what she knew and disclosed it to the police. After Jeppe left her atelier, Jenny had most likely gone straight to the school and waited out in front. One little shove and the problem was solved.

And all for money, to be able to keep her atelier and hold on to her art and her dreams. One misstep had led to the next in a slippery slope of mistakes with fatal consequences.

When you're passionate about something, you become unscrupulous. When you love, you hurt. Even in the best of families there's greed and deception, and even in the most profound love, you find hooks and grief.

Jeppe just had to grit his teeth and move on. He had tried failure before and knew it would ultimately make him stronger. Or at least more hardened. That it wouldn't kill him even if it felt like it now.

He hung his towel over the railing and slipped the sandals off. Then he walked out to the end of the dock and jumped in.

ACKNOWLEDGMENTS

THANK YOU!

Naively, I thought that publishing books would get easier over time, that anxiety would decrease with each publication. I was wrong. It only gets worse. Which is why the massive amount of support I receive from readers and collaborators becomes more and more valuable.

Thank you to Dorthe Vejsig at the Copenhagen district attorney's office; Klaus Bo from Dead and Alive Projects; Thorvaldsens Museum; and Ernst Jonas Bencard, professor of forensic medicine; Hans Petter Hougen; Claus Vilsen and Trekroner fort caretaker Hans Poul Petersen; Peter Cummings; Jens Borregaard from the Technical and Environmental Administration; and Cathrine Raben Davidsen.

To ARC for the tour of the plant and for putting up with all my questions. Special thanks to process engineer Jørgen Bøgild Johnsen. I hope you will pardon my fanciful treatment of the incineration process, and I accept full responsibility for exaggerations and murderous machinations.

Thank you to everyone in my ring corner: Salomonsson Agency, especially my agent, Federico Ambrosini, and to all the amazing people at Scout Press: Jackie Cantor, Jessica Roth, Abby Zidle, Jennifer Long, and my dear friend Jennifer Bergstrom.

Also my profound thanks to Sysse Engberg, Anne Mette Hancock, and Sara Dybris McQuaid for feedback and support. To publisher, editor, and friend Birgitte Franch: without you, no books—it's as simple as that. And last but in every sense first: Timm and Cassius, when it comes to you guys, no amount of thanks is enough. You're everything to me.